Critical acclaim for David Baldacci's novels

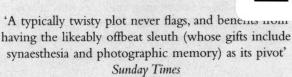

The Atlee Pine thrillers
by David Baldacci

  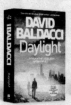 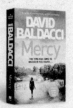

Long Road to Mercy

Thirty years since Atlee Pine's twin sister, Mercy, was abducted, Pine starts the pursuit of a lifetime to finally uncover what happened on that fateful night.

A Minute to Midnight

Seeking answers in her home town, Pine's visit turns into a rollercoaster ride of murder, long-buried secrets and a revelation so personal that everything she once believed is fast turning to dust.

Daylight

When Pine's investigation coincides with military investigator John Puller's high-stakes case, it leads them both into a global conspiracy from which neither of them will escape unscathed.

Mercy

FBI agent Atlee Pine is at the end of her long journey to discover what happened to her twin sister, Mercy, and must face a final challenge more deadly than she could ever have imagined.

Mercy

David Baldacci is one of the world's bestselling and favourite thriller writers. A former trial lawyer with a keen interest in world politics, he has specialist knowledge in the US political system and intelligence services, and his first book, *Absolute Power*, became an instant international bestseller, with the movie starring Clint Eastwood a major box office hit. He has since written more than forty bestsellers, featuring, most recently, Amos Decker, Aloysius Archer, Atlee Pine and John Puller.

David is also the co-founder, along with his wife, of the Wish You Well Foundation®, a non-profit organization dedicated to supporting literacy efforts across the US.

Trust him to take you to the action.

DAVID BALDACCI

Mercy

PAN BOOKS

First published 2021 by Grand Central Publishing, USA

First published in the UK 2021 by Macmillan

This paperback edition published 2022 by Pan Books
an imprint of Pan Macmillan
The Smithson, 6 Briset Street, London EC1M 5NR
EU representative: Macmillan Publishers Ireland Ltd, 1st Floor,
The Liffey Trust Centre, 117–126 Sheriff Street Upper, Dublin 1, D01 YC43
Associated companies throughout the world
www.panmacmillan.com

ISBN 978-1-5290-6173-4

1 3 5 7 9 8 6 4 2

A CIP catalogue record for this book is available from the British Library.

Typeset in Bembo by Jouve (UK), Milton Keynes
Printed and bound by CPI Group (UK) Ltd, Croydon, CR0 4YY

Visit **www.panmacmillan.com** to read more about all our books
and to buy them. You will also find features, author interviews and
news of any author events, and you can sign up for e-newsletters
so that you're always first to hear about our new releases.

*To the memory of the mighty and beloved
Finnegan, this man's best friend.
You will always be in our hearts.
Thank you for being a wonderful part of
our family for fifteen years.*

FBI SPECIAL AGENT PROFILE

Name: Atlee Pine

Age: Thirty-five

Place of Birth: Andersonville, Georgia

Marital Status: Single

Physical characteristics: At five eleven, Atlee
is a tall woman — she got it from her mother.
Solid and muscular, which comes from pumping
iron religiously. Her features come together in a
particularly attractive, almost bewitching, manner.
Shoulder-length dark hair and blue eyes. Her body
is a canvas of scars. The one on her left temple a
reminder of when her skull was cracked when she was
six. Bullet wound on the back of her calf. Knife
slice on left triceps. Surgery on her lower back
from her time as a weightlifter has left its mark.
Delt tats: Gemini and Mercury with the words 'No
Mercy' on each. You could say the woman wears her
heart on her sleeve and her delts.

Relatives: Mercy Pine (twin sister) — abducted from
the Pine family home when she was six. The main
suspect being the notorious serial killer Daniel
James Tor, now behind bars. Atlee believes it was
Tor who cracked her skull that night and left her
for dead in the sisters' bedroom. It broke the
family up, as Atlee's parents divorced shortly after,
principally because of what happened that night.
Atlee is now estranged from her mother. Her father
killed himself, on his daughters' birthday no less.

CONFIDENTIAL

Career: The abduction of her sister has haunted her life. After her parents' divorce her existence seemed aimless until she resolved to live the life her sister never did. Her physical size, natural strength and athleticism led her to be a star sportswoman in high school. She excelled at weightlifting and was on her way to joining the Olympic squad but just missed out on being selected. Instead she joined the FBI and is now a Special Agent, patrolling the rural, remote areas of southwest America.

Notable Abilities: An expert in MMA and kickboxing. Immense physical strength and endurance that have been learned and enhanced with one aim in mind: survival in a profession that is largely a man's world. An excellent criminal profiler and was offered a slot at the Behavioural Analysis Unit at the Bureau, which she declined. She doesn't want to profile monsters, she wants to catch them herself.

Favourite film: _Thelma & Louise_, although she would dearly hope to see a derivation of another popular film that speaks to her and those like her: _A Few Good Women_.

Favourite song: 'Big Girls Don't Cry' (Fergie)

Dislikes: Serial killers and politicians, but she repeats herself

Likes: Cold beer, fast cars and her Beretta Nano backup pistol

Mercy

1

Inch by solid inch, Atlee Pine watched the battered coffin being lifted to the surface from where it had rested six feet down for nearly two decades. Coffins and bodies were not supposed to be retrieved. They were supposed to stay right where they were planted, at least until a dying sun lashed out across space and bid farewell to all on earth.

But, for Pine, it was just that kind of day.

Just that kind of year, actually.

She gazed over at a black crow as it stridently cawed from its perch on the branch of a sickly pine overlooking the pierced grave. The bird seemed to think its meal was being delivered up as a boxed lunch, and the creature was getting impatient.

Well, I'm thirty years impatient, Pine thought.

Pine was an FBI special agent. Five eleven in bare feet, she possessed a muscular build from years of lifting massive amounts of weights, first for athletic glory, and currently to survive the rigorous demands of her occupation. Some agents spent careers mainly on their butts staring at computer screens or *supervising* agents on the streets. Pine was not one of them.

Her normal beat was in Arizona, near the Grand Canyon. It was a lot of ground to cover, and she was the only FBI agent out there. Pine preferred it that way. She hated bureaucracies and the paper pushers who lived and died by their stifling mountain of rules that got you nowhere fast. Certainly not with putting bad people away, which was really the whole point for her.

She was currently in Virginia working on something personal. This was her one shot to get things right in her life.

Next to Pine was her administrative assistant at the Bureau, Carol Blum.

Pine and Blum were searching for Pine's twin sister, Mercy Pine, who had been abducted from their shared bedroom in Andersonville, Georgia, when the girls were just six years old. Pine had nearly been killed by the abductor, surviving by a combination of sheer luck and, Pine supposed, her absolute unwillingness to die. She hadn't seen Mercy since. It was an incident that had destroyed the Pine family and stood as the one traumatically defining moment of her life.

They had tracked Mercy's whereabouts to a place near Crawfordville, Georgia, in Taliaferro County, the most rural and least populated county in the state. She had been given the name Rebecca Atkins and had been kept as a prisoner until she'd escaped many years ago. Now the trail was as cold as a morgue freezer.

Joe Atkins, one of her captors, had been found murdered the day after Mercy had escaped. His wife, Desiree, had disappeared at the same time. Pine had unearthed that her sister's kidnapper was a man named Ito Vincenzo. He was the brother of Bruno, a mobster who had held a grudge against Pine's mother, Julia. She had acted as a mole for the government in its successful attempts to bring down several New York crime families back in the 1980s. Members of crime families did not like to be brought down. They held it against you. The Vincenzo family had certainly held it against the Pine family. At the urging of his murderous brother, Ito Vincenzo had tried to obliterate the Pines, and had largely succeeded.

The Bureau had recently put out a PSA using an image of Mercy captured at the exact moment she had broken free from her improvised prison cell. Pine had hoped that if Mercy was alive she would see the notice and come forward. That had not happened, so Pine had decided to work on a different lead.

Years ago, her mother had told Pine that her father, Tim Pine, had killed himself. Subsequently, she had learned that Tim was not her biological father. A man named Jack Lineberry was. Lineberry had been nearly killed in an attack aimed against Atlee Pine in an unrelated case. The revelation that he was her father had stunned Pine, but what she had found out recently had shocked her just as much, if not even more. That was why she was here.

I know all families are dysfunctional, but mine seems to be the undisputed world champ in that competition.

The coffin finally reached the surface and was shifted away from the hole and set on the grass. Its metal carcass was visibly damaged by water, and also by sitting in the earth all those years. She wondered how preserved the contents would be.

A forensics team hurried forward, quickly prized open the coffin, and placed the human remains in a body bag. They zipped it up and loaded it into the back of a black van, which was quickly driven away. Pine thought she knew who was in that grave. But thoughts weren't enough, certainly not for an FBI agent, or a grieving daughter, hence the exhumation. DNA identification was as definite as it got. That would reveal who had been in the coffin, of that she was certain.

Pine had never been to this grave in rural Virginia, for the simple reason that her mother had lied to her about where her father's supposed suicide had taken place. Her mother had also told her that her father had been cremated and his ashes scattered by her at some unknown place. All lies. But then again, it seemed everyone had lied to her about her past.

She now believed the man in the grave was none other than Ito Vincenzo. He had apparently discovered Tim Pine's whereabouts and come to exact revenge on him. Only he had ended up being the one to die.

Pine had also been led to believe that her parents had divorced because of irreconcilable differences related to their guilt over Mercy's disappearance. Now she knew that Tim had faked his death, and her mother had voluntarily left her remaining daughter shortly thereafter. Julia Pine had in fact joined her ex-husband, and they had vanished together.

And left me all by my lonesome. Thanks, guys. What great parents you turned out to be.

2

Pine looked at Carol Blum. In her sixties, a mother of six grown children, and a longtime employee of the Bureau, Blum had become something of a surrogate mother to the federal agent, to some degree taking the place of the one who had abandoned her.

Blum stared resolutely at her boss, who had her hands shoved deep into her jeans pockets, and whose features held a frown that seemed to run out of room on her face.

"How soon will they know if it is Ito Vincenzo?" asked Blum.

"Hopefully a couple of days max. I gave them samples of his DNA."

"How'd you get those?"

"From his son's and grandson's bodies. A familial match under these circumstances constitutes a slam dunk."

"Yes, of course," Blum said quickly. "There's no other way a DNA connection to the Vincenzo family could be in that grave."

They walked back to the car and drove off.

"So what now?" asked Blum.

"We have some time, since the Bureau has given us an official leave of absence."

"It was the least they could do after you and Agent Puller solved that case in New York."

John Puller was an Army investigator who had teamed with Pine to run to ground a blackmail operation that had reached into the highest levels of the country's power structure. Puller had been shot in the process, but he was on his way to a full recovery.

"You were in on all that, too, Carol. And you almost lost your life because I screwed up."

"You also *saved* my life."

"After needlessly putting it in danger," countered Pine. As she turned out of the cemetery she added, "If Mercy sees the PSA she might come in. That would be the ideal scenario."

"And if she doesn't?"

"Then it could be that she's . . . no longer alive." Pine shot a glance at Blum. "I've accepted that possibility, Carol. A long time ago. I know Mercy was alive when she got free from the Atkinses. But a lot could have happened in between."

Blum said, "And it doesn't seem like the Atkinses did anything to, well, to educate her or . . ." Her voice trailed off and she looked uncertainly at her boss.

"Let's just acknowledge it—she looked like a wild person," said Pine slowly. "And I'm not sure how she could manage to function in society on her own, at least mainstream society. And people who live on the fringes with no support can be exploited." Pine looked out the window and said dully, "The person I saw in that video . . . could be exploited."

"But she was resilient and resourceful, Agent Pine. Look at how she survived the Atkinses and then outsmarted them and escaped."

"And Joe Atkins ended up dead with a knife sticking in his back," replied Pine.

"I already told you how I feel about that. He deserved what he got."

"I'm not disagreeing with you, Carol. But I am saying that if Mercy *did* kill him, if she is violent, then the intervening years might not have been kind to her. She might have done other things."

"You're thinking that she could have hurt other people?"

"Or, more likely, had been a victim of violence," Pine said.

"Which brings me back to my original question: What do we do now?"

"Her last sighting was near Crawfordville, Georgia. She got away that night, or at least it appeared she did."

"What do you mean 'appeared'?" asked Blum.

"Desiree Atkins has never been found. There are at least three scenarios that I can see." Pine counted them off on her fingers. "She killed her husband and fled. Mercy killed her and fled. Or Desiree killed Mercy and fled."

"Why would Desiree kill her husband?"

"By all accounts, she was a sadistic nut. We heard a gunshot on the video and just assumed it was Joe firing at Mercy. But what if Desiree had the gun and was doing the shooting? What if Joe tried to stop her? He gets the gun away but she stabs him."

"So you think Joe might have wanted Mercy to get away? I just don't see that. When the truth came out they *both* would have been in a great deal of trouble."

"I'm saying it's possible, not probable. She might have managed to kill Mercy, then Joe got nervous and wanted to call the police, so she stabbed him and fled with Mercy's body. Only it would have been a real chore for her to lift the body into Joe's truck. Desiree was tiny, and Mercy looked to be over six feet and probably outweighed her by seventy pounds. And they brought cadaver dogs in after we found out what happened there. There are no bodies buried anywhere in that area. So that option is out. But what if Joe helped her get rid of Mercy's body, then got cold feet or regrets? Then Desiree plunged the knife in his back."

Blum mulled over this. "Or, like you said, Mercy could have killed both of them. She left Joe's body and maybe took Desiree's remains and buried them somewhere far away."

"It's possible. But that would mean Mercy would have had to drive the truck."

Blum said, "Surely she could have figured that out."

Pine shook her head. "The truck has a manual transmission. I don't know anybody, particularly someone who has been kept in a hellhole for years and never attempted to drive *anything*, who could have figured out how a clutch works. Certainly not under such stressful conditions. And I can't see the Atkinses having taught her."

"So what are you saying then?"

"I'm saying, Carol, that I think it was *Desiree* who took off that night in the truck. But I think she went alone."

"Because the jig was up, you mean?"

Pine nodded. "Yes. So, to answer your initial question of what to do now, I think we head back to Georgia and see if we can pick up a very, very cold trail."

"And Jack Lineberry? Will you stop in to see him while we're in Georgia?"

To that, Pine said nothing.

She had mixed feelings about her biological father. And their last encounter had been disastrous. She was not expecting anything better the second time around. But ultimately the fault lay with him, not her. That's just what happened when every word out of your mouth was a lie.

3

Pine stared out the window of the rental car at Crawfordville, in densely wooded Taliaferro County, Georgia. Here, you'd never see an assailant coming before it was too late. Thick foliage was a killer's best friend, whether they were hunting deer or people.

They had flown into Atlanta from Virginia, rented the car, and driven here. They had already checked in with Dick Roberts. He was the retired, straight-as-an-arrow county sheriff who had helped them when they were down here the first time. It had been Roberts who, years before, had answered the 911 call and found Joe Atkins's body. The question had always been—who'd stuck the knife blade there? Roberts also had been with Pine when they had discovered Mercy's old prison cut into a knoll some distance away from the Atkinses' house, and when they had found and viewed the video chronicling her sister's escape. Roberts knew that Mercy was Pine's sister, and that this case was personal to her.

No, it's not just personal. I'm betting my entire

professional life on finally solving this thing. There is no going back for me.

A sense of panic seized her for a moment, like a swimmer who realized they were caught in a riptide with a limited and risky way back to shore. Then she glanced out the window, drew a long, calming breath, and silently chastised herself to get a grip, that she was acting like a child.

Roberts had given them the route that the Atkinses' truck had to have taken that night to where it was later found. They were now retracing that route. It was along a rural road; all the roads here were rural and winding and devoid, for the most part, of living things, except for the critters residing in the woods. They counted only five homes along the way. Three of them were occupied; two were abandoned. They stopped and asked their questions and found out that none of the people living here now were there during the relevant time period.

After the last interview, Pine and Blum drove to the spot where the truck had been found. It was an old Esso gas station long since abandoned, with the four letters and the neon tubes backing them having been used for target practice over the intervening years; only the sign's metal spines survived. It was a bare, eroded filament of civilization in a forest that looked determined to reclaim its own. They sat in the car next to where the gas pumps used to be. Pine took a look around, and the view was as desolate as her hopes. But then something occurred to her.

"Okay, the truck and Desiree ended up here," said Pine. "But why *here*?"

Blum gazed around. "I think this is a place to *meet* someone. 'Hey, so and so, come get me at the Esso station.' It was probably the only such landmark around. Desiree didn't know when the body would be found. She wanted to get away, but not in a vehicle that could be traced."

"And the 'so-and-sos' are pretty limited. In fact, there are only two possible choices, to my mind."

"Len and Wanda Atkins, her in-laws," replied Blum. "But Sheriff Roberts said that he talked to them after Joe was killed and Desiree disappeared. They both said they hadn't heard from Desiree."

"And they were both probably lying to save their own asses. You saw the picture of Mercy with them. They *knew* she was being held against her will. They knew if this all came out, they were going to prison. That's why they got the hell out of here pretty soon after Mercy escaped and Joe was killed. I'm now certain that Desiree called them that night and told them what had happened. They arranged to meet her here where she abandoned the truck. They drove her somewhere, maybe a bus or train station. And off she went to start a new life with a new identity. Then they went back to their trailer and were there when they got the word the next day about their son." She eyed Blum. "Any of that seem unlikely to you?"

"No, it all sounds spot-on, Agent Pine."

Then Pine's eyes narrowed and her look became less certain. "But it *does* seem unlikely that they would just take Desiree's word for it that he was dead. They might have thought they could still save him, or that she was even lying about it. But if he *was* dead, they would have been terrified that animals could have torn Joe's remains apart overnight. And we know that didn't happen."

"So maybe *they* were the ones to make sure their son's body wasn't desecrated?"

"Which means we need to find Len and Wanda Atkins and ask them that directly."

"*If* they're still alive."

"If they are, they would be getting Social Security and Medicare. We could find them that way."

"And he was a Vietnam vet. He was wounded. So . . ."

Pine picked up this thought thread. "That means he might be in contact with the VA for meds and treatments and the like. That would actually be faster for us than going through the HHS bureaucracy, because I don't really have good contacts there."

She pulled out her phone.

"Who are you calling?" asked Blum.

"Who else? John Puller. He already helped me get Len Atkins's military records."

She spoke with Puller, who told her he was recovering quickly from his injuries. He also said he knew several people at the VA because of his father being in one of their facilities, and he would do all he could to help her locate Len Atkins.

She thanked him and clicked off. "Okay, we'll let him work his magic."

"While he's doing that, do you think you should go and visit Jack Lineberry?"

Pine's expression hardened and she glanced out the car window. Lineberry's image swelled up in her head like a nightmare. "You asked me that before."

"And you never answered me, which is why I'm asking again."

"Why should I go see him?" asked Pine, her tone heated.

"Like it or not, he is your biological father. And the way you left it with him?"

"Look, I'm not proud of what I did."

"And now it's time to move on to another level with him."

Pine glanced sharply at her friend. "And why do I have to do that?"

"Because you're going to need his help, whether you find your sister or not."

Pine looked even more confused. "Come again?"

"I presume you still want to find your mother. And Tim Pine, now that you almost certainly know he wasn't in that grave. And Jack can be a valuable asset in helping you do that. However, I'm not asking you to cut him any slack."

"Good, because I don't intend to," interjected Pine.

"But," continued Blum imperturbably, "I think he is trying his best to do the right thing. And he *is* your father. And if you don't at least make an effort to have a relationship with him, I think you're going to regret it later."

"I regret a lot of things, Carol," said Pine. But she put the car in gear and headed on to see the man who had lied to her more than any other person in her life.

Except for my damn mother.

4

Jack Lineberry's estate was an hour south of Atlanta. He had made an enormous fortune in the financial world and owned, in addition to this main residence, a penthouse in Atlanta and a pied-à-terre in New York, as well as a private jet. It was a lifestyle that most people would be thrilled to enjoy. Pine was not among them.

If you need that many toys to enjoy life, then you're still a child.

They had already called ahead and arranged to meet with him. They checked in at the front gate, were admitted into the house, and escorted to Lineberry by one of the maids. He was still in bed, the woman told them—which alarmed Pine, because it was well into the afternoon.

They entered the room and the maid left. The space was dark and overly warm, with all the window shades lowered. It was like a tomb with wallpaper and carpet, and living people. The effect unnerved Pine.

"Jack?" said Pine.

Something stirred on the bed. A pajama-clad

Lineberry struggled to sit up, and finally managed to do so. Pine and Blum drew nearer and looked down at him. Their features betrayed their alarm at the state of the man. He looked like he had aged two decades since the last time they had seen him. A tall, handsome man in his sixties, he looked shrunken, withered, fragile, and, most tellingly, done with life.

Blum said, "Jack . . . what happened?"

He focused on her with a pair of weary, bloodshot eyes, his brow crinkling in annoyance approaching anger. "Nothing . . . happened. I'm . . . doing okay."

"You don't *look* okay," Pine said bluntly. "You don't look okay at all."

"That's *your* opinion," he replied testily.

"That would be any reasonable person's opinion," countered Pine.

"I was *shot*, Atlee. It's not like I have a case of the flu. Nobody just pops back from that. Particularly not someone my age."

"I realize that," she began before glancing at Blum. "And I know I was mad beyond all reason after my last visit here."

"You had every right to be as angry as you were. I feel like I got off easy, actually."

"Don't go all chivalrous and make this harder than it has to be," she said in a lighter tone.

He held up his hand before she could go on. "I've been doing a lot of thinking, Atlee. At this time in my life it's imperative to do so."

"Thinking about what?" she said sharply, not liking his fatalistic tone.

"About you, about Mercy, about your mother and Tim. And, finally, about me."

Pine drew up a chair next to the bed and sat down. "And what have you concluded?"

Part of her didn't want to know his answer, but in life you needed to listen to things you didn't want to hear, maybe those most of all.

"Well, first of all, I'm leaving everything I have to you and Mercy."

Pine immediately shook her head, recoiling at this news. "Jack, I don't—"

"Please hear me out. Please. It's important!"

Pine shot Blum another glance, and the woman nodded with a pleading look on her face.

She sat back, folded her arms over her chest, assumed a stubborn expression, and said, "Okay. I'm listening, but that's not the same as agreeing."

"I *am* your and Mercy's father. That gives me certain responsibilities, none of which I have lived up to."

"You didn't know where—"

He interrupted. "I knew more than I let on. And what I didn't know I could have found out. The bottom line is, I have behaved abominably throughout this entire thing. I doubt any man could have been a worse father."

He was so distressed that Pine felt her anger at him start to fade. She sat forward and laid a hand on his arm. "Jack, you were between a rock and a hard place. There was nothing simple about the situation."

"Well, it's simple for me now. I have two daughters. You are my only family. Parents often leave what they have to their children and that's what I'm going to do, too. If you don't want it, that's fine, give it away to whoever and whatever you like. But you can't stop me from doing it," he added sharply. "I've already had my lawyers draw it all up and it's signed. There's nothing you can do about that."

"Okay, Jack, if that's what you want."

"It is."

"But you've got a lot of years ahead of you. So this is sort of premature."

"No one knows what tomorrow will bring, Atlee, we both know that better than most." Before she could say anything he asked, "Have you found out more about Mercy, or your mother and Tim?"

Pine told him about the grave being exhumed and awaiting confirmation that the body there was indeed Ito Vincenzo's. She informed him of their steps to track Desiree Atkins that night, and their deduction that she had met Len and Wanda and they had helped her to flee.

"You mean the people who were in that photograph with Mercy?" said Lineberry.

"Yes."

"Do you really think you can find them after all this time?"

"With the technology and databases available today, it's hard to stay hidden."

"And you're hoping they can tell you what happened to Desiree?"

"That's right. And if we can find Desiree she might be able to shed some light on that night and even on where Mercy might have gone."

"She might not have any incentive to tell you," Lineberry pointed out.

"There are ways she can be persuaded. She's looking at prison time for what she did. And if she murdered her husband or . . ." Pine drew a quick breath. "She'll talk."

Lineberry, with an effort, sat up a little straighter. The conversation seemed to have animated him. "There's one more thing," he said.

Pine looked at him warily. Her real father had already thrown one curveball at her with the inheritance thing; she had no interest in another one. "Yes?"

"I know that you've been doing all of this searching on your dime."

Pine's brow furrowed. She hadn't been expecting this. "So?"

"It's not fair that you continue to do so. I have the resources that—"

She got his meaning. "No, Jack, this is my search for—"

"It's mine too!" he snapped, so unexpectedly they

21

all simply froze. Lineberry actually looked stunned that he had the energy to do it. He continued more calmly, "If you use some of *my* resources, you might get to the truth faster. For instance, the use of my jet to get around."

Pine began to shake her head but Blum said, "Go on, Jack. We're listening." She gave Blum a glare but remained silent.

"And I know you've been using rental cars and the like. That is not necessary. Take the Porsche SUV. It's just sitting in the garage doing nothing. And . . . and I've opened an account with funds in it that you have the authority to access from anywhere." He slid open the drawer on his nightstand and took out two pieces of plastic. "One debit, one credit. There is no limit on the amount you can charge. The four-digit PIN for the debit card is your birthday, month and day."

"Jack, I can't take your money."

"It's not my money, Atlee. It's *our* money. And it's not like you're going to be using it to go on vacation. You're using it to find your sister and my daughter. And your mother and Tim. I presume that when you're working as an FBI agent, the more resources you have to accomplish the job, the better. Am I wrong?"

"Well, no," she said slowly.

"Then I don't see what the damn problem is, do you?" he added bluntly, as though daring her to conjure a reason that would thwart his will.

Well, thought Pine, he had niftily turned the tables on her this time. She even felt a grudging pride for how he was handling this.

Meanwhile, Blum reached out and took the cards. "There is no problem, Jack. Your very generous offer of help is much appreciated. Isn't that right, Agent Pine?"

Pine looked at her and then at Lineberry's weary yet hopeful features, and her expression softened. "Thank you, Jack. That *is* very kind and very helpful."

He sat back, obviously relieved.

Blum handed the cards to Pine, who put them in her pocket.

Lineberry said, "And if you won't stay here, I would like you to use my place in Atlanta as a base. And you can fly in and out of there if need be on my jet. I'll ensure that it's ready to go at all times. I certainly won't be using it for a while."

"Okay, Jack," said Pine. She glanced at Blum. "That will be fine. But we may not be staying there much. We need to go where the leads take us."

"Understood," he said quickly.

"But I don't want people waiting hand and foot on us. We can take care of ourselves."

"I thought you might say that, so I have already given the staff there three months' fully paid leave. You'll have the run of the place all on your own."

"That is very generous," said Blum.

"It's only fair," said Lineberry emphatically. "For everybody."

Pine asked, "Is there anything you can remember that might provide a lead as to where my mother and Tim could have gone?"

Lineberry gazed solemnly at Pine. "In answer to that, I'm going to give you something that your mother asked me *never* to let you see."

Pine sat up straight now, every muscle tensed, her adrenaline spiking to such a degree she found it difficult to form her one-word response. "W-what?"

He once more reached into the drawer and this time pulled out a gray envelope. "When you read this, I want you to keep in mind that you must do the exact opposite of what your mother writes in here."

"When did she send it to you?" said Pine, ignoring this curious piece of advice.

"It was around the time she left you. It just turned up in my office mail one day. I had given Tim my contact information when I saw him in Virginia. The letter has no return address. But you can see that the postmark is Charleston, South Carolina. I think she might have been on her way to meet up with Tim when she sent it to me from there."

He held out the envelope to Pine. She stared at it like it was a gun being pointed at her. Then she took it, albeit grudgingly. She looked at the handwriting on the envelope. It was clearly her mother's.

"I . . . I think I'll read this later," Pine said in a hushed tone.

In a shaky voice Lineberry said, "I should have given it to you before now. There really is no excuse except that for a large part of my adult life I was steeped in the art of keeping secrets. It's not an excuse, you understand. It's just . . . reality. At least it was for me."

"Does this give any indication of where they might have gone?" asked Pine.

"Not that I could find."

"What did you mean when you said I should do the exact opposite of what she writes?"

"Now *that* will be clear when you read it," said Lineberry.

5

Pine drove the Porsche while Blum piloted the rental to the drop-off location at the airport. After that they headed to Lineberry's penthouse apartment in downtown Atlanta. Pine had been there before to have a drink with Lineberry, but it was the first visit for Blum.

"Oh my God," said Blum when the private elevator opened directly into the penthouse suite's vestibule. "This is something right out of a dream."

"Yeah, I know," said Pine glumly.

Blum eyed her. "Oh come on, Agent Pine. This is a lot better than the motel we stayed at last time. The heat didn't work and the shower ran at a trickle."

"He let us use his place in New York. Now we're driving his Porsche and staying here, and we have the use of his private jet, and he wants to leave me all this money and—"

"Yes, I really do feel sorry for you having to face all *that*," Blum said with a look that made Pine feel about an inch tall.

Pine sighed. "I know, I know, Carol. Most people would feel like they'd won the lottery."

"But you're not most people," said Blum, growing serious.

"I don't care about stuff like that. I never have. My apartment back in Shattered Rock is perfect. I've got my really cool vintage Mustang convertible. It's all I need. I'm not a private jet sort of gal."

"That's fine. But let's just use what Jack has offered in order to get where we need to go as fast as possible, like he said."

"Right, okay."

Blum looked at her watch. "It's dinnertime. With the 'staff' on leave, should I head to what I am sure is a fabulous kitchen and whip something up? I bet the fridge and freezer are fully stocked."

Pine took the credit card out of her pocket. "Or how about I treat you to dinner instead? Or at least Jack can."

The building concierge gave them several recommendations, and they decided on a French bistro within walking distance of their building.

They ordered a bottle of wine and their meals and spent two hours at a table in the back mostly talking about innocuous things. It felt refreshing to Pine, but she also felt some remorse. Pretty much every waking moment lately had been devoted to finding her sister. Deviating from that, even for a little bit, felt like a betrayal of Mercy.

"We *are* making progress, Agent Pine, but we do need to take a break every now and then," said Blum, apparently reading Pine's thoughts.

Pine nodded and then glanced around the restaurant, eyeing people who she was sure had their own share of problems, maybe not as dire as hers, yet problems still. But she was afraid, despite the "progress" Blum had mentioned, that either her problem would never have a resolution, or the conclusion would be finding her sister's body.

Can you handle that, Lee? You told yourself you could. But were you lying?

They were walking back when Blum said, "Will you read the letter tonight?"

Pine nodded. "Yes. I have to, although part of me is dreading it."

"I can understand that. Although there might be some clue in there."

"Maybe," Pine said doubtfully.

Back in the apartment, Pine took a long, steaming hot shower, put on a pair of sweatpants and a T-shirt, and climbed into bed.

She took the letter out and stared at the envelope for a little while. With her finger she traced her mother's lovely cursive handwriting, which was quite familiar to her. Pine sat back against the pillow and then abruptly stood, grabbed her phone, left her room, and walked down to the wine cellar that Lineberry had shown her on their previous visit. She snagged a bottle of Italian wine. It was the same vintage that he had served Pine here before. She'd decided she needed some more alcohol to make it through the reading of her mother's letter. A lot more.

She went out onto the terrace that wrapped itself around three sides of the penthouse. There was a glass wall rising nearly chest high enclosing the space. All-weather wicker furnishings and exquisite plantings and fountains and a large fire pit surrounded her. It really was a paradise. And she felt enormous guilt.

I wonder where Mercy is right now. I seriously doubt in a place like this.

Pine opted to just sit on the floor after using a remote control to ignite a gas fireplace enclosed by stone and textured ceramic tile. She moved closer to the flames and set her phone down, then opened the wine bottle, poured a generous amount into her glass, and took a long sip.

Okay, no more stalling, Lee.

She would sometimes refer to herself by the name she'd had growing up. She'd been given it because Mercy had trouble pronouncing "At-lee" and just started calling her Lee. The name had stuck until Pine had gone to college. Now she would dearly love to hear her sister call her by that name even once.

She took out the two-page letter and unfolded it. She frowned when she saw her hand shaking. She took another sip of wine to calm her nerves. It didn't work.

Come on! It's just a stupid letter.

But, clearly, it was far more than that. This would be the first example she'd ever seen of what her mother was thinking about things since she had abandoned her daughter all those years ago. Pine finished the glass of wine and poured another.

So here goes, Pine thought, taking a deep breath and holding it, like she was about to go underwater for a while.

Dear Jack,

Once again you have come to the rescue and Tim and I can't thank you enough. It was terrible, horrible, what happened in Virginia. The person obviously wanted to either hurt me by killing Tim, or thought I might be there with Tim. I am still shaking after almost losing him.

Here, Pine almost put the letter down. She had no desire to hear her mother's thoughts on almost losing her husband when she had chosen to walk away from her daughter. But something made her continue.

And then came the even harder part. Leaving my beloved Lee. I can't believe that I'm even writing this, Jack. She is really all I have left. After Mercy was taken, which was entirely my fault, as we both know, Lee was all that kept my life going. I know that

I smothered her, at the same time I put up a wall between us. I felt that if I let myself get too close to her that I would let something slip that would put her in danger. I couldn't do that to my little girl. Sitting next to her in that hospital bed, not knowing if she was going to live or die, not knowing what had happened to Mercy, my mind just shut down. I couldn't process anything other than the well-deserved guilt I was feeling. When my girls needed me, I wasn't there. There is no more basic duty for a mother. And I failed that duty miserably. She has now grown into a very smart, accomplished young woman I'm so proud of. And she did it all on her own. I know that she sees how I have shut her out and this just deepens my guilt. To withhold love from someone you love more than life itself, it does something to you, Jack, something irreversibly painful. But I can't make myself change course now. I just can't. The truth is if Lee thinks I don't love her then she won't miss me when I'm gone. At least that's my hope. Now, I have come into some money, I won't tell you exactly how, but I figured out something and when I confronted the person I turned out to be right. This money will fund Lee's college and also help provide for her later in life, and also give Tim and me something to live on. It is with a heavy heart that I am leaving her, but I feel very confident that she will be safe now.

When you recruited me all those years ago I was younger than Lee is now. I was scared to death.

I didn't want to do it, but you showed me how much good would come of it. And I suppose it has. For others. But not for the Pine family. I fully accepted that. Tim did as well. But not Mercy and Lee. They had no choice. All I know is, even though Tim and I will be together, I will be more alone than I ever have been before. Without my daughters, I am nothing. I thought that I had sacrificed everything for them. In the end, I simply sacrificed them. No mother could have done any worse than I did. So much so that I don't deserve to even be called one, not anymore. I think of Mercy and Lee every day and I will until the day I die. They were both my little flowers that I let wither. But I will spend the rest of my life trying to make up for what I did, for the poor choices that I made. At least I can try.

Thank you for everything, Jack. If you ever see Lee, please don't mention me to her. Don't say anything that will dredge up memories she should just forget. I'm not worth the trouble. She just needs to get on with her life and never look back.

And then she had signed the letter with her real name, Amanda, as opposed to Julia.

The tears that had fallen from Pine's eyes had stained the pages in several places. She read it through three more times, clinging to different words and phrases with each pass. She finally folded the pages and set them next to her as she watched night fall over the lighted Atlanta skyline.

Her family was out there somewhere, but the reality was all three of them could be dead now. If so, would finding their graves, if there even were graves, be enough for her?

I don't know the answer to that. I can't possibly.

Her phone dinged. She looked at the screen. It was a text from John Puller.

She sat up straighter. Leonard Atkins *was* receiving aid from the VA. And it was going to an address in Huntsville, Alabama, that Puller had also provided in the text. Pine Googled the location. It was about three and a half hours by car from Atlanta.

She went back inside and climbed into bed.

Her last thought before she fell asleep was, *Just keep plugging, Atlee. Every day. And you'll eventually get there. You'll find them, one way or another.*

6

When the woman rose from the chipped wooden stool, she stood a statuesque six foot one in her long, bare feet. She flexed her right hand and then her left. The fingers were callused and strong, just like all the rest of her. She felt pops, twinges, and creaks as bones and cartilage resettled into appropriate grooves; more cantankerous elements refused to fully reset, but grudgingly moved a bit closer to normal. She stretched her long, muscled neck, rolling it one way and then the other. She pushed her sculpted shoulders away from her neck, and her ripped traps and delts thanked her as the release of tension was both palpable and immediate.

She wore a frayed black sports top with a faded Nike swoosh, and a chest protector under that along with a pair of faded black Lycra athletic shorts. Both pieces of compression clothing sharply defined her long, muscular, and scarred physique.

The short, trim man standing next to her helped the woman slip on her gloves, and then he commenced rapidly massaging her long, ropy arms.

"You ready?" he asked, looking up at her.

She glanced down at him with a frown. "I'm here, Jerry. So what the hell do you think?"

He put in her mouthguard and then made the sign of the cross. He always did that, and it always irritated the crap out of her.

"Who you trying to signal, dude, your bookie?" she muttered through the mouthguard.

"See you on the other side, El," said Jerry as he hurriedly left the ring.

Eloise "El" Cain was getting a bit long in the tooth for what she was about to do, though she did it only when she really needed the money. Her opponent tonight was four inches shorter, but a real stud; at 190 pounds she outweighed the taller Cain by ten pounds. And, like Cain, almost all of it was bone, gristle, and muscle displayed across her broad shoulders, sinewy core, abs like rows of stacked bricks, barrel-thick thighs, muscled glutes, and diamond-hard calves. She could destroy 99 percent of the guys out there and give the other 1 percent a run for their money. Her technique was rock-solid: She could fight all day, could absorb terrific punishment, and had crushing power in all four limbs. She was over a dozen years younger than Cain, and many thought she had a shot at the big time. The only question marks were her fighting smarts and mental toughness. And the fact that the women's UFC world topped out at featherweight, or a 145-pound limit.

Cain had always thought that was sexist bullshit. There were some women out there who could fight with the best of them. The men had heavier weight divisions in the UFC, so why were the bigger women ruled out? Maybe they would just have to start their own league, or the larger women would have to make the jump to boxing, with its far heavier weight divisions. But ultimately it wasn't fair, and, like always, the women got the short end of the athletic stick, Cain believed.

Her opponent had more tats than unmarked skin, Cain observed. The general theme of the skin art seemed to be violent death, with sadomasochistic torture running a close second.

Cain knew she was here just for the woman to notch a win on her career belt as she moved up in the land of mixed martial arts.

Well, maybe I have different plans.

This was decidedly not the big time. No cage match televised on pay-per-view happening here. No Ronda Rousey, Holly Holm, or Cris Cyborg within a thousand miles of this dive. No million-dollar payoffs or eye-popping commercial endorsements. This was small-time, local stuff. But the rowdy, hard-drinking crowd numbered well over two hundred, and the excitement of what they were about to witness was palpable. The site was an old factory where stuff used to be made by the locals until the world changed and the country stopped making any stuff at all. Now it was a tinpot relic that was used for myriad purposes, none of them authorized and some of them patently illegal. But who was going to deny folks a little fun and a way to make some money on the side?

And I can earn my little pot of gold tonight.

The official purse was five grand. If she won, Cain would get only a thousand of it. The loser got three hundred bucks flat for getting her brains scrambled. Just how it was at this level. What Cain called it was kicking the shit out of someone while they kicked the shit out of you, while the crowd guzzled beer and sucked in weed, cheering and jeering. The rest of the cash would go to assorted males on the food chain who added no value and took no risks and raised not one finger. But they had power and influence behind them, so they got their pound of flesh.

Yet the possibility of a thousand bucks for one night's work was more than enough incentive for Cain to be standing where she was, mouthpiece in, fists gloved, strategy mapped out, adrenaline spiking.

The women met in the middle of an improvised ring, where fence posts had been cemented into huge tractor trailer rims to hold them upright. The chain-link fence around the ladies was eight feet high with a padlocked gate. Unlike a UFC octagon ring, the chain link was not coated with soft vinyl and the metal posts had no safety coverings. You got rammed into that, it was not going to feel good. The floor was not springy canvas, just concrete, so ditto for sudden collisions there. But Cain didn't mind. This was a piece of cake compared to other things she'd endured in life, although the locked cage door always bothered her. But if need be, she could climb the fence.

She glanced at her opponent, who was giving Cain her version of the intimidating dead-eye stare, which differed from the way that men did it. While testosterone-spiked guys always overplayed their hand and abilities in mental confrontations like this, women usually understated how badly they were going to mess you up.

"In your dreams, buttercup," Cain said. She tacked on a broad smile at the dead-eye, which really seemed to piss the gal off.

If I get in your head, all the better.

The setup was three five-minute rounds, unless one fighter was knocked out or otherwise was no longer able to defend herself. Cain had never been knocked out, but there was always the chance. The lower number of rounds meant that the fight would be high intensity pretty much from the get-go. There was no cruising in this ring of human mayhem. The crowd wanted punishment and blood and lots of it. Like watching the NFL, it was far more American than baseball and apple pie ever would be. The tough and vicious won, and everybody else was a loser.

The only people inside this temporary prison where the max sentence was fifteen minutes were the fighters and the ref. This one was a stout, arrogant piece of work who had the deserved rep of being a misogynistic creep who was not below feeling up a gal who had been knocked off her feet and/or robbed of consciousness. He had tried that on a momentarily dazed Cain in one fight, and she had communicated her displeasure by nearly biting off one of his fingers. He had never tried it with her again, but she didn't hold out hope for the jerk to call anything fair her way tonight.

But Cain also wasn't overly confident. She had assorted injuries that had never healed properly, including a rotator cuff that had the tendency to seize up on her when she needed it the most. And her opponent wouldn't need much of an advantage to knock Cain right on her ass, lights out.

The ref gave his brief instructions, shot a glare in Cain's direction, wiggled his permanently damaged index finger, and the ladies stepped back, awaiting the commencement of the match. It came a few seconds later via air horn, and the fight was on.

7

The women charged forward and met once more in the middle of the ring, with flared nostrils, cocked and locked limbs, and lethally intent eyes, while the crowd noise revved higher as the old, rusted guts of the factory rose up behind them. The whole scene was bolstered by ear-piercing music. "Eye of the Tiger" was running on a loop, and someone had set up seventies-era strobe lights and even a smoke machine that was already starting to peter out. It was tackiness taken to a whole new level, and everyone in attendance apparently loved it, except the two women about to do serious battle. They had other things on their minds, like survival. And money.

While the volume of the crowd spiked, Cain and her opponent took just a few seconds to feel each other out. Cain threw a jab and a snap kick to gauge the other woman's tendencies, power, skill level, and reaction time. Her opponent did the same. The woman landed a crisp shot to Cain's left oblique. Cain made her retreat by looping a kick in the woman's direction. But she did not stretch her long leg to its maximum range of motion.

Cain took a right cross to the chin and a knee to her other oblique. Both blows stung. The chick was faster than Cain was, she had to admit, her muscle twitch superior; none of that was unexpected. She could tell that the lady was not maxing out, not yet. She had the fuel to dump Cain on her ass, that was without doubt.

Cain feigned a short left and then hit her opponent with a right uppercut straight to the gut. But the woman's ab wall was stone. No damage done there, not really. Cain observed a sharp exhale of breath come out of the lady's mouth with the impact, like air from a popped balloon. But the eyes remained clear, and her expression looking more assured of victory. She must have assumed Cain had used max power on that blow. But the arms were your weak limbs. True strength, the real knockout power, Cain well knew, was housed lower.

Two rounds passed with hundreds of punches and kicks and knees thrown and painfully landed, and blood and sweat released. And it was a lot of blood and a lot more sweat, as their bodies collided, separated, and slammed against each other again and again like grizzly bears ripping at each other.

The concrete floor quickly became littered with the droplets of both women's blood and sweat, which their constantly moving bare feet had fashioned into blurry, ill-defined patterns that looked like an early-stage Jackson Pollock masterpiece. Welts and purplish bruises covered their arms and legs and torsos. Cuts littered their faces. You didn't do this sort of thing if your looks really mattered to you. A forearm to the nose or a foot to the chin was going to land you on the floor, not a magazine cover.

In a brief clinch, Cain said tauntingly through her mouthguard, "Come on, kid, you're supposed to be the next big thing. You haven't even knocked me down once, cream puff."

The angry woman tried to arm-bar her, but Cain roughly shoved her off and got a snarl in return. Her opponent leapt forward, and Cain took a hard shot to the head. She fell back a bit, but not in a defenseless way that would encourage the woman to immediately charge after her, hoping to land blow after frenetic blow until the ref stepped in and ended it. And this ref would do that in a heartbeat against Cain, just to deprive her of the cash.

Not tonight, jerk-off.

But then her rotator seized up and Cain couldn't lift her arm high enough to guard her face; the pain was etched on her features. The other woman immediately noted all this and came in for the kill.

She pounded Cain with everything she had, her fists moving so fast Cain could barely see them, much less block them. A cross caught her on the side of the face, staggering her, a hook battered the other side of her head. An uppercut tore into her chin and she fell back, trying to keep it together, and attempting to unlock her rotator.

But then the other woman made one mistake, and that was all it took inside a cage match. The mistake was stepping back and dropping her hands just enough, because she thought she was out of Cain's range. She was regaining her breath after her onslaught of blows, and taking her time in deciding how best to knock Cain out, which she now assumed was a foregone conclusion.

This was what Cain's intentionally shortened range of motion maneuvers had laid the groundwork for all throughout the fight. After a minute or so of jousting, even competitors at this level could mentally measure every millimeter of the ring and tack onto that the exact outer limits of their opponent's reach. But the latter calculation didn't work if the opponent let you see only what she wanted you to see. And with every kick launched, Cain had methodically done exactly that, never letting the gal see her full range of motion, which really was the whole ball of wax. Now, with her rotator betraying her, the moment had come.

The woman's trainer, more adept at this sort of thing than his protégé, and having seen Cain fight before, screamed out a warning through the chain link. It was a warning his fighter never heard because it came a second after Cain slammed her size-thirteen right foot—hard as a tree branch—into the woman's jaw. Even with all the noise, everyone in the crowd heard the sound, like a watermelon smashing on pavement, as the jawbone gave way to the foot bone.

The fighter was lifted several inches into the air with the force of the blow, her head snapping back far more rapidly than heads were designed to do. When she came back down the woman toppled like a chain-sawed pine to the cement, because her consciousness had just left the building.

All the ref had to do was bend down and see that the limp body held not a shred of anything that constituted a fighter capable of continuing. He waved the contest over after two minutes and thirty-four seconds into the final round. More of the crowd groaned in disappointment than screamed in delight. Clearly, the majority of bettors here thought Cain was going to get her ass kicked tonight.

The fallen lady was briefly revived with a cracked capsule of ammonia inhalant, hauled to her feet, and stood there, almost entirely held up by her pissed-off trainer as the ref grudgingly raised Cain's hand in victory. Then the beaten fighter immediately collapsed and was carried out of the ring on a stretcher.

Blood trickling down her face and out of her nose, Cain stalked out of the ring without saying a word to anyone. She had nothing she wanted to say, or anyone she wanted to say it to.

Cain just wanted her damn money.

8

In the dingy, filthy bathroom that held no shower, Cain stripped off her sweaty clothes and ran a soapy wet towel over herself to remove the stink and the blood, both hers and her opponent's. The bruises on her face were nothing; they would heal. She then briefly eyed her long naked body in the cracked mirror under the popping, unforgiving glare of fluorescent lights that had been all the rage a half century ago.

Only the best for this gal.

Not a single tattoo was grafted onto her skin. She didn't need them. She had scars, burn marks, lumps, painfully deep knife cuts and other disfigurements; they were all there, hand-tooled into her. She didn't grimace in resentment or disgust as she looked at these old wounds, she smiled in triumph.

I survived it all.

That had always been her attitude. Throw everything you got at her and she'd still be standing even if you weren't. She especially liked it if you weren't.

Cain ran a hand over dark fuzz cut so close to the

scalp that it almost looked shaved. She had done that last year. She should have done it long before then. Long hair had made her angry. For as far back as she could remember, which wasn't *all* the way back. She knew there were holes, gaps, blanks. Once she had hoped to fill them all in. Now, she appreciated the gaps. She had no more interest in discovering anything about her past because what would be the point? Only today and tomorrow and the day after that counted. And right now, she was a winner of a thousand bucks. So this was one of her best days in a long time.

Cain had finally got her rotator unseized, iced where she'd taken the hardest shots, rubbed ointment on her cuts, and put on her underwear and bra, faded jeans, and a tattered sweatshirt. Flip-flops went on her feet though it was cold outside. With the prize money she would buy some new casual shoes, but thirteen double wide wasn't routinely available, at least in something that didn't look like footwear for clowns. She slipped the sleek fifteen-shot Glock 19 with the black matte finish she always carried to these fights out of a padlocked cabinet and into her belt clip. She stuffed her other things into a small duffel, slung it over her shoulder, and went in search of her winnings.

She found it in the form of a small, thin man in a cheap, wrinkled suit with flint chips for eyes and a mustache that kept twitching like something was living inside it. He was standing in the hallway right off where the fight had taken place. An unlit cigarette dangled from his lips like an afterthought. The crowd was gone. It might just be her and him, and Cain wanted this over as soon as possible. A man, a woman, and money to be given, all in solitary isolation, was always complicated.

She held out her hand. "Let's have it, Sam. I got an early morning."

He lifted a worn envelope from his inside coat pocket and held it up tauntingly. "You suckered her pretty good, El. But she's smart. She'll figure it out. Unlike you, she's going places."

Cain didn't take the bait for the simple fact that she didn't care. "Right now the only place she's going is the hospital for a concussion check and to have her jaw wired. If she's really smart she'll take a coding class and leave you and this shit behind."

She dropped her duffel, grabbed the envelope, and opened it.

"It's all there," said Sam. "You think I'd cheat you?"

"Yeah, I do, because yeah, you have."

"That was before."

"Before what?" She caught him looking at her Glock. Cain said, "Hallelujah for open carry and no background checks. All a girl needs not to get screwed by jerks like you."

"Right," he sneered. "You have trouble passing a background check, El?"

She finished counting the cash and put it in her duffel. "I'd pass it as easy as you would, *Sam*."

"You made a few folks a ton of money tonight. Most bet against you."

"Yeah, well stupid them."

"You're past your prime. Maybe if you'd taken it seriously ten years ago. You got a lucky kick in tonight. She would've decisioned you easy, and she almost knocked you out. She was ahead in the first two rounds, and in the third, when your bum shoulder locked up, she was kicking the shit out of you. She's just better, admit it."

"How would you know anything about it, Sam? You've never been in the ring, have you? See, that takes a bunch of things you'll never have." She glanced at his crotch. "Starting with balls bigger than peanuts."

He didn't seem to be listening to Cain. He gave her the once-over. "You know, if you fixed yourself up, got all that damn shit on your skin taken care of, wore some decent clothes now and then, didn't shave your scalp like some dopey skinhead, and for a few hours acted like a girl instead of an attack dog, you could be attractive to a guy. You do that, maybe you and me could have some fun. I can be fun, with the right gal." He stroked her arm.

The next moment he was thrown against the wall, with the muzzle of Cain's drawn Glock pressed against his cheek.

"You ever try to lay another hand on me . . ." She racked the gun's slide to chamber a round and pressed the muzzle so far into his skin, it rode up against his cheekbone.

"You're batshit crazy, bitch," cried out a terrified Sam.

"And don't ever forget that." Cain stepped back, holstered the Glock, grabbed her duffel, and walked off.

She signed a few autographs for some stragglers in the parking lot who were probably too shit-faced to even know who she was. After that Cain climbed into her dented 1990s-era two-door Honda Civic hatchback, with enough miles on it to have circumnavigated the world nearly ten times. Off and on over the years this car had also served as her home as she crisscrossed the country.

Great old car, thought Cain as she started the engine. *What would I do without you?* She patted the dash like it was an old friend. And when you didn't have many friends, sometimes a car would do just fine.

The drive didn't take long because Cain lived in a nearby area that had not been gentrified. She supposed there were too many undesirables around.

Including me.

9

Cain parked out front and entered through the only door to her place after unlocking the rusted padlock. She relocked it on the other side because folks around here didn't abide by the same laws most human beings did. She knew at some point the owners would kick her and the other residents out and turn this place into something that would make them real money. For now, it was just a series of makeshift pods separated by thin walls having been put up during its transition from commercial use to residential. In that way the place had been inexpensively reborn from the hulks of semi-attached dilapidated buildings, where the current residents were one step up from being homeless. But it was a damn important step, she knew. You could always take a home for granted, until you didn't have one.

She had a roof, a bed, a toilet, a microwave, enough heat to get by, and windows and a floor fan in lieu of AC. She had a cell phone that she had "found" by stealing it, and WiFi that she had lifted from a nearby network after learning its password. There were rats all over, but they left her alone for the most part. The dump cost her four hundred a month in rent plus utilities, and that was a blessing to her because she couldn't afford a penny more than that.

Her legal name for a long time now was Eloise Cain. Eloise had come from a book she had read as a child. She didn't go by Rebecca Atkins anymore. Not since that night in Georgia. And she had had another name before that, but couldn't remember what it was. *How did I get so lucky to have all these names?* she sometimes thought when she'd had too many beers or too much weed, or both. *Most people only have the one.*

And Cain? That just came from reading the Good Book. Desiree Atkins had said the scriptures were all she needed to know in the way of learning. That she had to repent her whole life for all the awful things she'd done and all the awful things she'd wanted to do. Well, she had certainly wanted to do awful things to Desiree, all right. But whatever she was willing to do paled in comparison to what the woman actually *had* done to Cain.

After escaping, Cain had basically lived at some of the best public libraries in the country for years. And it wasn't necessarily about reading and learning, at least not at first. She had found, as a rule, that the more books you read, the longer they let you stay. And when it was freezing cold or mercilessly hot out, that was important. And if you read a lot of books, and even helped out, she had found that kindly librarians had often become informal teachers, helping her to read better and to write—and on top of that, they fed her, too. Because without something in the belly the mind didn't work too good. Those years had constituted her formal instruction, for better or worse.

She really had no clear memory of anything prior to going to live with the Atkinses. Except for one thing.

But it was a big thing. A really big thing.

She dropped her duffel next to the mattress on the floor. A box next to the mattress represented her closet. She could have flicked on a light, but she preferred the dark. Counterintuitively, for her, things somehow seemed to have greater clarity in total darkness. The stark distractions of life were filtered out by it, allowing one to fully focus as though one's life depended on it, which it often had for Cain.

She took a loose board out of the floor and opened the lid of the tin box she kept there. The money went in and the board went back. Also on the floor were stacks of books. All had been taken from libraries, some with permission, most without. But she had read them all, multiple times, so there was that. Books were meant to be read, not displayed on a shelf for decoration.

She sat on the mattress and rolled a joint. She lit it, sucked on it, drank in the smoke's fumes, as the night deepened and the weed siphoned off some of her pain from the fight. Over the years she'd torn through all of the hard stuff: coke, crack, meth, heroin, synthetics, exotic street mixes. Then she'd almost died from an OxyContin pill laced with fentanyl. It had taken three pops of naloxone spray from an EMT to bring her back, or so she was told. After that, she'd walked away from it. It was a bitch to kick, but she'd kicked harder than that. The bottom line was nothing was going to control her ever again.

She focused on the memory from long ago.

They don't want you anymore, the man had said that night to the little girl she used to be with the name and history she no longer remembered. As they sat in his car he had said, *They sent me here to take one of you. Your mother and father told me to kill you. But I'm not going to do that. I'm taking you to another family that wants you. You'll be safe there.*

She remembered the older couple, Len and Wanda Atkins. That was who the man had taken her to. Then she had been quickly passed on to Joe and Desiree Atkins. What they had done to her—well, Desiree mostly—she had tried her best to forget. But she never really could.

Slave. That was what she was. Slave, prisoner, piece of property, human meat; she had read about that stuff in books. Blacks used to be slaves in this country, she had read. Whatever the term, it was all she was back then.

How many trees had she chopped down for

firewood? How many logs carried, how much brush cleared? Floors and windows scrubbed, dishes washed, carpet vacuumed, grass cut, garden tended, bushes trimmed, vines and crap cleared, walls painted, clothes laundered, toilets and sinks cleaned, beds made, meals prepared that were never for her? How much shit hauled from one spot to another, or "Do this, do that, NOW!" orders just because they could make her?

She had read the fairy tale about Cinderella.

I was her, only I never found a prince. And my feet are way too big for a glass slipper.

Human beings were funny, in a very unfunny way.

She grew tall, very tall. Her parents must have been tall; she couldn't remember. And her life had made her strong: She could lift a truck, and she possessed stamina out the roof, able to work her ass off for days and not feel it. And not an ounce of fat was on her frame, because they fed her just enough to keep her hungry. And her pain tolerance? What she had endured tonight? It was painful, for sure, but really nothing compared to what she had endured in the past.

Desiree had really liked to burn shit. Dogs, cats . . . but mostly El.

And mentally she was stronger than she otherwise ever would have been. Every day the same. First the locked room in the house. Then her final destination was the little prison in the woods. Another fairy tale with a monster attached. The chain. The smell of rotting clay. She'd stayed focused in her mind to survive it. Played the mental games required not to lose her sanity. She obsessed over mundane stuff so she could bury the total absurdity of her current existence in the black hole of her mind while she doted over minutiae: the counting of seconds, the drip of water, the arrangement of her rag clothes on her grimy shelves, the cleaning of dishes, the fixation on just where to place the first cut on a tree limb. Or the sighting of a fawn that drove her to tears, or the spying of a hawk enjoying the lift of air currents along with the best view in the county.

A bird with more freedom than she had.

Each day she was alive to see the sun rise and then fall was an enormous victory. It truly was the little things, particularly when all the big things had been denied you. The long days and nights of labor, the knock-knock on the door for her two daily meals. Her with the food, him eventually with the gun. Because she had grown far bigger than both of them. They were afraid of her; she could see that in their wide eyes and how Joe clutched the weapon, how the vein at his temple bulged while that door, that damn door, stayed open. Never seeing another living soul except the scaredy-cat Joe and the bug-eyed and vicious Desiree, and occasionally Len and Wanda, who would come with sad eyes and leave with sadder ones. Cain had passed from terrified kid to cool-eyed adult. She was a prisoner even though she'd never been tried and convicted of anything.

Until *that* day came.

The escape, timed just so. She'd distracted him. He'd forgotten about the padlock, failed to secure it after doing exactly that year after year. She smiled at the thought. She knew about the camera. But she'd waited for them to get back to the house, counting off the strides in her head. She knew their routine better than they knew their routine, because they had a whole other life to think about and she didn't. She just had *this*. Then she had hit the door with all her strength, and she was so damn strong, like a lion, like a wild-ass lion that was about to break out, after years in captivity.

You humans better run like the living hell 'cause something not human is coming for you. The monster in the fairy tale is breaking out tonight, you muthas.

And she had slammed into that door, again, and again, and again, and . . . just like that—

Freedom.

She puffed on the joint, sucked in the smoke, and opened the small fridge she'd found in a dumpster and repaired and cleaned up. She pulled out a Budweiser, popped the top, and drank her fill, the beer irritating her busted lip. She pressed the cold can against it and then her oblique. Broken-Jawed Bitch really packed a wallop.

But there she was that night, charging to freedom, not knowing where she was going. Not caring about that in the least. After all those years. Then there had been Joe Atkins, looming up in her field of vision like the big, bad boogeyman. Only she was bigger and badder than Joe would ever be. He was a gnat to be squashed.

She lifted the beer can until it was upside down and she finished it off, wiped her chin, and pinched the joint out, saving the rest for later. She breathed in the reefer-scented smoke drifting in the air, like lines of miniature cumulus in her room, with the added benefit of making her high.

Yes, there had been Joe. And then he had been there no more.

Squashed. Freedom.

She lay back on the mattress, kicked her flip-flops off, and wriggled her long toes.

She had cash, she had a single credit card that she used very sparingly, she had a place to live, wheels to go to other places. She had jobs that she did, crap that she pulled. Not all legal, but so what? Nothing done to her had been legal.

Survival. She fell asleep thinking only of that. Just like pretty much every other night.

It didn't make her feel worse and it didn't make her feel better. But at least it made Cain feel something.

Hallelujah, you survived it all, El. Now go to sleep and get ready for tomorrow.

Just in case it comes.

10

Her phone alarm dinged at six a.m., and Cain rolled over and yawned. She sat up and opened the window to get out the final dregs of any lingering pot smoke. But she wasn't too worried. While they had random drug testing at her first place of work today, they used a blood test. A blood test could only detect THC, the component in pot that made you feel high, for about three hours after use. A saliva test could do it for between twenty-four and seventy-two hours. A urine test could nail you for up to thirty days after use. Hence, many employers used saliva or more likely a blood test as their testing tool. Otherwise, they'd test their way right out of business because they'd have no bodies to do the work.

That was the dirty little secret of the crap work world where millions labored every day. And the savviness of addicts who needed a job.

She opened her fridge, cracked three eggs into a glass, and drank it down raw. She had seen this done in an old movie about a down-and-out boxer named Rocky. Protein, apparently, which helped your body recover and build. Which was good, Cain thought, because it tasted like shit and had the texture of snot.

She changed into the outfit she had fought in—blood, sweat, and all—covered that with a hoodie and sweatpants, and slipped on a pair of worn sneakers. Then she left her place, padlocking the door on the other side. She ran for miles, her breath forming visible clouds with every exhale. Winter was coming with speed. But she would be snug in her little place, hopefully.

She liked to run, and her long legs and frame were built for eating up massive quantities of ground. Cain had been running her whole life. Sometimes for real, other times just in her mind, especially when she'd been locked up all those years. She would jog in place and let her imagination take her to any place other than the one she was in. The things she did in her mind to keep going, it was some wicked shit. Taught her stuff. Demonstrated that your mind could get you through anything. Anything. Because it had done so for her.

Psalm of my life: If you can't live in the world you have, make one up.

She stopped at five different "tents and boxes" and handed out cash from her prize money at each one. These were not boozers or druggies, at least not mostly. They would use the money for food and other necessaries, because they all had young kids living with them in their distress.

"Thank you," said one young mom, who was white but looked brown with the sun and the dirt. Cain could relate. This was the "tan" of homelessness. It was unlike any other skin tanning ever, Cain knew. It fried your brain as well as your outside. It never really came off you because you worried every minute it could happen again. It was like you were a fugitive for life and your only crime was bad luck or bad choices. When the rich and powerful made a mistake their lawyers and PR folks took care of it.

Cain waved the woman's thanks off and kept running. The next family was black, the next one after that, too. The next ones spoke Spanglish and shivered in the chill. The next family, she couldn't really tell what they were, not that it mattered. They were breathing, they were human. *They look like me in that way.* That was enough. Boxes were meant to house stuff, not put people in. Not until they're dead, anyway. Most people looked at them and felt either sorry or disgusted, or both. Not Cain. She just saw folks who needed some help.

At the end she had given away over half her winnings.

She knew what the term "Good Samaritan" meant, but only because of the Bible reading. But that was not why she was doing it. She did it because today she had money and today they didn't, but needed it. *Keep it simple* was Cain's motto. When you thought too hard about it, you tended to want to keep what you had and dare others to try to take it.

She got back to her place and completed her daily workout with pushups, floor dips, chin-ups on a bar wedged in a doorway, lots of ab and core work with a medicine ball, and exercises with a kettle-bell she'd gotten for a buck from a gym going out of business. Then bodyweight lunges and squats and calisthenics followed by shadow boxing; she finished with some heavy-duty stretching.

The strong and vigilant don't always survive, but it damn sure improves your chances.

She showered in cold water because that was all there was. She had started her period late last night. She had had her first period at age eleven while she was with the Atkinses. She thought she was dying when the cramps came and the blood dripped from down there. She had begged Desiree to help her. The woman had laughed and thrown her a roll of paper towels, telling her that it would come every month, like clockwork. She had added, "They sell stuff for it, but the paper towels will do for you. It's not like you're going anywhere. So deal with it."

And Cain had dealt with it using the paper towels. Until Wanda Atkins had explained to Cain what was really going on, and given her boxes of tampons. That had been an eye opener. She remembered asking Wanda if boys had periods, too.

"No," she had said. "Good thing, because they couldn't handle it."

Cain believed she spoke the literal truth.

Wanda had been nice to her, sneaking her books, taking care of some medical needs, bringing her some extra food. But she never once made any effort to free her. There were limits, Cain supposed, to people's generosity. And morals.

11

For twenty-five hours a week and nine bucks an hour Cain operated a forklift loading packing crates onto tractor trailers. They wouldn't allow her full-time work, because that came with benefits and other rights. All the guys there—she was the only female— were also part-timers.

She parked her Honda outside the terminal, put on her hard hat and protective shoe coverings and safety goggles, punched the clock, and climbed into her little rig. They could have gotten plenty of guys with heavy equipment operating licenses to do this, and who had been laid off in the recent downturn. But Cain was a lot cheaper and didn't demand full-time work. People like her were a hot commodity in the free market right now. She was a worker who didn't mind getting screwed: Employers loved her.

She liked the work because she didn't really have to talk to or deal with anyone. She just climbed into her seat, manipulated her ride hauling the crates and boxes, and did her thing. Years before, she had earned a good living doing similar work. Then she'd been injured on the job and the painkillers had helped a lot, so she kept taking them. Then came the day when she couldn't stop taking them. And then it wasn't just painkillers. It was anything she could snort, swallow, or stick herself with. And there went her job and everything else.

Someone had suggested counseling. She had gone to one person but when he'd asked about any troubles in her past, she got up and left. It wasn't worth it. Cain knew if she waded back into that, she'd just slit her wrists. There was only one way for her to go and that was forward. Some psych guy could write a book on her, but Cain would never read it. She had lived it. One ride through hell was enough.

Cain had never been to prison, only in jails for short periods for stupid crap she shouldn't have done. Petty thefts, DUIs, drug possession, throwing a drunk accountant through a plate glass window for grabbing first her ass and then her breasts, only to have his buddies swear it was all her. Stuff like that. Shit happened; shit just happened to her more than to a lot of others, it seemed.

Each time she was arrested she'd been afraid that her ID and manufactured past would not pass muster and uncomfortable questions would follow. Yet she had found that the police in real life were not quite the stuff you saw on TV. The computers were old and boxy, the offices drab, the clothes they wore drabber still. There wasn't an ounce of sexy among the whole crew, the morale was low, and the energy to go above and beyond on low-end cases like hers was virtually nonexistent. She was one piece of dull paper in a billion. Just shuffle her through because who really gave a crap.

Thank God for that.

She clocked out on the dot. She was about to get into her car when a new guy came up to her. His job was to fuel and detail the trucks, or at least she had seen him doing that.

He was lean—too thin, really—with a scraggly, ill-groomed beard, twitchy eyes, and a conceited expression, at least to Cain.

"Hey," he said.

"Yeah?"

"Hear you don't like guys."

"What makes you say that?"

He grinned. " 'Cause you've never gone out with none of the boys here."

"You talking about the one guy who has teeth, or all the others?"

"Hey, that's bitchy," he said, frowning.

"What the hell do you care?"

"I don't know. Look, forget it. Shit, I mean, what the hell is your problem?"

Cain said, "I got no problem. Just here doing my job. And now I'm going to do another job."

His expression changed from angry to curious. "Yeah? Where is that?"

"Why?"

"I make chump change here. I clean offices at night. But that pays shit, too, and it ain't regular work. Look." He glanced around nervously and then lit up a cigarette. His hands were shaky. "Look, I . . . I got me a kid. And my old lady ain't doing too good. Rehab, y'know? Meth, it's a bitch."

She looked him over and decided his old lady wasn't the only one fighting a meth addiction. Cain saw all the signs because she'd been there, too. "Detailing trucks and cleaning offices? Not much future. Same goes for meth. You don't kick that, nothing else matters because it gets in your head and you can't do anything else but worry about the next pop and how to get it."

"Shit, I know that! So what else do you do?" he asked.

She looked him over. "I do group Lyft rides three times a week in the afternoon. My car's not pretty, but it takes people who don't have a lot of dollars where they need to go. Not great money, but it's something. Then I go home and sleep. Then four nights a week I work security making rounds at a gated community a few miles outside of downtown. Ten to six in the morning. I'm on duty tonight, in fact. They used to have their own private police force, but then they outsourced it to save money. See, even the rich pinch pennies sometimes. It pays eight-fifty an hour, no real bennies, but there's no heavy lifting. And you get a little car to drive around in. I've been doing it for six months and the only thing that happened was I had to roust some pothead kids out of a rich dude's pool."

"Security job! I can't pass no background check and if I have to pee into—"

She interrupted. "They don't do any of that. No pee cups. No tests, at least they never have with me. They're supposed to, I guess, but the place that hired me? I went in for an interview at four in the afternoon and was on duty at ten that night. The only thing they asked me was what size uniform I took and whether I wanted a gun. They just want bodies riding around in a uniform looking like they know what they're doing. *Optics*, they call it."

"No training, really?"

"If they had to get people to pee or pass a background check they might as well close up shop. No Ivy Leaguers are applying for this stuff."

He took a puff on the cigarette and slowly blew the smoke out while he stared at the ground. "I guess that's right."

"And anyway, all the homes have these fancy security systems and surveillance cameras out the ass. We're just gravy on top of the mashed potatoes."

"And did you want a gun?"

"No."

"Why not?"

"For eight-fifty an hour, I got a gun, they got a gun, they're more likely to shoot me."

"I think I'd go for a gun."

She looked him over. "You know how to use one?"

"Sure. How do I apply for a job?"

She pulled out a piece of paper and pen from her glove box, spun him around, and used his back as a desk as she wrote a phone number down. She handed it to him. "Here. Tell 'em El Cain sent you. It might help. I know the extra cash comes in handy. After they take out taxes and crap it's around two-twenty a week."

"Shit, that's more than I make here. They pay me under the table so it's less than minimum, but they feed me lunch and there's usually some leftover donuts for breakfast."

"There you go. You can buy your own donuts."

He looked at the paper and said, "Thanks, I mean it, really."

"No problem. Hope it works out."

He looked at her bruised face, apparently focusing on it for the first time. "Damn, what happened there?"

"Got in a fight."

"Who with?"

"Some other chick. She ended up in the hospital to get her jaw wired and to hopefully think about something else to do with her life. I ended up going home and having a beer."

He chuckled as though he thought she was kidding. "But *do* you like guys?"

"I like some guys some of the time. I don't like most guys most of the time."

He grinned and stuffed the paper into his shirt pocket. "You're not like what they said."

"I'm not like what anybody says, because nobody really knows me. And that's how I want it."

12

"You, a rental cop? Now that's a good one."

In the rearview mirror Cain was staring at herself in a plain gray uniform with chevrons on the sleeve signifying absolutely nothing. It was just more optics. She was perched in her tiny two-door Smart Car, with the name STEELE SECURITY SERVICES airbrushed on the side panels in nifty colors. There was an orange bubble light on top of the car that she would turn on from time to time and then she'd speed around just to break up the boredom. She had the seat all the way back but with her long legs she still felt cramped.

She had been on duty for about two hours; it was a bit after midnight. She had made several rounds over her area of responsibility and found zero cause for concern. Certainly, the rich were sensibly afraid that someone would try to take what they had, but the truth was most thieves went for easier targets, like the poor and working class and sometimes reaching up to grab on to those in the middle of the economic pecking order.

There was a gatehouse on the only road into the community and it was manned by an armed guard 24/7. There were also two cars patrolling the neighborhood during the night, one of which was hers. The homes had all the latest gizmos in security, with more cameras than a Hollywood back lot. All in all, this was one tough nut for someone to crack. You made a 911 call from here, the real and rental cops would show up before you put down the phone. Someone had broken into an apartment she'd had once in Detroit in an area that could have been generously called "in transition." She called 911 but the cops hadn't even bothered to come. They were probably scared to.

She started on another round through the subdivision. And even though she'd seen them many times before, Cain found herself still marveling at the size of the homes, or *estates*, that were located here. They looked like mini-hotels. They all had landscaped grounds, lavish in-ground pools, guesthouses, and elaborate statuary, with each owner clearly trying to outdo his neighbor, if the amount of remodeling and new construction work being done was any indication. But, hey, you had to do something with the cash. She had no idea what the homeowners did to earn enough to live in places like this, but she knew she would never be among their number. And she was okay with that. She didn't want to live in a place so big that she might get lost.

Later, she pulled off the road, had a cup of luke-warm coffee poured from her thermos, and pecked in notes on the iPad the security firm gave her to use. The observations were perfunctory and were really only meant to show that she was actually doing something. She seriously doubted anyone read them. And if they did, it was a massive waste of time.

Nearly hit squirrel. Heard dog bark. Saw rich white girl sneak out and jump into clunker hatchback with poor brown boy and they drove off. Saw drunk homeowner pawing equally drunk woman half his age and not his wife as they stumbled into house getting naked along the way.

Same old crap.

Cain turned on the radio, drank her coffee, and scrolled through her phone. Amazing things, these phones. When she'd first learned of the internet it had blown her away. That was some seriously cool shit. There was so much she didn't know that she had had to prioritize and focus on the things she needed in order to get by. That was it. All the rest, she just winged it.

Cain wanted to smoke some weed for the chronic pain she suffered from, but that would get her fired if her employer somehow found out. And she couldn't afford to blow such a cushy job. She doubted after her last fight, and bust-up with Sam, that she would be getting any cage matches for a while. Besides her rotator issue, one doctor had told her she had an irregular heartbeat. She should be on meds for it, but meds were for people with insurance. She also needed some dental work done and she had to take care of a few other medical issues, too. But without health coverage, you just had to deal with it until you had the cash. She had already spent pretty much all her savings on having an old back injury remedied. She'd refused to put it on her plastic, not that her credit limit would have been enough. She'd asked the surgeon if she really needed to do it. He had told her, "Not if you don't care about being in a wheelchair in five years."

When she got really sick she went to the emergency room. They did what they did, then billed her a shitload of money that she couldn't and didn't pay.

It is what it is, I guess.

The Atkinses had not believed in doctor and dentist visits, at least for her. The first time Cain had seen either was when she had been on her own for two years. Three rotted teeth had come out of her mouth and two implants had gone in, and a month later she'd had surgeries for a hernia, a torn muscle, and a broken arm that dated back to when she was ten and had never gotten proper medical attention. The dentist, GP, and surgeon, respectively, had quizzed her as to why her parents had not addressed these issues before then.

She had lied and told them her parents were dead and she'd been raised by her grandmother who was not quite right in the head. They all had let that pass, which was good, since she didn't have a backup lie at the time. She'd since gotten much better with her web of fabrications. The dentist, GP, surgeon, and hospital had then sued her for the unpaid bills because her checks bounced like basketballs. She had skipped town, which was the only thing she could think to do at the time.

She looked down at her left foot and quickly wriggled it as the pain shot through. The copperhead had bitten her there when she was thirteen, while she'd been picking up wood from a stack to carry into the house. Her damn foot had swelled up, the venom started eating her skin away, and a serious infection had set in. Desiree had poured what she called "magic water" over it and spoke some gibberish Cain couldn't understand, and she doubted Desiree could, either. Three weeks later Cain had come out of a coma, a term she had learned about later. Wanda had been there when she came to. Wanda apparently had some medical training. Cain's foot had been heavily bandaged and there were some bottles of medicine next to her bed. The dressings smelled strongly of what she now knew was antiseptic. The skin on her foot would never look the same, but she didn't care. Cain had lived. What more could she hope for?

These musings abruptly stopped when Cain heard the announcer on the radio.

Rebecca Atkins. The FBI was looking for a Rebecca Atkins from Georgia in connection with a matter from the early 2000s. Anyone with information about her was to call the number provided by the FBI, and there was also an email address provided.

When she had been held captive all those years, a cold dread would come over Cain whenever she heard the footsteps coming closer. This was when she was younger and unable to defend herself. What would happen when the door opened? What was Desiree's mood? Cruel? Batshit? Drunk and docile? Or doped up and mean? Was Joe going to be regular Joe or monster Joe? How bad would it hurt? Would she cry? It was a feeling like your stomach had turned in on itself. That your blood had solidified, and where your hearing became so acute you could hear grass bending into the wind at a hundred yards. Your entire world was condensed to the shape of a door with your heart pounding at the thought of what would come through it. The monster of every fairy tale nightmare, only this monster lived in the house with her.

She hadn't felt the "freezies," as she had called them, since she had turned fifteen. When she had grown to her full height and was as strong as a horse, the comings of the Atkinses no longer terrified her. After that, she had terrified *them*. But she still had been a prisoner.

Now the debilitating freezies were settling in all over her body.

The FBI was looking for her about an incident in Georgia from the early 2000s. There could only be one incident involving Rebecca Atkins from Georgia during that time.

She took out her joint and lit up, sucking the smoke into her lungs like these were the last pops of weed she would ever take. The PSA ended and the radio channel went on to something else, but for Cain there was no going on to something else. Headlights suddenly slammed against her windshield like a wave of water. When she saw it was her colleague in the other Steele Security clown car, she lowered the joint out of sight, but did not roll down the window, though he opened his. She held her phone up to her ear as though she were on a call. He smiled, nodded in understanding, and drove on.

For the next six hours Cain drove around and around like she was on some giant carousel that didn't have an Off button. But she wasn't seeing any of the houses, or random car or person, even though they were all there. All she could think was: The FBI was looking for her in connection with an *incident*. Her shift ended, and she aired out the car before dropping it off and getting back into her ride in the Steele

Security parking lot. She had a sudden thought and used her phone to go online and Google "FBI" and "Rebecca Atkins."

This took her to the FBI's official website, and caused her another shock as a fuzzy still photo came up on the screen. It was her after she had just burst through that door on her way to freedom.

I . . . I look batshit. And I probably was. No, I definitely was. But I was also cunning. I was focused in my total madness. I just wanted out. Who wouldn't have?

She looked in the mirror again and then stared at the image on her phone screen. She breathed a sigh of relief. There was no way anyone would think those were the same person. Her hair was long. Her face was thinner and drawn and filthy. She looked like a lifetime member of some insane asylum. While she didn't necessarily look normal now, she didn't look like *that* anymore, either.

Cain sat back and thought about those first few months of freedom. She had hitchhiked across the country, putting as much space between her and Georgia as she could, finally stopping at the Pacific Ocean, which she didn't even know was called that. She didn't even know how many states there were. She didn't know what California was. It had taken her years to build up even a semblance of basic knowledge.

I had to teach myself to drive a car, take medicine, and read something other than picture books, though the librarians over the years had helped me a lot with that. I had to learn how to write my name in something other than block letters. To add and subtract. Hell, what was a credit card? Or a rent payment? Or an email? Or a smartphone? Or a computer and the internet? Or a million other things that everyone else took for granted but I never could?

She leaned her head into the steering wheel. *You've overcome so much, El. Think about that.*

She drove home to get ready to go to work. She would sleep later, after her forklift gig. She would bag working out and being a cheap chauffeur today.

She didn't like people looking for her. She didn't want to be found. Only bad things could happen from that.

And haven't enough bad things already happened to me?
Well, apparently not.

13

Son of a bitch!

Cain had returned to her home to find that the padlock she used had been removed and another put in its place. And her clothes, books, and other possessions had been tossed on the ground right outside her residential pod. That included her beer and what little food she had up there and that was now rotted and also torn up by animals. Tacked on the wall next to the lock was an official-looking notice proclaiming that any trespassers would be prosecuted to the fullest extent of the law.

Still in there, under the floorboard, was all her cash, her stash of pot, and her Glock.

"Assholes," the voice said.

She turned to see the elderly man walking up to her. He was too thin, too shaky, and he looked ready to drop dead at her feet. He was also her neighbor and a good, kind person.

"What in the hell happened, Saul?" she asked.

"They came last night, El. Tossed all my stuff out along with *me*. Ruined my only good pair'a pants, and all my bottles of Ensure are for shit. And that cost a pretty penny. Assholes." He spat on the ground.

"Who are *they*?"

"Said they were hired by the folks that just bought this place. Some people on the West Coast, they said. Plan to turn it into 'luxury condos' or some such."

"But my rent's paid through the end of the month."

"So's mine. I told them fellers that. They told me it wasn't their problem. I could go to court and sue."

"Right, like we can afford to hire lawyers. But I still got stuff in there."

"I don't know what to tell you, El. They threw my ass out last night around midnight. Scared the shit outta me. Just cut my lock clean in two. They done it to everybody here. Had the cops with 'em, just in case."

"Cops! But how can they evict people if they've paid their rent? I thought there were laws."

"Hell, laws are for the rich folks. You think anybody gives a shit about us? And when I tried to argue the point one of them said the rent money we 'supposedly' paid wasn't. That we were illegally squatting."

"That's bullshit. What else did these guys tell you?"

"Told me if I come back they'd toss me in the can."

"But you *are* back."

"Hell, I never went away. I slept next to the dumpster."

"Where are these 'guys' now?"

"I think they're coming back tonight. They said something about fencing in the whole kit and kaboodle then."

"What are you gonna do now?"

"This was the only place I could afford. Just got my Social Security and whatever I can earn. Guess I'll check out one of the homeless shelters. But last time I did they was full up. And they got some mean suckers in there. Do stuff to you, take your things, what little you got. I'll probably go to the underpass. Or maybe down by the river. They got a little shantytown there. Least till I find something else. Well, good luck."

He tottered off to move on with his life. She had to admire his pluck in the face of losing basically everything he had.

Cain picked up all her things and carried them to her car. She returned to the building and looked at the padlocked door. She was calculating how best to do this.

"Hey!"

She turned to see the man striding toward her. He was in his thirties, about her height, around two hundred muscular pounds. His blunt expression was as serious as a man about to go to war. He had a holstered pistol and wore the uniform of a private security service.

"Hey right back," said Cain.

He stopped cold when he saw her uniform. "Who are you?"

"Who the hell are you?"

"Dwight Talbot. I'm on duty here to secure this place."

"Well, so am I. Name's Donna White. I just got called up to come here. And that's after pulling a graveyard shift."

He looked at the logo and name on her uniform. "Steele Security? I used to work for them. They lowball the guards."

"Tell me about it. When did you make the switch to Douglas?" she said, noting the name and logo embroidered on his sleeve.

"About six months ago."

"Smart man. I might do the same."

"I didn't know Steele was on this job, too."

"I just go where I'm told, you know how it is."

"Yeah, I damn well do."

"West Coasters putting up luxury condos here, so I heard," she said smoothly.

"Hell, I was wondering what they were doing with this pile of crap. When I was a kid they made furniture here, least I think."

"Well, we'll never be able to afford to live here. I don't have *luxury* in my future."

"Me too. That's the damn truth."

"Look," said Cain. "I know they cleared everybody

out last night, but have they checked out all these buildings?"

"Dunno, why?"

"Because when I got here, I could have sworn I heard somebody inside this one."

"Shit, really?"

"Yeah, but the door's padlocked. You want to call the cops? Although if I'm wrong we might get our asses handed to us. But if I'm right and we score the prick ourselves?"

"We might cop a bonus," said Talbot.

"What I'm thinking."

"How you want to do this?"

"You got a key for the lock? I was supposed to get a copy, but in all the rush they never got it to me."

Talbot pulled out a key on a large ring from his pocket. "This is a master. Fits all the ones they put on last night."

"Cool. Okay, hand it over. I'll pop the lock and let's go in. You got the gun so you cover my back, okay?"

"Okay." He passed her the key and took out his pistol.

"Just don't shoot me by accident, Dwight."

He grinned. "Hell, Donna, that ain't gonna happen, hon."

"Just checking."

She unlocked the door, and they quietly made their way inside and up a short flight of steps. The

interior was tiny with only two doors. Cain knew
one led to her bedroom, the other to the bathroom.

"You check that door," she said, pointing to the
bathroom door. "I'll do the other."

"You sure you want to split up?" said Dwight.
"You don't have a gun."

She slid out her baton. "I got this and I do MMA."

"For shit, really?"

"Yeah, just won a match the other night."

"Well, you look like you can take care of yourself,
that's for sure. Just holler if you need me, hon."

He went left and Cain entered her room on the
right. She eyed the floorboard and thought quickly.
She opened the window and then stepped back. "Hey,
Dwight, come quick," she called out.

Talbot bolted into the room. "There was nobody
in the bathroom," he said. "What's up?"

Cain pointed at the window.

"Just saw the asshole running into the woods
behind here. He must've gotten in and then out
through this window when he heard us coming. You
look faster than me. Go after him and I'll call this in."

"Right! I'll get the son of a bitch."

Talbot bolted outside. As soon as Cain heard the
door bang open she lifted up the floorboard, took out
her cash, gun, and pot, put the board back, and ran
down the stairs and out the door. She put all her stuff
in her car and was back at the building when Talbot
came huffing back.

"H-he must'a got away," said Talbot, bending over and sucking in air. "Y-you call it in?"

"Been trying. Damn cell phone's got no bars. You're going to have to do it."

"O-okay." He straightened and made the call.

When he was done, Cain looked down at her phone. "Hell, *now* I get a call coming in? I hate AT&T." She put it to her ear. "Yeah? What, yeah, this is Donna White. You're shitting me, right? No, really, you're shitting me? Okay, well screw you, too."

She put the phone away in her pocket with a disgusted look on her face.

"What was that all about?" Dwight asked anxiously.

"Steele just canned my ass. And you want to know why? Because they saw on the film from last night that I dozed off for like ten seconds. Like no rental cop's ever done that."

"Sorry asses," exclaimed Talbot.

"So, they just told me to get my butt back and turn in all my stuff. Yeah, I'll turn it in. I'll throw it in a fucking dumpster."

"What I would do, no lie, hon," said Talbot.

"Well, hang in there, Dwight, don't let them screw with you."

"Okay, Donna, hey sorry, gal."

"Yeah, everybody's got problems. But I'm still breathing, right? And look, don't even mention I was here to anybody, okay? They'll probably try to pull some bullshit about something that happened so they can screw me out of my last paycheck."

"Hey, my lips are zipped."

She fist-bumped him, went to her car, climbed in, and drove off.

Oh, Dwight, what a dumbass you are. And thank you for that, hon.

She settled her gaze on the road. Now she just had to find a new place to live. And she still had the little matter of the FBI looking for her.

She needed to do something about that, only what?

14

Atlee Pine and Carol Blum pulled into Huntsville, Alabama. Located in the Tennessee River Valley, it was a stately, historic southern town with a growing population and a modern veneer over the aged, antebellum underbelly. It had rich parts, poor parts, and in-between parts, just like every other town. Its economy had moved from cotton mills to textile plants to the space program and now centered on biotechnology. It was an interesting mix of old and new, storied families with long lineages and old sprawling homes with pillars out front and water views out back, facing a wave of diverse newcomers coming for good-paying jobs, interesting work, and cheaper housing than could be found in the Northeast, California, Florida, or Texas.

After skirting the downtown area and driving for a while, they pulled into the gravel drive of a one-story brick-and-siding rancher. It covered about twelve hundred square feet in a neighborhood of seventies-era homes that had probably cycled through several generations of families, and would probably cycle through several more before all was said and done.

Pine knocked on a door that had peeling paint and a tarnished and dented brass foot plate. A few moments later they heard a woman's raspy voice through the closed door. "Yes?"

"Mrs. Atkins?"

"Yes?" The voice was now both worried and intrigued.

"I'm with the FBI. I'd like to talk to you."

"The FBI? Is this some sort of joke?"

"No, it's not." Pine took out her shield and placed it against the dirty sidelight next to the door. She could see a woman's blurred, wrinkled face studying the FBI badge through the glass.

"Okay, what is this about?"

"Your son, Joe Atkins."

"Joe? He's long since dead."

"I know. That's what we want to talk to you about. Please, it's important."

They could hear the lock being turned back and the door slowly opened.

Wanda Atkins was nearly eighty now, shriveled and withered by the years into something both hard and soft. She had on khaki pants and a white blouse, and wore thick white orthopedic shoes that looked as though they weighed about two pounds each. She was also using a metal cane with a curved handle and a wide bottom for support. Her hair had been permed beyond all reasonable recovery, with tufts missing and revealing pink scalp underneath. Her face was a mass of embedded concentric lines, and her eyes were set deep in the shrunken hollows of the sockets. Still, they were youngish eyes paired with the tanned skin and bedlam of wrinkles; the effect was a bit unnerving, like Pine was watching the woman age right in front of her.

She had a cannula in her nose, and a long oxygen line connected to it went down to the floor and then out of sight into the house.

"Now what is this about Joe?"

"May we come in?" asked Pine.

Atkins glanced at Blum, who said, "We're just here for information, Mrs. Atkins."

Perhaps comforted by Blum's age and innocuous appearance, Atkins stepped back so they could move into the house. They were immediately hit by mingled odors of bleach, mustiness, and fried foods.

"You'll have to excuse me. I have to give Len his medication," said Atkins, moving past them. "He needs them right on time."

They followed her into the next room. The house was cluttered with cardboard boxes stacked up and piles of unread, folded newspapers and magazines and what looked to be insurance and medical papers. Dust had accumulated on every surface that Pine could see. Two large oxygen tanks sat in holders against one wall, along with a portable oxygen concentrator that was connected to the line attached to Atkins's cannula; there were also boxes of tubing and what looked to be a CPAP machine on a table. Two aluminum walkers were perched against a wall. A blood pressure monitor hung on a stand, and a gurney with collapsible sides was set against another wall. Prescription bottles lined one table and sat next to an elongated pill dispenser organized by days of the week. The dispenser's bins were chock-full of pills.

It looked like an ICU room in the suburbs.

Strapped into a wheelchair was, Pine assumed, Len Atkins. His bald head and withered body listed to one side, his tongue was hanging out, and he was drooling onto a bib tied around his neck. He looked like the roughened shell of a human being nearing its expiration date.

Atkins poured some liquid from a brown bottle into a small measuring cup, eyeing the dosage carefully, and then poured that into a glass of water. She then placed a straw in the glass.

"Len? It's time, sweetie. You need to drink this."

Len perked up a bit, his gaze running around the room until it found his wife standing right in front of him. She put the straw in his mouth and he started to suck on it. It took about a minute but he got the liquid down. She wiped his mouth and put the glass down.

She turned to them and said in a very low voice, "He had a stroke last year. The doctors say this is as good as he's going to be. He can't walk or talk or do much of anything else, really. I think he can understand most things. We have an aide that comes in four times a week. But on days she's not here, it's tough. Most times I get the lady next door to help. She's in her thirties and very strong. And I'm not without disabilities, either." She glanced at the oxygen tank. "I have pretty bad COPD. Please, God, never pick up a cigarette. It's not pretty. And I'm ashamed to say I still can't kick the nicotine habit. But what the hell does it matter now?"

Pine said, "Well, with all this oxygen around, it might matter a lot if some of it leaks."

"That's why I vape. No need for matches. We can leave Len here if you want. And talk in the kitchen about Joe."

"You said he can understand things?" said Pine.

"Yes."

"Then if you don't mind, I'd prefer that he listen in."

Atkins stiffened at this remark, but raised no objection.

15

Pine shifted stacks of papers and mail out of the way to make room for her and Blum to sit. Atkins perched on a piano bench in front of an old, scarred upright, its row of white keys yellowed by time, too much sunlight, and lack of care.

"Now what's this about Joe?"

"We've been to your old trailer in Georgia," began Pine. "It's full of snakes."

She scowled. "I'm not surprised. We didn't even bother to sell it. We just left. Nobody would have wanted that thing. Over the years we got all new furniture."

"And you moved here about, what, eighteen or so years ago?"

"Something like that. Look, what is this about?" she added sharply.

"It's about this." Pine took something out of her pocket. It was the photo of Len and Wanda Atkins and Mercy that Pine had found in the attic of Ito Vincenzo's beach house in New Jersey.

She held it up for Atkins to see. The woman

blinked rapidly and then let out a little gasp, her shaky hand going to her quivering lips.

"That's you and your husband. And this is a woman that you called Rebecca Atkins. But her real name is Mercy. She was kidnapped by a man named Ito Vincenzo from her home in Andersonville, Georgia, and brought to live with you. We know that Ito and your husband served in Vietnam together, and Len saved Ito's life. So that's why he brought her to you, I suppose. I'm not sure, but he might have been under the mistaken impression that your husband could never father a child because of the wounds he suffered, not knowing that you already had a son. But at that point in your life I suppose you didn't want to care for a six-year-old, so you turned her over to Joe and Desiree."

Atkins's eyes filled with tears and she put a hand over her mouth and started to cough uncontrollably. Blum rose and hurried into the kitchen, and Pine could hear water running. Then Blum came out with a full glass of water and handed it to Atkins. The woman drank it down and composed herself, taking long breaths, greedily sucking on the supplemental oxygen provided by the cannula.

Pine put the photo away and looked expectantly at the woman. Now that she was finally facing a key person in her sister's life *after* the abduction, she was not leaving without making significant progress in her search.

Atkins pulled out a Kleenex from her pants pocket and rubbed her eyes and nose, shifting the cannula to the side to do so.

"Didn't realize how chunky I was back then," she said. "I've lost quite a bit of weight since that picture was taken, but Len is just as bald as ever." When she saw Pine staring stonily at her she hurried on. "You're right. Len knew Ito and *did* save his life. But we had Joe *before* Len went to Vietnam. And Ito and Len kept in touch over the years. He knew about our having Joe."

"Then maybe he came to you because you were the only ones he knew who lived close to Andersonville. But I'm more interested in what took place when Ito brought Mercy to you."

"He showed up in the middle of the night, pounding on the door, waking us up. Scared the hell out of me. I remember it so clearly. Ito was really shaken up, nervous as hell, almost out of his mind with panic."

"Where did he say he got Mercy?"

"He said Becky, or Mercy, had been abandoned. That she didn't have anybody."

"And did he say how he came to have her?"

"He said he found her on the side of the road, just walking along."

"And she didn't tell you otherwise? She was six. She could talk. She knew things. She didn't tell you that her name was Mercy and that Ito had taken her away from her family?"

"Not that I recall, no," said Atkins, not meeting her eye. "She was very quiet, didn't say nothing. I tried to get her to eat or drink something but she wouldn't. She seemed terrified."

Pine sat back. "And later you didn't see all the news coverage and flyers and everything with Mercy's picture on them? You lived barely two hours from where she was taken. The state of Georgia was saturated with news about her abduction."

Atkins glanced anxiously at her husband. "I . . . I don't . . . It was such a long time ago and all. And there wasn't anything about it when Ito showed up with her."

"Because no one knew she had been abducted at that point. But now comes the big question. Why didn't Ito, or you, take Mercy to the police? When you find an abandoned child, that's what you do, right?"

Atkins looked extremely nervous now. "I . . . I asked Ito that. I said, well, we need to call in the authorities, they'll know what to do."

"And how did he respond to that?" asked Blum.

Atkins twisted her hands in her lap and sucked heavily on her oxygen. "At first, he . . . he said that he had been in foster care growing up and that it would be a nightmare. He said the authorities would do that to her. And she might be abused and heaven knew what else."

"But that didn't have to be the only option. They

could try to find her parents and see why they had abandoned her, as he claimed," countered Pine.

"I said that very thing to Ito. And that they might find other relatives who could take her in."

"And his response?"

Blum added, "And you said, 'at first'? Does that mean his story changed?"

"Yes, it did. That's when things started getting really weird. Ito next told us that she really hadn't been abandoned. He moved us away from the girl so she couldn't hear and said that the parents had been trying to kill Mercy when he happened by. He rescued her from them, and they ran off. He said they were probably clear out of the state by now."

"They were trying to kill their own daughter and Ito just *happened* to be passing by?" Pine said, her tone full of derision. "And why would he care if she heard that or not? If it had really happened, she would have *known* her parents were trying to kill her!"

"I know how it sounds now," said Atkins in a defensive tone. "But we had just been woken out of a deep sleep and had a child dropped on us. We weren't thinking too clearly."

"I'm sure no one would have been," said Blum in a soothing tone.

"Thank you for saying that," said Atkins with a grateful look. She wiped her nose with the Kleenex. "It was all a nightmare."

"So you believed what Ito said?" asked Pine.

"He was very convincing. And why would he lie? Why would he show up at our place with a child like that?"

"He lived in Trenton, New Jersey. Did he say why he was in *Georgia* running around in the middle of the night?"

"He said he was coming to visit us. As a surprise."

"Andersonville is south of where you lived," said Pine. "He would never have reached that town if he were simply coming to visit you."

"But we didn't know that because he never said anything about Andersonville. He never told us where he'd found her."

"Okay, so you took Mercy?"

"Yes. We didn't know what else to do. Len wasn't thrilled about it, but I couldn't see any other way."

"And what happened to Ito? Did he leave that night?"

"Yes, he said he was going back to where he'd gotten Mercy to see what was going on."

"Yes, that's exactly what he did," said Pine. She knew that the next morning Ito Vincenzo had gotten into a fight with Tim Pine outside their house. He had accused Tim of kidnapping and killing his own daughter, even though he knew that was not true.

"And did you ever see him after that?" asked Pine.

"No, he never came back. But he wrote letters and

he sent some money every year. I would use it to get Becky things."

"Yeah, I know about the payments he made. That was how we found out about you in the first place. So you never contacted him about Mercy? Never asked him to come and get her? Or whether he had found out anything else about her?"

"Well, he never called us about anything, and we didn't think trying to pressure him would do any good."

Pine shook her head, looking incredulous. "Okay, let's get back to the photo I showed you and fast-forward in time. Are you saying you couldn't tell from the state of Mercy that day that something was wrong? She was filthy and had wounds and bruises and marks on her skin."

Atkins's eyes once more filled with tears. "Look, I don't want to get into trouble."

Blum said, "All we want is the truth, Mrs. Atkins."

Pine added, "We know more or less what happened the night your son died. What we don't know is exactly *how* he died, or what happened to Desiree and Mercy."

"Why would you think we would know about that?"

They heard a grunt and turned to see Len Atkins holding up a stiff arm and pointing at his wife. He grunted again. He apparently had been listening to the entire conversation and was not happy with the direction it had taken.

Atkins seemed to be able to decipher this. She put her hands in her lap and said in a resigned tone, "It was Desiree, you have to understand that. Joe had his issues, but Desiree? That woman was the devil. Not at first, not when they got married, but later, that's when her true colors came out."

"We've talked to the former sheriff where you used to live, Dick Roberts. He told us about . . . Desiree. He called her the 'voodoo lady.' He said he was called out one night because Desiree was torturing a dog."

"Dick was a good man. And he was right about Desiree. She was pure evil."

"Did you know they were holding Mercy in a prison out behind their house?"

Atkins's top lip trembled. "Am I going to go to jail?"

"Not if you answer our questions *truthfully*," replied Pine, trying to keep both her emotions and patience in check. "Let's go back to the beginning for a minute. What happened after Ito dropped her off with you and then left? How did she end up with Joe and Desiree?"

Atkins scrunched up the Kleenex and laid it aside. She glanced once at her husband and then began: "The next morning, in the cold light of day, we were frantic. I mean, we believed what Ito had said, but there were still so many questions. And we didn't want to get into trouble. And we didn't know what to do with the child. She was scared and dirty and confused. We kept her for a few days and were wondering what the hell to do. Len found Ito's number and called him, but no one answered. He left messages, but Ito never called back. We were thinking about taking her to the police and telling them what Ito had done. I mean, we couldn't keep her. Then, when Joe and Desiree came by, we told them what had happened. Joe immediately said, 'We've always wanted kids. We'll adopt her and raise her.' Well, that seemed like a good solution to me and Len."

Pine gave her an incredulous look. "Mrs. Atkins. How could you possibly do that without checking to see whether Ito Vincenzo was really telling the truth? We're talking about a human being, not a puppy. A guy shows up in the middle of the night with a kid? And you just take her and that's it?"

"I know, I know," said Atkins miserably. "But Ito seemed very earnest. And he really seemed to care about the girl. And we couldn't think of a reason why in the world he would have kidnapped a child and brought her to us. We trusted him."

Pine sighed heavily and sat back, scrutinizing the woman. "Did you know that there was another little girl involved that night? Mercy's twin sister. Ito did a nursery rhyme, 'eeny, meeny, miny, moe,' to choose which one to take. Then he struck the other little girl so hard he shattered her skull. She almost died."

Atkins's hand flew to her mouth and fresh tears sprouted from her eyes. "Oh dear God. Why would he do that? Why?"

"He did it for his brother, who was a mobster with a grudge against Mercy's family. He took Mercy and almost killed her sister to punish the parents."

"A m-mobster? Ito?"

"No, Ito ran an ice cream parlor in Trenton. His *brother* was the mobster in the family. He shamed Ito into doing what he did. But it doesn't excuse Ito's crimes."

"No, no, of course not. But we knew nothing about any of that."

"So Joe wanted her, and you let Desiree take the girl even though you knew Desiree was, as you said, evil?"

"Well, we didn't know that then. Back then, she was just sort of odd. I actually thought having a little girl to dote on and raise would be good for her. And I believed Joe would make a good father. They had been trying for kids and it hadn't worked, so this seemed like a blessing. And Desiree seemed eager to have her, too. It was her idea to name her Rebecca."

"But did you ever question *Mercy* about where she came from?"

"Well, yes, now that I recall."

"And what did she say?"

"Well, she said that Ito had taken her from her parents because her parents wanted her dead, which matched up with what Ito had told us. It was all so horrible. Poor little child. Can you imagine parents saying that?"

"Mercy really told you that her parents wanted her dead?" said Pine skeptically.

"Well, come to think, I believe she said that's what *Ito* told her."

Pine shook her head at the woman's obliviousness. "And in the days that followed you never thought that this girl could be the same child who had been abducted in Andersonville? Because it was all over the news by then."

"Look, Len and me, we kept to ourselves. We didn't watch the news and we didn't go out much. If you've been to our old trailer you know we didn't have any neighbors. I'd never heard the name Mercy till you mentioned it. I swear."

They heard moaning behind them and turned to see tears sliding down Len Atkins's cheeks.

Atkins rose and stroked her husband's cheek. "It's okay, Len. We . . . I just have to tell them, okay?"

He jerkily nodded and she resumed her seat.

Pine refocused on her. "Did you know how Joe and Desiree were treating Mercy?"

Atkins stared down at the floor. She said slowly, "At first things seemed normal. They seemed to be settling in as a family."

"Did they formally adopt Mercy?" asked Blum.

"They said they did."

"But you never saw any paperwork, a certificate?"

"No."

"Go on," said Pine.

"Then it got to be that whenever we would come over to see her, they would scramble around and whisk the child away to dress her up and get her room clean. But I would talk to her and play with her and things still seemed fine, though I could sense there was something strange going on."

"How so?"

Atkins looked up, a pained expression on her face. "See, the thing was, Desiree never left us alone. She was always hovering. And Becky always wore long pants and long sleeves, even when it was hot and humid, like it is a lot in Georgia. And then, after thirty minutes or so, they'd swoop Becky, I mean Mercy, away, and that would be that."

"And then at some point you found out the truth?"

Atkins nodded. "We made a surprise visit. Not to catch them doing anything but just to stop by. I had found a cute dress for Mercy and wanted to give it to her. This was maybe two years after they got her. We heard screaming coming from the house. We both of us rushed in. And . . ." Here Atkins stopped for a moment and drew several long breaths, sucking on the oxygen coming into her nose like it was a line of crack.

"What?" prompted Pine.

Another moan came from behind them. When Pine turned to look, Len Atkins was pantomiming something. He was pushing the fingers of his functioning arm into his damaged one.

Pine whirled back on Atkins. "What is he trying to tell us?" she demanded.

"Mercy was tied down to a table. And Desiree was sticking needles into Mercy's arms and legs. Dozens and dozens of them. She was screaming in pain."

16

Pine wiped the water off her face with the hand towel in the Atkinses' bathroom. She looked at her reflection in the mirror over the sink. She almost didn't recognize the reflection staring back at her. She seemed transformed into something hollower than she had been before knocking on the Atkinses' door, as though a core part of her had been ripped away. She drew a long breath and tried to settle her nerves. She had had to abruptly leave the room and come here after Wanda Atkins had told them about Mercy being tortured with needles.

She went over to the window and looked out. A hawk was lazily flapping its wings as it made its way across the sky. She heard the sounds of children playing from another yard. A truck rumbled by. There was a car horn. And the blustery noise of a motorcycle starting up somewhere. A white-haired woman was taking laundry off the backyard clothesline next door. All normal, all regular.

And none of it had anything to do with how she

was feeling, which was anything but normal. It was all ragged and piercing and traumatizing.

And it's nothing compared to what Mercy endured.

She shivered once, squared her shoulders firmly, though she in fact felt no spine in her body or soul, and returned to the front room to find both Atkins and Blum staring anxiously at her.

Pine retook her seat after saying, "Sorry about that. I just had to take . . . a moment. I've . . . I've gotten personally involved in this case." She did not want to reveal to Atkins her familial connection to Mercy for a number of reasons.

Atkins said slowly, "Yes, well, I can understand that, sure." She glanced apprehensively between Pine and Blum.

Pine cleared her throat and said, "And did you think to take Mercy from her after you saw what Desiree was doing to her?"

"We were certainly stunned. But then Joe explained it away."

"How could he *possibly* do that?" said Pine between clenched teeth.

Atkins kneaded her thighs with her hands in her agitation. "He . . . he said that Mercy had terrible pains and that what Desiree was doing was sort of like that, oh what do you call it when they stick the pins in you?"

"Acupuncture?" suggested Blum.

"Yes, that's right."

"Acupuncture doesn't make you scream in pain," pointed out Pine, her cold gaze square on the other woman. "The needles they use aren't anything like regular needles."

"Well, I believed my son," said Atkins defensively as she looked away.

"And did you know about them moving her from the house to the prison in the woods?"

Atkins winced at this. "They . . . they told us she was uncontrollable. That she would hurt herself and others. They had to take precautions. It was to keep *her* safe, too," she added.

Pine drew out the photo again. "So this girl standing right next to you was uncontrollable and would hurt herself and others?"

"Joe said they had given her something to calm her down that day."

"Well, *Joe* seemed to have an answer for everything. Did you go out to the prison cell?"

Atkins looked up at her. "I did."

"Why?"

She spread her arms and said in a near wail, "Because . . . I felt so sorry for her. I brought her food and books and I talked to her about things, read to her, did numbers with her. I'm no teacher or anything, but I did what I could. I . . . I just wanted her to have a friend."

"But you never told the authorities about what

Desiree was doing to her?" interjected Blum. "That she was being held prisoner?"

Atkins shook her head. "I . . . I was afraid. Len and I could go to jail."

Pine said impatiently, "Talk to me about that last night. When Joe was killed."

"We had no idea any of that had happened. We only found out about Joe the next day."

"If you lie to me, I *will* arrest you."

"What do you mean?" said Atkins, looking severely shaken.

"We know that Desiree vanished. We know she drove their truck to the location where it was found by the police. Her husband was dead and Mercy was gone. Who would she call except you and your husband? You're the only ones who knew what was going on, who knew of their *criminal* acts." Pine stared the woman down. "So you need to tell us the truth."

Atkins eyed her husband, who had grunted at her and then added a nod of his tilted head to that.

Atkins turned back to Pine with a resigned expression. "She called while Len and me were watching TV, a rerun of *Gilligan's Island*. Funny how you remember things like that."

"Go on," said Pine impatiently.

Atkins said in a rush, her words coming out like beans spilled from a jar, "She said Becky had gone crazy, had broken out and killed Joe and then run off.

Desiree said she had to get away or else they'd arrest her. She was out of her mind with panic."

"Why would you agree to help her at that point?" asked Pine. "With your son dead?"

"We were completely paralyzed by what she told us." Tears slid down the old woman's cheeks. "My God, she had just told me my son had been murdered. And then that evil bitch threatened us. She said if we didn't help her, that she would tell the police we knew all about it. She said she'd tell the police that *we* had tortured Becky. Len and I didn't know what to do. We were scared out of our minds. Desiree can lie better than anybody. So we helped her get away."

"How exactly did you do that?"

"We drove her all the way to Atlanta. She got a bus out."

"To where?"

"I don't know. She wouldn't tell us. We haven't seen her since."

"Or talked to her?"

"No. And good riddance."

"And what did she tell you about Joe's death?"

"She said that Joe tried to stop Becky, I mean Mercy, from leaving. And . . . they fought."

"And Mercy killed him?" said Pine.

"That's what Desiree said."

"And you believed her?"

"I didn't know what to believe. It was all a blur by then."

"And the sheriff told you about Joe the next day?"

Atkins's eyes filled with fresh tears. "I already knew he was dead, but I had to pretend to be shocked. It was the worst day of my whole life."

"And what did the sheriff tell you about Joe?"

"He was sure that Desiree had killed him. I mean, he had no idea about Mercy living there. We told him we hadn't seen or heard from Desiree."

"So you lied to him and obstructed the investigation," said Pine bluntly.

Atkins nodded, her features full of misery. "I . . . I suppose we did, yes."

Pine eyed Len Atkins, who looked back at her mournfully. He slowly shook his head. "I think your husband would like you to tell the truth."

Atkins glanced sharply at him. "I *am* telling the truth."

Pine said firmly, "So your son's body lay outside all night long and was untouched by animals? Not one bite taken out of him, according to the police."

Atkins put a trembling hand to her face. "Please, stop. Please."

Len grunted. Pine glanced at him once more. He was staring fiercely at his wife.

Atkins looked at him, drew in a sharp breath, and said, "Okay, we went over there . . . and saw Joe's body. We had to. He was our son. We had to make sure. We didn't know if Desiree was lying or what. When we saw he was . . . dead . . . we . . . we couldn't leave our son out . . . out there alone." She teared up again. "It was horrible . . . Len had his shotgun and he kept watch and scared the critters away . . . but . . . but the flies . . . they were all over h-him." She let out a gush of air and took some time to calm while Pine and Blum waited.

Atkins wiped her eyes with her sleeve and said, "*I* met Desiree at the old Esso station, and drove her to Atlanta while Len guarded Joe's body. The next morning he was going to call 911 from a pay phone and tell them about Joe without identifying who he was."

"Why wait until the next morning?" interjected Pine.

"Desiree wanted time to get away. But then early the next morning, before I got back from taking Desiree, Len heard someone coming and hid. A man was walking his dog. He found Joe's body and ran off, obviously to call the police. I got there about ten minutes later and Len told me what had happened. We drove back together to the trailer. When the police showed up later we acted all surprised."

Pine studied her. "Did you look at the body closely?"

"It was our son, if that's what you're asking."

Blum interjected, "We know this is hard, Wanda. But we're trying to find Mercy. Anything you can tell us about what you observed that night will help."

Atkins wiped her eyes and said firmly, "There was

a knife sticking in my son's back, and he was *dead*, that's what I saw."

"Anything else?" asked Pine.

"I don't know. I was so upset." She paused. "He ... he had a lump and some blood on his head. I remember that."

"Did you see signs of a struggle?" asked Pine.

"No. But I'm not sure what I would be looking for."

"What did Desiree say actually happened? As detailed as you can recall."

"That Mercy got away somehow. And Joe tried to stop her. And she attacked him. And stabbed him. And then ran off."

"Where'd she get the knife?"

"Desiree didn't say."

"There was a gunshot," said Pine. "On the surveillance tape we heard a shot."

"I don't know anything about that. Desiree never mentioned a gunshot."

"Did Desiree have a shotgun when you saw her at the Esso station?"

"No."

"Did she tell you where she was going? Are you sure you haven't been in contact with her over the years? Not once?"

"No. I don't want to ever see that awful woman again," Atkins snapped.

"And then you moved away?"

"Yes. We sold Joe's house. With Desiree gone, we were next of kin. We used that money to buy this place. Joe also had money in some bank accounts from his business. All of that came to us, too," she added, shooting them nervous glances.

"I see."

Pine rose, took out a couple of her business cards, and handed them to Atkins. "You think of anything else, or if you hear from Desiree, please call me."

"I doubt we'll hear from her after all this time."

"Oh, you just never know, do you?"

17

As they drove away from the house, Pine said, "She was lying."

"How so?" asked Blum.

"Desiree would never walk away and leave them all that money from the house sale and the bank accounts. If she was going to start over, she needed financial resources. I'm betting Wanda knows where she is and they keep in contact just in case someone like us shows up asking questions. And I think the shotgun Joe had was the same one that Len used to guard his son that night."

"If you're right, what are we going to do about it?"

Pine glanced in the rearview mirror. "If they are in contact with her, our visit must have really shaken up old Wanda. In fact . . ." Pine suddenly pulled off the road, put the Porsche in park, and said, "I'll be back in a minute."

She climbed out and hustled back down the street. Before she reached the Atkinses' home she cut through a stand of woods and came up on the rear of the property. She jumped over the chain-link fence and headed up to the back of the house. There was an open screened window that looked directly into the kitchen. As she peered through it, Pine had to suddenly duck down.

Wanda walked into the kitchen looking pale and distraught. There was a phone hanging on the wall directly across from Pine. It had enlarged number keys to help those with vision challenges. Wanda walked over to it. Pine pulled out her phone, turned the video recorder function on, placed it against the screen, and zoomed in on the phone's numbers.

Wanda held up a small notebook, squinted at the open page, then put her glasses on and slowly punched in a phone number as she kept referring back to the page. She finished and waited. Pine kept her video recorder on and also listened through the screen. Thankfully, Atkins's back was to her.

"It's me, Wanda," said Atkins into the phone. "Why am I calling? Well, I'll tell you why. The FBI was here. Yes, the FBI was here asking questions about Becky. That's right. *Becky*. They know all about what you and Joe did. And they're looking for her and *you*! They know you're alive and how you got away that night."

At this point Wanda lowered her voice considerably and didn't do much talking, just nodded her head. Pine put her phone away, retraced her steps, and a minute later climbed back into the Porsche.

She told Blum what had happened and handed her

the phone. "Get the number off there, call up the Bureau, and ask them to find out who that phone is registered to and to get a physical address for it."

Blum did so and a few minutes later clicked off. "They're working on it. They said the area code shows that it's a western North Carolina number."

"Okay, that's a start. If they can get us Desiree's current name—I'm sure she's using an alias—and an address, we can make some progress for sure."

"What do you think she can tell us?"

"What really happened that night, for starters."

"But Desiree has every reason to lie. And the statute of limitations for what she did to Mercy has probably expired, as unfair as that is."

"But there is no statute of limitations on murder."

"Murder? You mean Joe?"

"Maybe not just Joe. There was a gunshot on the video we listened to the night that Mercy escaped from her prison. Joe didn't have a gunshot wound."

"So you think . . . ?"

"I have to think of every possibility, including that Mercy might have been killed that night, too, and that's why Desiree fled. Everything we've learned about the woman points to her being a sociopath."

"I . . . I guess that is possible."

"But it's *only* a possibility. And that doesn't make it true."

As Pine put the SUV in gear and they drove off, her phone buzzed. It was Jack Lineberry calling.

"Jack?"

"Atlee, something has happened." He sounded frantic.

"What?"

"Oh my God," he exclaimed.

"Look, just take a few deep breaths and calm down."

He ignored her advice and she forgot about it as soon as he spoke. "The police were just here."

"What police?"

"The Georgia State Patrol and a detective from Virginia."

"Virginia? What did they want?"

"The body in your father's grave was positively identified as Ito Vincenzo."

"Okay, no surprises there."

"Yes, but now they know that I lied about identifying the body as Tim Pine, Atlee. I think they're going to arrest me for obstructing justice in a homicide investigation."

"Homicide investigation? What the hell are you talking about?"

"When I told them that Tim had called me and told me what happened, they asked did I have any *proof* that he actually killed Vincenzo in self-defense. They asked how I could be sure that Tim didn't *murder* him."

"And what did you tell them?"

"What could I tell them? I didn't have any proof.

I just knew what Tim told me. And the fact that he disappeared and Vincenzo was buried in his place? I can tell you that the police are highly suspicious of that. They said something about him now being a fugitive."

"Do they know the whole story about my parents and the mob bosses? That would make them understand why Vincenzo would want to kill Tim."

"They didn't seem to. And, legally, I'm still not really allowed to disclose anything about that. But it might all have to come out depending on how this plays out."

"Did they say what they were going to do?"

"They said they were putting out an arrest warrant for Tim Pine. They're going after him, Atlee. My God, after all these years."

Pine could only stare dumbly out the windshield.

Well, that was one I didn't see coming.

18

The woman said to El Cain, "Just so you know, we require a week's worth of rent in advance. Cash, no checks, no credit cards 'cause the folks who stay here are dishonest as hell, and they keep ripping us off."

She was short, pudgy, and thick-boned, in her early forties, with long, dyed blond hair parted in the middle, where her dark roots were waging a come-back. She had a spiteful look, and her tone was aggressive and unfriendly. She was dressed in faded jeans, a pair of black flats, and a sweatshirt silk-screened with, ironically, the image of a smiley face.

"Nice to know I'm moving into such a high-class place."

"Thought you would've figured that out before you walked in here."

"Do you live here?" asked Cain.

"God no. It's not safe at night." The woman added, "They did put a charcoal grill in the back, but you got to bring your own charcoal and lighter fluid. And you take full liability for any fires out of control or shit like that. And let me tell you, some drunk bastards have come close to burning this place down more than a few times while grilling hamburgers and hot dogs."

"I'm a vegetarian," Cain quipped. "And I never touch alcohol."

"R-right," said the woman, giving her a dubious look.

Cain paid the money and took the key to her new home. After doing her forklift gig, Cain had looked around and finally found this dump. It was in a horseshoe-shaped motel built in the 1970s that had been "renovated" into longer-term living arrangements, or so the woman had told her. Which meant, basically, that nothing had been done to it besides changing the name so they could charge more, a week at a time. The asphalt parking lot had long since been given over to dirt and weeds. She unlocked the door to number 110.

The room's width was a little under twice as long as her height. The bed was a twin with a gauzy veil for a coverlet and a pillow that looked as flat as a gambler without a stake. The only other furniture was a small nightstand that leaned to one side, a scarred desk with a shiny green Gideon Bible on it, and a chair with its back partially hanging off. There was no carpet, but they had left behind the gray, scratchy underneath pad for what reason she didn't know, other than it would cover the concrete slab below. The missing carpet's tacking strip was exposed where the wall met the floor, its pointy nails like rows of puppy teeth. There was a tiny closet with a few metal hangers. The bathroom was basic: ancient toilet, stained sink, phone booth-sized fiberglass shower. Someone had left a half roll of toilet paper and what appeared to be permanent pee stains on the toilet seat. The window was open. Cain closed it and tried to lock it but that was a no-go. She would have to fix that.

She put her duffel and other few possessions on the desk, took out her Glock, and lay back on the bed with it in her hand. She was tired, worried, and fearful, not because of where she was now living. She was scared because the FBI was after her. There was no statute of limitations for killing someone; she knew that from watching *Law and Order* episodes.

But could they really get her for murder? They had kept her locked in a cage. Didn't that give her the right to free herself and to defend herself against the Atkinses? She didn't know. She wasn't a lawyer. And people did whatever the hell they wanted and got away with it. Just like the Atkinses had for so many years.

The immediate years after her escape hadn't been much better. She was a very tall nineteen-year-old with the mental awareness of a preteen and the emotional maturity of someone even younger. Her naivete had led her into treacherous situations. Her fear of the authorities had steered her to groups that had exploited her, damaged her further, chewed her up, and then spit her out. And then one day Cain had woken up and said to herself, *Enough*. And then she'd said it even more forcefully to the biker gang member she was shacking up with, leaving him a bloody, pulpy mess. It was the least she could do after months of beatings from him. After that, it was her, solo. It would be her solo until the day she died, she had promised herself.

Cain slept fitfully for a couple of hours and awoke ravenous. She splashed water on her face, and since the room rate obviously didn't include towels or a washcloth, she used a spare sweatshirt to dry her face. She had purchased a new pair of shoes with her MMA purse and now slipped them on.

She drove to a nearby Wendy's and had a chicken sandwich, fries, and a vanilla milkshake. She looked around at the other tables and saw moms helping kids with their food, wiping mouths and noses, and cleaning up spills, just normal stuff. Still, she felt something odd in her head. Funny scenes appeared there. She had had them before. Dim memories . . . of something . . . someone. A girl laughed and put her hands over another girl's face. The other girl screamed with giggles. It was like a dream so vivid, it gave you the sweats. Yet when you woke up you could really remember nothing about it.

She left and drove back to her new home. The first thing that confronted her was the scream. It was loud, scared, and when it died out, she opened her car door and looked around for its source. There were other residents around, some sitting on fold-up outdoor chairs or on the ground, or on overturned five-gallon paint buckets while smoking and drinking and shooting the breeze. Two others were playing cards with piles of quarters as chips. Not a single one of them reacted to the screams. Cain wondered why. And she meant to find out.

Cain walked over to one of them, a burly guy in his fifties with thick gray hair poking out from under a John Deere ballcap and wearing a dirty T-shirt and old-style white painter's pants covered with colorful splotches. He had a can of Bud in one hand and a cigarette in the other. His eyes were red and unfocused, and she wondered how many Buds he'd downed.

"What the hell is going on?" she asked him.

"What?" he said, looking confused at the query.

"The *screams*."

He shrugged. "Ain't none of my business, sweetie."

"Not what I asked."

He pointed his smoke at room 104, about the time another scream sounded from within. "Girl's getting her punishment again."

"What girl?"

"Ken's girl."

"And why is she being punished?"

"Cause Ken says so."

"And who the hell is Ken?"

At that moment the door to 104 burst open and a young woman came running out, her hands over her head. She was dressed in her underwear and was barefoot. She was Hispanic, in her early twenties, with beautiful features and a sleek, lean body.

Coming out after her was, Cain assumed, Ken. He was in his thirties, about six feet tall, around 250 pounds, and built like a bowling ball. He was shirtless, which showed off his powerful arms and thick, heavily tatted shoulders, and muscular forearms. His beer belly was impressive, Cain thought. He looked pregnant with triplets. His shaved scalp and forehead had a large skull tat embedded on it. Among the other tats was a swastika on his right forearm. He held a belt in his right hand, and a cigarette dangled from his mouth. A knife rode in a holder at his waist.

"Get back here, Rosa; don't make me chase you, girl. It ain't gonna be good for you if I do. You ain't got no clothes on, you dumb bitch. Ain't you got no shame, woman?"

Rosa turned, spat at him, and hurled a machine gun's worth of Spanish, none of which Cain could understand, nor, did it seem, could Ken. Cain could see the bright red marks on Rosa's arms and legs where the belt had struck her. Cain involuntarily rubbed her arms where Desiree had struck her innumerable times with her damn belt.

Ken took out the smoke and ground it under his

boot heel. He snapped the belt like a whip and growled, "I told you before, you speak *American*. You gonna make double trouble for yourself, you stupid tacohead." He laughed at his insult.

"*You* are tacohead!" barked Rosa. "That's why you're so *fat*. You eat too many, you pig."

His smile faded as his poor attempt at humor was thrown right back at him; he looked around at everyone staring. Cain knew that men like Ken had only one reaction to such public insult. His lack of wit and deep-set insecurities quickly gave way to his abundance of brute physical strength, and uninspired knee-jerk reactions, which would always be violence-based. Grim-faced, he advanced on her, while Painter's Pants Man hurriedly retreated, and most of the other people got up and fled inside their rooms.

Cain turned to her left and saw the woman from the office staring at them outside the glass doorway and wearily shaking her head. Then she moseyed back inside like this was simply a daily event. And Cain clearly understood that it was. The Kens of the world all had the same playbook and never deviated from it. That made them dangerous, but predictable. And that made them imminently beatable, if you approached them just right. And Cain had a PhD in the subject of idiot boy-men.

As he advanced on a defiant Rosa, Cain stepped into his path. "Put down the belt, go back inside, get your head clear, and don't do anything else stupid," she said.

Painter's Pants Man took another long step back and muttered, "Oh, hell, you dumbass woman."

Ken didn't say anything back. He just swung a lumpy fist at Cain's head.

19

Cain sidestepped the blow and drilled a razor-sharp, thunderous uppercut right into Ken's diaphragm. He doubled over, and his face turned crimson as every ounce of breath in his body got kicked out into space from the staggering blow. While he was dealing with that, Cain launched an elbow strike into his right kidney. It connected with the ferocious impact of a two-by-four with a nail sticking out. He screamed and, his adrenaline spiking and overcoming the pain, he threw another fist at her. She easily blocked it with her forearm, gripped his wrist and elbow, pulled in opposite directions, and Ken screamed again. She pushed him to the ground and said, "Walk away. Last warning, dickhead."

Ken staggered to his feet, his big belly sucking in and out as he tried to get his breathing and his pain under control. He whipped out the knife. Before he could raise it, though, Cain lunged forward and kicked it out of his hand. The knife sailed ten feet away.

He grabbed his damaged hand. "You broke my finger, you stupid bitch."

"Unless you knock this shit off, that won't be the only thing I break."

He roared and bull-rushed her, his thick arms spread wide.

She easily sidestepped his charge, clenched his left arm as he went by, and ripped his elbow up even as she brought his wrist inward at a drastic angle. When he tried to pull free, she drove a bony knee into his already damaged right kidney. Ken yelled out in pain as she used his arm to lever him to the dirt once more, while he screamed obscenities at her.

He reached with his other hand to his back and a pistol appeared in his hand. He shrieked in fury, "I'm gonna kill you, you mutherfu—"

He didn't finish his sentence because Cain let go of his arm, grabbed both sides of his head, and pulled him toward her; at the same time she smashed her very hard knee directly into his face. He fell back with the blunt impact, but still managed to bring the gun up, and fired. The shot passed within a few inches of her head.

As he staggered up, Cain charged forward and hit him with two quick jabs to the jaw and a left hook to the oblique, which again dropped him to his knees. She gripped his wrist and struggled to break his hold on the gun. The son of a bitch was strong as a bull, she had to give him that.

He suddenly lunged for her, hitting her in the throat with the crown of his head. She fell back, her breathing labored from the blow, but she had managed to wrench the pistol away from him. Then he grabbed her hand and tried to pull the gun free.

This was getting way past critical, she thought.

Cain brought her knee up and hit him right in the chest with it, twice. He staggered back but pulled her with him, both of them still holding the gun. His finger managed to reach the trigger and pulled it. The shot blasted out of the gun and smacked into the wall of the motel.

Okay, Cain thought, *I need to end this*.

The move she was contemplating was complex, but she'd done it a few times in a cage fight. Still holding on to the gun with one hand, she got a headlock on him with her other and used that as a fulcrum point. She lifted herself off the ground so that he was supporting her entire weight as well as his. She arched back, her face pointed to the sky, and pulled with all her strength. He flipped over her as she went under him. At the last possible moment she let go. His head slammed into the dirt as she managed to lithely roll through on the other side.

A moment later Cain rose holding the pistol, because the torque on the flip move had forced him either to let go or blow out his rotator.

Cain stepped back, her chest heaving, and looked down at the pile of Ken on the ground bleeding and unconscious.

"Holy shit!"

Cain gagged, spit up, and rubbed at her bruised throat before looking over at Painter's Pants Man, who was standing there goggle-eyed, his Bud still in hand.

"What?" asked Cain.

"You just kicked the crap out of Ken," he said in disbelief.

"So?"

"But you're a girl and he's a guy."

"That's not an answer," she said in a croaky voice.

She knelt down and examined Ken. He *was* unconscious, but she checked his pulse. It was strong. She tugged on his arm and one of his legs. Though unconscious, his body reacted to the pull and the limbs involuntarily jerked back.

Okay, didn't seem to be any spinal damage from his head hitting the ground.

She rose and looked at Rosa. "You okay?"

Rosa was staring down at Ken with stark fear.

"*Madre de Dios.* He . . . he will kill me when he wakes up."

"Go get your things," said Cain.

"*Qué?*"

"You got any kids? Any . . . *niños?*"

Rosa shook her head. "We're not . . . married."

"Okay, go get your things. I'll take you to a place where you'll be safe."

Rosa ran back into her room and they could hear her banging and slamming things.

"Hey!"

Cain turned to see the office woman striding toward her.

"Hey what?"

"You assaulted Ken."

"I was defending myself."

"I don't think so. I'm going to have to call the police," she said.

"I thought you might do that when he was beating the shit out of Rosa."

"He was just disciplining her. You shouldn't have butted in."

"Well, the fact is, we're leaving," said Cain.

"Who's leaving?"

"Me and Rosa."

The woman said stubbornly, "You're not getting your money back. No refunds."

"Yeah, I can see how you might think that."

" 'Cause it's true."

"How long has Ken been here?" asked Cain.

"A month."

Cain pulled out her phone. "Then *I'll* make the call to the cops."

"What the hell are you talking about?" the woman exclaimed, utterly thrown by this abrupt change in the discussion.

"Ken broke his parole. So I'm notifying the cops that he's here and that you've been harboring him for a month."

"Shit, are you drunk or what? How do you know he's on parole?"

In answer Cain pointed to a tat on Ken's arm. "That's the membership symbol for the Aryan Brotherhood. They're a prison hate group. You get that tat when you go inside. I can tell it's a prison tat because it's a shitty job; they use melted-down junk for ink and crappy, homemade shivs to do it. Now Ken's on the outside. He's a young guy. Parole is usually for quite a few years. That tat looks almost brand-new. But he's got a knife and a gun. And he just assaulted a woman. Triple-strike parole violations. And you just admitted that you know he does this regularly. So that makes you an accessory. That'll get you at least a year in jail, too."

The woman took a step back, her confidence draining away along with all the color in her face. "How do you know so much about all that?"

Cain knew all about that because she had been picked up hitchhiking and then assaulted by one of these "Brothers." She'd briefly been held against her will before escaping, and had left the dude looking a lot like Ken did right now.

But she said with authority, "I'm a cop."

"Bullshit! Show me your badge. And what would you be doing here?"

"I'm undercover investigating some of the lowlifes in the area, so I'm not carrying a badge. Besides, you think every gal could take out somebody like Ken without special training?"

It was sometimes stunning to Cain how easily she could produce lies that sounded authentic, like she had with the security guard that morning. But for most of her life Cain had been in situations where coming up with an alternate reality on the fly and under stressful situations—and making it sound so real that sometimes she believed it herself—was the only thing that allowed her to keep breathing.

Practice makes perfect. And practice under penalty of death makes better than perfect.

Painter's Pants said, "She's talking truth to you, Beth. I mean, you can see that with your own damn eyes, gal. Hell, I bet she's like ex-military or something with all that damn ninja training."

Cain said, "So, *Beth*, go get my money, *all* of it, and bring it here to me. And I won't call the cops. Not because I don't want to see you and Ken go to jail, but because I don't want to waste time filling out the paperwork. I have better things to do."

Beth stood there for a moment, wavering. Then she ran back to the office and came back with the money. She handed it over to Cain, who counted and then pocketed it.

Cain went to her room, grabbed her things, and met Rosa outside. She had put on jeans and a white long-sleeved shirt and carried a small duffel.

They drove off while everyone else stared at the unmoving pile of Ken.

20

Cain got Rosa into a women's shelter that Cain had used when she had first come to town. She pressed a hundred dollars into Rosa's hands and said, "Don't ever go back to that guy. He *will* kill you, okay? The dude's just bad."

"I swear I won't. And . . . thank you."

Cain said nothing in reply because she wanted no thanks, from Rosa or anyone else. She just wanted to be left alone and wondered why she kept inserting herself into other people's troubles. Maybe because no one had done that for her, and she understood quite clearly the catastrophic results of looking the other way.

She decided to splurge a bit and checked in at a local Marriott using her credit card. Cain took her things up to her room on the fourth floor and closed the door behind her. She took a long shower with actual hot water, letting it soak into her and using all of the complimentary toiletries the bathroom had to offer. It took her only a few seconds to dry her hair. She put on a clean pair of jeans, to replace the pair dirtied from the fight, with a white T-shirt and a loose-fitting straw-colored sweater over that.

After that Cain sat on her bed and stared at the floor. The day was not yet over and she had covered a lot of ground, from being thrown out of her lodgings, to having to vacate her next home, to arriving here. She didn't have to work as a security guard tonight, and tomorrow was payday for the forklift job. She would get her check and cash it, and put the money with her other money.

She lay back on the bed and used her phone to once more access the notice from the FBI. She brought up the image of herself on the screen: wild-eyed and long haired and both thrilled and terrified at her sudden liberation after all those years. She put the phone against her chest, closed her eyes, and conjured up that final night with the Atkinses.

She had run toward the house, not because she wanted any sort of revenge, but because she knew that was where the road out of this nightmare was. She knew she had limited time because of the camera outside the door. Joe Atkins had told her time and again that *I'm always watching you, Becky, always. Don't you even think about trying to get away, you hear me, girl?*

When she had first gone to the Atkinses to live, it had been with Len and Wanda. But that had been for only a few days. They had treated her all right, but then she had gone to live at Joe and Desiree's place. And that was when her ordeal began, although it had not started that way. At first they had been somewhat kind to her; however, everything about her life before that was garbled, like the bad connection on a phone. She knew she had been taken from somewhere by the man. That her real parents had wanted her dead for some inexplicable reason, at least that was what he had told her. Now she didn't have strong enough memories of her previous life to know whether this was true or not.

However, the day had come when the Atkinses' behavior toward her had changed. Well, it had been Desiree, really. Joe had mostly worked outside the home, so it was just her and Desiree. They never had any visitors except, occasionally, Len and Wanda.

It was small things at first, bouts of sharp, inexplicable anger, the taking away of privileges, time-outs that turned into verbal and then physical abuse. When she was around eight, Desiree started playing what Cain now knew to be mind games with her. Planting things in her young head that would have been warnings to someone older and more mature. At first, Joe had defended her, but he'd never really forced Desiree to change her ways.

Don't hit her that hard, Desiree, he would say. *Feed her more than that, that's not enough for a cat. Put her in better clothes, Desiree, what's the matter with you?* But then, Joe's attitude changed too. Cain thought it was Desiree's doing because Joe would storm into her room and say, *I know what you've been doing, Becky. I know! And you're not going to get away with it*. One day he had come in and said, *You are never to bite my wife again*. And then he'd belted her in the face. Of course, Cain had never bitten Desiree, though she'd wanted to.

Then the time came when she went from the house to the prison cell carved into the side of the knoll. They had come into her room, woken her up, and said it was time for her to live in her new home. Cain thought they were giving her to another family, and she hoped and prayed they would be nicer, because now she was being beaten regularly, verbally terrified, worked to death, and fed hardly enough to keep her alive.

But that was not what had happened. As they dragged her into the woods, Cain was sure they were going to kill her and bury her body out there. She had screamed and tried to get away, but she couldn't, and there was no one to hear her cries. They took her inside and Joe had used his flashlight to show her what was there. It was meager and dirty and cold, and Cain thought she could hear things scurrying around on the floor.

This is your new home, Becky, Desiree had said tauntingly. *This is where you will sleep every night and where you will wake up every morning, unless you disobey me and are bad and then you will never wake up again.*

At that point the young Cain was so panicked she couldn't process what was happening. When they locked her in she pounded on the door, screaming for them to let her out, that she would be good from now on. Then she had heard Desiree's voice coming from right against the other side of the wood: *If you make any more noise, I will let the snakes inside with you. I see two right now who look very hungry. And they will bite you until you are dead. And then they will swallow you whole, Becky. Do you understand me? Do you hear them hissing? I will do it. You know that I will. They grow snakes big around here.*

A terrified Cain had slowly backed away from the door as far as she could, all the way to the dirt side of her prison as it notched into the knoll. She had sat down on the mattress and never made another sound. She heard them walking away and leaving her there; she had stayed up all night in the dark, waiting to hear the hiss of the snakes who would come to bite her dead and then eat her.

Cain sat up and rubbed at one of the burns on her arm as the painful memories seeped from her mind. Desiree would strap her down in her bed and then light the cigarette and hold it over her, suddenly sticking the burning ember into her skin, making Cain scream before pulling it away and then drilling it into another part of her body until the girl cried out even louder.

Please stop, Desiree, please don't hurt me.

I'm your mother, you will call me mother. And another burn would follow.

Mother, please don't hurt me.

And Desiree would burn her again and cackle, *Your mother doesn't love you, Becky. She has never loved you because you don't deserve it, not like other children who are good and pure, which you are not. You are wicked and nasty and not to be trusted.*

Cain jumped up and rushed into the bathroom, where she upchucked her burger, fries, and milkshake meal into the toilet. She washed off in the sink and stumbled back into the bedroom and collapsed on the bed.

She lay there, breathing deeply until she fell asleep. In the swirls of a misty dream she saw a face with features that resembled so remarkably her own that it was like staring into a mirror. The gap in the front teeth, but dirty jeans instead of a dress, a resolute chin, a fierce look, a small hand clenched into a stubborn fist. A name kept calling out to her, but it was a muted voice in the midst of a hurricane. She just could not make it out. However, it gave her calm, a certain, necessary strength; it always had.

Cain awoke and the image vanished. She sat up and cursed. Why did it disappear as soon as she opened her eyes?

She looked outside and was surprised to see that it was pitch-dark. She'd been asleep longer than she had thought. Cain took the elevator down to the hotel bar. She sat at the end away from the live band and moodily drank her beer. The bartender was black and in her early forties with pink and purple hair, an athletic build, stylish forearm tats, an efficient manner, and a twinkle in her eye.

"You look like you need that beer, girl."

"This one and a dozen more."

"Hope you're staying here then."

"I am."

"You in town on business?" the woman asked.

"No, just passing through from somewhere else."

"Ain't we all."

She moved on when another thirsty customer held up a hand.

The TV mounted on the wall was on a news channel, and Cain choked on a mouthful of beer and spilled some of it from her glass when she saw her picture come up. The notice said that the FBI was looking for this woman, the image was from 2002, that her name is, or was, Rebecca Atkins, and that any information about her whereabouts should be sent via phone or email, and that information then flashed up on the screen.

Cain slowly put her beer down and wiped off the residue from her chin.

The bartender came over with a towel and sopped up the spilt beer from the bar. "You okay?"

"Went down the wrong way."

Cain laid some cash down for the beer and included a healthy tip. She got up and staggered off.

The bartender turned and looked at the TV where

the picture of Rebecca Atkins still filled the screen. Then she looked back at the disappearing Cain.

And she frowned as she picked up the cash.

After checking out of the hotel the next day, Cain did her work at the truck terminal and got her paycheck. She then called the trucking company and told them she would have to take a few days off. The man told her if she didn't show up for work she was fired.

"Okay, I'm fired." Cain hung up. She sat down, counted her money, made a rough calculation, and made the same call to the security firm. The manager there was a good guy, a grandfather with a soft spot for her.

"I got twenty laid-off bums waiting in line for the job, Cain, and ten of them have college degrees. You sure about this?"

"I'm sorry, but I got some place I gotta go. I can't get out of it."

"Okay, good luck. If you ever come back, let me know. I'd take you over some philosophy major any day."

She filled the gas tank and set off. Cain had no idea if her decision would lead her to salvation or a prison cell. But something very powerful inside her told Cain she had to do it. After all these years, the gap in her memories had to be filled in, one way or another.

She pointed the car south and hit the gas.

Back to nightmare time.

21

Many hours later Cain slowed her car and felt her breathing accelerate as she drove into Crawfordville, Georgia. This was not because of the surroundings. She had never passed any place here that was recognizable to her because the Atkinses had been careful never to bring her into town, or anywhere else. They obviously didn't want anyone to know that they had her. At first, Cain didn't know why that was the case. As the years went by the reason became very clear.

Cain stopped for a late dinner at a small diner with half its blinking neon lights out and with an exterior faded by time and probably shallow pockets. She wasn't really hungry but just needed a bit of time to deal with the fact that she was back in this place.

The waitress poured out her second cup of coffee and watched as Cain listlessly poked at her food.

"Not to your liking, hon?"

Cain glanced up. The woman was well into her seventies and looked too tired and frail to still be working. The smell of stale cigarette smoke rose from her pores like a morning fog. Her teeth were nicotine stained, but her features were kind and her smile was sincere.

"No, it's fine. Just sort of lost my appetite."

"Haven't seen you around before. You new in town, or just passing through?"

"Just passing through."

"Yeah, that's what they all say," noted the waitress wistfully. She tucked a strand of gray hair back inside the blue cap she wore. "I'd like to say I'm just passing through sometimes, and I was *born* here. Born here and never got out of jail. Where you coming in from?"

"Atlanta," Cain lied.

"Been there once, thirty years ago. Bet it's changed a lot. Now this here place never changes. Some days that's good, most days not so good. But it's all I've got or ever known, so . . ."

"Change can be good," said Cain.

"You sound like you speak from experience."

"Well, experiences are all *I've* got."

"Hope they were good ones, sweetie."

Cain paid her bill and left without answering.

She had learned the street address for the Atkinses when she had lived in the house and seen letters addressed to them. For some reason, that address had been lodged in her memory ever since.

The Google maps app on her phone was guiding her to that destination. When she turned onto the road she finally saw something she remembered. The massive live oak up ahead. It had obviously gotten even bigger over the intervening years; its canopy was so broad it almost blocked out the sky, it seemed to her. This was the tree under which Joe Atkins's body lay. She wondered if the last thing he ever saw was that tree, knowing it would outlive him.

There were no other homes down here, as had been the case when Cain lived here. As she passed by the house, the sweat started popping up on her face, under her armpits, behind her knees. Her stomach started to churn. The freezies were taking over with the power of a fully loaded freight train. She hit the gas, blew past the house, jerked to a stop a quarter mile down, put the car in park, then got out and threw up coffee and stomach bile behind a raggedy bush.

This is ridiculous, El, pull yourself together.

She got back into the car and drove back down the road, passing the house slowly. It looked mostly unchanged. There was a large blue tractor trailer rig out front. It seemed to dwarf the modest house. The rusted metal carport next to the house was empty. She could see no lights on inside. She pulled farther down, parked on the dirt shoulder, and got out. With a flashlight she'd taken from the glove compartment, Cain set off into the woods with a very specific destination in mind.

My old home.

She knew if she could endure this, she could make

it through anything, because here was where she had made it through everything.

Cain recalled every step since this was the same path, albeit in reverse, that she had taken on her way to freedom. She turned to the left and came out into a clearing. She needed to be very careful right now. She looked back in the direction of the house. She couldn't see it from here, but she wanted to make sure no one was coming from that direction.

She continued on, having to fight her way through the wilderness that had grown up in the path since she had last been here. But she paused and studied some broken branches, demolished bushes, ripped-apart saplings, and how the earth underneath her feet had been disturbed by numerous feet plowing through here.

She started sweating again.

The video. People have recently been here. They were heading where I'm going right now. The cops. The FBI.

The freezies started up again, and she leaned against a tree and took deep breaths. Lactic acid was drying out her mouth and enfeebling her limbs. That had happened to Cain in her very first MMA bout. She had been so nervous that she could barely move. The woman she was fighting had knocked her flat on her ass and then tried to arm-bar her. Cain had been so pissed at herself that the lactic acid got blown up in the spike of fury-spawned adrenaline. The ref had finally had to pull her off the woman, whom she had beaten into unconsciousness.

She blew air and acid out all over the Georgia forest until her limbs were freed of their lethargy and saliva returned to her mouth.

When she reached the next clearing, she stopped and looked ahead.

Her old home rose up out of the darkness like some creature that carried only despair in its maw. It was smaller than she remembered, but that was normally the case when folks revisited the haunts of their childhood, and for Cain the word *haunts* was spot-on. The door was closed, but when she shone her light, it was revealed that there was no padlock. The ivy around the front had been pulled down, exposing the rusted surveillance camera.

She gathered her nerves, stole up to the door, knelt down, and put her ear to it. She heard nothing from inside. Then Cain looked up at the camera and was seized with a terrible thought. Was it still functional? She reached up and pointed it away from her. She fled into the woods and waited for about twenty minutes to see if anyone appeared. When no one did she crept back over to her former prison, steeled herself for a moment, then opened the door and went inside.

Cain shone her light around and was instantly engulfed with thousands of horrible memories; the effect was suffocating, as though the room suddenly lacked all oxygen. She sat down on the floor and guided her light around.

She winced and drew back at the sight of the chain secured to the wall. They had used that on her until she had grown too big and defiant.

And dangerous. They didn't dare get that close.

As soon as she was fully grown, it became about two things: keeping their distance, and the gun. Desiree hadn't been able to torture her anymore. But she had done plenty of it over the years. Enough to leave Cain permanently disfigured.

She looked at the filthy mattress on which she had slept for thousands of nights; then there was the shelf with odd objects on it, all treasures to her back then. She had given names to all of them and they had been her only friends during those years. She talked to them, had tea parties with them, then, as she grew older and bolder, she formed an imaginary gang with them that did mischievous things to drive the Atkinses crazy.

She breathed deeply, and the smell of wet clay and mold and rotting wood filled her lungs like water in a bucket. As a captive here, she had breathed this air every day. But every day that she had been alive *to* breathe was a victory.

There were items she didn't recognize. A pair of boys' sneakers, a baseball mitt, a deflated soccer ball, some girly magazines. Maybe the people living in the house now had kids and they had found this place and used it as a hideout or something. In fact, the more she thought about it, maybe that was how the place came to be found by the cops.

And then she saw it.

Sally, her doll, which lay in a corner on the floor. She went over and picked it up. It looked so tiny in her hand now, though the last time she had held it she was nearly fully grown. She had come to regret leaving it behind, but in the heat of the moment, in the sheer exhilaration at being free, she had forgotten all about Sally. She stuck it under her bulky sweater. Sally would not be left behind this time. She rose and left, closing the door behind her.

And that was when the voice called out.

"Hey, what are you doing here?"

22

The teenage boy held a flashlight in his hand and was pointing it at Cain. He was medium height and skinny with a mop of unruly hair. She estimated he was around fourteen or fifteen.

She found her voice and said, "Hey there. Look, I just heard about the stuff that went on here. I was driving by and decided to take a peek. Sorry, I didn't mean any harm."

His expression softened, but his look remained wary. "O-okay, I . . . I guess I'd be curious, too."

"You live around here?"

He looked over his shoulder. "In the house back there. This is *our* property."

"Wow, okay. Did you use to hang out in there?"

"Yeah, me and my brother, when we were younger."

"What's your name?"

"What's yours?" he said sharply.

"I'm Donna."

"Okay, I'm . . . Kyle. And . . . and I don't think you should be here."

Cain had shifted Sally to the back of her sweater, so Kyle couldn't see the lump. "Look, you have every reason to be freaked out, but I'm sort of freaked out, too, you know?"

His features softened. "Yeah, I guess. I mean, you're a girl and I'm a guy. Don't worry, I won't hurt you," he added hastily.

Cain almost smiled at this because she could have knocked Kyle out with one lazy kick.

"Thanks, Kyle. I really appreciate that. So, I saw on the local news the FBI was on the case. Damn, that's not something you see every day. Were they here, too?"

Kyle came forward, his features now full of excitement. "Yeah, they were. It was like being in the middle of a cop TV show. They were asking about some girl. And about the people who used to live here before us. I forget their names. Anyway, I remembered this place. And *I* was the one who showed them," he added proudly. "My dad talked to the cops and it seems like they were keeping a girl out here. I guess they were weird-ass people. I mean, she was like a prisoner or something." He frowned. "Totally sick stuff."

"Totally. Somebody I know said she saw a picture of the girl on the news."

"That's right. It was on a tape. You see that camera there?"

"Yeah."

Kyle frowned as he looked at the camera pointing the other way now. "Hey, somebody moved it. Maybe it was the cops. Anyway, the asshole who used to live here had a cable that ran all the way back to our house. I found it. And there was one of those old VCR things under the floor. And there was a tape in it. We played it and that picture was on it." He shone his light on the door. "That girl they made live in there busted out."

"Wow, no way," said Cain.

"Oh, yeah. And that's not all. The dude who owned the house? He got killed. My dad said the girl might've done it and that the jerk deserved it."

Cain felt something like a molten lava rock in her stomach. "Did they say how he died?"

"Not that I remember."

"And was there anyone else involved?"

"The dude's wife. She disappeared. They don't know what happened to her. Or the girl."

"But I guess the cops are looking for her, the girl, I mean."'

"Yeah, I guess so. I mean, if she killed that guy, she should get a medal, least I think so. But I guess if she killed him she broke the law, too. Probably why they want to find her." He looked up at her appraisingly. "Man, you are tall. Like that FBI lady."

"FBI lady?"

"The one who was here asking about everything. But you're taller."

"Yeah, I'm taller than most girls, unless they play basketball. Again, I'm sorry I trespassed, Kyle. I don't want to get into trouble."

Kyle waved this off. "No problem. I won't tell anybody. Hey, you want me to show you around in there?"

"No. It looks way too creepy."

Kyle nodded. "I know. When me and my brother found it, we thought it was creepy, too, but it was a cool place just to hang out. That's why we didn't tell our parents. But when we found out some little kid was being held in there? They must've been really, I don't know, screwed in the head. That's what Dad said, anyway."

"I think your dad's probably right about that."

"When we were watching the video and the girl busted out of that door?" Kyle grinned. "I don't know. I mean, it was scary, but now that I know why she did it? It was so dope. I was like rooting for her to get away."

"Yeah, you'd think most people would think that. But then again, the law can be funny."

"Yeah, I guess so."

"What are you doing out here so late?" she asked.

He pulled a camera out of his jacket pocket. "I'm putting together a little video about all this for my Instagram account. I'm going to call it Flight to Freedom, or something like that."

"Right. Okay, that sounds cool. Well, thanks, Kyle, it was nice meeting you."

"Same to you, Donna."

Cain turned and walked quickly off. She made her way back to her car and sat there for a couple minutes as she steadily processed all she had just learned.

The FBI was looking for her. They probably thought she had killed Joe, and possibly Atkins. Maybe it would be justified and maybe it wouldn't be. To Cain's mind, she had done nothing wrong. But she had had enough experience with the law to know that they saw things in a different way. And that way of thinking could land her right behind bars. She'd already been in a prison once, for committing no crime at all. She didn't intend to ever go back again.

She drove toward town and took a room at a motel.

She stripped down to her underwear and lay on the bed. She closed her eyes and immediately all she saw was the interior of that cell in the woods. Every detail was seared into her mind. She had been gone for nearly two decades now, but after being back there, it was like she had never left.

She remembered asking Desiree why they were treating her this way.

You're a wicked girl and you must be punished, Desiree had said.

But what wicked things have I done? Cain had asked right back.

I'm not going to waste my breath going into them. You don't deserve that, you little evil creature. You just keep in mind that you are being punished and you deserve every bit of it. And for good measure she had added a slap to Cain's face.

Once, when the lady Wanda had come by, Cain had asked her the same question.

Wanda had patted her hand and said, *There are wicked people in the world, Becky.*

So am I wicked, then? Cain had wanted to know. *Like Desiree says?*

I'm not talking about you, dear. I'm talking about others.

Cain had remembered asking Wanda for help, to get away, but the woman had just burst into tears and said she couldn't. Something about her son, not wanting to get Joe in trouble. So she had just let Cain rot there.

She didn't blame Wanda, not really. She could understand why she did what she did. It was all about survival. What more to life was there, really?

She reached over to the nightstand and snagged her old doll. She pressed the mildewed toy against her chest. "You were my only real friend, Sally. And maybe you still are."

23

The next morning Cain rose late and showered and took a few moments to look at herself in the mirror. She examined the burns on her left arm, and then the ones on her right. She could recall with absolute precision when each had been done and the means used. The person was always Desiree Atkins. Joe apparently didn't have the stomach for it. Desiree, on the other hand, apparently had no limits to what she would do.

The woman had often used lighted cigarettes. She seemed to like watching the skin blacken and bubble. Cain could remember looking at the woman even as she was shrieking in pain. The louder she yelled, the more Desiree smiled, the longer the burning went on. It didn't take Cain long, young though she was, to realize that if she marshaled all her focus and did not scream in pain, then Desiree would soon lose interest and stop, even though Cain's body would be shaking all over in agony. Desiree apparently liked to *hear* the terror. And sometimes Desiree would bring out the needles and the knife and carve things into Cain's skin. But her next favorite torture device had been the belt. When Cain had seen Ken holding his belt to threaten Rosa, all those memories came flooding back. But again, if Cain did not cry out, Desiree would stop enjoying it and leave Cain to quietly sob over her fresh wounds.

There was only *one* reason that Cain could focus during all that and not cry out. She had one image that she held in the safest, most remote spot in her mind. She hid it away, she told herself as a little girl, because she was afraid Desiree might find it and take it away, and leave Cain with nothing to fight back with.

The image was vague, yet powerful. A little girl was sitting in the dirt, wearing a colorful skirt, her long hair in her face. And she was looking up at something in a tall tree. A woman whom Cain could never really see was calling out to someone in the tall tree.

"You get down here right now, young lady. You have no business up there. You'll fall and hurt yourself."

And Cain would hear the little girl wearing the dress reply, "It's okay, Momma, it's just Lee being Lee. She'll find her way down. She always does. Don't be mad at her, Momma."

Who Lee was, Cain didn't know. Why she was up a tree, Cain didn't know. She suspected the little girl with the long hair and the dress was herself, but she didn't know that for certain.

She'll find her way down, Momma, she always does.

For some reason that curious image had fully consumed all of Cain's attention to such a degree that she could not feel the burns or the blows or the cuts and needle stabs that Desiree was inflicting. It allowed her to survive. Cain had felt a burst of pride for this Lee person. She apparently did what she wanted, took risks, figured things out, and she came out all right in the end.

Just like I needed to do.

But what was Lee? A figment of her imagination? Nothing at all? Or maybe someone important?

Should she be thankful for this Lee, or hate her?

Was Lee really me? I was being tortured every time this image appeared in my head. Was I just reaching for something, anything, to get through it? Because a person would, whether it was real or not.

Cain splashed cold water on her face, dressed, and went out to eat breakfast, choosing the same diner where she'd picked at her dinner.

She sat at the counter and looked around the place. It was mostly elderly people having their coffee, bacon and eggs, toast, and grits. Working-class folks like her, and as unlike her as it was possible to be. Some were clearly old enough to have been here when she had been living with the Atkinses. The sign outside said the diner had been here since 1960, so it was here long before she'd been born.

Could any of these people have helped her? Could they have found out about her? How could people keep someone prisoner in a place like this and no one know about it? Although Cain had read of a man in Ohio who had kept women prisoners in his house smack in the middle of a neighborhood. How the hell had that happened? Did people just not give a shit?

"Hope you enjoy your breakfast better than you did your dinner, hon."

Cain looked up into the face of the same waitress from last night. "Yeah, I'm pretty hungry, so I think I will."

She ordered, and when the waitress brought the food back over Cain said, "I was wondering, do you remember anyone named the Atkinses who used to live around here? They'd be around your age."

"You mean Wanda and Len Atkins?"

"Yeah, that's right."

The wrinkled face crinkled into a sad smile. "Well, that takes me way back, hon. I was good friends with Wanda. My husband, God rest his soul, and Len were in the VFW together. They've been gone a long time. They left after their son got killed."

Cain feigned surprise. "Really, he got killed?"

The waitress put her elbows on the counter and leaned down. "Joe Atkins was murdered. And his wife, Desiree, did it. I'm as sure of that as you're sitting right there. She lit out after it happened and no one's seen her since. And she was one strange lady. Sadistic, if you ask me. I saw her deliberately run over a dog with her truck. How sick is that?"

"Pretty sick. So she's gone, too?"

"Oh, yeah, years ago. How do you know the Atkinses? You said you weren't from here."

"I think my dad knew Mr. Atkins somehow. When I told them I was going to be passing through here he told me to look them up. I guess Mr. Atkins had told my dad that he lived in Crawfordville, but my dad didn't know if they were still here or not."

"Well, like I said, they moved away a long time ago."

"He'll be disappointed. I think he wanted to get back in touch."

The woman pursed her lips in thought. "Oh, wait a minute, where's my brain? I can help you out."

"How?"

The waitress pulled out her phone. "Wanda and me exchange Christmas cards. Hell, I got her address in my phone right here. She and Len are over in Alabama now, Huntsville."

She held out her phone with the contact showing, and Cain took a picture of it with her phone.

"Wow, thank you so much. This will make my dad's day."

"Old friends are sometimes the best friends. And in this day and age, we need all the friends we can get."

Yes we do, thought Cain. *I hope to find one someday.*

24

A battered Ken Buckley lay in the hospital bed, still unconscious. A monitor showing his precarious vital signs was set on a rolling stand next to the bed. The surgeon had addressed as many of the injuries as he could in the short time period, but there was more to be done, and Ken was not out of the woods yet. The fact that he was still not conscious was most problematic.

The man sitting in the chair next to him was Peter Buckley, Ken's older brother. He was in his forties, six one, fit and lean. He wore a tailored dark suit with a colorful pocket square, an immaculate white dress shirt, and no tie. His nails were well-groomed, his skin healthy and unmarked. The shoes on his feet were made of supple leather and cost a thousand bucks, the sleek suit over twice that. His hair was dark and wavy and neatly trimmed. His face was hairless, and his features were sharply defined. His pale blue eyes sometimes appeared dead white in a certain light. He had a quiet intensity and confidence about him that drew one's attention, something he didn't necessarily like. He crossed one leg over the other, revealing patterned burgundy socks, and stared at his little brother. Ken was the youngest, Peter the oldest, with several brothers and two sisters in between.

Two of the brothers were dead; the third was a guest of a state prison in the south. The sisters had long since disappeared, happy enough to get away from the Buckley clan. Their father, Peter Sr., had been severely wounded decades before in a chaotic shootout with federal agents at the family compound in a remote part of the country. Their mother had been injured in the same melee and then arrested along with her husband. But she had turned on her spouse, and her testimony had sent him to prison for several lifetimes, while she was put in witness protection with her children. Buckley's father hadn't made it through his first year in prison, because another inmate had sliced his throat from ear to ear. After that, Buckley's mother had abandoned her children, and Buckley had never seen her again.

Buckley's father had led a large group of followers who believed in segregation based on race and ethnicity, independence from outside laws and social mores, and adherence to a code of conduct that extended to all members, except the senior Buckley. He was free to do what he wanted, and to whom he wanted, because he was the leader, the chosen one, the man with a vision.

And they had also trafficked in stolen property, and

sold drugs and guns, because the money was necessary to fund their preferred way of life.

However, the federal government had come calling one night after some bodies were found. The dead were people who had once followed, but now disagreed vehemently with, Buckley Sr. And he had responded not with words but with guns, knives, and ropes. And shallow graves for prematurely and violently ended lives.

And the feds had destroyed his father for it, for merely standing up for what he believed in. Not nice, thought Peter Buckley. But then there were many not nice people in the world.

After his father's death and his mother's abandoning them, he, as the oldest sibling but still a child himself, had taken over the leadership role with respect to his remaining family. When he reached adulthood he had spent all his time expanding on his father's ambitions in a far more sophisticated way, choosing to learn from his father's mistakes rather than repeating them.

Over the years, he had created a far greater empire, and hidden the criminal elements of it behind a complex web of entities. At the same time, he had inserted himself into the fabric of mainstream society behind a consortium of perfectly normal businesses, while also building a reputation as a philanthropist. He supported myriad candidates for political office and had many friends who held both high and more mundane offices. He had found that only the latter could actually accomplish the things he needed done. Power at the national level was hopelessly gridlocked. But if you needed a residential development approved, or wanted the contract for garbage pickup, or required rezoning for a commercial project, the locals were far more powerful than even the president of the United States.

Several years before, he had bought back the land on which his family's compound had been situated, and he had rebuilt some of the facilities. He had put in a private airstrip and would fly in there from time to time, and stay there all alone for a few days. He would walk the site, sleep in the facsimile of the house in which he had been raised, and imagine how life could have been had the law not destroyed the Buckleys. That was his therapy, his respite from a world that he had learned to dominate on his terms but also would never truly belong to.

He had tried in vain to teach his brothers that real change meant playing the game until you got to the point where you controlled the game. Outsiders did not make real change. You had to become an insider, and you did so through a series of steps: ingratiate, annex, dominate, and then consolidate. Let the changes be so incremental that they would never see what really was coming until it was far too late.

However, his ill-educated brothers had not listened to their older sibling's advice. Since his teens Ken had been in prison. He had only been recently released from his last stint for another stupid and meaningless crime. Ken was particularly unteachable, his skin tatted with crap he probably didn't even understand. He was a loser and not really worth worrying about.

His sisters, like their mother, had abandoned the family when they reached adulthood. Buckley had never forgiven them. He had also never married or had a serious relationship with a woman, because he knew them to be totally untrustworthy. When he required sex, he paid for it. The night passed and the lady was not there in the morning. And that suited him just fine.

But Ken was still family, so Buckley *did* worry about him. When he got the call about what had happened from a police officer who had found his phone number among Ken's personal belongings, he had flown in on his jet two hours later. He had sat through Ken's first surgery. And he had gone to the motel to find out what had happened, and had also spoken to the local police.

A woman, of course, had done this to his brother. A tall, strong woman who had given no name and paid for her room in cash. She had told the woman at the motel that she was an undercover cop. Yet the police had no knowledge of her; Buckley, in his friendly, nonthreatening way, had asked for details about this, and the police had been very accommodating because Buckley was Ken's brother and looked and acted eminently respectable. So the woman had lied. And she had nearly killed Ken. Buckley had also confirmed that the woman had done all this to Ken with her bare hands. A formidable woman, physically, because Ken was no lightweight when it came to a brawl.

The surgeon had said that they would have to run more tests and do more imaging to make certain there would be no lasting damage to his body or his brain.

Buckley would take care of his little brother, even if it meant hiring people to change his diaper and feed him through a straw. And the woman needed to be found and punished appropriately. In Buckley's mind, there was no other possible outcome.

He left the hospital, climbed into a rented Mercedes, and drove back over to the motel. He was a man who was usually driven places, but he had come here alone. This was family business. When others needed to be called in, he would call them in. First, he had to do some more digging.

And a thought had occurred to him.

Beth, the woman at the motel's front desk, seemed pleased to see him again.

"Have they caught her yet? I gave a description."

"Unfortunately, no. But when I was here last time I noted the camera out front. Is it functioning?"

"Oh, damn, I forgot about that. Yes, it is. The cops didn't even ask about that."

"May I see the film?"

She showed him to a back room and had him sit in front of a computer. A few moments later scenes appeared on the screen, and Beth sped up the video until she got to a certain point. However, there were numerous blurry and totally blacked-out segments.

"That's her car," she said in a triumphant tone, hitting a key to return the video to normal speed. "The gray Civic."

Buckley took out his phone and keyed in the license plate number and then took several photos of the car. "But where is the woman? If you have the car, you should have her as well on the security footage."

"It's this lousy system," whined Beth. "It jumps around and doesn't film everything. And the camera is really old and half the time doesn't even work." She ran it back and then played it forward again. "You see there, and there? Where it's all blurry and gray? That was probably when she came and went to the office. This is the only good shot of the car. But at least we got that."

He thanked the woman with a hundred-dollar bill.

"I hope you get her," said Beth, eagerly taking the money. "She's a real bitch."

"And the woman with Ken whom you mentioned earlier?"

"Rosa? Yeah, the bitch drove her out of here. Said she was taking her somewhere safe."

"Do you have a picture of Rosa? I hope we don't have to rely on security footage again."

"We don't. I have it on my phone."

Buckley looked intrigued. "And why is that, I wonder?"

Beth looked embarrassed. "One day she . . . she had on a dress I liked. I was thinking of getting one, so I . . . I took her picture."

He looked over her frumpy clothes and pudgy frame. "I see."

She showed him the photo, and he took a picture of it with his phone.

"Very lovely woman," said Buckley. "Thank you."

"Are you going to try to find her?"

"Yes, I want to let her know about Ken's condition."

"I doubt she cares."

"I will do so anyway. Any ideas where she might be?"

"Like I said, the big gal mentioned she was taking her someplace safe. Now, there's a women's shelter in town. You might want to try there. It's on Everson near Fuller Street."

"Thank you again."

He got back into the car, and texted the images of the license plate to an associate and asked him to run down information on it. Then Buckley drove off to look for Rosa.

He had a great many other things of importance

on his plate right now. But he had set all of them aside for this. His family, granted, wasn't much. Yet it was still his family. And in Buckley's world, family could not remain unavenged. After his father's death, his whole life philosophy had revolved around one concept: You can never turn the other cheek. So Ken's attacker had to be found and beaten badly enough to be hospitalized.

In Buckley's world it was as simple as that.

25

Beth's information proved to be spot-on. However, Buckley hadn't been able to enter the women's shelter and directly talk with Rosa due to their visitor safety protocols.

He sat in his car for several hours and watched women come and go from the shelter. Finally, his patience was rewarded when Rosa walked out, turned left, and entered a café a block down from the shelter. He got out and followed her in. She had taken a table at the back, and he walked over and introduced himself.

She looked frightened when he told her that he was Ken's older brother.

"I'm not supposed to be talking to anybody like you. They said I could come here for a few minutes just to stretch my legs, but I have to go right back. They know where I am and if I'm not back—"

He interrupted her to say disarmingly, "Please, I wish you nothing but the best. I *know* my brother is an idiot and dangerous. He always has been. He's been getting into trouble for so long I have given up on him. I really have. But he called me and told me what happened and I came in to see him. I was close by, you see."

"He called you, so he's okay then?" she said nervously.

"He was beaten up pretty badly but, yes, he's okay. He, of course, disclaimed all responsibility, but I know better and I talked to the people at the motel. They were very clear that he was at fault and that the young woman who came to your aid was quite the heroine."

"She was. She saved my life probably."

"May I sit down?"

She hesitated for a moment, but then looked at the crowded café and probably decided it was safe enough.

"Okay, sure."

Buckley sat across from her. "I have made it very clear to Ken that if he ever comes near you again, you will press charges and have him sent to jail for a long time."

She looked at him wide-eyed. "And you'd be okay with that?"

"Ken *belongs* in jail."

"How did you even know where I was?"

"The woman at the motel mentioned this women's shelter. It was a shot in the dark, but, quite by luck, as you were coming out, I was pulling up in my car."

"But how did you know what I looked like?"

"Again, the woman at the motel described you in detail. She said you were quite lovely, and she was right."

Rosa looked down and a smile crept across her lips. "Thank you."

Buckley ran his eye over the woman and quickly summed her up, having known dozens just like her. Sexy and she knew it, feisty, not well-educated, capable of being physically dominated, and also susceptible to just the right sort of talk, encouragement, and flattery, but with a red line that could not be crossed. He marveled at how his obtuse, one-dimensional brother had managed it with her. Probably through brute strength, which only worked for a time with women. Then the woman either wised up and fled or pissed off the man enough to where her death followed.

Or his.

The waitress came over and they ordered coffees. Buckley waited until they were delivered to start speaking again. "I do have a question. Ken is not subtle or complex. His anger issues are quite apparent. With that in mind, why were you even with him?"

Rosa shrugged. "He was different, in the beginning. He was nice and treated me nice. Then he changed. Like overnight. I was going to leave him. Nobody deserves to be treated like that. I gave him lots of chances."

"I'm sure you did. I gave him lots of chances as

well. So it was fortunate that this woman showed up when she did."

"Yeah. See, Ken was beyond pissed because he said I'd looked at another guy for a couple seconds. I mean, as if. I'd never do that because he'd kill me."

"Yes, I'm sure. So what can you tell me about your *savior*?"

"Why?" Rosa said cautiously. "Look, I don't want her getting into trouble. She told Ken to cool it and walk away. But he was going to knife her and then he pulled his gun."

Buckley spread his hands in a disarming gesture. "I'm not here to get her into trouble. But the police *are* looking for her. I want to make sure that she knows Ken won't be pressing charges against her, because I also made that clear to him. As you also pointed out, Ken was going to hurt *her*."

"Hell yes he was. He *said* he was going to kill her. He fired two shots from the pistol before she knocked him out. So why are the police looking for her then? If she didn't do anything wrong and Ken isn't pressing charges?"

"There is one small problem that goes outside of anything having to do with Ken. She apparently told people that she was an undercover cop. The police frown on that. I believe that's why they're looking for her. For identifying herself as a police officer."

"She only said that to get that witch at the front desk off her case."

"Nevertheless, I'm just telling you what I've been told. So do you have any idea where she is, or what her name is?"

"No, she never told me her name. And I didn't ask. But I think she was from around here. I mean, she knew where the women's shelter was. We drove straight there."

"Do you believe she might have stayed there at some point?" asked Buckley.

"I guess it's possible. I mean, why else would she know where it was?"

"Unless she worked there at some point?" suggested Buckley. "Or had a friend who stayed or worked there?"

"Yeah, I guess that's true."

"What are your plans?" asked Buckley.

"I'm not sure I have any right now."

"What is your line of work?" Buckley asked.

"I used to be a receptionist. But I can do nails. And I did some personal fitness training."

"Yes, you look very fit. So you did that before Ken came into your life?"

"I . . . I had some problems with stuff that sort of messed me up for a while," Rosa replied, averting her gaze. "Ken and I met at a party. We hit it off, so . . ."

"Were they substance abuse problems?"

"Why do you say that?" she asked, giving him an offended look.

"Because that's the problem most people have that

messes up their lives. But I'm not judging you. Lots of people get addicted for all sorts of reasons."

"Well, I kicked it, at least I'm pretty sure I did."

He took out his wallet, counted out a thousand dollars, and handed them across.

"What's this for?" Rosa asked with a stunned expression.

"Call it a down payment on financing your post-Ken life."

"You don't have to do that."

"No, I feel that I do."

She quickly put the cash in her jeans pocket. "Thank you. That's really sweet of you."

"You're welcome."

She gazed admiringly at him, obviously attracted by his good looks and expensive clothes and cultured and generous manner. "I can't believe you're Ken's brother."

"We were always very different. But if he had made better choices, he could have become what I did. Or perhaps even better. He had some talents."

"I wish I'd met you instead of him," she said coyly, gracing him with a smile as she toyed with a lock of her hair and leaned forward to show a flash of cleavage. "Look, I'll leave you my number, in case you have any more . . . you know, questions. Maybe we could have a drink?"

"Maybe we could. Shall we head back?"

He walked her to the shelter and watched as she

disappeared inside after giving him a smile and a little wave.

"Saw you give her that money, mister."

Buckley turned to see a woman standing there. She was in her fifties and had clearly suffered a hard life. Her clothes were dirty and disheveled and her eyes unfocused and her body wobbly. She said, "I live here, too." She pointed to the shelter. "I heard you talking to that pretty Mex girl over coffee. I was having coffee too, with my *last* dollar."

"I see," said Buckley. "Perhaps you can earn some money, too."

The lady looked at her falling-apart shoes. "I was here when El brought her in."

"El?" said Buckley.

"El Cain."

"Is El short for something? Ellen, Eleanor?"

"Don't know about that."

"Exactly how do you know her?"

"She used to be here, years ago. I come here off and on. You don't forget El. Tallest woman I've ever met. And tough. She don't take shit from nobody."

"What else do you know about her?" asked Buckley.

The woman eyed him funny. "Saw you give her money," she said again.

Buckley produced ten twenty-dollar bills and passed them to the woman.

She pocketed the money, looking warily around as

though to check who might be watching, and said, "She's a good person. Helped me."

"Do you know anything about her background? Where she came from? What she does for a living?"

The woman thought for a moment and then snapped her fingers. "She does that kickboxing stuff. You know? That MM–something."

"MMA? Mixed martial arts?"

The woman pointed at him. "Yep, that's it."

"Where does she fight?"

"There's a place on the south side of town. Old shoe factory or something like that. Went there one time to watch two gals near kill each other. Never saw El fight, but I bet she was good. Don't take shit off nobody, like I said. She told me she fought there."

"She apparently is a very good fighter. When was the last time you saw her?"

"Well, when she brought in the Mex gal."

"Anything else?"

"She's a good person," she said again.

"I'm sure she is. Thank you."

26

Buckley made some calls and finally located the old shoe factory. There was a fight scheduled the next night. He spent the day with his brother at the hospital after he'd undergone another surgery. As he stared down at his unconscious brother, Buckley had the sensation that this might be as good as it got for Ken. And that saddened him more than he thought it would.

The next night Buckley headed to the fights. The venue had an invitation-only list that he circumvented by passing the bouncer out front a hundred dollars.

"Go right in, sir" was the bouncer's immediate reply as he tacked on a big smile.

The place held about two hundred people, who were both fired up and drunk. The fighters were two men with shaved heads and chiseled physiques, and tats that covered more of their exposed bodies than not. Buckley did not care about the fight. He made discreet inquiries among the staff and quickly focused on the man named Sam.

After the fight was over he cornered Sam in a back hall.

"El Cain?"

"What about her?"

"I'd like to know more about her than I do right now."

"What's it to you?"

"I'm a curious man. I understand she's a good fighter."

Sam shrugged. "Yeah, although she's past her prime if you're in the business and thinking about taking her on. But she's sneaky. And do not get in range of her kicks. Man or woman, it don't matter. She brings a load."

"Any idea where she is now?"

"Again, what's it to you?"

Five one-hundred-dollar bills answered that question.

"She lives in an old building they rehabbed into cheap units. It's not that far from here. Or at least she did. Heard they just got rousted out by the new owners. So I don't know where she's hanging now."

"What do you know about her past?"

"Heard she came in from out west years back. She showed up here one day. Said she could fight and wanted in on the action. Physically, she looked like she could handle herself, but just being tall and strong don't make you a fighter. So I put her through a little test. I got her in the cage with one of my guys. He was in his forties back then, way past his prime, but he was still good and he was a dude."

"What happened?"

Sam lit up a cigarette and grinned as he blew out the smoke. "Buddy, what happened was, she knocked my 'tough' guy out in about a minute. He woke up a half hour later wondering how a truck could've hit him *inside* the building. Well, after that, I told El if she really got serious about fighting she could go some-where. Have to be boxing or some unofficial stuff like we do here 'cause UFC don't have weight classes that heavy. But she only did it locally when she really needed the dough. She fought recently against a real stud, an up-and-comer. El snookered the lady and broke her jaw with one of the hardest kicks I've per-sonally ever seen, guy or gal. She grabbed her thousand bucks and walked out of here. Haven't seen her since."

"She ever tell you about herself? Her family?"

"As a rule, El didn't talk about herself. But let me give you a warning, friend. The last time she was here she pulled a gun on me because I told her if she dressed up a little and acted a teeny-weeny bit femin-ine, me and her might have a good time. I mean, some dinner and drinks and wham-bam-thank-you-ma'am and all. I saw the look in her eyes. She would've blown my damn head off without a second thought."

"Goodness, and after you had expressed yourself so eloquently to the woman."

"Exactly."

"Thank you for the advice. I will watch myself when I find her."

"*If* you find her."

"No doubt that's what I meant."

He got the address of where Cain had last lived. He drove over there to find a fence erected around the property and guarded by security who could tell him nothing of the people who had once lived there.

"They're all gone now," the guard said. "And good riddance. They were all lowlifes."

As Buckley got back into the car his phone rang. It was the hospital. He listened carefully, thanked the person, and said he would take care of all arrangements.

He didn't start the car. Buckley stared out the windshield into the darkness as he thought about what the doctor had just told him. An undetected and now ruptured brain aneurysm. Nothing they could do. Ken was gone in under a minute. They weren't sure if it was connected to his recent beating, but they couldn't rule that out. In any case, they were very sorry.

Buckley started the car and put on his seat belt harness. So now he had to bury *another* brother.

This was no longer a matter of putting El Cain into the hospital.

It was now a matter of putting the woman into a grave.

27

Buckley checked into an upscale hotel and ordered a late dinner from room service. He made phone calls and sent emails and texts while he ate his meal and drank his wine and thought about the details and decisions ahead of him. Ken would be cremated. There would be no religious ceremony; such spectacle would have been wasted on both brothers.

Buckley would scatter his youngest brother's ashes at the site of their father's brutal attack by the government. From human being, to a corpse, to residence in a jar before being sent headlong into the winds. All in the matter of the blink of an eye, really. It gave one pause, thought Buckley. Or it should.

His room was immaculate and comfortable, having all the expected high-end accoutrements. Buckley had grown up with none of these things, for his parents, despite the money coming in from their disciples and assorted business dealings, insisted on living simply, and thought that any largesse spent on their children was out of bounds strictly on principle. Buckley had resented that as a child. But he had come to agree with his parents' philosophy that people needed to earn what they had. However, the living simply part was not something he had adhered to.

Buckley had acquired the ability to purchase such luxuries not all that long ago. These included multiple residences, luxury cars, a yacht, and a private jet. It had been a hard slough, but he had gotten there in the end. But these were just toys at the end of the contest. Prizes, nothing more. The real thrill was in gaining the money, in acquiring the power, in beating others out for it. The rest of it left him uninterested, even depressed.

He had been nearly killed four times, starting from the shootout at the family compound—a DEA-fired round had embedded itself in the wall an inch above his head as he lay on the floor—plus three other instances when he had been an adult and was forging his own path in life. And each time, he had never felt so alive as when he had been minutes, or even seconds, from death.

He took out an envelope from the drawer, and put five twenties in it for the maid the next day. He made a habit of taking care of working-class people because he related to them more than he did the folks with whom he did business. Many of these people had been delivered into the world already on third base and thought it was their own effort that had gotten them so close to scoring. They believed themselves entitled to the best because they had, through no effort of their own, always been given the best of everything. That made it all the sweeter when he outsmarted this "elite" class of what really turned out to be overentitled simpletons far out of a league they stupidly believed they owned.

He liked the power that money provided. He liked to make as much of it as possible because he wanted as much power as possible. But he had started making money because he had siblings to feed, and the only thing between them and starvation was . . .

Me.

It made a man careful. It made a man think before he acted. Because one mistake could be fatal, on any number of levels. But having thought things through, you were more willing to take a risk, because it was a highly calculated one.

El Cain, though he'd never met her, struck him as that sort of person, based on all he'd learned about the woman. Under different circumstances, he might have hired her to work for him. She seemed like a downtrodden person who had risen above all that life had thrown at her. He believed she would be interesting and resolute and capable of great things, given the chance. But she would not be given the chance, if he had anything to say about it. Ken had to be avenged. If Buckley let that pass, what next? Before long, he would have no principles left.

He went down to the pool area, lit a Maduro cigar, drank his wine, sat by the water, and read the responses to his previous communications. He demanded much of his associates. In return they were well paid and he had their backs, come what may. He required absolute loyalty, but unlike many in his position, he returned that loyalty. Not necessarily because it was right or fair, but because, in the end, it was in *his* best interests. If you threw those who sometimes disagreed with you under the bus, then they wised up, and all you were left with were sycophants. And that was like inbreeding; it made everyone stupid and weak.

He didn't care for women like Rosa, who could have handled things so differently with Ken, or not shacked up with him in the first place. It was clear from her clumsy pass at him that she would have jumped into Buckley's bed if he so desired. That showed no loyalty to Ken and a lack of respect to Buckley. And actions resulted in consequences. He sent out an email with Rosa's photo attached, to an associate he had put on standby after learning of Ken's death. The man answered and things were quickly arranged.

He went up to his room and slept deeply, with a clear conscience but a burdened mind. He rose the next morning, had his breakfast, and tidied his room, folding the used towels, laying them neatly in the corner by the tub. He checked out of the hotel, liberally tipping people along the way and receiving smiles and thanks in return.

He drove off in his rental and used the car's

Bluetooth feature to check in with his people. The results were promising.

Rosa had relapsed in her drug addiction, taking an overdose with fatal results in an alleyway behind the women's shelter. The police were investigating, but it seemed clear that the matter would go no further than that. Buckley's thousand dollars had been retrieved from the corpse, so no questions would arise from that. They might make inquiries into the gentleman who had been talking to Rosa yesterday in the café, but no one other than Rosa knew about his connection to Ken. And even if she had told someone about him, Buckley had a wall of respectability around him. And there was nothing unusual about a recovering addict overdosing. So that chapter on Rosa was now closed.

He received another call five minutes later.

"We ran the license tag on the car," said the voice. "The owner is *Eloise* Cain. I'm sending you her personal details, to the extent we could find any. She's done some jail time, had some drug problems. Curious thing is, there's nothing on her until she was about nineteen or twenty. Before that, it's a black hole."

"Then dig into the black hole," ordered Buckley. "And how do we find her?"

"She has a credit card. We're using our resources and contacts to track both. She used her card to stay at a Marriott after she attacked your brother."

"And her cell phone? She must have one. She can be tracked that way."

"She has no registered account. She could have stolen a phone and just uses local WiFi and other free sources to enable calling and internet services, or it might be prepaid minutes or a burner phone or a hybrid thereof; there're lots of ways around that. Her credit card is registered to an address that's no longer valid. There's a Gmail address listed on the account, but she hasn't used it recently, and there's no really good way to track it. So we're keeping a hawk's eye on the credit card activity."

"If you have her car information, can't you hack into her satellite mapping service and pinpoint her location that way?"

"It's an old car and doesn't have that feature."

"Send me the information on the Marriott; there's probably more than one in this town. And get me a picture of the woman. Maybe a copy of her driver's license."

"On it, sir."

When Buckley received the hotel info, he drove to the Marriott and checked in. He spent the day walking around the property and talking to staff members about El Cain. He explained that he was her father's attorney and needed to get in touch with her about an inheritance. No one questioned his credibility after looking over his professional appearance and listening to his earnest, cultured voice. However, no one had seen a woman matching her description.

Until he walked into the hotel bar that night.

He sat on a stool and ordered a bourbon and soda on the rocks. The same bartender who had served Cain was now serving him. He described Cain generally and asked his question, using his cover story.

The woman nodded. "Yeah, she was in here. Looked like she could use some good news."

"Do you have any idea where she might have gone?"

"No. She didn't really say much." The woman wiped down the counter and attended to another customer while Buckley waited patiently. When she came back over she said, "But something was weird."

"What do you mean?"

"There was this thing on the news. On the TV right there."

Buckley glanced at the TV and then looked back at her. "Go on."

"The FBI was looking for a woman. They had her image up on the screen. They said her name but I don't remember it. Anyway, they were looking into something that happened to her in Georgia in the early 2000s. Well, the gal on the TV looked like some wild animal, she really did. She was tall with these batshit eyes, with long hair down to her butt."

"Why is the FBI looking for her?"

"They didn't say."

"And the connection to Ms. Cain?"

She placed her elbows on the bar, leaned forward, and said in a confidential tone, "Inheritance, huh?"

"Yes."

"Big money?"

"Yes."

"Go figure. Some of that money coming my way, mister? Because I could sure use it."

Buckley placed three hundred dollars on the bar.

"I like your style," she said as the money went into a fanny pack on her belt. "I'm a bartender, we have to be observant, read body language and expressions, see if people are three sheets to the wind, you know."

"Yes, I know."

"Well, she was staring at the woman on the screen and looking scared as shit. She even spilt her beer. And when she got up to leave, I watched her go. She'd only had the one drink, but it was like she couldn't walk straight. Whoever the lady on the screen was, that gal knew her somehow, I'm sure of it."

28

Asheville, North Carolina, was home to the Biltmore Estate. At nearly 180,000 square feet it was the largest private residence ever constructed in America, and it was still owned by the descendants of the Vanderbilt heir who built it. It was now open to the public for tours and other events, and it brought a great many people to Asheville every year. The town also possessed a thriving arts and wine and food community. The western part of the Tarheel State was picturesque, with the Blue Ridge Mountains providing a brilliant backdrop to the town.

As Pine and Blum rode into Asheville, neither one was thinking about any of that.

They had in their sights one person and one person only.

As the FBI had finally told Blum after some delay—probably because it wasn't connected to an official case—the phone number that Pine had seen Wanda Atkins input to her phone was attached to a specific address in Asheville. The Bureau had now provided that information, and Pine meant to make good use of it.

Dusk was coming quickly, and the streets they passed were filled with people sitting in outdoor restaurants with gas-fueled heaters providing warmth; art galleries were ablaze with light and activity, and cars and pedestrians were making their way to a flurry of destinations. People of means seemed to be having a good time trying to figure out where to plunk down their hard-earned cash.

"I've never been here," said Blum. "It looks quite lovely."

"Only we're looking for the dark side right now, not the lovely," replied Pine. Following the navigation instructions, she turned right and then left and slowed the Porsche. "And that's it, up on the right with the white siding."

"How appropriate," said Blum, eyeing the sign out front as they passed by. "Desiree Atkins runs an *occult* shop. I didn't think she'd be baking cupcakes."

"She goes by the name Dolores Venuti now," said Pine. "At least the phone is registered in that person's name. But it's Desiree, I'm almost sure of that."

They had previously gotten Desiree's file photo from the Georgia DMV. The picture showed a stern-faced woman with protuberant eyes that Blum had proclaimed were "downright creepy."

"But that photo is really old," Pine had pointed out after seeing it for the first time.

"I doubt she would have changed that much," said Blum. "People like her never do. Except to get even creepier."

The occult shop was in a small bungalow that one reached by going up a set of warped wooden steps. The large sign out front read in exaggerated calligraphy: THE DARK MOON RISING OCCULT SHOP: PSYCHIC READINGS, CLASSIC WITCHCRAFT PRODUCTS, POWER CRYSTALS AND CANDLES, PROTECTION SCARVES, LARGE APOTHECARY SELECTION, AND MUCH MORE.

"Protection scarves?" muttered Pine. "People really buy that crap?"

"More than you think. There's a large occult business in Arizona, in fact."

"How do you know that?"

"One of my friends is in the business. She's also a tarot card reader, has a psychic hotline, and does workshops for aspiring occultists. She makes far more money than I do."

"Then the world is truly upside down, Carol."

Pine pulled to a stop down the street. "The place looks dark." She checked her watch. "I don't see the hours posted, but she's probably closed for the day."

"It doesn't look large enough for Desiree to live there, too. And I doubt this area is even zoned for residential."

"You're probably right—she may very well live

somewhere else. And she may not have a home land-line. More and more people don't."

"I guess there are ways we can find out where she lives."

"It's all a matter of speed and finding the point of least resistance."

Blum eyed her keenly. "Why does that make me think you're about to do something not quite legal?"

"Oh, Carol, you know me like a book. Wait here."

Pine hopped out of the SUV and walked back down the street. She looked around and found this section of the street pretty empty. *Good.* She tried the shop's front door and found it locked. She looked through the door glass for evidence of an alarm system, but didn't see any. Maybe Desiree had put a protection spell on her shop in lieu of contracting with ADT, thought Pine.

Pine walked around to the back of the building and sized it up. One door, two windows. Large, mature trees ringed the small, park-like area that ran behind all the shops here. An old picnic table sat under the tree canopies.

She tried the back door but it was locked, as were the windows. Until Pine worked her knife through the gap on one of them and pushed the simple lock back. She slowly lifted the window, ready to run if an alarm sounded, but fortunately none did.

She slipped through the opening and closed the window, after lowering herself softly to the floor. Her nostrils were instantly breached by mingled pungent scents. She slipped a small flashlight from her pocket and manipulated the lens opening so that only a small, core beam was produced. She shone it over the walls. They were covered with shelves, which, in turn, were loaded with all sorts of things, many of them grotesque, at least to Pine. A bottle of fake shrunken heads was a real eye-grabber.

At least I hope they're fake.

Boxes of tarot cards were stacked haphazardly on a table. And they were on sale! A full-sized skeleton coated with dust hung from a holder in one corner. One could take it home for the sale price of $599. Astrological charts in various sizes and colors hung in lopsided, chaotic patterns on the walls, along with prints of creatures that Pine did not recognize. There were books with titles like *Witchcraft at Home* and *Self-Healing Tonics*. Pine looked through the latter one and doubted that the FDA would have approved. The place was disheveled and unorganized and there was junk piled around, including unopened cardboard boxes with the shipping labels still on them.

She moved into the next room. It was small and looked to be the office. This space was also littered with papers and boxes; a laminated desk was wedged into one free corner with a computer on it. The computer required a password, so Pine ignored it and went through the desk drawers. She found some stationery with the store's name and address.

And under a stack of junk she also found a check-book with the name Dolores Venuti printed on it, along with another address in Asheville.

Pine certainly believed that Desiree and Dolores were one and the same, although she would have liked absolute confirmation of that. She found it when she looked at some photos taped to the wall. One was of a person who could only be Desiree. She fit the description Pine had been given and, more important, the DMV photo. She was standing in front of the occult shop and was smiling. Written in Sharpie at the bottom of the picture was the inscription, "Welcome to the neighborhood, Dolores." It was signed by various people, and the shops named under those signatures were probably part of the local retail community.

She took a picture of it with her phone.

Pine copied the address from the checkbook onto a piece of paper and left the way she had come.

She climbed back into the SUV and handed Blum the paper with the address.

"Plug this into the GPS."

"What is it?"

"Hopefully, it's where we'll find Desiree Atkins, aka Dolores Venuti."

"What was the shop like?"

"Creepy, just like I'm sure she is."

"If she's home, what are you going to do?"

"Stop myself from strangling her, and then start asking my questions."

"And if she won't answer?"

"Then maybe I won't stop myself from strangling her."

"You can't mean that."

Pine put the SUV in gear. "Don't bet the farm on that, Carol."

29

"Okay, I don't like the looks of this," said Blum as they pulled down a long gravel road with thick woods on either side. A patch of fog was rolling in, and the only light was from the SUV's headlights.

"This is right out of the opening scene of every slasher movie I've ever watched."

"Don't let your emotions run away with you, Carol," said Pine.

Blum glanced at her boss. "Aren't you a little nervous?"

"I think Desiree should be more worried about *me* than I should be about her."

"You believe she'll be there?"

"We're going to find out pretty soon."

They rounded a bend. In the distance they could see the lights coming from a small split-level rancher built of brick and siding. It had a forlorn look, as though it were lonely without any other homes around. There was a metal carport next to the house with no car under it. The light they saw was coming from the front room.

"Great," said Blum. "The little house in the dark woods. I wonder if Hansel and Gretel are inside about to be eaten."

Pine pulled the SUV to a stop and killed the lights. "Wait here."

"I don't want you going up there by yourself."

"I'm armed and I'm a federal agent who is more than a little homicidal right now. Put simply, Desiree is a munchkin and I'm an Amazon. But slide over into the driver's seat. Keep the doors locked and your phone in hand."

Pine climbed out and made her way toward the house, keeping off the road and sidling along the tree line with careful strides. She then veered toward the front of the home and peered into one of the lighted windows. She saw furniture, pictures on the wall, a burgundy-and-blue rug on the floor, and not a person in sight. She edged around the corner and entered the backyard. She spied a small toolshed with gray siding and a shingled roof. She made her way over there and shone her light in one of the windows. It looked empty except for some tools, a wheelbarrow, and a step-ladder. She tried the door, but it was locked.

She slipped over to the rear of the house and walked up a flight of wooden steps that led to a deck, built onto the back, which held some old patio furniture. The door there was locked as well. She used her light to see inside the rear door and check for an alarm panel.

Shit.

There was one, and she could see that it was armed. Why have one here and not one at her business?

She stepped back and looked around.

Okay, that might be a way.

Pine hustled to the toolshed and used her knife to force back the lock. She ducked inside and came back out a moment later with the ladder. The grade of the property dictated that the home had a high foundation in the rear covered by a brick veneer. She stepped back up on the raised deck, set the ladder next to the back door, and climbed the ladder to the spot that all the warning labels implored should never be touched by a human foot. She gripped the edge of the gutter and did a chin-up, praying that the gutter would hold her weight. It did, and she swung her legs up onto the roof. She gripped the edge of an asphalt shingle and used that to pull herself fully on top of the roof. She walked across it to the upper-level section of the house where two dormer windows presented her with possible entry points.

Most home alarm systems did not arm upper-level windows. She was about to find out if this place broke that norm. She inserted her knife between the sash to pry back the clasp. If the window was armed, this far out in the country she figured she'd have time to search the place, make and drink a cup of coffee, and get away long before the cops showed up.

Fortunately, no alarm went off. She slipped through the window and closed it behind her. She shone her light around the bedroom she found herself in. It was meticulously neat and furnished sparingly. She checked the closet and found that all the pieces of clothing would fit someone of Desiree's age and petite stature. She inspected the bathroom situated in the hall next to the bedroom, then looked into the other bedroom on the other side of the bathroom. This space was empty except for two boxes stacked on top of each other. She looked through them, but they just contained some old clothes and other odds and ends.

It seemed clear that Desiree lived here alone.

Pine walked back into the bedroom. She had never seen a place so neat and organized. The bed was made up with decorative pillows arranged just so and military-level tight corners. She poked her head back in the closet. It looked to be one of those California Closets jobs, with two tiers of hanging rods, glass-fronted cabinets, deep drawers running on smooth slides, and open shelves for all the footwear. It held stacks of sweaters so neatly arranged they could qualify as store displays, and pants and shirts and dresses and skirts on hangers that seemed to be arranged by type and style. Scarves, shoes, underwear, and socks were all scrupulously sorted and organized. In the bathroom, toiletries and other items were in perfect order. The bathtub/shower was sparkling clean, the floors and countertops scrubbed and smelling of disinfectant. Towels were arranged in order of size and color in the linen closet.

She made her way downstairs to find that it was laid out simply but was, if it was possible, even more organized and clean than the upstairs. The wooden furniture in the main room was highly polished, the cushions plumped without a stain or smudge visible. The tracks in the rugs laid over oak hardwood floors showed they had been recently vacuumed. The knickknacks on the shelves were dusted, and the windows held not a streak of dirt.

She started searching the other rooms down here. Each one she got to was model-home organized. There was one door that was locked, but when she put her ear to the door she could hear the rumbling of the air handler. Probably just the furnace room.

The small powder room across from the foyer looked like one you would find in a high-end hotel, right down to the decorative tissue box holder and copper soap dispenser and framed artwork, plus a fancy toilet paper holder in the shape of a cat's long tail.

The kitchen was small but it sparkled. The travertine tile floor looked clean enough to have a picnic on without the blanket or even dishes. The counters were wiped down, the table set with a plate, cup, and cutlery in a rolled napkin. Canisters on the counters were arranged by height. The stove top's six burners glistened with not a speck of grease on their surfaces.

Pine opened some of the cabinets and drawers and found everything so organized she felt like she truly was in a model house where everything was on display, no one actually lived there to do any damage, and thus all was perfect. The contents of the refrigerator were so carefully arranged that it made her own fridge back in Arizona look like a dumpster. But that really wasn't a high bar, Pine conceded.

The thing that was bothering her was that she could understand Desiree being a neatnik, maybe even OCD. But then why was her shop so messy? Normally, a person with that condition didn't let their desire for organization stop at the front door of their home.

Off the kitchen was a small laundry room. A basket on top of the dryer held scrupulously folded clothes. She glanced at the items and then looked away, but only for a moment. Then her gaze swung back to the stack of clothes. She took a pair of jeans off the top of the pile and held them up.

Desiree had been described to her as being very short, under five feet, and her driver's license had confirmed this. Pine held the jeans against her own legs. They would have been too short for her, but they were also far longer than someone Desiree's height could have worn, even if she had on heels.

And the style and narrow hip cut of the pants were for someone a lot younger than Desiree.

The blood seemed to solidify in Pine's veins.

No way. No way in hell.

She put the pants back in the basket and left the laundry room. She raced back upstairs and made a more thorough search. She noted the pulldown attic door in the ceiling in the unused bedroom. She yanked on it, and a set of hinged stairs collapsed downward. Pine locked the steps in place and hustled up them. She shone her light around in the darkness and called out, "Hello? Is anyone up here? I'm with the FBI. Hello?"

There was no answer, no sound. She hit the entire space with her light and found nothing there.

She climbed back down and lifted the stairs up. They receded into the attic opening, and the access door banged shut behind them.

Pine felt something moving across her head. She was standing underneath a ceiling vent. The heat had just come on again.

The heat?

She ran down the stairs and over to the locked door. She put her shoulder against it and pushed. She felt the lock start to give. She pulled a small lockpick kit from her jacket. She didn't bother picking the simple lock. She just used one of the tools to merely slide the door bolt back. She opened the door and turned on the light. As she had guessed, the home's

HVAC system *was* located in here with the ductwork shafted into the unfinished ceiling where it headed on to the rest of the house. She looked around the space. There were a couple of shelves off to the side, all stacked with boxes. The floor under the HVAC was cement.

Had she been wrong in her assumption? But then why lock the door?

She then walked behind the shelves to a small space. She stopped and stared when she noted that the floor here was *not* cement. It was tongue-and-groove wood. Was it just wood flooring laid over the cement? But why bother with that for a room like this, into which no one other than a repairman would ever really enter?

In the farthest corner sat a hand truck with a large box perched on its lip.

Pine moved the hand truck away, then bent down to examine the spot the box had covered.

Pine felt like she had been gut-punched.

Recessed into the floor was a keyhole. As she looked over the area, she saw the parameters of the trap door. There was a lift handle inlaid into the floor next to the keyhole.

Okay, here we go again, thought Pine.

30

"Is anybody down there?" called out Pine through the wooden trapdoor.

When she was met with silence, she stomped on the trap door. "Hello, is anyone down there?"

Nothing.

Pine looked around and saw it. On one of the shelves' metal supports was a single key attached to a magnet.

She pulled it free, knelt down, and put the key in the lock. She turned it and then grabbed the recessed handle. The door came up easily on hydraulic hinges.

The space she was looking at was completely dark.

"Hello?" she called out again.

This time she heard a noise. No words, just a scuffling sound.

Pine shone her light into the dark. A set of steps was revealed.

"Hello, my name is Atlee Pine. I'm with the FBI. Is anyone down there? I'm here to help."

The sound she had heard could have been rats. But

you didn't have a secret space to keep rats in. And they didn't wear jeans.

She started down the steps, the light in one hand, her pistol in the other.

"Hello? Please show yourself. I'm here to help you. Are you being held against your will? Where is the woman who lives here? Dolores Venuti?"

Now Pine could hear heavy breathing and whimpering, as though whoever was down here was terrified beyond belief. For a moment she thought it might be Desiree. But this couldn't be a hiding place for the woman. She had looked at the underside of the trap door. The key only worked from the *outside*.

"I'm not going to hurt you. I'm here to help you."

She reached the bottom of the space and had to bend low because the height of the rest of the room was only around four feet. This had to be the rear of the house, where the grade dictated the high foundation. She decided to squat on her haunches and illuminate the area with her light. She shivered because it was chilly down here. The space obviously wasn't climate controlled, and she figured the outside was right on the other side of the wall. She pointed her light to the left and slowly went to the right.

She saw, with growing horror, the elements of someone living down here. Plywood and cinderblock shelves with clothes piled on them. A torn bean bag chair with a pair of worn lime green Converse sneakers lying on top. A battery-powered lantern. A stack of magazines. A mattress with covers and a single pillow strewn haphazardly over it.

Then Pine tensed when she saw the sock-clad foot. She slowly lifted the flashlight and the beam traveled upward, along the legs clothed in jeans, past the waist, rode up the baggy sweatshirt, and finally came to rest on the young, terrified face staring back at her, the eyes squinting as the beam drilled into them.

Pine lowered the light and said, "I'm with the FBI. I'm here to help you"—she looked around at what was obviously a prison—"get out of here."

The girl balled herself up tighter and shrank deeper into the corner in which she was cowering. She had a blanket half wrapped around her because of the chill. As Pine raised the light beam to show the girl's face, it shook back and forth as though answering Pine's statement with disbelief and also a refusal of the offered help.

Pine put her gun back into its holster and took out her badge. She turned the light on herself, so the girl could see both Pine's face and the shiny FBI shield.

"I'm with the FBI. Do you know what that is? I'm a federal cop."

Pine turned the light on the girl once more to see her reaction. She looked even more terrified, if that was possible.

Pine slid over, snagged the lantern, and turned it on. The light feebly illuminated the space, but it was strong enough that Pine could put her flashlight away.

She sat cross-legged on the floor across from the girl and studied her. To Pine, she looked to be around thirteen or fourteen, with gangly arms and legs, about five five. Her skin was as pale as milk, her build scrawny. There were bruises on her face, and a cut on her lip. Her hair was blond, stringy, and dirty looking. The eyes were of someone who distrusted everyone and everything.

"Can you tell me your name?"

The girl hugged herself and shriveled back.

Pine said quietly, "I can get you out of here. Do you want to be . . . free?"

The girl shook her head and finally spoke. "N-no."

"Why not? You can't possibly want to stay here."

"S-she'll be m-mad."

"Who, Dolores?"

The girl nodded.

"You let me worry about Dolores. We can leave right now. I can take you to a safe, *warm* place."

Pine reached out a hand but the girl shrank back. "N-no. Th-the d-dog. It'll b-bite me."

"What dog?"

The girl pointed upward.

"I've been through the whole house. There is no dog."

"O—outside," said the girl, her eyes widening.

"I came from the outside. I saw no dog. Do I look like I've been attacked by a dog?"

The girl ran her gaze over Pine and for the first time looked more confused than scared.

"Dolores told you there was a dog?"

The girl nodded.

"What's your name? I'm Atlee."

"I'm G-Gail."

"Okay, Gail. I saw no dog. Dolores lied to you."

Gail sat up straighter and wrapped the blanket around her lower legs.

"But I hear it barking when I'm down here."

Pine thought about this for a few moments. "Does she let you out of here?"

"Only when she's here. I do the cleaning and cooking and stuff."

"I thought you might. But did you ever feed the dog? I mean, I saw no dog bowls or dog toys. And if it's kept outside, there was no doghouse or a chain."

"No, I never fed the dog. I'm scared of them."

"When the dog barks, does it always sound the same?"

Gail shrugged. "I guess. I mean, it was a dog barking. And I heard it like an hour ago."

"Tell me something, does it always happen at the same time when Dolores isn't here and you're down here?"

Gail thought about it. "Maybe, yeah."

"Right. Well, there's technology that allows someone to do that. With a recording set on a timer."

"There's really no dog?"

"No. Have you ever left the house?"

"Not since I came here. Dolores said I couldn't. It wouldn't be safe."

"Why wouldn't it be safe?"

Gail said, "I stole some food and other things from a store. And the police are after me."

"Who told you the police were after you? Dolores?"

"Yes."

"*After* you told her you stole the things?"

"Yeah. She asked me a bunch of questions. And I told her about it."

"How did you come to even be here?"

"I was hitchhiking and Dolores stopped and picked me up."

"When was this? How long have you been here?"

Gail shrugged again. "I'm not sure. Maybe six months. Maybe longer."

"Where's your family?"

"Don't have any. My mom and dad died. Overdosed."

"I'm sorry. Didn't you have any other family who could take you in?"

"No. So they put me in foster homes. That . . . that didn't work out too well. So, I ran away."

"Then Dolores brought you here. And made you live down here?"

"Not at first. I slept upstairs on the couch. But then she said I had done some bad things. I didn't know what they were, but she kept on and on about them. I work really hard for her. I keep the house spotless and I cook and do the laundry. I do what she tells me to do. But then she said I had to come down here and sleep. But she said if I did better, I could move back upstairs where it's warm."

"Why does she even have a space like this?"

"She said it was like a safe room. She had it put in when someone broke into her house once. Least that's what she said."

"Okay," said Pine. "But the door only locks from the *outside*, so it's not much of a safe room, is it?"

Gail looked confused. "Oh, right. I never thought about that."

"Does anyone ever come by here?"

"Not that I know of. I've never seen anybody except Dolores."

"So you've never tried to get away?"

"I wouldn't have anywhere to go and I thought there was a d–dog."

She burrowed her face into her knees and started to sob.

Pine slid over and put her arm around her. At first, Gail jerked back, but then she slowly leaned into Pine's shoulder.

"Okay, look, first thing we need to get you out of here. I have a friend waiting in a car outside. We'll take you to where we're staying and get you cleaned up and buy you a meal, okay? You look hungry."

"Dolores said I'm so skinny I don't need to eat much."

"Yeah, I'm sure she did. Put your sneakers on and grab whatever else you want to bring with you."

"There's nothing, really."

"Okay, let's go."

Pine led the girl up the steps and out of the room.

They had reached the foyer when the two women stepped out from the shadows.

Pine saw Blum first.

And Desiree second. The little woman was holding a gun to the side of Blum's head. She had put on weight, and her hair was long and gray and clung to her head like strings of weighted beads. The face was hard and tight and full of venom.

She looked at Pine and said, "You're not going anywhere."

31

"I'm sorry, Agent Pine," Blum said, even as Desiree Atkins dug the muzzle deeper into the woman's temple. "She was on me before I knew it."

"Shut up." said Atkins, before she glared at Gail.

"What the hell are you doing up here? Do you want the dog to get you?" she added shrilly.

Gail shrank back behind Pine.

Now Atkins leveled her gaze on Pine. Her brow wrinkled. "You look really familiar to me. Do I know you? You look like trouble."

Pine said, "I probably look like a lot of people who you think are trouble."

Atkins nodded but her suspicious look was still present on her features. "I have a surveillance camera set up at the end of my driveway. I got an alert and saw on my phone when you drove in. Joe taught me all about surveillance. But the stuff they have nowadays? All wireless with a phone app. It's how I disarmed my alarm system before coming in just now."

Pine just stared at the gun.

"Wanda told me you were snooping around."

Pine said nothing. She just kept her eyes on the pistol held against Blum's head.

"Wanda said you were looking for Becky."

Now Pine spoke. "Her name is Mercy. Not Becky. That was the name *you* gave her."

"Well, whatever, she was Becky to me." She glanced at Pine's waist. "You're FBI, so you got a gun. Take it out and put it on the floor. Real, real slow. I know how to use this gun real good."

Pine took out her Glock and, holding it by the muzzle, knelt, and set it on the floor. Pine had a Beretta Nano in an ankle holster as her backup weapon, but it was useless so long as Atkins had the gun against Blum's head.

Atkins smiled in triumph as Pine stood. "Now, that's real good. No trouble from you I can see. Becky was a badass. A real troublemaker. You, not so much."

Pine just stood there looking at Atkins.

The woman said, "Now, you two are going to get in Gail's little hidey-hole."

"And then what?" asked Pine.

"And then I'm leaving. I'm all packed to go, suitcase in the car. I was as soon as Wanda called me."

"And Gail?"

"She'll be coming with me. She needs me to take care of her, don't you, Gail?"

Gail glanced up at Pine with a hopeless expression.

"You don't have to go with her, Gail," said Pine.

"Hey, hey!" cried out Atkins. "You don't tell her shit like that. You do that again, your friend here gets it good." She shoved the muzzle so hard into Blum's face that the woman moaned.

"Okay," said Pine. "Okay."

"That's better," said Atkins, clearly enjoying this. "Now move."

Pine led the way with Atkins bringing up the rear, her gun still pointed at Blum's head.

They entered the HVAC room where the underground space was.

"Okay, you can hold up right there," said Atkins. She shoved Blum toward Pine. The woman staggered and nearly fell, but Pine was quick enough to catch her.

Now Atkins pointed her gun at Pine as her finger slid to the trigger.

"I take it we're going down into that space *feet* first," said Pine.

"Well, I can't very well let you live to tell people things. I guess somebody will find you eventually. By then, I'll be in another country."

"It'll be tough to get out of the country with Gail."

"Who said she was coming?" Atkins said brusquely.

"So you're going to kill her, too?" said Pine.

"Gail is a little scared mouse. She'll do what I tell her to do and—"

The next instant Atkins cried out because Gail had jumped forward and bitten down on the hand holding the gun. She scratched and clawed at the woman's eyes. They struggled until Atkins brought the gun down on Gail's head, and the girl gasped and fell away.

Then a far stronger hand gripped Atkins's gun. She looked up into the face of Pine.

Pine couldn't help but smile as she cocked her arm back and then slammed her bony fist into the woman's face. The massive blow flung the much smaller woman against the wall, where Atkins slumped to the floor, unconscious.

When Atkins woke up about ten minutes later, she moaned and slowly sat up. Her eye was blackened and swollen shut, and her right cheek was heavily bruised. She looked up with her good eye at Pine, who towered over her.

"Get up," said Pine.

"I . . . I don't think I can. I'm—"

Pine gripped her under the arm and jerked Atkins to her feet.

She pulled the woman over to the box on the hand truck, and pushed her down on it.

Gail cowered in a corner, holding a washcloth filled with ice against her injured head. Blum stood next to Pine.

Pine said, "Your little mouse turned into a lioness, Desiree. I saw a little girl do that after being kidnapped by a creep in Colorado. He never thought she would do what she did, because she was young and a girl. He's currently in a state pen for the rest of his life."

Atkins glared at Gail and rubbed her swollen cheek. "I need a doctor."

"You're going to need a lot of things, including a lawyer. But even that won't be good enough to save your ass."

"You broke into my home and I was defending myself."

"And Gail?"

"I have no idea who she is. Was she hiding in here? I never come into this room."

Pine gave Atkins a condescending look. "Three witnesses against you, Desiree. And the fact that you have a hidey hole where Gail was forced to live. And then there's the little matter of what happened back in Georgia."

"What happened back in Georgia was that bitch Becky killed my husband," Atkins barked furiously. Spit flew out of her mouth along with the words.

"Now there's the real Desiree Atkins. I knew you were just hiding the psychopath in there somewhere." Pine leaned against the wall. "Why don't you tell me what happened that night?"

"Why don't you go to hell?"

Blum stepped forward. "You're going to prison. The only question is for how long. If you cooperate, it won't be as long as it otherwise would be."

When Atkins didn't answer Pine pulled out her

phone. "Okay, let's just get the cops in here. They'll charge you with kidnapping, unlawful imprisonment, and attempted murder, among other felonies, and then we'll call the Georgia police. They've been looking for you for a long time, Desiree. You fled a murder scene. There's no statute of limitations on murder. And you imprisoned Mercy. We have video proof, and Wanda will testify as well. You've got no chance."

Pine started to punch in the number.

"Wait!" exclaimed Atkins.

Pine looked at the woman while her finger hovered over the phone. "I'm listening."

"What do you want to know?"

"We know Mercy broke out of her prison. Then what?"

"She attacked us. She knifed Joe and went after me. But I got away."

"Where'd she get the knife?"

"She had it with her."

Pine held up her phone. "If you keep lying I *will* call the police and it's all over."

"I'm not lying."

"Mercy had no knife. We saw the tape."

Atkins knitted her brows. "She . . . she must've found one on the way to the house."

"Yeah, I'm sure you leave butcher knives lying all over the ground. Who fired the shot?"

"What shot?"

Pine held up her phone again but said nothing.

"That . . . that was Joe. He . . . Becky jumped him and he shot at her, but missed."

"You don't miss with a shotgun, not at close range."

Atkins looked panicked, glancing this way and that.

"Let me tell you what I think happened," said Pine. "Mercy was running toward the road because that was her escape route. But before she could do that, she ran into you and Joe. There was a confrontation. Joe and Mercy went at it. She hit him in the head and fled. Somehow a shot was fired. Then something happened. And Joe ended up dead from a knife in his back. Then you got your stuff together and called the Atkinses. Wanda met you at the Esso station, drove you to Atlanta, and put you on a bus, and you got the hell out of Dodge. You ended up here and got yourself another slave because that's just the sort of sick person you are."

"You have no proof of anything that happened in Georgia."

Pine shook her head. "You're going to prison. It's long overdue."

"What if I told you your precious *Mercy* was killed that night?" sneered Atkins.

"You can tell me, but that doesn't make it true. The fact is, if she was dead, you'd have had no reason to kill Joe, and if you hadn't killed him you'd have had no reason to run, would you? Because the cops didn't know you were holding a young woman prisoner.

You'd just bury her in the woods and that would be that."

Defeated, Atkins looked away and said nothing.

Pine stared at her for a long moment, disgust dripping from her features. Then she called the police.

32

"We've contacted Gail's family, Agent Pine," said Deputy Sheriff Tate Callum. Pine and Blum were at the Buncombe County Sheriff's Office in Asheville. The battered Atkins was just down the street at the county detention center after having been arrested and formally charged.

Callum was in his late thirties, trim, with a brisk manner and blue eyes topped by close-cropped blond hair. He was heading up the North Carolina piece of Desiree Atkins's crime spree.

"She told me that her parents overdosed and were dead."

Callum nodded thoughtfully. "That's true. But we found an aunt and uncle. Apparently, they were in no financial condition to take Gail in when her parents died. Now they are and they want her to come live with them. They're coming here to get her, in fact."

"That's wonderful news," said Blum.

"What about Desiree Atkins?" asked Pine. "Or Dolores Venuti, as she's known around here." Pine had filled in Callum on Atkins's true identity and her being sought on suspicion of murder in Georgia.

"Fact is, once she gets a lawyer and he sees what the evidence against her is, she'll probably do a deal. But there's more. My deputies are at her shop right now and they've been reporting in what they've found. Kidnapping and imprisoning Gail is bad enough. But they found evidence of what looks to be a drug distribution operation in a secret room at her shop. I guess the occult business wasn't making enough money. She's looking at a minimum of twenty to life when all is said and done. And that doesn't take into account the Georgia piece you told me about. I plan on calling the Georgia folks tomorrow."

"Can we see Gail now?"

"Sure thing. If you hadn't come along, I'm not sure what would have happened to her. I know she's been through a lot but she's showing some real pluck."

Callum led them to a small office where Gail was seated and eating a sandwich and a bag of chips and drinking from a bottle of water. There was a bandage on her head from where Atkins had struck her with the gun.

Callum left them and Pine and Blum took seats opposite the girl.

"How's your head?" asked Blum.

"It's fine." She smiled weakly and rubbed the spot. "Dolores has hit me lots harder than that."

"We heard about your aunt and uncle, that's really good news," said Pine.

"Yeah, I guess."

"Did you have a good relationship with them?"

"They didn't live that close to us. I suppose that's why I went into foster care. But they have a daughter my age, Sarah. We used to get together way back."

Pine said, "It was very *brave* what you did. You saved our lives."

Gail put her sandwich down and took a drink of the water. "I couldn't believe she was just going to abandon me like that. It made me so mad. After all I'd done for her."

Pine and Blum exchanged a nervous glance. Blum said, "She's not a good person, Gail. You're far better off without her. Just put her out of your mind. She's not worth thinking about anymore. She's really not."

Pine added, "You can see that, right?"

Gail looked up at her. "I just don't want to be left alone again. It's . . . scary."

"You won't be. But after what happened to you, you're going to need some counseling."

"Counseling?" Gail looked terrified.

"Just someone who's trained to help people through some bad events in their lives. The person will just talk to you, Gail. And you can talk to them about . . . things. It's only meant to help you put this awful experience behind you, and get on with your life in a positive way."

"Oh, okay." She munched on her sandwich, but still looked wary of the whole thing.

"And like you said, you have a cousin your age. You can grow up like sisters. It'll be fun. Always someone to talk to and share stuff with."

Gail looked intrigued by this possibility. "I never thought about having a sister. Do *you* have a sister?"

Pine said slowly, "Yes, I do. A *twin* sister, in fact. It's . . . pretty cool. She was . . . she *is* my best friend."

Gail smiled. "That's pretty dope. A twin. Are you identical?"

"I . . . I, uh, think you could probably tell us apart now."

"Okay."

Pine handed her a card. "This is my contact information. Any time you want to, please give me a call. I mean it, okay?"

They exchanged hugs with the girl and left her there.

"Do you think she's going to be all right?" asked Blum.

"Right this minute, there's no way to tell. She was with Desiree only six months, so maybe the damage won't be permanent. She's been through a lot for someone so young. She probably just needs time to heal."

As they walked down the corridor Blum said, "Are *you* okay?"

"I will be okay. If I ever find my sister."

"And if we don't find Mercy?"

"I'm not going to think about that possibility right now."

"What do we do next?"

"We need to talk to Desiree again, hopefully for the last time."

33

The detention facility was clean, sleek, and modern looking, but it still had bars and secure doors to keep the bad people away from the good. Pine had learned there were more than five hundred prisoners kept here in the main facility and in a jail annex. She was only interested in one.

Callum had called ahead, and they were quickly led to Desiree Atkins's cell by one of the guards. As the door opened and then clanged shut behind them, Atkins never once looked up. She was sitting in the one chair in the room that was bolted to the floor, and was dressed in prison duds.

She was staring at her hands like they contained all of her problems and none of the solutions. She had a bandage taped over her cheek, and the skin around her eye was now yellow and purple.

Pine leaned against the upper bunk while Blum stood near the door. The jailer had moved away to give them as much privacy as one could expect in a place such as this.

"What the hell do you two want?" asked Atkins, glancing up. "Come to gloat?"

"We came for a chat," replied Pine.

"Go screw yourself. And I'm suing your ass for assault. I might have brain trauma."

"Yeah, you definitely have something off in your head, but it had nothing to do with me. And you have the time to talk since you won't be leaving here anytime soon. No bail because you're a flight risk," said Pine. "And they know all about Georgia."

Atkins' eyes glittered with hatred. "Good. And I can tell them how Becky killed my husband. They need to put her in prison for murder."

"You can try, but your imprisoning her for all those years will mean whatever you say will not pass the smell test," said Pine. "Even if she killed Joe, she had every right to. He was just going to lock her up again. Enslaved people have an absolute right to do whatever it takes to get free. We actually fought a civil war over that."

"What do you care about Becky? It's been, what, almost twenty years? Give it a rest."

Pine curled her long fingers around the bunk support post primarily so she couldn't form a fist with them and have another go at the woman.

Blum noted this, stepped forward, and said, "Why did you do it, Desiree? Why did you treat Mercy the way you did?"

Atkins snarled, "What exactly did I do? I'll tell you!

I took the kid in when no one else wanted her. This guy plopped her in Wanda's lap. Like she could take care of a six-year-old? Give me a break. She smoked so many packs of cigarettes a day she got winded going for the mail. The kid would've died but for me. I should be getting a medal, not a prison sentence."

Pine said, "You abused her. You tortured her. You locked her in a hole in the wall in the woods. You call that doing her a favor?"

Atkins turned pink with indignation. "She was wild. She was uncontrollable. We had to lock her up. If you had only seen her back then."

"So she wouldn't escape, you mean?"

"I don't have to tell you anything else."

"But if you do, I can put in a good word for you."

"Right, shave two years off whatever I'm going to get? No thanks."

"Did she ever mention her family?" persisted Pine. "Did she ever tell you what happened to her? What her real name was? Did you ever even ask?"

Atkins waved all this off. "I had my own problems!"

"You can tell us nothing?"

"I can tell you plenty. I choose not to. That's my right! And there's not a damn thing you can do about it, bitch."

"Wanda told us you tried, but could never have kids of your own," said Blum.

Atkins shot her a cruel look. "What's your role

here, Granny, to be the good cop? Guilt me into saying something? Don't waste your time, *hag*."

"I mean, you must have *wanted* children. You took Mercy in, like you said," Blum added, while Pine watched her with a curious expression.

"Damn right. I took her in when nobody else would, like I said. I did her a favor. And what did I get out of it? Heartache and misery."

"So you did care for her, at some point?"

Atkins calmed a bit and the vindictive look in her eyes faded somewhat. "I took care *of* her. I dressed her and fed her. She was clean. Until . . . until we moved her where we did."

Blum sat down on the bunk opposite Atkins and said in a quiet voice, "Because she was unruly? Because you were fearful of what she might do? That's understandable."

Pine shot Blum a look but remained quiet.

"Yes! She terrorized us. By the time she was eleven she was taller than Joe. When Becky hit thirteen she grew like a weed. She was huge. At fifteen she was over six feet and strong as a horse. Joe always took the gun when we went out to the woods. I insisted on that. And when he was gone during the day, I had to keep the gun on her while she was doing work for us. It got so we had to make her do most of her chores after Joe got home because I was scared to be around her alone, even with the gun! If we'd let her stay in the house she would have killed us in our sleep. It was like . . . having a wild animal around. Even when she was out in the woods, I barely got any rest. I was a nervous wreck all the time."

Pine inwardly seethed at these callous remarks. As though Atkins's misery had been greater than her sister's. As though Mercy was at fault somehow. But she said nothing. Blum was obviously working on something, and Pine wanted to let it play out.

"And she probably kept secrets from you," said Blum. "People like that often do."

"She did!" said a now-animated Atkins. "Exactly. Joe said she didn't. But what did he know? He tried to trust her when she was still little. She just suckered him."

Blum said, "Men are clueless about reading women. We both know that. When you get to a certain age, like we both are, it becomes very clear."

Atkins pointed at Blum and grinned. "You hit it right on the head. Men! They're moronic when it comes to women. They don't know how we think. The head games we play. The manipulation we use." She said in a little-girl voice, "'Oh, big, strong man, you're so much smarter than me, can you come over here and do *everything* I tell you to do?'" She grimaced. "And see where that got Joe? An early grave."

"But you weren't fooled," said Blum.

Atkins shook her head and tacked on a cackle. "I saw right through her. I knew what she was about. She

229

didn't fool me for one minute. All this innocent crap. Trying to get Joe on her side. It was disgusting."

Pine reached into her pocket and her fingers closed around her phone. She slid it out but kept it behind her back.

Blum noted this, but Atkins didn't. She was staring at the floor, lost in her own self-pity. Blum rose and moved so she was in front of Pine, blocking Atkins's view of her.

Pine quickly flicked through her screens and tapped on a couple of images.

Blum said, "But unlike Joe you were probably able to get her to talk. To reveal things she didn't want to reveal because you were smarter than she was."

Atkins looked up with a desolate expression. "Joe never gave me credit for anything. I was the one who told him to go into the security business when he lost his job. I helped him get started and then got him clients. And I was the one who told him we needed to put that girl in a cage. I knew she was nuts. The man that took her? Wanda said he told her Becky's parents wanted to kill her. And they probably had good reason. I came to see that. He saved Becky from whatever she was involved in, but he did us no favors, that's for damn sure."

"It must have been really intrusive for you."

"At first, I thought it might be okay, you know. Having a kid. You're right, I did want children, but I had a problem there and couldn't. But I wasn't sure this was the right way."

"But you still took her in. That was good of you."

"At first Joe thought it was so great. See, he was the one who *really* wanted her. A frilly little daughter to dote on. But six months after she came into our lives, it was like I didn't exist. All Joe saw was cute little Becky," she added in a derisive tone. "He totally ignored me. And then she grew up. That cute little puppy turned into a wolf. A monster!"

"That all must have been difficult to accept," said Blum in a supportive tone.

Atkins exclaimed, "It was impossible. Who was this stranger? What right did she have to come into our lives and take my husband away from me? What right? Oh she was so cute, so pretty. And I was what, a lump of coal?"

"Yes, I see that."

"Well, Joe didn't. Made me so mad. I wanted to kill him. And her!"

"But you talked to Mercy? You learned things about her?"

Atkins smiled slyly at Pine. "I *knew* that was her name. She told me it was. But then I spent years wiping that out of her memory, out of her *life*."

"How did you do that?" asked Blum, keeping her gaze on Atkins. "It must have been difficult."

"I had my ways," said Atkins with a wicked grin. She mimicked a little girl's voice again. "'Don't,

Mommy, don't do that. Don't burn me. Don't cut me.' 'Your name is Becky,' I would say. 'Becky. Only Becky. Mercy is dead, do you understand? Mercy is dead.' Over and over and over. It finally got through. Finally. No more Mercy." She smiled. "See, I won. I beat the little brat. She thought she was so smart. Well, *I* was smarter."

"Did you have to make her forget anything else?" asked Blum.

Atkins's features calmed and she looked down again. "There was one thing I could never make her forget," she said.

Pine tensed and said, "What was that?"

"Eeny, meeny, miny, moe." She glanced up at Pine. "Stupid nursery rhyme. She read it in a book we had. She went ballistic. She tore the book apart. She was screaming. Joe had to come in and hold her down. And she was only seven or eight at the time. I had no idea what the hell that was about. Crazy, stupid kid. Worst mistake of my life taking her in."

Blum glanced at Pine, who had closed her eyes and looked away. Blum turned back to Atkins. "So the night Mercy escaped . . . ?"

"Idiot Joe forgot to lock the damn door. Before we knew it here she comes, running past the house. Joe had seen it on his TV screen. He went after her. But the moron didn't take the gun. I remembered it, though. I went after her with it."

"Because you couldn't let her get away?"

"Of course not. We'd go to prison if she did."

"But I don't understand. If you had the gun, why didn't you stop her?"

"Joe grabbed her but she slugged him, and he fell and hit his head on a rock. Blood was everywhere. He tried to get up but I think he had a concussion. He fell back to the ground and didn't move. Mercy saw the blood and him lying there not moving, and she ran like a damn racehorse. I don't think her feet touched the dirt."

"What happened next?"

"I fired twice at her, both barrels. But she was already into the trees. I was going to go after her and finish her off. But then Joe came to, got up, and tried to stop me. He tried to take the gun away."

"Why?" said Blum. "He must have known what would happen if Mercy got away."

"He was soft," Atkins said in a disgusted tone. "He didn't want to kill her. He wanted to let her get away instead, if you can believe that. Said enough was enough. The idiot!"

"That must have upset you."

She smiled maliciously. "So I told him, 'Look, Joe, there she is, she's coming back.' When he turned, I picked up the stone and hit him in the head. Knocked him cold. I wanted to shoot him, but the shotgun was empty. So I ran into the house, got a knife and . . ."

". . . finished the job?" said Blum.

"When it was done, I wiped my prints off the

knife and called Wanda. I told her Becky had killed Joe. And then I grabbed my stuff and they helped me disappear."

Pine swallowed nervously and asked in a tentative voice, "And Mercy got away? She was alive?"

"Yes, the bitch damn well did."

Pine gripped the bed post hard, her eyes shut, her heart soaring with hope.

Atkins suddenly looked alarmed, as though she had just come out of a trance. She stared at them stonily. "But I'll deny everything I just said, and you can't prove otherwise."

"Oh, I think we can," said Pine, opening her eyes. She held up her phone and then hit the Play button on the recorder function. Atkins's voice came through loud and clear.

Realization of what had just happened spread over Atkins's features, and then her face hardened. "You can't do that. You . . . you tricked me. It's illegal."

Pine shook her head. "Technically, I'm not the arresting officer. You've been read your rights, including the right to remain silent. If you choose to spill your guts that's up to you. And you haven't engaged counsel yet nor stated that you wanted one. This wasn't an interrogation. You just spoke of your own free will. And I just happened to have my recorder on."

"I'll get that thrown out, you bitch!"

"Well, you can try," Pine said. "I'm sure the

Georgia police will be in touch. Particularly since you made their job of convicting you so much easier."

Pine stepped forward and leaned down so she was eye to eye with Atkins.

"And just keep in mind that Mercy took the best you had and still kicked your ass. And she's out there somewhere free and living her life. And you're going to spend the rest of your sorry life in a place a lot worse than this. And I wish you many, many more years of living."

Pine called the jailer, and she and Blum left.

As they were walking down the corridor Pine said, "Great job on getting her to open up."

Blum unexpectedly sighed. "I still wish you could have kicked her butt."

Pine put her arm around her friend's shoulders. "Oh, we did better than that. Way better."

34

Cain pulled her car up to the curb and looked over the modest rancher in a working class neighborhood outside of Huntsville, Alabama. It was a place where Cain could have grown up. Playing with dolls and riding bikes and kicking soccer balls in the backyard, having barbecues and running under the sprinkler in the summer, roasting marshmallows and building snowmen in the winter, although she doubted it snowed all that much this far south.

Normal.

She snorted at the thought.

Right. That was some fantasy.

She had blown out a tire in a remote area halfway through her drive from Georgia. Cain had no spare, and it had taken well into the night to first find a tire shop and then for the shop to get a replacement tire, since her car was so old. After that she had driven until she was exhausted. She finally spent the night in her car just outside of Huntsville before waking up, having a hot cup of pretty bad coffee, and finishing her journey. And now here she was.

The air was warm, the sun shining, the birds were swooping around, and Cain felt like she was on the way to attend her own funeral. She headed to the front door.

She knocked and waited as footsteps approached. She wasn't sure how she was going to handle this, but maybe that was a good thing. Ever since her escape from the Atkinses she'd been winging things for the most part. Sometimes it had worked and sometimes it hadn't. But why change now?

Wanda Atkins opened the door with an e-cigarette in one hand. She stared up at the towering Cain and her free hand flew to her mouth, almost dislodging the cannula in her nose as she recognized her visitor.

"Oh my God, it's . . . you."

"It's been a long time, Wanda. And even with the lack of hair and the years piled on I guess I haven't changed so much."

Wanda started to shake. "I'm . . . I'm so sorry for everything, Becky."

"It's El now, short for Eloise."

Wanda looked startled for a moment and then a sad smile eased across her face.

"Eloise? Like the book I brought you?"

"Yeah, only it was Eloise at the Nightmare House. My own little fantasy," added Cain. She looked at the cannula in Wanda's nose and the attached oxygen line. "You sick?"

"Smoked too many cigarettes." She held up the e-cig. "Now I vape." She eyed the tall Cain warily. "What are you doing here, Be—I mean, Eloise?"

"Can I come in?"

Wanda looked uncertain about that, so Cain just stepped past her and into the house. And there was nothing she could do about it, which made Cain feel immeasurably powerful.

Wanda followed her into the living room, where Len Atkins was asleep in his wheelchair.

There were stacks of folded laundry on tables and chairs and some dirty dishes piled on an ottoman. The mingled smells were fuggy. To Cain they smacked of old and sick.

"Sorry for the mess," Atkins said in an embarrassed tone.

Cain shrugged. "This is a lot better than where I used to live, right? The walls aren't dirt. And when you want to open the door, it opens, right?"

Atkins coughed and glanced nervously at her husband. "I, uh, I guess you remember Len. He, uh, he had a stroke a while back."

"Whatever," said Cain brusquely. She didn't care about strokes or Len's or Wanda's problems. This moment was all about her.

Wanda quickly moved some items off the couch so Cain could sit. She sat across from her in a chair and studied the younger woman. "Why did you cut your hair off? It was so beautiful."

"Not after my time with Desiree it wasn't," Cain replied, tacking on a grim look at Wanda. "She had fun pulling it out by the roots, or setting it on fire. But then you know all about that."

The older woman shrank back under her fierce gaze, like a flower getting hit by a sudden burst of frost. "I think about you a lot," she said lamely.

"You did some nice things for me, Wanda."

"But I never did anything about—"

"No, you never did," said Cain in a harsh voice, but then she shrugged. "It wasn't your problem, right? And in the end I took care of it myself."

"I . . . Joe deserved whatever you did to him."

"I knocked Joe down when he tried to stop me, and he hit his head on a rock. If he died, it wasn't my fault. Then I just ran for it. Somebody fired a gun at me and missed. Had to have been Desiree because Joe was already dead. Then I just ran harder. I kept going for miles and miles until I was able to hitch a ride."

Wanda looked at her with a startled expression.

"What?" asked Cain.

Wanda composed herself and said slowly, "Joe didn't die because he hit his head on a rock."

"Well then, what happened to him?" said a now-startled Cain.

"Joe died because someone stuck a knife in his back. He was deliberately murdered."

"A knife?" said Cain, now visibly stunned.

"There's no doubt. It punctured his heart."

Cain sat back, and it was like a great weight had been lifted off her.

Then I didn't kill him. So why is the FBI after me?

"I didn't stab him. But I bet you know who did."

"I always thought it. I mean, Desiree was so—"

"—evil? Yeah, she was. Do you know where Desiree is now?"

"I have a phone number, but no address." Atkins looked nervously at her. "And you don't want to go down that road, Eloise. It . . . it would not be good. You have to stay away from the past. I don't want you to be hurt, not again."

"I was hurt a lot. While you stood by and did jack shit. I'm still hurting, actually." She rolled up her sleeve so Atkins could see the knife etchings, the lumps, and the burns that would be with her till she died. "You think this shit ever stops hurting? Not to mention how she messed with my head. That was even worse than this crap."

Wanda's eyes filled with tears, and she put a hand to her mouth to stifle a sob.

"You can cry, Wanda. All you want. It won't change anything. It won't change how I feel about you or old Len in the wheelchair over there. *You* got to live your life. You got to walk in and out your door whenever you wanted. But not me. You ever think about that when you went home and left me where I was?"

"Are you here to . . . hurt us?" Wanda looked over

Cain's large, muscled physique, her eyes swelling with the fear that physical harm was imminent.

"Fortunately for you, no. But I know that the FBI is looking for me."

"They were here."

Cain looked alarmed. "Here? When? How did they find out where you were?"

"She didn't say."

"She?"

"A younger gal around your age, and an older woman. They were asking questions."

Cain thought about what Kyle, the teenager in the woods, had said about the tall FBI agent. "What sorts of questions?"

"About what happened that night. They said they had a video of you."

"Yeah, I saw that on the TV. What exactly did they ask about?"

"About you, how you got to where you did. What happened on the night you got away. But they also told me some things."

"Like what?" asked Cain.

"That your real name was Mercy. And that a man kidnapped you from your house."

"Mercy? I . . . I was *kidnapped*?" said Cain.

"Yes. A man named Ito Vincenzo. He and Len were in Vietnam together. He told us that your parents wanted you dead and that he, well, that he rescued you. But according to the FBI gal, he was lying. He took you from your parents for his own reasons. It had something to do with a grudge he had against your mother. The mob was involved or something or other. It was truly bizarre." Wanda paused and said, "And he left the other child. He apparently did a little nursery rhyme to pick which one of you to take. Eeny, meeny, miny, moe. How sick is that?"

35

Cain felt her heart start to pound and an intense pain shot through her head along with a cascade of repressed but still ill-formed memories. It was like her brain was moving so fast, it was burning itself out, all safety valves blown right through. She glanced at Len.

Am I having a stroke?

She now remembered going berserk when she had read that nursery rhyme in a book while she'd been with Desiree. She had come upon those words and it was like something exploded in her head. She had never known why. But *the other child?* Then she felt stupid. The rhyme was a *choosing* rhyme. Of course there had to be someone else. And then something else clicked in her mind. The rare memory she had always carried with her that allowed her to survive Desiree.

It's okay, Momma, it's just Lee being Lee. She'll find her way down. She always does. Don't be mad at her, Momma.

"Eloise, are you okay?"

Cain came out of her musings with a jolt and stared at the old woman, but her heart was racing like she'd just snorted a dozen lines of coke. "Something just occurred to me, that's all. So my real name is Mercy?"

"Yes. Do you remember that at all?"

Cain shook her head. "Desiree did a really good job of making me forget things." She looked darkly at Wanda. "But then you knew that, too, didn't you?"

Wanda quickly looked away. "I guess you hate me. And you have every right."

"I don't think you're important enough anymore for me to hate, Wanda."

Wanda glanced up. "What have you been doing all these years?"

"Surviving." She glanced at Len. "Will he always be like that?"

"Yes. And it's just me to take care of him, really."

"Well, I guess you both are living in your own little prison now, aren't you? Tell me, how does it feel?"

"I'm very, very sorry, Eloise."

"Yeah, you already said that. But then words don't cost anybody anything, do they? What else did this FBI lady say? Why do they want to find me if I didn't kill Joe?"

"I think they want to help you. You were kidnapped, after all. And I looked that up after they left. The FBI deals with kidnappings."

"All these years later?"

"It's a cold case, that's what they call it on TV. Maybe you should go and see them."

Cain eyed her closely, her suspicions running high.

She wasn't ready to believe any of this, particularly coming from this woman. "Are you sure they don't want to arrest me for Joe's murder?"

"Well, I don't think so."

"You don't *think* so? That's not good enough."

"I don't know any more than that."

Which means I'm still screwed.

The weight of the world seemed to reappear on Cain's broad shoulders.

"What about Desiree?"

"What about her?"

"Give me the phone number. I want to call her."

"But why?"

"I don't think you have any right to ask that. Just give me the damn number." Cain rose and looked down at the woman.

Wanda stared back up, obviously frightened.

"It's good to be scared, Wanda, when you're around me. I'm not normal. No one would be normal after what happened to me. Give me the number. Now! Or I won't be responsible for what I do to you or the prick in the wheelchair."

"Are you going to try to find Desiree? And hurt her?"

"That's my business. You don't have a say in that, not now. Not ever."

Wanda rose, slipped an address book out of a drawer on a side table, and tore out a page. "Here, just take it. I never want to talk to that woman again."

Cain took the paper. "Does Desiree know about the FBI visiting you?"

Wanda nodded. "I called her."

"Why, to warn her?"

"Something like that."

"Blood really is thicker than water."

"Desiree is not a blood relative of mine," said Wanda petulantly.

"Really? Well, pardon me for being confused on that shit."

"Can you . . . can you forgive us?" asked Wanda.

Cain shook her head. "The only reason I'm not going to hurt you both is because you're not worth the trouble." She held up the paper. "But if this number is not Desiree's, then I'm coming back. And everything that bitch did to me, I'm going to do to you. And I haven't forgotten a single thing. Trust me."

After she left, Wanda collapsed back into her chair, sobbing.

On the way to her car Cain stopped and launched a powerful side kick against the lamppost next to the sidewalk, sending it crashing to the ground. Then she climbed into her car and looked down at the paper with the number on it.

She had never been this close to Desiree before. And she knew she had to keep out of the range of the FBI. But now that she had made the decision to do this, there was no turning back. If she was going down, so was Desiree.

36

Cain had no intention of *calling* Desiree. She drove into Huntsville and stopped for something to eat. She also searched on her phone for a way to find the address attached to the number Wanda had given her. She quickly found it, and for a small fee to allow herself premium status, the internet search service she had found spit out the name Dolores Venuti and a physical address in Asheville, North Carolina.

Dolores Venuti must be her new name.

Cain plugged the address into her phone GPS. It was five hours if she didn't stop.

It was mostly interstate, and the hours went by fast as she drove through the Blue Ridge Mountains. The peak fall colors had passed and many trees had dropped their leaves, but it was still an inspiring sight. If Cain hadn't been so oblivious to her surroundings.

She listened to the radio for any additional mention of "Becky from Georgia," but there was none. About an hour out she stopped once to pee at a rest stop, then sat outside at a picnic table and drank down a bottle of G2 and ate a banana she'd bought. She stretched out some kinks in her back and legs before she got back into the car.

Before she drove off she opened the glove box and eyed the Glock in there. She'd had the gun for three years. She'd only fired it at shooting ranges. She pondered whether she could actually fire a round into Desiree's head.

She came away unsure, but that was progress, only Cain didn't know what kind.

The woman had tortured her for all those years, piling one despicable act on top of another. And Joe had done little to stop her, so she had no reason to feel any sorrow at his death. Yet she had been relieved to know that she hadn't killed the man, after all these years of thinking she had. But the fact that his true killer and her years-long torturer, Desiree, had gotten away scot-free was just too much to take.

What she was doing might cost her whatever life she had left. But she also knew she could never enjoy another second of living while Desiree breathed air. All those years ago Cain had simply wanted to get away. Now she wanted something more. You could call it payback, revenge—justice, even. She wasn't sure which one was applicable, if any. But she was sure that, whatever it actually was, she had to get it, or die trying. It was like all the emotional bills pending from that time in her life were now coming due. And she was the debt collector.

Within another hour she pulled into Asheville. The

address was a shop. One of those weird-ass occult shops, observed Cain as she drove past and saw the sign.

Figures.

And there was a police van parked in front of Desiree's place. The front door of the occult shop opened and two people dressed in blue scrubs and booties came out carrying what looked to be trash bags, while a police officer stood guard at the front door, his fingers curled around his gun belt. The scrubs opened the rear doors of the van and put the bags in the back.

She pulled down the road and parked a block away. Then she got out and walked back toward the shop. A woman came out of another storefront about four doors down. She was in her fifties, heavyset and with gray hair tied back in a bun. She had on jeans and a long green apron with the name "Organic Alley" stenciled on the front. It matched the sign over her shop.

Cain walked up to her and said, "What's going on there?" She indicated the occult shop.

The woman looked up at her. "Dolores Venuti was arrested, at least that's what I heard."

"Dolores? Really?"

"Yes. She owns that shop."

"What was she arrested for?"

"I walked over there earlier and asked some questions. They really wouldn't tell me anything, but I hung around and I heard some of the policemen talking."

"What did they say?"

"And who are you and what's your interest?" said the woman, her look now suspicious.

"I'll tell you. I drove all the way up here from Alabama because Dolores offered me a job in her shop. I've done occult retail before. I'm sort of into it."

The woman looked over her appearance and said, "Yeah, I guess I can see that."

"So I quit my job and came here. And now it looks like I'm SOL. So, *that's* my interest."

The woman clucked in sympathy. "Oh, you poor thing. But it might turn out to be a good thing for you because I heard the police say that they found *drugs* in her shop. You don't want to be caught up in all that. And they mentioned something about a young girl that Dolores had done something to. I even heard the word 'kidnapping.' I mean, you think you know people. But she always gave me the creeps, to tell you the truth. And between you and me, she struck me as being a little bit mean."

"Wow, who knew," said Cain with feigned surprise, which was maybe the most complex bit of acting she'd ever attempted. "So I guess Dolores is in jail?"

"Yes, the detention center on Davidson Street. It's not that far from here."

"Well, hopefully they keep her behind bars, right?"

"Oh my God, yes."

Cain turned and walked back to her car and sat in it. She looked up the detention center address on her phone, drove there, and stared up at the place.

This was the closest Cain had been to the woman in a long, long time. She felt chills all over her body.

She can't hurt you anymore, El.

El?

Apparently my real name is Mercy. That's what Wanda said the FBI had told her, and I suppose they wouldn't lie about that.

She sat back against her seat and closed her eyes.

"Mercy." She said the word out loud. It was a strange name. Why would her mother have named her Mercy? And the other child. The one on the other side of the nursery rhyme?

Cain scrunched up her brow as though that would make her damaged memory suddenly light up and tell her all. It didn't. Nothing came out. Except for one thing.

It's okay, Momma, it's just Lee being Lee. She'll find her way down. She always does. Don't be mad at her, Momma.

Was Lee my sister? Was she up a tree and I was telling our mother not to be mad?

The weight on her chest was suddenly crushing. It felt like when she had overdosed the first time. She was panicking; she felt she couldn't breathe.

She got out of the car and proceeded to run. She ran faster and faster down the street, turned right, then left, and reached what looked to be a small park.

Cain plunged directly into the thicket of trees and ran until she could run no more. She stopped at one massive oak, wrapped her arms around it as though to prevent herself from lifting off the ground, and slowly slid to the dirt.

She lay there for she didn't know how long.

Cain wept so hard, it got to the point where she could form no more tears. Her chest stopped heaving, and she was able to stand by gripping the tree trunk and hoisting herself a few inches at a time, like she was climbing a slicked pole.

She composed herself and walked unsteadily back to her car; she almost couldn't find it, but when she climbed in and shut the door, she felt a bit better.

She hadn't been this way in years. After escaping from the Atkinses, every fourth or fifth night of freedom would end in night terrors. She would awake certain that Desiree was right on top of her ready to drag her back to hell.

She drove off, found a hotel, and checked in. The place was more than she could really afford, but right now she wasn't thinking about that. Later, Cain had a drink in the bar and some dinner at a restaurant a short walk down the street, because she just needed some brisk air to chew on. After that, she walked back to the hotel and wondered what she was going to do now.

Desiree was in jail. There was no way to get to her.

Mercy

And even if she did, what was she going to do? Kill the woman with her bare hands? Scream at her? Torture her like she had tortured Cain? And then what?

I go back into another prison for the rest of my life?
Has all this been for nothing?

37

For the twentieth time, Buckley studied the frozen image on his computer screen. His first viewing had filled him with curiosity and even sympathy. The woman, who he now knew had been called Rebecca Atkins, was obviously scared; he could easily see that in her features. The wild eyes, the unnatural stretch of her jaw, the bulge of her cheeks, the chaotic gap in her mouth—all spoke of crisis. But there was also just the tiniest hint of something else there too— exhilaration, perhaps?

Her physical state was deplorable. The long, thick hair was bushy and filthy, the clothes were near rags, her skin was dirty and scarred; clearly the woman had been through a long ordeal.

Next, Buckley had researched online an "incident" related to the Atkinses in the early 2000s, in a rural Georgia county. It had not been hard to find the account of Joe Atkins having been found dead, and his wife, Desiree, missing and either presumed to have killed her husband or else been a victim of his murderer.

He reclined in the desk chair in his hotel room. There was an extremely curious point to all this. These news accounts had made no mention of a Rebecca Atkins. The most obvious reason for this would be that the authorities were not aware, back then, of the woman's existence. So how could that possibly have come about?

Buckley once more looked at the woman's image on his computer screen. Back then there had been no ubiquitous wireless home surveillance camera technology tied to smartphones. So why have a security camera in rural Georgia nearly twenty years ago?

Buckley enlarged the image and studied the edges of the picture. A tree branch, the murky outline of a bush, a darkened path; all of this was behind the woman who was staring at the lens. She was in the woods, which in rural Georgia was not unexpected.

He enlarged the image even more and now could see the wall of the place. It looked dilapidated, with vegetation growing around it.

Not a traditional residence. A cabin in the woods, maybe? But with a camera covering the door? What would be the point unless something of value was kept in there? His first thought was maybe some sort of illegal operation. Maybe they were running moonshine? Or smuggling drugs? Or selling guns? Or perhaps people? Like this woman?

Were the Atkinses running a human trafficking operation? That didn't seem likely to him. Most times such operators quickly moved their "merchandise" by truck to locations all over the country. They got their full compensation when the product was delivered. This woman looked like she had been a prisoner for a long time. Unless *she* had been delivered to the Atkinses as a slave.

He looked down at his phone screen where an associate had previously sent him a copy of Eloise Cain's current driver's license.

The face that stared out at him seemed carved from granite. There was nothing "happy" about the features. The long dark hair swirled around her shoulders. The photo, not particularly good to begin with, and even grainier as a digital copy, was some years old.

He sipped his drink and made a phone call. Buckley told the man what he wanted done.

Two hours later, through a text, Buckley received copies of the Georgia driver's licenses for both Joe and Desiree Atkins. Buckley checked the physical descriptions. He was most concerned with height.

Joe Atkins was five five. Desiree was four eleven.

He looked at Cain's driver's license. Her height was listed as six one. And in the image he had seen of her on the TV, she looked every inch of it.

Unless a serious genetic aberration had occurred, or there was some ancestor of considerable height lurking in the family tree, Rebecca was probably not the Atkinses' biological daughter. Height was one of the most predictable genetic traits passed from generation to generation. Short parents typically made for short offspring, the same for tall parents. He looked at the images of the Atkinses on their driver's licenses. There were no similarities between their features and Rebecca's, and the hair color, while not decisive, was nowhere close.

So either she was adopted or she'd been abducted and provided to the Atkinses—unless *they* had done the abducting.

He focused on another aspect of the case. A news article from back then detailing the loss suffered by Leonard and Wanda Atkins, Joe's parents and Desiree's in-laws. Buckley reasoned that they had to know about Rebecca. They lived nearby and were the only family Joe had. And they were the only survivors, other than Desiree, mentioned in the news article and the related obituary. The article also said that Leonard Atkins had fought in Vietnam. Buckley checked Len Atkins's age at the time, which was given in the article, and added on the intervening years. He would be well into his seventies now.

He sent an email with another information request. An hour later he received a reply. It turned out that Atkins was registered with the VA and was getting treatment after having had a stroke. And the reply included his current address. Buckley didn't know how his associate had obtained this info so fast, but he thought that the VA needed to seriously upgrade its cybersecurity firewalls.

But then don't we all?

However, this time, he wasn't complaining.

Buckley was wheels up on his jet in a few hours. When they landed he drove a waiting rental car to a hotel where he had made a reservation. He checked in, went up to his room, and spread his case files out on the desk.

He had some wine from the minibar and pondered what to do next. This was all growing extremely complicated. And intriguing. He opened his laptop and brought the image up. He flicked his finger against Rebecca Atkins's/El Cain's picture on the screen.

She would not be easy. He smiled at the challenge.

And since the FBI was now involved, he had a unique asset that he could call on to help him in his quest to find the woman. It was late, but he could always leave a message. He hit the name in his contact list, and a voice answered within two rings.

"Hello, Peter, I trust you have something worthy of me. I've been rather bored lately."

"I do indeed. In fact it has to do with your former employer."

"The Army or the FBI?"

"The latter," Buckley replied.

"Excellent, I always love to stick it to the Bureau when given the chance."

"They're looking for a woman named Rebecca Atkins, aka Eloise Cain. And so am I."

"And your interest in her?"

"Entirely personal. She killed my brother, Ken," said Buckley.

"Sorry to hear that."

"I can send the jet. Just give me a location and a time."

"I'm a bit tied up at the moment. Just finishing something up. I can be ready to go tomorrow morning around eight. I'm in DC currently. I can go out to Dulles to catch your ride."

"All right. They'll fly out of the Signature Terminal."

"And where are you?"

"The great state of Alabama."

"Okay, and what is there of interest to you in the great state of Alabama?"

"I'll fill you in when you get here," promised Buckley.

"Private jets are so convenient. I wish I could afford one."

"Well, you'll always have the use of mine."

"Aren't you sweet. Look, I really have to go. A few things to tidy up, like I said."

"Right, see you soon, Britt."

He clicked off.

38

Britt Spector put her phone away and looked down at the body on the floor. A few minutes ago it was a living, breathing human being. Now she had transformed it into a corpse via a broken neck that would make it look like the very elderly and long-serving and high-ranking congressman had fallen down the stairs of his lovely home, in a stately old neighborhood in northwest DC. The tox report would show that the man had had too much to drink, and was already unsteady on his feet due to some neurological ailments and cognitive debilitation, although he had won his reelection by a landslide. And the forensic trail the fall had left would not suggest foul play, because while she had nudged him down the stairs, it wasn't enough to change the trajectory of his descent, alerting the police that something was amiss. Then it came down to finishing the job with a slight but classic maneuver on the man's already extensively damaged vertebra that the Army had taught her. And he had died.

Simple and easy.

Spector had no sympathy for the fellow, who was cruel and corrupt. For over four decades he had sold his influence in hundreds of different ways, with wired funds sliding into foreign numbered accounts, or substantial favors and hidden payments handed out to those he favored, relatives, friends, mistresses. Sometimes it was as simple as making sure a law *wasn't* passed; indeed, he was known as a particularly efficient bill killer. And the laws he made sure would never see the light of day usually would benefit the masses, who had little money and no power. Thus, the result of his either stonewalling or passing a bill always benefited the wealthy and the connected because they *could* reward him. That was how the game was played, and he played it better than most.

And his growing net worth had been explained away through well-designed investment devices, or lucky business gambles that had nothing to do with luck. His real wealth was outright hidden from view in those numbered accounts in faraway places. However, he had gotten too big for his britches and made a fatal mistake in deciding to renegotiate a deal that was already done, for far better terms.

Spector's employer on this job had had this done to them once too often by the man. Before, they had agreed to his demands. This time, they had decided to cut their losses and also take the congressman out of any more deals, as well as the remainder of his years. And with his declining health, he was getting far more difficult to trust and control. And there was growing concern he would let something slip that would spark an investigation that would turn out to be *inconvenient*.

The far younger man replacing him at this pinnacle of power would not be nearly as duplicitous. Or stupid enough to think that he could get away with anything. They were all cookie-cutter drones. The only principles they believed in were the ones that benefited them. The question was simple: How much would they cost? They were just another line item in a budget, though that line item would *never* officially appear in any budget. Yet that made it no less critical.

The calculation was a simple one: Laws equaled money. If you made the laws, you made the money.

And this immoral and corrupt man, whose political decisions had harmed many ordinary citizens in myriad ways, would be buried, and his loved ones would mourn him; but then they would immediately fight over his money, the only thing of value he would leave behind.

Good riddance, thought Spector.

She finished with the body and took her time erasing all traces of her presence there. After that, she made her way out the way she had come, via an impossibly high window and down a wall that seemed to have no visible means of support for such a climb or descent other than a copper gutter. But that was for the average intruder, not Britt Spector.

There were no signs of forced entry. And that would make it certain that the police would conclude the man's death was an unfortunate accident.

She walked down the darkened street and arrived back at her hotel in short order. She took a shower, had a drink, and sent an encrypted message to her employer. Then she waited and checked an electronic bank account to make sure that the remainder of the agreed-upon funds had been deposited. When this was verified, she went to bed. She rose at six the next morning, showered and dressed, packed her bag, checked out, and was on her way to Dulles via an Uber.

She liked working for Peter Buckley. He was a class act who paid extremely well. And he never called her in for something that was not aligned with her elite abilities.

Spector caught the Uber driver checking her out in the mirror. Spector knew she stood out. Five ten, lean and willowy, she had driven herself hard most of her life to achieve her goals. Her features were exotic due to her Filipino father and Scandinavian mother. Her skin was olive and her hair blond. Her father had been an Olympic-caliber judo athlete. Her mother had been a tall, rangy biathlete, and she had taught her daughter how to both ski and shoot at the same time. Her parents' athleticism had passed to their daughter, though she had not followed their paths in life. She had other goals.

She looked at the man's hungry gaze in the mirror. Any woman would easily be able to read that look.

"You like what you see?" she said.

He nodded. "Very much."

"Well, life is full of disappointment," she replied. She turned away and thought no more of him.

Yes, men were easy. Women, women were hard. And apparently Peter had found a challenge for her to take on.

This was exactly what rocked Britt Spector's world.

39

The wheels of the Bombardier jet solidly gripped the tarmac and held as it landed at the business aviation park. The aircraft taxied to a stop, the door stairs dropped down, and off stepped the sole passenger. Spector carried her black leather duffel over one shoulder, with a confident swagger in every stride.

Before joining the Bureau, she had completed college and then enlisted in the Army, jumping out of perfectly good airplanes with the 101st Airborne Division. Before every mission they would smear any exposed part of their skin with multicolor camo paint. It was a difficult process, and you had to get it just right or the entire purpose would be defeated. Irregular diagonal lines across the face. Two colors on the lips, nose, chin, etc. Don't forget the ears, neck, eyelids, hands. Done right, even if the enemy hit you with a light, you would still be invisible. You could kill them before they killed you. Done wrong, you were a sitting duck with a Hollywood premiere-grade spotlight shining on your soon-to-be dead ass.

Yet the Army had never understood or appreciated

her. When the promotions didn't come as fast as she would have liked, and after some of her extracurricular activities had drawn the ire of those in command, she'd gotten her honorable discharge and moved on. She'd then taken her talents to the FBI. She'd stayed there long enough to realize it was also not a good fit for her personal goals. So she had become a freelancer in a field she had very much made her own. In doing so, she was deploying the same skills she had gained and burnished first in the military and then at the Bureau, but making far more money in the process. And, best of all, it was a life of her own making.

While her parents had been exemplary athletes, they had truly been disasters as parents and at providing for their only child. Thus, Spector had grown up poor and physically and verbally abused by a mother and father who had never achieved their dreams of athletic glory and had taken that failure out on her. After escaping their yoke, she had worked for all she had, and never wanted to be poor or abused again.

She climbed into the passenger seat of the waiting black SUV, and as soon as her butt hit the leather, they were off.

Driving was Peter Buckley, immaculate in pearl-gray slacks, a classic navy blazer, collared shirt, and pocket square. He turned to her and said, "Good flight?"

"Beats the hell out of a jump seat on a C130

wondering whether a SAM was going to blow you out of the sky."

"Your work in DC went well?"

"As well as possible, thanks."

"But now you're on my clock," he said.

"Same terms as before?"

"Double."

She slid her sunglasses down to peer at him. "I sometimes forget what an attractive man you are, Peter, dear. But why double?"

"Because this job, I think, will be worth it."

"You mean doubly hard?"

"You live for the challenge, or did I remember wrong?"

She slid her shades back up and looked out the window. "You never do anything *wrong*, Peter, do you?"

He handed her an iPad. "On the drive read the file I've put together. We'll eat in my hotel suite. I've already booked you a room. You still like champagne with your niçoise salad?"

"Is there any other way to have it?"

As the SUV drove along Spector read the file once, then twice, and then a third time, which, she had been trained, was where the truly useful knowledge and nuance was gained.

"Who's the FBI agent on the case?"

"That I don't know."

"Shouldn't be hard to find out. I still have contacts there."

"Even after what happened?"

She looked up from the iPad. "Nothing officially *did* happen. And I don't burn bridges. At least not with people who matter."

"Okay, see what you can find out, but leave no fingerprints."

Spector smiled to herself, perhaps thinking about her last assignment. "I never do, Peter. Now that I've read the file, tell me what you think."

He went through his theories about the woman named Rebecca Atkins being a prisoner in Georgia. When he showed her Atkins's image, Spector scrutinized the screen and nodded. "Wooded area, the terrible state of her, surveillance camera, that would be my conclusion. So now she's calling herself El Cain."

"And she killed my brother, Ken, as I told you."

"I never met Ken, but I'm sure he was tough."

"He was. But with someone who knew what they were doing? Like you? He wouldn't be much of a match. One man I talked to said Cain tore through a professional fighter with a ferocity he'd never seen before. And she pulled a gun on this same man, and he said she would have blown his head off without a second thought."

"Tell me, why did she kill Ken?"

"Does it matter?"

"Just trying to get the full flavor. But if you'd rather not answer . . . ?"

"My brother was with a woman, Rosa. He was beating her. This woman, let's call her El Cain for consistency, intervened. She gave him multiple opportunities to walk away, but he grew increasingly incensed. When he pulled a gun on her, well, she took it to another level." Buckley glanced at her. "Does that make a difference?"

"No. But would it be impertinent for me to say that your brother got what he deserved?"

"It would not be."

"So why are you doing this, then?"

"If you had grown up in my family, you might understand."

"I might, and then again, I might not. What's the next move?"

"Find El Cain."

She touched the iPad's screen. "And we talk to Leonard and Wanda Atkins, currently residents of Huntsville, Alabama, which explains why we're here. Do you think the agent on the case has been by to talk to them?"

"I would be stunned if they haven't."

"And if the Atkinses won't cooperate?"

"I have ways of making them do so—I'm talking money, of course—and if my methods don't work, I'm sure you can think of some."

"You appear to be all-in on this. Otherwise, I doubt

you'd be taking such personal risks by going after her with the FBI already involved."

He glanced over at Spector, frowning. "I've taken personal risks my whole life, Britt, just as you have. You do so when the stakes are worth it."

"Well, you like a challenge, too. Maybe you've been stagnating."

Buckley nodded, looking thoughtful. "There's no maybe about it. I *have* been. The earlier years were the best, when I was building something. Even when I had nothing there was a dream in place. I guess there was nowhere to go but up, and it all depended on me. Now I go to board meetings or sit in on video conferences. I listen to stupid, boring people say stupid, boring things, and I wonder why I'm even bothering. They make their money and I make my money. But one can only make so much money."

"Spoken like someone who has far more than he'll ever need."

"Then I'll triple your fee, but don't ever think money will replace the thrill of living, Britt."

"I never said it would, Peter. That's why I do what *I* do."

40

"We might be too late," said Spector as they walked up the sidewalk to the Atkinses' front door that afternoon.

Spector had checked into her room at the hotel and had her champagne and salad in Buckley's suite. Then Buckley had made numerous phone calls and sent texts and emails. Spector had gone to the gym to engage in her intense daily workout, which had left her sweaty and breathless. She had showered and changed, and they had then driven over here.

Spector examined the knocked-over lamppost. "That looks very recent."

They hurried up to the front porch, and Buckley rapped on the door.

Wanda Atkins opened it and stared up at them, bleary-eyed.

"I hope you're not selling something, because I'm not buying."

"It looks like you need to *buy* a new lamppost anyway," said Spector, pointing to the demolished one.

Atkins stared at it and her eyes bulged. "Well, damn."

"How did it happen?" asked Buckley.

"Excuse me, but who are you folks?" asked Wanda suspiciously.

Buckley said, "We're trying to find a woman named El Cain, but you might know her as Rebecca Atkins."

"How do you know anything about all that?" demanded a stunned Atkins.

"May we come in?" asked Buckley.

"No, no, I don't want any visitors now."

Buckley took out his wallet and pulled out a fistful of cash. "It will be worth your while, Mrs. Atkins. We just have some questions. You *are* Wanda Atkins, correct?"

"Yes, yes I am, and I don't care who knows it. I got nothing to hide. But what do you want with Becky?"

"This would be much better discussed privately," said Buckley smoothly.

"Well, all right," said Atkins, staring at the bills clutched in his hand.

She led them into the living room. Len was sleeping in his wheelchair.

"Mr. Atkins?" said Buckley.

"Yes, he's had a stroke. I don't want to wake him. He can't talk anyway—he just grunts," she said bluntly.

"All right," said Buckley, with a glance at Spector, who was drilling Atkins with a hard look.

They all sat down, and Buckley said, "Have you seen Cain lately? Might she have been the one to knock down your lamppost?"

Spector added, "That would have taken a lot of force."

"Well, she's a big woman, bigger than you," said Atkins before she caught herself.

"So she *has* been here then?" interjected Buckley.

"You mentioned money?" said Atkins.

Buckley placed two thousand dollars in hundred-dollar bills on the coffee table. "And depending on what you can tell us, I'll double that amount."

"But what I don't get is why everyone's all so interested in Becky now."

"Like who?" asked Buckley.

"The FBI has been here. Couple of gals."

"*Female* FBI agents?" said Spector quickly.

"Well, one was I guess. The other woman was too old. I think the agent said she was an assistant."

"Interesting," noted Spector. "That's not usually how the Bureau conducts investigations. What was the agent's name?"

"She left me her card." Atkins rose, went into the other room, and came back out with one of the business cards Pine had left her and handed it to Buckley. He looked at the name and then passed it to Spector.

"Did you know this Atlee Pine?" asked Buckley.

"No, but there're almost three thousand female special agents at the Bureau."

"Are you with the FBI, too?" asked Atkins, who was listening closely to this.

"No, but I know some of the agents."

Buckley said, "What did you tell Agent Pine?"

"She already knew a lot, but I filled in some blanks."

When she didn't seem inclined to say any more, Buckley pushed the pile of cash toward her. "And we look forward to you doing the same for us, filling in blanks."

"But what's your concern in all this?"

"We have been tasked with finding El Cain. She's wanted in connection with a crime."

"What sort of crime?"

"The worst of all, I'm afraid—murder."

"Murder? Who was killed?"

"We can't go into that right now. But she is wanted by the police. What we're trying to do is find her and convince her to turn herself in. That way no one gets hurt."

"My God. She never mentioned a murder."

"I'm sure she wouldn't."

"Wait a minute, you're not talking about my son, Joe, are you? Because Becky didn't kill him."

"No, I'm talking about a murder that just happened

recently. Now, we've made inquiries. And we need you to validate our conclusions."

Atkins's face screwed up in confusion. "I'm afraid I don't understand."

"That your son and daughter-in-law kept Rebecca prisoner in a cabin in the woods and, from the looks of things, abused her emotionally and physically. She escaped from there. Your son was killed by, perhaps, his wife. And both his wife and Rebecca disappeared. And that you and your husband knew about it. And that you left Georgia after it all happened. And Rebecca is now calling herself El Cain."

Atkins said accusingly, "You've talked to that Agent Pine, haven't you?"

"Because that's what she said as well, you mean?" interjected Spector.

"Yes. She seemed to have it all figured out."

"How was Cain tortured?" asked Spector, drawing a sharp glance from Buckley.

"I . . . I'm not sure . . ." Atkins stammered.

"We need the truth, Mrs. Atkins," said Spector. "Or it will not turn out well for you. We are working with the authorities on this."

Atkins glanced at her sleeping husband and said, "Desiree liked to burn things. And stick things with needles and carve . . . *things* with knives."

"By 'things' you mean Cain?" said Spector sharply.

"Yes. When she was here Becky, I mean Mercy—"

"Mercy?" said Spector sharply.

"Yes. Agent Pine told me her real name was Mercy, and she was kidnapped from her parents and brought to us in Crawfordville, Georgia."

"And her last name?" asked Buckley.

"She didn't say."

"Why would the kidnapper bring the girl to you?" asked Spector.

"He was an old friend of my husband's. They fought in Vietnam together. But he said Mercy's parents wanted her to die. But . . . but I guess that was a lie. The thing is, we believed him. And since we were too old to take care of a child, my son and Desiree took her." She shuddered. "Mercy showed me some of the scars from what Desiree did to her."

"The mental scars will be far worse," said Spector, staring the woman down.

With another curious glance at his companion, Buckley interjected, "Do you know where Cain is now? Did she say where she was going after she left here?"

"I gave her Desiree's phone number."

"Do you know where Desiree is living?"

"No, I just had her number."

"We're going to need that," said Buckley.

"I gave it to Becky. I don't remember it."

"Mrs. Atkins, let me remind you this is a murder investigation. If you obstruct the investigation in any way, you could go to prison." He glanced at Len Atkins. "And then who would take care of your husband?" Buckley knew that if Atkins looked at this with calm reason, his explanation for their being here would seem ridiculous. He wasn't the police. She needn't tell him anything. And yet most people, particularly in stressful situations, were not even remotely calm or rational; they were, instead, vulnerable. And the power of suggestion went a long way with vulnerable people. As did a pile of cash.

But Atkins said, "I don't have it. I gave my only copy to Becky."

"I'll give you another thousand dollars."

She looked agonized by this. "You can give me all the money you have and I still won't have the number."

"Do you at least remember the area code?"

She gummed her lips and looked at the ceiling. "My short-term memory is just about shot. Comes with getting old."

"All right," said Buckley, looking frustrated.

"Do you think she's going after Desiree?" asked Atkins.

"Wouldn't you?" said Spector.

Atkins kept her gaze on Buckley. "But why would Becky kill anyone?"

"We're not sure. That's why we want to find her. To ask her. And if she is going after Desiree we need to stop her. We don't want anyone else to get hurt."

Spector said, "Why didn't you stop them from *hurting* Becky?"

Atkins seemed surprised by the question. "What? I . . . I didn't . . . I didn't know what to do. I was afraid."

"How young was she when Rebecca became a prisoner?"

"Six."

"So you were too afraid to help a little girl?"

Buckley glanced questioningly at Spector. He didn't seem to understand where his colleague was going with this.

"I'm not proud of it," said Atkins.

"Is there anything else you can tell us about Cain when she came to visit you?" asked Spector.

"She hated me for what I'd done. She probably wanted to kill me. As big and strong as she is, she could have easily. But she didn't. I . . ."

"What?" said Spector.

"I was surprised that she turned out . . . as . . ."

". . . normal as she did," said Spector.

"Y-yes. She seemed to . . . to have herself together okay."

"With no help from you."

"I did what I could," Atkins said indignantly.

"Right."

"Yes, well, thank you," said Buckley hurriedly. "We'll be in touch."

On the way to the SUV, Buckley said, "What the hell was all that about, Britt?"

"Nothing. She just rubbed me the wrong way is all."

"Okay. Just don't let it get in the way of what our goal is."

"It won't, Peter. But you have to admit, it was disturbing."

"*Life* is disturbing. But put it behind you. I need your A game for this."

41

Back at the hotel, they walked to their separate rooms.

Spector sat on her bed for a long time staring into space, something she almost never did. Reflection for her was painful and thus counterproductive. She mixed herself a gin and tonic from the minibar and sipped on it, while she looked out the window at downtown Huntsville. She had killed a number of people during her career. Some while in combat in the Army. Once as an FBI agent when a suspected serial killer they had tracked down pulled a gun and was going to empty it into Spector's partner. She had shot him dead. Then, in her new career, she ended the lives of others she had no quarrel with, solely for payment.

So what right do I have to question Wanda Atkins's ethics, or morals?

She finished her drink, sat on her bed, and took a photo out of her wallet. It was of her parents. Her father had been short and heavily muscled, but immensely flexible, with superb range of motion. In martial arts that was key, she knew. Her mother had been tall and lean; Spector had taken after her

280

physique-wise. She stared down at their unhappy countenances.

They had brutalized their daughter, making her childhood a misery. Her father had drunk himself to death. Her mother had died by her own hand with a rifle similar to the one she had used to compete with in biathlons.

Spector couldn't say she missed either of them. Constant beatings just did that to a child. Part of her—Spector's surprisingly frail emotional side—wanted to return to the Atkinses for a little visit and end the lives of both Wanda and her crippled husband; it would be easy. But the professional side of her said that was not possible.

She lifted the sleeve on her right arm and stared down at the mark that had been carved into her skin as a seven-year-old by her drunken father while her doped-up mother held her.

El Cain had apparently put herself back together, at least to a certain extent.

I'm not sure I can say the same.

Unlike Cain, she had undergone plastic surgery to erase all the other marks inflicted on her, except for this one. Because it had been the first, and because she wanted it with her always, so that she would never forget.

Not that I ever could.

She had never met Cain. She would kill her when the time came because that was how she made her living. But after learning what the woman had gone through, she would take no pleasure in it. In fact, she was starting to regret taking this job at all.

Give her a corrupt politician to get rid of, or a cartel chieftain, two of which she had sent to the hereafter. Or a dictator from a troubled nation who had killed and robbed his people for decades until she had been sent in to hurry him off to an afterlife by the leader of another country. Her employer had been as bad as the dictator, but that was no concern of hers.

But this one was different. Still, she had committed to doing it.

Even with that, she could only lie on her bed and stare at the ceiling, wondering about her life decisions and not coming away with a single good answer.

In his room, after having some wine and doing some other work, Peter Buckley was staring down at his notes from the interview with Wanda Atkins. It was a setback that they didn't have Desiree's phone number or address, but they would have to work around that. And if they could somehow get to Desiree first and then await Cain's arrival? But she had the woman's phone number and might already be well ahead of them.

His smartphone buzzed as a text dropped into his inbox. When he looked at the screen he couldn't believe his good fortune. A transaction had been made using Eloise Cain's credit card at a hotel in Asheville, North Carolina.

He pulled from his file a copy of her driver's license. He had two associates standing by for just this sort of eventuality with immediate access to his private jet. He gave them the necessary information, then he took a snapshot of Cain's driver's license and sent it to them.

Fly there now, find her, and take her, he said in the message. *And let me know when you do. I'll arrange for a place for you to bring her and text you the location. I'll be there as soon as I can.*

He made a call and had one of his people attempt to charter a private plane from a local provider in Huntsville. Unfortunately, nothing was available, and all commercial flights leaving that day had long lay-overs. He clicked off and then texted Spector with the news; he added that they would be driving to Asheville, a little more than five hours away, and she should be ready to leave in ten minutes. He received a single thumbs-up in reply. He frowned at the response. He was unsure what was going on with the woman, but he didn't like it.

He called another associate and told him to find a private place on the outskirts of Asheville and to do it in the next hour or so. It seemed a difficult task, and it was. But Buckley paid for people to do difficult things all the time. And they either succeeded or they no longer worked for him.

He packed his bag and left twenty dollars for the maid. Then he met Spector in the lobby, and they headed to the rental car.

42

"Hello?"

"Agent Pine?"

"Yes, who is this?"

It was the evening and Pine was in her hotel room sitting on her bed when the phone had rung.

"Special Agent Drew McAllister. I'm out of the WFO," he added, referring to the Washington Field Office.

"What can I do for you?"

"I've been assigned to the Ito Vincenzo homicide matter."

Pine kicked off her shoes, leaned back against her headboard, and thought back to Jack Lineberry's frantic phone call. "And this has become an FBI 'homicide matter'?"

"Yes. And I'd like to ask you some questions."

"Okay, go ahead."

"I meant in person. Where are you?"

"Asheville, North Carolina."

"I can be there in the morning."

"I'm not really sure what I can tell you. And why

isn't this an investigation for the local cops? I understand that police from Virginia and Georgia are
already involved."

"You know how these things roll. The Bureau has
an interest, so I have an interest. Can you give me the
address in Asheville?"

Pine did so, and then they arranged a time to meet
in the morning. She clicked off and tossed her phone
down.

"Shit," she muttered and then rubbed her temples
because she felt a sudden fire there. They really were
going after Tim Pine in connection with Vincenzo's
death.

*Well, they might actually find Tim and my mom for me.
And then send them and Jack to jail. Great.* She audibly
groaned at this possibility.

Pine needed to do something, something to burn
some energy. The weights room at the hotel didn't
have enough iron to challenge her, so she ran out to
a shop down the street and bought a one-piece black
bathing suit. She returned to her room, put on her
jeans and a T-shirt over the swimsuit, and headed to
the pool. She dove into the water and swam lap after
lap, focusing on her strokes and her breathing—a
form of cheap therapy.

Exhausted, she finished, pulled herself out of
the pool, and climbed into the in-deck hot tub situated on the pool deck. She let the hot, jet-propelled
water envelop her and thought about what questions

Special Agent Drew McAllister would ask her tomorrow. And, more critically, what answers she would or could give.

She climbed out of the hot tub, went into the changing room, stripped off her bathing suit, dried off, and then changed back into her clothes. As she was leaving the pool area she glanced through the window of the adjacent space where the workout room was located.

There was only one person in there. A tall woman with a buzz cut. Probably in the military, Pine thought. She was outfitted in loose-fitting sweats and was moving all the stacks the universal weight machine had to offer.

Pine went back to her room, showered, and changed into another pair of jeans and a fresh sweatshirt. After a room-service dinner, she sat in her chair looking out the window and then debated whether to take a walk to further clear her mind. With Desiree in jail, she wasn't sure what direction to head in now. But finding Mercy was still her only priority.

A moment later her phone rang. She snagged it off the nightstand.

"Yes?" she said.

"Agent Pine? This is Wanda Atkins. I hope it's not too late for me to call."

"No, not at all. Did you remember anything else?"

"No, but I thought you needed to know that she was here."

"Who was there?" It couldn't be Desiree, Pine knew.

"Beck—I mean Mercy, she was here. She tracked me down somehow."

A dumbfounded Pine stood there shaking.

"*Mercy* was at your house?"

"Yes."

"When?"

When Atkins told her Pine barked, "And you're just calling me now!" Pine felt like her head was about to explode. She could barely breathe.

"She was very upset. Which made me very upset. I've been crying for what seems like days. But I finally decided I needed to call and let you know what happened."

Pine got her nerves under control and refocused. "What did she want?"

"She wanted to know if I had a way to get in touch with Desiree."

"And what did you say?"

"I . . . I had a phone number. I know I should have told you, but I didn't. I'm sorry."

"Forget about that. It doesn't matter now. Just tell me, did you give Desiree's number to Mercy?"

"Yes, I did. But she doesn't go by Mercy. She goes by Eloise now, El for short. She didn't tell me her last name. Eloise is from the children's book. That's what she told me. I brought her a copy of it while she was . . . with Joe and Desiree. I . . . I did try to help her, you know," she added in a pitiful tone.

When Pine said nothing, Wanda added, "Why would she want the phone number? I really don't think Desiree will talk to her. I mean, why would she?"

"That's not why she wanted it," said Pine.

"What do you mean?" Wanda added, her voice now laced with panic. "Wait, can she track Desiree down from just her phone number?"

"Yes," said Pine, who had a sick feeling that that was exactly what Mercy was going to do and might already have done. In fact, Pine could have gotten that information faster through paying to access an internet search database than waiting for the Bureau to provide it. She wouldn't make that mistake again. "There are ways on the internet to get a physical address from a phone number."

"My God. Then she might already be wherever Desiree is, if it's not too far away from Huntsville."

Pine was almost in a trance. Her heart soared because as of this morning her sister was alive. But if she was going to try to get to Desiree? Her throat was so dry she had trouble talking. She put a hand against the wall to steady herself because her legs seemed to have lost their ability to support her. A simple question occurred to her. "What . . . what did she look like?"

"Tall, even taller than you. And very strong looking.

But she was always that way. And her beautiful hair was all gone. She had cut it so close to her scalp, oh, it was sad. She looked like she was—"

"—in the military," said Pine, suddenly remembering something.

"Yes, exactly, now I'd also wanted to let you know that some other people were here asking questions and—"

Pine heard but really didn't register these words. She dropped her phone on the bed and rushed from the room. She banged off the walls in the hall and didn't even bother with the elevator. She took the stairs, leaping three steps at a time. She hit the main floor, burst through the door, shoved two attendants and one guest out of the way, and sprinted through the lobby on her way to the hotel's gym.

Please, please, please. Mother of God please.

One needed a hotel key card to access the gym. Pine didn't bother to use hers, she simply kicked the door open. She looked frantically around and her hopes plummeted. The only person there was an elderly man reading an iPad on a recumbent exercise bike. He had nearly fallen off it when she forced the door open. Pine ran over to him and described Mercy to him.

He shook his head. "No, ma'am. The place was empty when I got here and nobody came in after." He looked at the broken door. "Except for you."

Pine raced to the front desk, where she flashed her

shield and asked about the room number for a guest with the first name Eloise.

"We don't give out—" the clerk, a young man, began.

"This shield says otherwise," barked Pine. "Do it!"

The intimidated clerk quickly checked the computer. "Yes. An Eloise *Cain*. She checked in today and is staying for one night only. Paid with a credit card."

Eloise—the same name she gave Wanda. It has to be her.

"What's her room number?" she said frantically.

"I can't—"

Pine grabbed his arm and jerked him toward her. "Tell me the fucking room number or you're under arrest!"

"Four-oh-four."

"Now give me a key to that room."

"I can't do that. I need to talk to a supervi—"

Pine shouted, "I don't have time to argue. This is a life-or-death situation."

The man paled, grabbed a blank key, charged it, and handed it to Pine.

"Do you know what kind of car she was driving?"

"No. We don't have valets. Just self-park. And I must say this is highly unusual."

"You're damn right it is," snapped Pine as she sprinted toward the elevator.

43

Pine ran into Blum in the lobby.

"I was going to take a walk before bed, what's happened?" she said, noting her boss's excited features.

She followed along as Pine quickly filled her in on Mercy's likely being at the hotel, and also about Special Agent Drew McAllister's arriving the next morning to question her.

"You really think that was your sister in the gym here? I mean, what a coincidence."

"The description Wanda gave me fit the woman I saw in the gym to a T. And how many six-foot-tall Eloises are out there?"

They reached room 404. Pine drew a long breath and knocked on the door. Her hand was trembling. They heard nothing from inside. She knocked again.

Pine leaned toward the door. "Mer-Eloise Cain? It's . . ." A suddenly stumped Pine thought frantically for something to say.

Blum called out, "It's your sister, Atlee Pine."

Pine stared wide-eyed at Blum for a moment

before thanking her with a weak smile. But there was still no sound from within.

Pine put the key card in the reader and swung the door open. They moved inside, and Pine turned the lights on.

"Mercy? It's Atlee. Mercy! It's your sister, *Lee*."

The bed was still made. They could find nothing that wasn't supposed to be in the room. A dirty towel and washcloth lay on the bathroom floor.

Pine said, "The front desk clerk said she checked in today and was only staying one night."

"I would say that she might have just gone out, but there's no suitcase or anything else of hers in here. Do you think she could have already left? But surely if she checked out the clerk would have told you."

"If she came here looking for Desiree she might have found out she's been arrested and is in jail. There would be no way for her to see her. She might have just left without bothering to check out." Pine stood in the middle of the room and put a hand over her face. "Shit, I can't believe I walked right past my sister and didn't even know it was her."

"My God, Agent Pine, you haven't seen her in thirty years. She wouldn't recognize you, either."

"But we're twins, Carol. Damnit, you'd think I would have—"

"What? Felt a tingling sensation? That's not how it works, Agent Pine. It was amazing luck she was staying at the same hotel. And it was just bad luck you didn't recognize her. There was nothing you could have done."

Pine went to stand over by the window and looked out. She had a sudden thought.

"They don't have valet service here, only self-park, but they might have a security camera."

They rushed back to the front desk where the same young man was standing. He started scowling as Pine approached him. He ducked into the room behind the desk and thirty seconds later, an older woman came out also carrying a scowl and a defensive posture.

"Can I help you?" she said stiffly.

Pine pulled out her shield. "I'm with the FBI. I need to know if you have video surveillance of the parking lot."

"Why do you need to know that?"

"Because I am trying to track down a guest who is staying here. She's not in her room. She might have recently left the hotel. I need to see if her car or her image is on the film."

"Do you have a warrant?"

"Why do I need a warrant?" asked Pine. "I'm not asking to search anyone's room."

"You've apparently already done that, or so my associate told me. Video surveillance is a form of searching. It invades someone's privacy, not only the person you say you're looking for, but our other guests as well. So, no warrant, no security tape."

"You sound like a lawyer," said Pine, who was impressed with the woman's argument, despite her frustration with her answer.

"For twenty years I was a paralegal to one of the best criminal defense attorneys in the state."

"Why are you working here, then?"

"If you must know, he died and I lost my job, and I'm apparently too old and too expensive to be employed as a paralegal anymore," she said bitterly.

Blum said, "Well, clearly those people are wrong and stupid."

The supervisor looked at Blum. "Are you with the FBI, too?"

"I am."

Now the supervisor looked impressed. Pine could almost see the woman's brain percolating.

"Well, that's . . . progress."

Blum smiled knowingly. "Yes, it is. But a lot *more* progress needs to be done. I think we both know that."

The woman eyed her for a long moment, before she glanced at Pine. "But I'm still afraid I can't do what you want without the proper legal process."

Pine's features calmed and she rested her elbows on the counter and looked at the woman, her expression one of desperation mingled with mental exhaustion. "Would it make a difference if I told you the woman in question is my twin sister? And that I haven't seen her since we were six and she was kid-napped from our home in Georgia?"

The woman took a step back and gave each of them a searching glance. "Is that really the case?"

"I would never make something like that up." Using Blum's phone because she had left hers in her room, Pine showed the woman the image of Mercy from the FBI PSA. "This is my sister at the exact moment when she broke free from years as a captive in a living hell. Now, I believe she's in this hotel. I've never been this close to her in thirty years." Pine handed the phone back to Blum and said pleadingly, "Will you please help me? If I have to wait for a war-rant, she'll be long gone. This may be my only shot."

A significant moment passed while the woman processed all of this. Then she nodded and said, "Would you like a tour of our security room? We sometimes offer that to our guests so they can see how we take ensuring their safety seriously. I can even have my personnel show some actual footage from the parking lot from today, say around the time your sister checked in?"

"Thank you," said Pine with a relieved smile. "Thank you so much."

"I'm someone's sister, too," the woman said demurely.

44

Ten minutes later Pine and Blum were sitting next to a woman in uniform in a small office near the hotel's business center. The woman was hitting keys on her computer, and footage was coming up on the screen.

"Okay, here we go." She manipulated the footage to speed it up to whenever someone appeared in the parking lot. They saw people come and go in their cars.

Then Pine said, "Hold it right there. There!"

The woman froze the footage, and Pine and Blum stared at a very tall person in a hoodie getting out of a car. The film quality was poor, black-and-white and grainy.

"It's hard to make out much," said Blum. "Including whether it's a man or a woman."

"Can't see the face at all," Pine added in a disappointed tone. "Only the profile. Can you let it go frame by frame?" she asked the woman.

The security officer nodded and hit some keys. They watched as the person walked slowly away from the car and toward the hotel, with a duffel in hand.

"Still can't make them out, and I couldn't see the license plate, either," said Pine. "Can you go back and enhance it?"

"Sorry, that's the best I can do," the woman said. "But the car's make and model are clear. It's a Honda Civic. Looks to be really, really old."

"Yes it does," said Blum.

Pine said, "Thank you for doing this."

"No problem. Hope you find the person."

Pine and Blum walked out and headed toward the elevator.

"I can't believe this. She was right there and now she's gone."

Blum said, "Why do you think Mercy is involved in all this now?"

"She must have seen the FBI's PSA. And that's a problem."

"Why?" asked Blum.

"The way the Bureau worded it, she might think they're after her for Joe Atkins's murder. Shit, I should have asked Wanda if Mercy was worried about that. But I can phone and ask her when I get back to my room. Since she called my cell I have her number in my phone list."

Blum said, "Can you get the Bureau to change the message? We know she didn't kill Atkins, not after Desiree confessed."

"I tried to do that before, but they wouldn't relent. You know they try to walk a fine line at all times.

I can try again after what we learned from Desiree, but I'm not going to hold my breath." She suddenly brightened. "When McAllister gets here tomorrow I can ask him about it. He might be able to persuade the higher-ups to go for that."

"In the meantime you can put out an APB for a Honda Civic."

Pine said, "I can and will, but would you like to take a guess how many of them there are? And we couldn't even tell the color."

"Well, you can put out a description of Mercy. She *does* stand out. And now we have an updated description of her."

"Yeah, I can do that, too."

"You don't sound hopeful."

"Oh, I am hopeful, Carol. And for one very good reason."

Blum nodded. "Now you know that your sister is alive."

Pine broke into a relieved grin. "It's weird."

"What is?"

"I've never been this happy and miserable at the same time. And who knows, we've already had one miracle. Maybe we'll have another one and Mercy will show back up at the hotel."

"My fingers are crossed."

Blum went to her room, but Pine decided to check on Mercy's room again. She figured she might have missed something. She had been too distracted to perform a thorough search.

She took a few minutes to look around and then picked up the discarded towel and washcloth and sat on the side of the tub holding them.

Would she ever again be this close to her sister? Would Mercy disappear again for another thirty years?

She had been euphoric for about two minutes. Now she had never felt this depressed. She dropped the towel and washcloth on the floor. "I'm sorry, Mercy. I was so stupid. I should have known that was you. I should have."

She rose and left. She turned to pull the door closed behind her.

That's when she felt a gun muzzle pressed against her spine and a voice said, "Come with us very quietly. Or you're dead right here. And if you make one move or try to get away we will kill anyone we run into. If you don't believe me, just try it."

Pine looked back into the man's hard, cruel features.

And believed him.

45

A blindfolded Pine drew a long breath. She could not see the pitch-darkness that surrounded her like a cage, but she could sense it. She was also bound and gagged. She didn't know how much time had passed, but for some reason she thought it was still nighttime.

Even with her feet and hands bound she had managed to sleep a little, if fitfully. She had no idea who had snatched her, or why. Or where she currently was. They had blindfolded her on the drive over to wherever they were. She had managed to gauge how long the trip had taken. About a half hour or so. In a mountainous area like Asheville, she could be in the middle of nowhere now.

She had heard noises every now and then, but the men had not come back. She had been helped down a set of steps, so she might be in a basement or a cellar.

Pine tensed when she heard footsteps above. There were the murmurings of conversation, then a raised voice was saying something she could not make out and then came more footsteps. A door opened and a light clicked on. With the blindfold on, the light couldn't dazzle her, but her heart started to race when the footsteps drew near.

Peter Buckley and Britt Spector stopped in front of Pine, and both gazed down at Buckley's hand, which held Pine's FBI shield. Spector looked quite upset at the prospect of having a kidnapped FBI agent in their midst, but Buckley didn't seem unduly disturbed by this. He glanced over at the two men who had abducted Pine and then turned back to her.

"What's your name?" he asked.

"FBI Special Agent Atlee Pine. Who the hell are you?"

Buckley pulled up a chair and sat down across from Pine.

"I am looking for someone named Eloise Cain. I understand that you have also been making inquiries about her. Why?"

"Answer my question first."

"To negotiate, one must have something to negotiate with. You have nothing."

Pine didn't respond to this.

"We don't seem to be getting anywhere," said Buckley quietly.

"What's your interest in Cain?" asked Pine.

"She killed someone."

"Who?"

"None of your concern," said Buckley.

"How do you know she killed the person?"

"There were multiple witnesses."

"Why did she do it?" asked Pine.

"Again, none of your concern," replied Buckley.

"Was it self-defense?"

"I've answered a number of your questions. I think it's your turn."

"She's part of an investigation I'm involved in," said Pine.

"I know about the FBI's PSA. You're looking for her. Her name once was Rebecca Atkins and she was from Georgia."

"That's right."

"I made inquiries into the matter. There was a murder. Joe Atkins. His wife, Desiree Atkins, disappeared. Is that the FBI's interest?"

"Yes."

"She wasn't their daughter. She was kidnapped by someone and brought to the Atkinses."

"You seem to know a lot," said Pine.

"I also know that back then her name was Mercy. What was her last name?"

Pine thought quickly. "We don't know that yet."

"You're lying. If she was kidnapped, she had to have a last name and the FBI would know it. What was the last name?"

"I can't tell you."

"What is the exact nature of your investigation?"

"I can't disclose that."

Buckley nodded at Spector and flicked a finger at Pine.

Spector stepped forward, drew a breath, and drove her fist into Pine's gut. Pine hadn't sensed something coming and wasn't prepared for the blow, but her rock-solid abs protected her somewhat. Still, the hard shot hurt like hell and she toppled out of the chair. One of the men lifted Pine up and slammed her back into the seat, where she pitched forward, trying not to throw up.

When she finally managed to sit up Pine gasped, "You're in a world of trouble for kidnapping an FBI agent."

"I agree" was Buckley's surprising reply. "Only my men mistook you for Cain. Tall and strong looking with long dark hair was the description that I took off a copy of her driver's license. To be fair to my people, you *were* coming out of her hotel room. Now we must make the best of it. I have kept you blindfolded so that we might have a peaceful resolution of this matter. You tell me what I need to know and we let you go. I have no wish to end your life unnecessarily."

"I have nothing to tell you because I don't know where Cain is. I'm looking for her, just like you."

"I know she booked a room at the hotel where you were staying. Have you already met with her? Where is she?"

"I didn't know she was at my hotel."

"As I already pointed out, you were coming out of

her room. My men confirmed the number from one of the hotel staff."

"Okay, I did find out she was there, but only *after* she had left. There was no suitcase, no nothing in the room."

"So why are you still in Asheville then? Is it this Desiree Atkins, the one who disappeared?"

"It doesn't matter," said Pine.

"Why not?"

"She was arrested in the last twenty-four hours, and she's in jail now, charged with some serious crimes."

"What was she arrested for exactly?" asked Buckley.

"I choose not to tell you."

On a sign from Buckley, Spector struck Pine another blow, this time via a spin kick to the side of her head. Perhaps fortunately for her, this time the blow knocked Pine unconscious.

Buckley looked at her lying there on the floor and then turned to one of his men.

"Find out about the woman who was arrested. I doubt it will be under the name Desiree Atkins. Do it now."

The man hustled up the stairs, while Spector bent down to check on Pine. She felt for a pulse and was relieved it was strong. She brushed the hair out of Pine's face and saw the large bruise forming on the side of her face.

She glanced over at Buckley.

"I didn't mean to hit her that hard."

"It doesn't matter," said Buckley absently.

"Peter, she's an FBI agent. Do you know how serious this is?"

"I look at it as an opportunity."

Spector straightened. "What does that mean? What opportunity?"

"You know of my personal history?"

"Some, yes."

"My father was destroyed by the federal government. They even managed to make my mother betray him."

"Peter, I understand that—"

Buckley barked, "This is my chance to make it right, Britt. This may be my *only* chance. And I'm going to take it." He looked at the fallen Pine. "There lies the shining symbol of the federal government in all its inept and disgusting glory." He looked at Spector. "Two birds with one stone, Britt. A lifetime of injustice rectified in one act."

As Spector stared over at the man, she tensed. His expression, his entire demeanor, had changed drastically. It was as though he were another person entirely.

"Where is all this coming from, Peter? I thought we were just after Eloise Cain. I didn't sign on to wage some symbolic war against the federal government because of what it did to your family."

He pointed his finger at her. "You signed on to do what I tell you to do. If you can't do that, you are of no use to me."

"I thought you said you were going to reach a peaceful resolution on this with regard to Agent Pine."

"I lied. Now, are you with me, or not?"

Spector glanced at the fallen Pine. "I'm with you, of course."

"Thank you. Now, I have a phone call to make."

He went to a corner and punched in a number while Spector bent over Pine and tried to revive her.

The call was answered five seconds later by a distinguished, baritone male voice.

"Mr. Buckley? Is something wrong?"

"I need you to come to Asheville, North Carolina. I'll send the jet."

"And what's in Asheville?"

"I have someone I want you to represent in a matter of great importance to me."

46

Two hours outside of Asheville, Cain pulled off the road, cut the engine, and just sat there. She rubbed her face and then rubbed it again. She felt dirty despite her shower after working out; she felt sick despite not being ill. She had come here to tear down her nemesis once and for all, only to find that her nemesis was sitting in jail.

But not before she had kidnapped another girl and held her prisoner. In her anxiety, Cain pushed against the steering wheel so hard she actually felt it start to bend. She relaxed and looked out the window. The darkness looked back at her without a trace of understanding or empathy, when, in all honesty, she was looking for both.

You have to put this behind you, El. You can't do this anymore. You won't make it.

But she had another dilemma. The FBI was still looking for her. She hadn't stabbed Joe Atkins, but there was no way that Desiree would ever say that she hadn't. She would try to take Cain down with her, that was for certain. In fact, she thought, with a sudden panic, she might use that as leverage to get a better deal on her current crimes. Trade Cain for a lighter sentence. Cain wouldn't put anything past the woman, because literally nothing was beyond her.

So where did that leave her? Tired and clueless and just not giving a shit. With Desiree behind bars all the energy seemed to have been sucked right out of her. That was why she had decided to just leave. But now she was rethinking that decision. Cain fingered the hotel key card in her pocket. She had blown good money on her room and she hadn't even slept there or even checked out. She decided to go back and get a good night's sleep. In the morning she would decide what to do.

She drove back to the hotel, went up to her room, and fell into bed. At least for a few hours her troubles would no longer rule her thoughts, but they might sneak back in the form of nightmares. As she closed her eyes, Cain simply decided to chance it. Nightmares couldn't really hurt you. It was only when you awoke from them that the real pain could come.

The next morning Carol Blum was getting worried. She had arranged to meet with Pine for an early breakfast, but Pine hadn't shown up, which was not like her. Blum had phoned both her cell and her room and gotten no answer. She had gone to Pine's room and knocked and also gotten no response. When she called Pine's phone, she could hear it ringing from inside the room. Something was definitely wrong.

She rushed down to the lobby to find out if anyone had seen Pine, when two men in blue FBI windbreakers strode into the hotel looking like they owned the place.

"Agent McAllister?" she said, going over to the men and instinctively focusing on the older one.

That man was well into his forties, salt-and-pepper haired, medium height, and with a trim build and alert manner. The other was in his early thirties, tall and lanky, with a jutting chin, a high, lined forehead, and blond hair. He looked at Blum with suspicion.

The older man nodded. "I'm Special Agent Drew McAllister. And you are?"

Blum quickly explained who she was and also that Pine was apparently missing.

McAllister quickly took charge and made inquiries at the front desk. One of the attendants led them up to Pine's room and opened the door for them. They quickly searched through the room and found that Pine's belongings were all there, except they couldn't find her guns.

"They might be in the room safe," said Blum. "I know she usually stows them in there." She opened the closet, and pointed out the safe. "It's locked."

"You're probably right," said McAllister.

"She had her shield with her when she was going back to her room last night," Blum told them.

"Well, maybe she never made it back to her room," said McAllister grimly. "Is your car still in the parking lot?"

"Yes, I saw it from out of my window."

"And she didn't contact you after you saw her last night?"

"No. I think you're right. I don't think she made it back to her room."

"Anything unusual happen here last night?" asked the other agent, who had been introduced as Special Agent Neil Bertrand.

Blum glanced at him for a moment, her mind spinning rapidly. She did not want to tell the FBI about Mercy Pine having been in the hotel last night. But once they made inquiries, the agents would find out about the questions Pine had been asking the previous night.

"We were following up some leads, but nothing panned out," she said, deciding to judiciously tell a semblance of the truth. She had been with the FBI for far too long to outright lie to two of its agents.

McAllister gave her the Bureau stare-down, which Blum handled with aplomb, having confronted it many times in the past.

"How long you been with the Bureau?" he asked coolly. When she told him, he said, "Yeah, I thought so." He cracked a grin. "You've got all our numbers, right?"

"I just want to find Agent Pine."

They went back downstairs, where McAllister and Bertrand methodically questioned the staff. They finally found one employee who was about to go off duty. He said he had seen a woman fitting Pine's description leaving the hotel around ten that night with two men.

"Did it seem like she was being taken against her will?" asked McAllister.

"I don't know," said the man. "But they were real close to her. One guy actually had his arm around her waist. And she didn't look very happy, now that I recall. But it's not like she was screaming or anything."

"Did you see if they got into a car?" asked Bertrand.

"No, I didn't go outside."

At that point McAllister called in the local police. The employee was given over to a sketch artist to provide a description of the two men. Security footage from the previous night was checked, but there was no sign of Pine on any of it. McAllister speculated that the men might not have been parked in the lot, but perhaps right in front of the hotel.

"But why would they have targeted her?" asked McAllister after they had finished with the local cops.

"I don't know," said Blum. She did explain about Dolores Venuti's having been arrested, and having gone to see her in the detention facility. "Besides having enslaved a young girl, she apparently was running some sort of drug enterprise. These men might have been working for her as part of that."

McAllister and Bertrand went to consult with the local cops about this possible lead, leaving Blum all alone in the lobby.

She walked around in a bit of a daze until she passed by the front desk. The clerk who had been on duty the previous evening walked into the lobby and spotted her.

"Ma'am?"

"Yes."

"The guest you and your friend were looking for yesterday?"

Blum instantly tensed. "Yes?"

"She came back last night."

"She did?"

"Yep. I recognized her. Eloise Cain. She sort of stands out. When I was driving in I saw her out jogging. When I pulled into the parking lot, she was going into the gym through the outdoor entrance."

"Thank you so much."

He smiled. "Hey, sorry we got off on the wrong foot. Where's your agent friend?"

"I wish I knew," said Blum. "How do I get to the gym?"

Praying with every step, Blum found the gym and approached the door. She peeked through the window and saw a very tall woman in a tank top and sweat-pants lifting a stack of weights on the universal machine. Her muscles were taut and defined, and for a moment Blum thought she was staring at her boss minus the hair.

She used the key card to access the door. When it opened El Cain looked over at her. She seemed puzzled, because Blum was clearly not dressed for working out.

Blum thought for a moment about how best to handle this. Finally, she decided, in the urgency of the moment, that the direct approach was best.

"Mercy Pine? Your twin sister, FBI Special Agent Atlee Pine, has been kidnapped from this hotel, and I need your help to find her."

47

Cain slowly rose, towering over Blum, who had stepped a bit closer to her.

"Who in the hell are you?" said Cain.

"My name is Carol Blum. I work at the FBI. My boss is Atlee Pine, your twin sister. We've been trying to find you for a long time now."

"I don't have a sister, twin or otherwise."

Blum took something from her purse and held it out to Cain, who snatched it and looked down at the photo. "That's a picture that Agent Pine had of you and her and your mother when you were living in Andersonville, Georgia. It's a Polaroid, the only one she had of you as sisters. I've been carrying it for her as we look for you."

Cain's gaze took in every aspect of the images. Things, murky elements in her memory, started to jostle back and forth, like bumper cars. The effect was as jarring as real bumper cars would be. "My mother?"

"Yes."

"And this Atlee, you say she's my sister?"

"That's right."

Cain thrust the photo back at Blum. "That's a crock of shit. I've never even heard of anyone named Atlee." She grabbed her hoodie and stalked off toward the door.

"But I'm telling you the truth."

Cain whipped back around and shouted, "Leave me the hell alone, lady. I don't need this shit, especially right now."

As Cain turned away from her Blum frantically thought for a moment and then cried out, "You called her *Lee* when you were kids."

On this, Cain froze in the doorway of the gym. She expected every muscle in her body to tense, but instead they relaxed, like a tired swimmer's did, after getting safely back to shore.

It's okay, Momma, it's just Lee being Lee. She'll find her way down. She always does. Don't be mad at her, Momma.

Cain now began to tremble. The calm was gone. The bumper cars in her head were now smacking each other with increasing velocity. It actually hurt, not like a headache. It was like someone had lit a match to her soul. But she needed more than a name and an old picture.

She turned to Blum. "There are lots of girls named Lee."

"Your mother's name was . . . Julia," Blum said tentatively.

Cain shook her head. "Means nothing to me."

She again turned to leave while Blum desperately

tried to think of something, anything to hold her. Then she remembered their meeting with Desiree, what the woman had said about the book that had driven Mercy into a frenzy. Maybe she would remember that.

"Eeny, meeny, miny, moe," Blum blurted out.

Cain whipped around. "What?"

"The nursery rhyme the kidnapper used to choose between the two of you. 'Eeny, meeny, miny, moe.' Do you recall that?"

Cain sagged against the wall and then abruptly sat down on one of the weight stack benches.

Blum said in a sympathetic tone. "I know this is all overwhelming. The truth is, the man who abducted you that night was named Ito Vincenzo. And we know why he took you. And that he gave you to Len and Wanda Atkins. Who, in turn, gave you to Desiree and Joe."

Cain said dully, "Wanda told me that. And Desiree is in jail here, I found that out."

"Your sister is the one who arrested her. Desiree had imprisoned another young girl named Gail. We freed her. Desiree is being charged with that crime, among others." She paused. "And we got her to confess to killing Joe Atkins, Mercy. We have the recording. She confessed to stabbing him to death."

Cain looked at her, blinking back tears and shaking her head slowly. "This . . . this is sort of . . ."

". . . too much to process?"

Cain nodded, her features pained.

Blum sat down beside her. "Of course it is, Mercy. Or do you prefer El?"

"Mercy really is my name?"

"Yes, it is. Mercy Pine."

"Then . . . um, Mercy . . . is okay."

Blum said, "I know you must have a million things running through your head right now, and I don't mean to add to your burden. But there are some things you absolutely need to know."

"Like what?"

"That other FBI agents are here at this hotel. They came to interview Agent Pine about Tim Pine. But they know nothing about your being here, too."

Mercy wrinkled her brow. "Tim Pine?"

"You and your sister believed he was your biological father. That was not true. Another man was your father, but Tim raised you with your mother until you were taken when you were six years old. He was thought to have killed himself, but now we know that wasn't true. The FBI now knows that the man killed wasn't your father but Ito Vincenzo."

"The guy who took me?"

"Yes."

"Wanda said he was connected to the mob or something and had a grudge against my mother."

"He kidnapped you and then years later he tried to kill Tim Pine. Only Tim was able to kill him

317

instead. The body was identified as Tim's by a friend and your mother. And Tim vanished."

"Jesus Christ," said Mercy, letting out a chest of air.

Blum patted Mercy's shoulder. "I know I've just dumped a lot into your lap. But my goal now is to keep the FBI away from you because I'm not sure how all that will play out."

"But you said Desiree confessed to Joe's murder!" Mercy exclaimed. "Doesn't that put me in the clear on that?"

"Desiree did confess, but the FBI doesn't know that yet. The proof of that is on your sister's phone. And it *will* put you in the clear, as you said. The problem right now is we have her phone but no way to get into it. So I want to keep you and the Bureau separate until we find Agent Pine."

"You said she was kidnapped?"

"Yes, from this hotel last night by two men. Now either they were working with Desiree, who was also dealing drugs, and are perhaps trying to use Agent Pine as leverage to get Desiree out of prison. Or they are tied to you somehow and took Agent Pine in order to make her tell everything she knows about you."

"But who would be after me?"

"I don't know. Do you have any enemies? Anyone looking for you?"

"I don't think I have enemies who would snatch an FBI agent. I mean, I'm not that important. I just have an ordinary life. I don't have any friends—or enemies, really."

"Then maybe it *is* Desiree. She might be working with some very dangerous people."

"How did you know I was here?"

"Agent Pine saw you in this gym yesterday, only she didn't know it was you at the time." She looked at Mercy's head. "She couldn't have known you would shave your hair off. She spoke to Wanda Atkins. Wanda told Agent Pine that she gave you Desiree's phone number when you saw her."

"I used that to track Desiree down here."

"Yes, that's what we thought. When Wanda told her that and described what you looked like now, Agent Pine immediately realized that it had to be you in the gym. By the time she got there you were gone. We found out your room number but you had left by then."

"I did leave. But then I decided to come back. I . . . I had spent a lot of money on the hotel room and I thought . . . I thought I should at least spend the night."

"I would have done the same thing," said Blum kindly.

"Do you have any idea where they might have taken Lee?" asked Mercy.

"No. We only have the statement of a hotel employee that it was two men who abducted her. He gave a description, and the FBI is working on it with the local police. But I'm not sure they have any leads to go on."

"And that picture of me on the TV?"

"Agent Pine had that put up. We found where you were being kept, and saw the last tape that Joe Atkins made. That's where that image came from."

"Desiree really did kill him, then?"

"Yes. Joe apparently was going to let you go. Desiree was having none of that. She stabbed him and ran for it. Len and Wanda helped her get away."

Mercy shook her head. "So now I know I have a twin sister and we come close to finding each other and now *she's* been taken. Just like I was all those years ago. How messed up is that?"

"Very," said Blum quietly.

Mercy glanced up. "Do . . . do I look like her?"

"You're a couple of inches taller, and she has long dark hair. But in the face and eyes, I can most definitely see it. Absolutely."

Mercy nodded and looked down again. "How do we find her?"

"I'm not sure."

"If Desiree is connected to this, she might know who took her."

"Yes, but she's in jail."

"Then let's go talk to her there. I've been meaning to talk to Desiree for a lot of years now." She glanced up at Blum. "And we have nothing to lose, right?"

"Right." Blum attempted a smile, but it never reached her eyes because she obviously did not like this idea at all.

Mercy rose, and her big hands curled into fists. "Then let's go."

48

"Is this your car?" asked Mercy as they climbed into the Porsche SUV. Blum had taken the keys from Pine's room.

Mercy had changed into jeans and another hoodie, and checked out of the hotel; she had put her duffel in the back seat.

"Good Lord, no. I can't afford this."

"Then it's Lee's?"

"No, she can't afford it, either. It . . . it belongs to a man named Jack Lineberry. He's very wealthy, and he let us use it."

"And what's his connection to all this? Why did he let you borrow his wheels?"

Blum put the key in the ignition and started the engine. "I suppose you have to know this, and now is as good a time as any."

"Know what?"

"Jack Lineberry is your biological father."

Mercy took this calmly. She nodded and glanced out the window. "So our mom was quite the guy magnet?"

"I don't think it was like that at all. He was her handler when she was working undercover to bring down some Mafia families. They . . . they had feelings for each other. Or something like that, and your mother became pregnant with you and your sister."

"So how did she end up with this *Tim* guy?"

"They fell in love. Jack is quite a bit older than your mother, and their . . . relationship might have had more to do with the work they were doing, at least for your mother. I have to say that Jack Lineberry was very much in love with your mother, and probably still is."

"And where is our mother?"

"With Tim, presumably."

"And Lee? Where is she in all this?"

"When your sister was in college, your mother left her without any real explanation. She doesn't know where your mother is." Blum studied her closely. "You're taking all this quite calmly."

"Well, it's no more earth-shattering than anything else you've already told me in the last ten minutes."

This blunt statement made Blum smile. "You are more like your sister than you know."

"Am I?" Mercy said dubiously. "My life has been very different from hers, apparently."

"I know some of what you went through with Desiree."

"I dreamed of killing her a thousand times."

"I'm sure you have."

"I came here to kill her."

"Yes, Agent Pine assumed that."

"Agent Pine, huh? FBI and everything? Didn't know they had many gals doing that."

"She's an excellent agent, one of the very best." Blum pulled out of the parking lot and headed toward the street.

"Good for her," said Mercy, but the voiced compliment rang hollow. "And you've been looking for me for a while now?"

"Yes. It's been quite the journey, with a lot of twists and turns."

"Yeah, I bet."

Blum glanced at her.

"What have you been doing all this time, Mercy?"

"Just surviving. Like everybody else."

"It will be difficult for you to see Desiree, won't it?"

"It may be more difficult for *her* than me."

Blum said sharply, "You didn't escape from that awful woman just so she could put you back in prison, did you?"

"I feel like I have every right to kill her."

"But if you do, she wins. And I know you're smart enough to know that. But if you can't promise me you won't attack her, then we're not going to see Desiree."

"She may be the only lead to find your boss."

"And your *sister*. So unless you're prepared to hold back your natural anger, we're not going to be able to find Agent Pine, which means she'll probably die."

"I should have more feelings for her," said Mercy, perhaps with a degree of honesty that startled even her. "But it's been a long time. And a lot of shit happened in between. And she got to stay home. I lost the rhyme. I got pitched into the nightmare."

Blum pursed her lips. "Ito Vincenzo, the man who kidnapped you, also cracked your sister's skull that night. She lay there all night with her brain bleeding. It was only a miracle that she lived after a long time in the hospital. That night destroyed your family. Your sister later thought Tim killed himself, but your mother lied about that. Then she left to join Tim, as I said, leaving your sister all alone. It seems that Vincenzo apparently thought he was taking you to a *good* situation, where you would be taken care of. He knew nothing about Desiree. So I think, at least in his mind, that you were the *winner* of the rhyme and your sister was the loser."

Blum looked over at Mercy to find her glowering at her.

"I wasn't a winner in any way, shape, or form."

Blum said hastily, "Of course you weren't. I'm only saying that Vincenzo meant to kill your sister, not you."

Mercy settled back in her seat and glanced out the window.

Blum said, "And, unlike you, Agent Pine has very firm memories of you. She's lived with that loss for the last thirty years."

Mercy said in a far calmer tone, "Desiree managed

to beat those memories out of me. I remember snatches here and there. The name Lee. The fact that somebody else was there, you know?"

"Yes, I can understand that."

"But it's not the same as having memories. It's just shit in your head you can't make sense of. Like somebody gave you a book to read but first smeared all the words so badly that you can only make a couple out. It's . . . a hard thing to live with, knowing it's there somewhere, but never being able to find it." She looked over at Blum. "Sorry if how I talk doesn't measure up. You said your boss went to college and everything. I may sound dumb, but I'm mostly not. I read a lot. Books got me through a bunch'a shit."

"You sound just fine to me. And I think given what happened to you, it's a miracle you're even alive."

"I don't give up. I never have. You hurt me, I just try harder."

"That is exactly who your sister is."

Mercy nodded but didn't comment.

"And Desiree?" asked Blum nervously.

Mercy didn't answer right away. "I won't lay a hand on her."

"And why is that?"

"Because you're right. I don't want to lose, especially to *that* bitch." A moment of quiet passed and then she added, "And maybe I'd like a shot at meeting my sister. Alive."

49

Mercy followed Blum, who was trailing Deputy Tate Callum down the hall toward the cell holding Desiree Atkins. And she was sweating. For two reasons. First, she was in a jail surrounded by cops; that was bad enough. She'd been in jail on the other side of the bars, and this was bringing back all those memories. Second, she was about to see the woman who had tortured and then very nearly killed her a long time ago. She knew which was worse: the flesh-and-blood woman easily won over the steel bars.

Callum glanced at Blum. "And where is Agent Pine today?"

"Tied up. She just wanted me to follow up on a few questions. *Agent* Cain here is assisting us."

They had come up with that story on the way over.

Callum eyed Mercy. "So, you work undercover, Agent Cain?"

Mercy smiled, ran a hand over her scalp, and touched her stained sweatshirt. "What was your first clue? Other than the fact that I don't have my badge with me?"

He laughed. "Right. Boy, they grow the ladies tall at the Bureau, don't they?"

They reached the cell door and Callum opened it and ushered them through. "Just let the jailer know when you're done." He closed the door behind them and headed back down the hall.

Desiree turned and saw Mercy. "Holy shit!"

Mercy said nothing. She just stared down at the woman.

Desiree backed up against the wall. "Don't you dare come near me." She glared at Blum. "What the hell do you think you're doing bringing this psycho here?"

"I thought it was high time you two were finally reunited." Blum failed to hide a smile.

Mercy looked around and then sat down on the lower bunk. "Nice, clean digs, Desiree. You should be able to make do in a place like this for, what, the rest of your shitty life?"

"They've got nothing on me. You just wait until I get myself a lawyer."

"Heard you pulled the same crap with another girl like you did with me. Sounds like she got away from you a lot faster than I did. You must be losing your touch."

"Shut up!"

"It's a wonder I was ever scared of you. I mean, you

look like a plump little mouse ready to be eaten. And I can eat a lot."

"I scared you well enough back then."

"Not that hard to do with a six-year-old. A lot harder to do with a sixteen-year-old. And damn impossible to do right now."

Desiree shook her head. "You're full of it! You had no idea who you were dealing with."

"The harder you tried to hurt me, the farther inside my head I went. Then your little fantasy fell apart and you left me alone. So guess who won the head game?"

"You think I care about any of this?"

Mercy smiled broadly. "I'll testify at your trial. I can be exhibits A to Z on your being a sadistic bitch." She looked over at Blum. "And now this lady wants to ask you some questions."

"Go to hell."

"That's not very nice," said Mercy.

Blum interjected, "If you help us, Desiree, maybe we can help you."

"How?"

"The police know you were running a drug operation. They want to know who you were working with. If you can tell them that, they can work a deal on your sentencing."

Desiree's face lighted up for a moment and then went hard again. "Well, they better make it a damn good deal or they get squat from me."

"What can you tell us?"

"Nothing, until I get a deal in writing." She smiled maliciously. "But the guys I work with, they are some bad hombres."

"Do you think they know you've been arrested?"

"They're not stupid, okay?"

"But you haven't spoken with them?"

She looked at Blum curiously. "Why do you want to know? And where is that other FBI bitch? Why isn't she with you?"

Blum looked at Mercy and then returned her gaze to Desiree. "I'll see what I can come up with. But if I do come back with an offer, can you help us?"

"Help you do what exactly?"

"I'll let you know once we have a deal in place."

Blum walked over to the door. "Officer?" she called out between the bars.

As the man headed toward them Desiree said to Mercy, "You think you're all high and mighty now?"

Mercy didn't even look at her. "Compared to you, I am."

"You're just big and ugly. An animal, that's all you'll ever be."

"And loving every minute of it."

They left her there and walked back down the hall to meet up with Callum.

They passed an older man with graying hair, thick jowls, and a pretentious expression, heading the other way. He was dressed in a sleek, dark blue suit with a red tie and a pocket square. He had a black leather briefcase in one hand. He glanced at Blum and Mercy and came away obviously unimpressed. The jailer escorting him said, "It's right down this way, Mr. Marbury."

As they were out of earshot Mercy said, "I don't trust people in suits who carry briefcases."

"Well, you just knocked out the entire legal profession."

"I know."

Blum said, "I'm not sure she'll be able to help us. I think she was lying about the bad hombres. That's why I didn't mention what had happened to Agent Pine. There would have been no point."

"But if the guys working with her didn't snatch Lee, who did?"

Blum said glumly, "I don't know. And we're running out of time. I can just feel it."

Back with Callum, Blum talked to him about a possible deal in exchange for information on Pine's whereabouts.

"I'm certainly sorry to hear about Agent Pine," said Callum. "But I don't think we can do any deals, at least not right now."

"Why?"

"Because the lady is represented by counsel now. He'll have to come up to speed and then we'll have to have the prosecutors meet with him. If we don't go by the book, we can jeopardize our entire case."

"Who's her lawyer? A local guy?"

"Nope. Guy named Marbury, Stephen Marbury. He's in from New York. You probably passed him in the hall. Older guy, gray hair, dressed in a suit that probably costs more than my truck."

Mercy said, "That's the jerk we passed in the hall. *He's* her lawyer?"

"That's right. Just flew into town, he said."

Blum thanked Callum for his help, told him not to mention them to the lawyer, and then she led Mercy outside.

They climbed into the Porsche and eyed the black Escalade that was idling out in front of the detention center, with the driver on his phone.

Mercy said, "Probably Marbury's ride. He looked like a guy who gets driven around."

"So maybe we wait around and see where that ride takes him."

"Maybe to my sister?" said Mercy.

"Maybe," said Blum in a distracted tone.

"What's the matter?" asked Mercy, glancing at her.

"Something Desiree said," Blum suddenly exclaimed. "Stay here, I'll be right back."

She hurried back into the facility. About two minutes later, she came out and got back into the Porsche.

"So what's going on?" asked Mercy.

"I just talked to Callum. He said Desiree has made

no phone calls since she's been here. And you recall she told us she was *going to get* a lawyer?"

Mercy nodded slowly, thinking this through. "So if she made no calls and said she was going to get a lawyer, she obviously had no idea this Marbury dude was even coming today."

"So if Desiree didn't send for this high-powered lawyer from New York, who did?"

50

Peter Buckley listened on his phone for a few minutes. He liked to listen. That was the way one learned things. When you talked, you gave away things.

He said, "Fine. But I want to meet face-to-face and you can give me a fuller briefing. I'll text you the address. I've arranged a place for the *very* short-term."

He put his phone back in his pocket and returned to the room where Pine was seated in the chair. They had tied her to it this time, so if any more beatings happened, she wouldn't fall off it. Britt Spector stood off to one side, watching, a nervous expression on her features.

"Agent Pine," said Buckley. "The woman you arrested is Dolores Venuti. She is accused, among other things, of kidnapping a child and holding her prisoner."

Pine said, "I know that."

"Why do I think Dolores Venuti and Desiree Atkins are one and the same?"

"Think what you want," replied Pine. "It's a free country."

"You won't confirm it?"

"No."

"I've also heard that Dolores will try to make bail."

"That'll never happen. She's a flight risk." Pine caught herself a beat too late.

Buckley allowed himself a brief smile. "Right. She's a flight risk because you told them about what happened in Georgia. Good, thank you for confirming my theory that Dolores and Desiree are one and the same. As for the bail, we will have to see. Court decisions are sometimes unpredictable."

"Not this time."

"But if she does make bail I will pay her to tell me what she knows."

"Desiree hasn't seen the woman in nearly twenty years. What could she possibly tell you?"

"One never knows until one asks."

"And if you talk to her, then you'll just drop me back at the hotel all safe and sound?" said Pine in a blistering tone.

Buckley eyed Spector before answering. "I will give you one more chance to tell me all you know about El Cain. Then, your death is not inevitable. You have my word."

"Your *word*? Don't think so. I pass."

"Are you sure?"

"What I'm sure of is that I was dead the moment

I let your goons get the drop on me. But if you're going to kill me anyway, you have no reason not to tell me why you want Cain so badly."

"I told you. She killed someone."

"But you didn't tell me who."

"That is no concern of yours."

"Come on. I give you *my* word, I won't tell anyone. Not that I'll be able to."

Buckley hesitated, his mind working rapidly, perhaps too rapidly. "My brother."

Spector shot him a disapproving look, but said nothing.

"And did he deserve it?"

"Without a doubt he did."

"So what's your beef with her, then?"

"He was my family. That's enough reason for me."

"I can see how you might think that. But thinking like that tends to get you killed."

"I like my odds better than yours right now."

"So when will you know if Desiree makes bail?" she said.

"Soon."

"Well, I've got lots of time then."

Buckley eyed her closely. "You are brave. I like that in a person."

"Thanks, now go fuck yourself."

Spector smiled at this comment, but turned away so Buckley wouldn't see.

"Are you sure you don't want to reconsider? It is

possible that you know a lot more about the matter than Desiree does. I'm a man who prefers as much information as possible."

"Repeat in your head what I just said to you."

A visibly frustrated Buckley turned and left, beckoning Spector to join him. Spector eyed Pine for a long moment. Judging by her expression, a number of troubling thoughts were going through her mind. Then she turned and followed Buckley out.

51

Pine listened as additional sets of footsteps followed those of the two people who had already left. Then another one after that. The light was turned off, driving her even deeper into darkness. The door was closed and locked. And then a few seconds later all became quiet as the sound of the footfalls vanished.

She waited a bit longer and then leaned so far forward in the chair that the back legs came off the floor. Her knees edged down to touch the concrete, so there was barely any noise. They had tied her ankles individually to the chair legs, but had not run the rope through the crossbeam. That was a big mistake. She slowly turned to the side and simply straightened her own legs to free them. Then she was able to stand with the chair still attached to her.

The blindfold had slipped enough with her maneuvers that part of it was close to her mouth. She bit down on the fabric and jerked her head to the left and right. The cloth slipped enough to where she could see. She looked at the wall, turned, and backed toward it until the chair bumped into it.

She bent forward so the lower half of the chair and the back legs were right against the wall. Then she slowly applied weight and thus pressure until she could feel the wood begin to give. She kept going, slowly. The last thing she needed was some explosion of sound to bring her captors running.

The left leg separated first and then the right. Then the bottom half of the chair came apart from the top. The next minute the whole thing was splitting apart at various spots. She got her hands free of the restraints and quietly pulled the chair off her. She ripped away the blindfold and looked around at the darkened space. No windows. Solid walls. One door in and out. Slab floor. She slipped over to the door, and put her ear against it. She could hear nothing. If someone had been on the other side, they would have already come bursting in here. She tried the door, but it was locked. She had no phone, no lockpick kit, no guns.

She was alone with no way to get help.

Instead of feeling hopeless, she saw it as a challenge, an obstacle to be overcome. And it wasn't like she had anything else to do while they were waiting to kill her.

Pine looked around the space and saw some boxes stacked by the wall. In one was an emergency radio with a built-in light and other features. She popped the battery compartment and snagged the old batteries in there; some had their ends ruptured where the

chemicals had seeped through. She laid out the batteries on their sides in front of the door, pocketed one
of them, and then stood on the chair Buckley had
used and unscrewed the light bulb. Then she climbed
down and went to stand by the door.

Pine stood there for more than an hour until she
heard footsteps—fortunately, only one set.

She moved back against the wall.

The door was unlocked and then it opened. She
saw in the darkness a hand move to the light switch
as the person entered the room. No light came on,
obviously. Then the feet reached the batteries under-
foot, and the person fell heavily.

That was the only opportunity Pine needed. She
could see his outline on the floor from the scant illumination coming from the next room. She smashed
her foot right into his diaphragm to keep him from
crying out. Her next shot was an elbow strike to the
head, which bounced his cranium off the concrete
with the same level of whiplash a rear-end car accident might inflict. The impact knocked him cold.

She searched him and pulled out his pistol. Fortunately, in his other pocket was her shield. She used
the rope from the chair to secure his hands and feet,
and then she slid him over to a corner of the room.

Pine looked closely at his face. This was one of the
men who had kidnapped her from the hotel. She
doubted this was the guy who had been talking to
her. That man was clearly the boss, and head honchos

seldom did the dirty work. She clocked him one more time in the face just for the hell of it.

She moved out into the next room after shutting the door behind her and locking it. Then she quietly made her way across the room and up the stairs, and reached the top landing. The door was partially open. She did a turkey peek that revealed nothing. She did a second look and saw a man sitting at a table looking at his phone with his earbuds in. He was the other guy who had snatched her. She stuck her head out and surveyed the rest of the room.

Empty. But that was not good enough. There was no room for error here; she only had one shot to do this right.

She took out the battery with her left hand and hurled it at the window behind the guy. As soon as it struck the glass, the man jumped up from the table, dropping his phone on the floor, and cried out, "What the hell!"

Pine waited three seconds to see if the tossed battery drew anyone else out into the open. When it was clear the man was alone, she stepped through the doorway and pointed the gun at him.

"On your knees, hands behind your head, then lie down face-first, legs spread. Do it now or I *will* shoot you."

The man saw the gun, fell to the floor, and put his hands behind his head.

Pine quickly moved forward and used the butt of

the gun to inflict two hard taps on his skull, knocking him out. He got the same trussed-up treatment as his partner downstairs, with a cord of thick twine she found in a cabinet.

She snagged his phone and called 911, told the dispatcher who she was and what had happened, and asked her to notify Tate Callum of her circumstances.

"Do you know where you are?" the dispatcher asked.

"Give me a sec."

She ran outside and looked around at the thick woods surrounding the house in which she'd been held captive. "In the middle of nowhere. Seems to be a lot of that around here."

"Okay, we can trace you by your phone. Just leave it on."

She looked down at the phone. "The battery is really low. It might die on me, and I'm not hanging around here, because some other people might show up. I'm going to walk out to the main road. That might give me a better idea where I am. Hold on."

Pine ran down the long, twisty drive, finally reached the main street, and found a mailbox with a number address on it and then a street sign farther down. She gave this information to the dispatcher.

The dispatcher said, "I'll have officers there as fast as possible. Be careful, Agent Pine."

Next, Pine was about to call Blum when—

"Shit." She looked down at the screen as the iPhone's juice ran out and it went dark.

The last thing she wanted to do was go back to the house and search for a phone charger. A moment later, an ancient, rattling Ford pickup truck with a license plate designating it as an antique appeared around a curve and headed her way. Pine stood in the middle of the street with her shield held up high. When the driver slowed and stopped, Pine rushed forward. Behind the wheel was a white-haired woman in her eighties, wearing faded bib overalls, a straw hat, and a wry smile.

"I'm an FBI agent," Pine said, showing her the shield. The woman squinted at it and then pulled up her glasses, which dangled on a chain, to see it better.

"My, my, that's very impressive, young lady."

"I need you to drive me to a hotel in downtown Asheville." She told the woman the address, then added, "It's an emergency."

"Sure, honey. I know where that is. Get in."

Pine jumped into the passenger seat and the woman said, "Do I get to break the speed limit since it's an emergency?"

Pine said, "Do whatever you need to do to get me there as fast as possible. Any cops stop us, I'll deal with it. Do you have a cell phone I can use?"

The woman shook her head. "Had one of them flip phones once, but I never got the hang of it. Every time that thing rang in my pocket, nearly scared me to death."

"Great," said Pine under her breath.

"Now, let's get going," the old woman said as she sat up straighter, took off her glasses, and rammed down the gas pedal.

The truck leapt forward but then settled into a sedate forty miles per hour pace.

The woman looked over at her and smiled. "This truck belonged to my father. Got it wound all the way up, missy. All hundred and forty horsepower. Can you feel it? We'll be there lickety-split. This is so exciting."

"Yes, ma'am" was all Pine could manage.

52

"There he is," said Blum.

Stephen Marbury had just walked out of the detention facility. He had a pleased expression on his face as he climbed into the back of the Escalade. As soon as the door closed, the vehicle drove off.

Blum put the Porsche in gear and followed at a discreet distance.

Mercy said, "You really think this is connected to Lee's disappearance?"

"I would be shocked if it weren't. But I've been to Desiree's house. If she was working with a drug ring that has this kind of legal muscle, I would have thought she'd be more affluent."

"She might be socking it away and living light to avoid suspicion," opined Mercy.

Blum glanced at her. "You'd make a good detective."

"I've lived life and learned my lessons," replied Mercy tersely.

The Escalade turned onto the main road and sped

up. Both vehicles traveled several blocks in moderate traffic before stopping at a red light.

"Do you remember anything of your life before you went to the Atkinses?" asked Blum. "Except what you've already told me?"

"I sort of remember my mother. She was tall, too. I remember Lee being up in a tree. And I went back to the Atkinses' place in Crawfordville, to my little prison. Found my doll, Sally, and took it. She's in my duffel."

"It must have been painful reliving all that."

"It was, at first. And then I remembered that I survived *all that*."

The light changed and they started up again.

"I wonder where he's going," said Mercy.

"Hopefully to a place that will lead us to Agent Pine."

"Do you like working with her?"

"It's the best job I've ever had."

"Lee sounds perfect," Mercy said with a bit of snark.

Blum glanced at Mercy. "If that was your impression from what I said, then I said it wrong. She grew up largely alone. Even when her mother was there, she told me that she really wasn't. After what happened, it was like your mother both smothered your sister as far as never letting her out of sight, but then cut her off emotionally."

Mercy looked over at Blum, her expression now

more nuanced. "That must've been tough. A double whammy, 'cause I kind of remember Lee liked to do stuff Mom didn't want her to do, but then Mom was really proud of her for doing it. That seemed to mean a lot to Lee, like they were real tight."

"I'm a mother. I know how important maternal nurturing is. Nothing comes close to what you endured, but Agent Pine has suffered the effects of that motherly absence, too."

Mercy nodded and looked thoughtfully out the window. "And my dad is this Jack Lineberry character? How exactly did that shake out?"

"He worked at a government agency. I'm not sure which one. As I said, he was your mother's handler. They developed feelings for each other and acted on those feelings. I'm sure it was a very difficult time for both of them. Jack was actually engaged to someone else, but then he fell in love with your mother. And . . . and then they . . . got together and your mother became pregnant with you and your sister."

Mercy smiled. "You have a nice, polite way with words, Carol. You mean they had sex and out popped twins."

"That's one way to describe it," said Blum primly. She turned left to follow the Escalade.

"And where is this Lineberry guy now?"

"He's at his estate in Georgia."

"Estate, huh? Must be nice."

"He's leaving everything to you and Agent Pine, by

the way. All his wealth. You will be a very rich woman when the time comes."

Blum glanced at Mercy to see her reaction to this. It wasn't what she expected. Or maybe it was.

Mercy was frowning. "I get by just fine. I don't need big bucks from a guy who screwed my mom."

"Well, it will come to you eventually. And you can do with it what you want."

"You're assuming I outlive the guy. Nothing is guaranteed," she added bluntly.

"No argument there."

Five minutes later Blum said, "It looks like we have arrived."

The Escalade had slowed and turned into a long drive that led up to a substantial home on about five acres.

"Well, whoever we're dealing with has some bucks of his own," noted Mercy.

Blum slowed the Porsche and pulled past the driveway the Escalade had turned into. Then she drove on and turned into the parking lot of a church that was down the street a bit. There were other cars in the parking lot, and she edged in between two of them so as not to stand out.

She stared across the street at the house.

"They might have Agent Pine in there."

"Maybe so. Now what do we do?"

"We could call the police, but we really have no

grounds to do so. And if they come and find nothing in there, the people will know we're on to them."

"I can go take a look," offered Mercy.

"No, it's too dangerous. If they are in there, they could capture or kill you."

"Then what—we just wait out here while they might be in there hurting Lee?"

Blum looked torn. "But you have no experience doing this sort of thing."

"Let me tell you something, I've kicked the shit out of more 'tough' guys than any gal you'll ever meet, including your boss. There's a lot to worry about with this, but me not being able to handle myself ain't one of them."

"But—"

Mercy started to open the door. "I'll be careful. I'll just go and take a peek. Okay?"

Blum's defenses crumbled away. "Are you sure?"

"As sure as my name is Mercy Pine." She leaned into the back seat, zipped open her duffel, and took out her Glock in the belt clip.

When Blum saw it she said, "Do you have a permit for that?"

"Where I got it, you don't need a permit or a background check. And North Carolina is an 'open carry without a permit' state. I checked that before I came here."

"Why did you do that?"

Mercy put the clip holster on her waistband and

covered it with her sweatshirt. "I don't like to get hassled by the cops if I can avoid it. What's your phone number? I'll text or call you if something pops."

Blum gave her the number, and Mercy put it in her contacts list. Then Blum opened the glove box, plucked out a pair of small binoculars, and handed them to Mercy.

"Thanks. I feel like a real spy now."

Blum said, "Please, please be careful. I don't want to lose both sisters."

Mercy got out, looked both ways down the road, then hustled across the street. She made a wide berth around the target property and promptly disappeared from sight.

Blum sat back in her seat, ran a shaky hand over her forehead, and started to pray.

53

A preoccupied Buckley sat in a chair in the dining room of the house, where the large furnishings still looked small in relation to the enormous space. Spector moodily leaned against the wall, while Stephen Marbury paced restlessly in front of them.

The house was closed for the season; its owners were at their other home in Colorado, which was probably even more splendid than this one. The property manager had been paid a large fee to allow them to use it for a couple of hours as a safe meeting place. No faces, no names, just cash.

"This puts *me* in a bit of a pickle, Mr. Buckley," said Marbury, who, while he paced, seemed focused on the state of his wingtips rather than the measure of his client.

Buckley was barely listening. The phone call he'd gotten had more than ruined his day. Agent Pine had escaped. His men had been found, revived, and relocated before the police arrived, thankfully, but that was small consolation for the problems Pine's gaining her freedom could potentially cause him. He said absently, "I never told Pine you had been hired by me. Only that Dolores Venuti would be seeking bail. I didn't even say you would be the one seeking it. The connection is tenuous at best."

"But I met with her today. They are bound to make the connection. And I had to identify myself to the police at the detention facility. They know who I am. They know I'm from New York. They can easily track me down."

Buckley said distractedly, "Then I suggest that a vacation is in order. In another country. I can make the arrangements."

Marbury started to whine. "It's not that easy. I have other clients. I have a practice. I have a family."

"Then go back to New York, and when the police question you, you will merely tell them that you received a cashier's check for ten thousand dollars to come here and meet with Atkins, or Venuti, rather. You don't know who sent it but you presumed she would know. When she didn't have a clue, you were as puzzled as she was. I can provide the cashier's check drawn on an untraceable account, backdated. You can say you hadn't cashed it yet because you weren't sure you were going to take the case. You came down here to get the lay of the land. Because you *are* a prominent member of the bar, after all. Now that you know the state of things, you want no more part in it. You have never officially appeared as her counsel or filed the requisite papers legally attaching yourself to her case. That will be the end of it."

Marbury stopped pacing and stared at him, impressed. "That actually might work." He added in an admiring tone, "You would have made a fine lawyer."

"Yes, well, I've always aimed *higher* in life," Buckley said tersely, drawing a smile from Spector. "And now that *your* personal welfare is accounted for, please provide me with the information I need."

Buckley had called in Marbury so he could meet with Desiree Atkins and milk as much information out of the woman as possible under the pretense of legally representing her. There were few ways to get in to see a prisoner, but being a lawyer was one of them. Buckley had no interest in Atkins's being granted bail. He had tried to use the lawyer's being able to talk to Desiree as leverage to make Pine provide him with information about El Cain, in exchange for sparing Pine's life. And now Pine was out there somewhere, no doubt gunning for him.

Marbury sat down across from him, placed his hands on the table, and then clenched them. He looked ready to commence either begging for mercy or lying on the witness stand.

"She is an abominable woman. Insufferable whiner. Everything was someone else's fault. She's not quite right in the head, in my opinion. Might make for a good legal defense, actually."

"Yes, yes, most assuredly, I think we can safely conclude that any person who imprisons and tortures another is not in their right mind," said Buckley.

When Spector glanced at him with hiked eyebrows, he read her mind and added, "If it's done solely for the sadistic pleasure of the person doing the torturing. But if it's done for the purposes of obtaining vital information? Well, even our very own government has done *that*."

He looked back at Spector with a superior expression and she finally glanced away.

Marbury looked puzzled by this back-and-forth, but ended up ignoring it and plunging on. "Since I told her the attorney–client privilege would protect anything she said, the idiot woman told me that an FBI agent and her associate had tricked her into confessing to killing her husband in Georgia on the same night that this Rebecca Atkins escaped from where she was being imprisoned. She was furious about that and wanted me to get the evidence thrown out."

Spector stepped forward and said, "Did she question who sent you to her aid?"

"Not in the least. She strikes me as someone who sincerely believes that aid will come whenever she damn well needs it. The fact is, since she's a fugitive from justice, no judge would cut her loose. She'd simply disappear again."

Buckley clearly didn't care about bail or Desiree Atkins. "What did she tell you about El Cain?"

"She hadn't seen her since that night in Georgia." Marbury paused to rub at his mouth. "Until Cain walked into her jail cell earlier today with an older woman."

Buckley and Spector exchanged a significant glance.

"You didn't mention that on the phone. How did it come about?" asked a frowning Buckley.

"They just showed up. She had no idea they were coming. The older woman and Pine had visited Atkins previously. They said that they wanted to discuss doing some kind of deal with her. She didn't know the details yet. They were going to get back to her."

Buckley glanced at Spector. "You really need to work your contacts at the FBI to find out more about *Agent* Pine."

"I actually found out some things. I was going to discuss them with you when all this happened."

"Well, I'd like to hear them now."

"Okay, first, Pine's apparently a world-class agent, but she's definitely a lone wolf. She could have climbed the Bureau ladder, but has no interest in doing so. Currently, she's assigned to the Grand Canyon area and lives in a town called Shattered Rock. It's a one-agent RA," she added, referring to a small FBI Resident Agent office. "Carol Blum, the 'older woman,' is her assistant there. But it's odd that she's out in the field with Pine on a case. That's not how the Bureau operates. And this El Cain matter is obviously a cold case, so I was confused as to why Pine was even involved at all. I mean, it's not her area of responsibility. I asked that very question, but my contacts had no answers." She added in a warning tone, "But by all accounts, Peter, Pine is good, I mean really, really good. We need to tread carefully."

"Well, considering she escaped from us, I would tend to agree with you."

Marbury looked very uncomfortable hearing this. "Mr. Buckley, please, I can't be party to any of this. I have to tread cautiously here to maintain my legal career."

"Don't worry, Marbury, none of this will come back to you." He gave the lawyer a piercing look. "And if memory serves, weren't you part of El Chapo's defense team a few years ago?"

"Well, everyone is entitled to a proper legal defense," Marbury said primly.

"Right. Now tell me, how and why would Blum and Cain think Desiree would be of any use to them?"

"It seems that in addition to imprisoning people, my 'client' also is involved in a local drug ring. She admitted that to me when I questioned her about this deal they were discussing. While they never told her what they wanted from her, and they certainly didn't mention to her that this Agent Pine had gone missing, she speculated that they knew about the drug ring and might want information about that. She told them she wanted a sweetheart deal presented to her first no matter what they wanted from her. They left it at that with, I suppose, the understanding that they would go back and try to get such a deal for her."

Spector said, "That would make sense, Peter, since they have no idea that *you're* involved in this. They can't possibly know that it's someone with a beef against El Cain that's behind this and not someone connected to Atkins and this local drug ring."

This should have been good news to Buckley, but it wasn't. He had let slip to Pine that his motivation in going after Cain was the fact that she had killed *his* brother. Unless Cain had killed lots of people's brothers, that would narrow things down considerably. He had been an utter fool to have disclosed that, but he had never envisioned Pine's escaping. Which was a lesson to never assume anything. The only saving grace for him, perhaps, was that Cain might not know that his brother had actually died.

He looked up and caught Spector eyeing him. She was a smart, clever woman, he knew. And her look was clear; she was now thinking the same thing he was. He had screwed up. But he also knew she had said what she just had in front of Marbury to cover up this angle. The lawyer had no need to know. And that was yet another reason why he liked working with Britt Spector. She got it, when most others didn't.

Buckley let his thoughts wander down this road a bit. *But if Cain and Pine and Blum joined forces, and Cain was able to connect Ken as my brother and learned that he had died? That would lead right to me.*

"What else, Stephen?" Spector said to Marbury while keeping her gaze on Buckley.

"Well, Cain is very tall, very tough looking, and her hair is nearly shaved, like a buzz cut."

Buckley came out of his musings and snapped, "Atkins told you this? About the shaved hair? The only picture we had of her was with *long* hair. That was one reason my men made the mistake at the hotel in picking up Pine instead of Cain. They mistook her for Cain because they looked so much alike."

This comment had an extraordinary effect on Spector. She backed away, pulled out her phone, and did a series of searches while Buckley and Marbury continued their conversation.

She read through screen after screen until she got to one that left her slack-jawed.

"Peter?" She gestured for him to join her in a far corner of the room.

"What?" he asked impatiently.

"What you said about your guys mistaking Pine for Cain?"

"Yes?"

She held up her phone. "You need to see this. Now."

54

Buckley joined Spector in the corner of the room.

"What is so important?" he demanded. "What do I have to see?"

She said, "Pine has a Wikipedia page. Not of her own making. It was apparently a fan thing. When she was in college she tried out for the Olympics in powerlifting and barely missed making the team. I had looked at it before but I didn't read the whole thing. I thought it was just fluff. That was *my* mistake."

"And how the hell does that help us?" snapped Buckley.

She handed him the phone. "Read the *last* paragraph of the very last page. It's a bit of her personal bio from a long time ago. Shit, I should have found this out before, but none of my contacts at the Bureau mentioned it."

Buckley read the last paragraph and then glanced sharply at her. "Mercy *Pine*. Kidnapped from Andersonville, Georgia, and never seen again. Mercy Pine! They're *sisters*?"

"More than that. They're *identical* twins. So your men could be forgiven in confusing the two. And that would explain why she's working this case. And that also explains my Bureau contacts' not wanting to answer that question. It was probably only a need-to-know about what she was doing."

This explained a lot, thought Buckley. And it also started a kernel of an idea in his mind that was rapidly formulating into a strategy that would coincide nicely with what he had decided this whole thing really meant to him. But with Pine's having escaped it complicated things. Still, there was always a solution to every problem.

While he was thinking about this, Spector left her phone with Buckley and rejoined Marbury, who was still staring curiously at his employer.

Spector said, "You were talking about Cain's shaved head?"

Marbury finally drew his gaze from Buckley. "Yes, Atkins told me about that, but as it turned out, I saw it for myself. I didn't know it at the time, of course, because I hadn't yet met with Atkins. But I passed Blum and Cain in the hall on my way to see Atkins. They had apparently just finished speaking with her before I got there."

Buckley heard this and looked up from the phone, leaving thoughts of his developing strategy behind for now. His gaze shifted first to Spector and then to

Marbury. He said to the attorney, "Do you mean they left the building *before* you did?"

"I suppose so, yes."

"Where were your car and driver parked?"

"Right in front," replied Marbury. "It was the most convenient spot for me. Very close to the front door. I have a gimpy knee."

Spector said to Buckley, "To do any deal they would have to get a sign-off from the local police. Blum and Cain could have gone to speak with them after they left Atkins."

"At which time the local police would tell them that they could do nothing about any such deal at the moment because . . ." He looked at Marbury.

Marbury got the point like a knife between his ribs. "Because she was now, apparently, represented by counsel. By me."

Spector flitted to the window, but kept out of sight.

Buckley didn't even look at her because he knew exactly what she was thinking. He said sharply, "Marbury, would you even know if you had been followed here?"

The lawyer looked astonished. "Followed? I . . . I . . . that didn't occur to me."

"Of course it didn't," Spector interjected derisively. She took out a small but powerful optical device from her jacket pocket and surveyed both the street and the area beyond on the other side street. She saw nothing until she reached the church. There were a number of cars there. She was about to look along the street the other way when she adjusted the device and was able to make out something interesting. "There's a red Porsche SUV parked in the church lot down the street. It has Georgia plates." She adjusted the lens again, increasing the clarity. "And that might very well be our Ms. Blum at the wheel."

Buckley joined her at the window. "Any sign of Cain?"

"No, but she might have left Blum to do some closer surveillance." She looked across the room. "In fact, she might already be in *this* house."

Marbury looked at them with a stricken expression. "Are we in danger or what?"

Spector drew a gun from her shoulder holster. "Peter, I can check the house. If she is in here, our task just got a lot easier."

Marbury looked alarmed by this comment, but was smart enough to remain silent.

Buckley took the optical device and Spector told him where to aim it. He looked through the lens at the Porsche. In spite of it all, he smiled. His adrenaline had spiked, and with the blood rush came the thrill he'd been missing for too many years now, after having felt it every day of his life for a very long time. And best of all, the possible strategy, in the flash of creative brilliance, had turned into a definite resolution. The only one that mattered now.

He handed Spector back her optics.

She glanced expectantly at Buckley and was confused by the look in his eye. Where she thought she would see frustration and even desperation, she saw something else entirely.

She fingered her pistol and asked, "So do we go after Cain, retreat from her, or wait for her to try to find us here?"

"None of the above. I have a far better idea."

Mercy sat on her haunches and studied the rear of the house through the binoculars. The place was almost entirely built of stone with a few odd timbers and other materials thrown in for interesting architectural measure. It was private and well shrouded from the street with no close neighbors. A good pick if you were doing something bad, she thought. The Escalade was parked in front of the three-car garage. She could see the driver still inside scrolling down his phone. What she couldn't see, through the tinted side windows, was whether Marbury was still in the SUV or not. She doubted it. Why come here just to sit on his butt in the driveway?

She had sounded more confident with Blum than she felt right now. While it was true she could go toe-to-toe physically with just about anybody, she really didn't know what she was doing here. And it wasn't like her brief stint as a cheap security guard had prepared her to become a crackerjack sleuth. She did have some experience with breaking and entering, though. And if it had been dark she would have been more comfortable trying to get inside the place through a door or window. Plus a home like this had to have a first-class security system, though it might be turned off now since it was daytime and people were inside.

Mercy decided that she was doing no good just squatting here like a lump, so she moved forward, keeping low and trying to stay out of the sight line of the row of windows on this side of the house. She passed by a pool that had its winter cover on. She stopped behind a clump of bushes and waited to see if anyone had seen her and was about to sound the alarm. That didn't happen, so she relaxed and looked around, trying to use her common sense and natural observation skills, which she had cultivated over the years. In the places she had lived, correctly gauging the mood of a room and the violent predilections of various people had saved her on more occasions than she cared to remember.

She wondered if this place had been recently rented for the short-term, because the pool chairs, chaises, and tables around it were covered and stacked up. The place had the feel of having been shut down for the season. The Escalade had not pulled into one of the garage bays, meaning it probably didn't belong to the place, she reasoned.

She poked her head over the top of the bush and scanned the house using her optics. She couldn't see anyone through the windows. But then she ducked down as Marbury came into view. Mercy slowly lifted her head up once more. He was talking to someone, and in the next moment Mercy saw clearly who that was. She had never seen him before, but he seemed like someone of importance.

He was in his forties, tall and lean and very well dressed, right down to the pocket kerchief. Mercy could make all this out because the lights were on in the room and the man came to stand by the window to look out for a minute or so. The way he was talking and gesturing with Marbury made Mercy conclude that he was the boss and the lawyer the underling. She supposed lawyers always made good underlings. Mercy had had several run-ins with lawyers, and none of those occasions had turned out well for her.

But there was something familiar about the boss man, in the jaw and eyes, yet Mercy couldn't place him. She dropped her head once more, then decided to get down on her belly and stare up from under the bush.

The man was talking while continuing to gaze out the window. Mercy didn't like that look. It was too observant, she decided. This was a man with something on his mind. And she knew what that was: Lee Pine. He had her somewhere, maybe here; she could just feel it. They were in cahoots with Desiree somehow.

When the man moved away from the window,

Mercy left her hiding place and sprinted toward the house. She planted herself against the stone wall and waited for a few moments. She had spotted a rear door that was hidden enough from view to hold possibilities.

Keeping flat against the side of the house, she reached the door. It was locked, which was not surprising. She looked toward the part of the house where the two people were and gauged it to be far enough away for her to safely attempt what she was about to.

She put one foot on the doorknob, stepped up, and grabbed hold of the home's façade, where there was enough irregularity in the stonework to provide a space for her strong fingers to grip. She did a pull-up and then brought her weight down fully on the doorknob. She felt it bend but not break. She did this same maneuver twice more, and the knob sheared off.

She dropped to the ground and looked at her handiwork. With the knob gone the inner workings of the lock were revealed. She stuck her finger in the hole and, using considerable strength, managed to move back the mechanism controlling the lock.

She gave a push and the door swung open.

The next moment she was inside and her gun was out. She surveyed the area.

Her speculation that the place had been closed down seemed to be verified by the stuffy air and the dust covers over the furniture. She quickly and quietly searched the rooms on this level. When she was done Cain listened for a few moments until she heard the footsteps overhead together with muted voices. She found the stairs and took each riser with care.

She heard more footsteps and more muted voices. She froze and waited for a bit. Mercy suddenly realized that she had no idea what her sister sounded like. She quietly slipped back down the stairs and waited at the bottom in case whoever was up there decided to leave this way.

Five minutes later and growing impatient, she made her way up and reached the door at the top of the stairs.

Mercy inched it open and peered through the crack. What she saw was an expansive space, lavishly decorated, but again with the furniture covered. She opened the door enough to squeeze through and bent low, surveying the field in front and behind her.

She started to take a step forward but then stopped. She hadn't heard any more footsteps or voices in quite a while. She straightened and started to race forward when she heard the vehicle start up.

She made it to the window in time to see an SUV roar out from somewhere and disappear between the hedges that lined the driveway. A moment later the Escalade followed suit.

"Damn," exclaimed Mercy. She was torn between searching the rest of the house and rejoining Blum.

Finally deciding that if her sister was here, they wouldn't leave her behind, she left the way she had come. She ran flat-out to where she had left Blum in the Porsche in the church parking lot.

Only neither the SUV nor Carol Blum were there any longer.

56

Pine leapt out of the ancient truck before it even stopped in front of the hotel.

"Thank you," she called over her shoulder.

The elderly woman tooted her horn, leaned out the window, and cried out, "Thank *you*, missy! Most fun I've had in years!"

Pine raced into the lobby and ran up to the front desk where the same woman from the night before was standing.

"My God, Agent Pine," said the woman. "They've been looking everywhere for you. We thought you had been kidnapped."

"I was but I got away."

"You're hurt!"

"What?"

"Your face. It's all bruised."

Pine touched the side of her face where she'd gotten kicked. In the spike of adrenaline during her escape, she hadn't even remembered it or felt the pain. Now it all came rushing back to her. She rubbed her oblique where she'd been struck the first time. It was swollen and hurt like hell. Whoever had done it packed a wallop.

She refocused and said, "Where's the woman I was with, Carol Blum?"

"I don't know. I haven't seen her. The FBI are here. They're in the dining area. An Agent McAllister?" She described him.

Pine hustled to the dining area and spotted a man who had to be Drew McAllister, and a tall, younger man with him. They were sitting near the back of the room. She ran over and they both gaped when they spotted her.

"Agent Pine?" exclaimed McAllister as he jerkily rose from his seat.

"That's me."

"I just got a call from Tate Callum and heard you got away."

Pine gave them a thirty-second down-and-dirty on what had happened to her and how she'd escaped. "I'm hoping the guys I trussed up can lead us to what's going on."

McAllister, surprisingly, shook his head. "That won't be happening. Callum told me that when they arrived at the address you gave them the men were gone."

Pine groaned. "Shit. Someone must have come and gotten them loose, because they weren't getting away on their own. And they were both unconscious."

He jerked a thumb at his partner. "This is Neil Bertrand."

Pine nodded at him. Bertrand said, "They roughed you up?"

Pine rubbed her swollen face. "I wasn't as cooperative as they would have liked."

McAllister said, "Look, we came down here to talk to you about Tim Pine, but since all hell has broken loose, maybe we need to pitch in on this thing first, whatever it is."

"Thanks, right now I could use all the help I can get."

"The locals will process the house where you were kept. They might turn up something."

"I need to call my friend, Carol. I left my phone in my room. I'll be right back."

"No, we got it right here. Ms. Blum turned it over to me. She's been trying to contact you." He handed it to her.

Pine snatched up her phone and unlocked it. There were several earlier calls and messages from Blum. She was obviously frantic about Pine's disappearance. She called Blum's phone, but it went right to voice mail. Cursing, she texted Blum, but got no reply.

"I'll be right back," she told McAllister.

She ran up to her room and grabbed her ID and guns from the room safe, then ran back down to the lobby and reentered the dining area.

"When did you see Carol last?"

"This morning right when we got to the hotel. She was the one who told us about your disappearance. But I don't know where she went after that." He glanced at his partner. "Neil, check into that."

Bertrand rose and left.

Pine sat down in his seat and looked at McAllister.

He said, "Blum thought it might be Desiree Atkins's drug ring associates who took you. What do you think?"

"That's not it. The man who's leading this up spoke to me. I can't ID him because I was blindfolded. But he told me that if Desiree Atkins got bailed out they were going to get to her and make her talk. That doesn't sound like her drug ring partners, if there even are any."

"Did he say what sort of information he wanted from her?"

"He wanted to find somebody."

"Find who?"

"Eloise Cain." Pine drew in a long breath. "Who is the same woman I'm looking for."

"Did he say why he wanted to find her?"

"He said that she had killed his brother. He wanted revenge, I suppose."

"And why would she kill his brother?"

"The man said his brother deserved it. But that it didn't matter because it was family. He clearly wants Cain dead."

"And why were you looking for this Eloise Cain person?"

Pine knew this question would be coming.

"She's a person of interest in a case I'm working."

McAllister looked put out by this. "That's what I tell *my* bosses when I don't want to loop them in yet. Is that really the best you can do under the circumstances?"

Pine looked at the man and held his gaze. "I just need you to trust me on this one. It's complicated, and we just don't have the time. Please."

He sat back and sighed. "I checked up on you before I came down here, of course. Nothing but superlatives. So for now, I'll let this pass. But at some point, Agent Pine, I'm going to have to hear the whole story."

"I hope by then I'm able to give it. And I mean the *whole* story."

She left him there and went back up to her room. She left three more messages for Blum, both voice mail and text. Something was clearly wrong.

Idiot. She hadn't even checked to see if the Porsche SUV was in the parking lot.

She rushed down to the lobby and headed to the exit door as a Lyft car dropped off a passenger in front. Pine pushed through the revolving door and stepped outside.

Then she stopped dead and turned to look at the

person who had just gone *into* the hotel through the revolving door.

She was standing just inside the lobby and was now staring at Pine.

The woman slowly walked back outside.

And for the first time in thirty years the Pine sisters were staring at each other with only a few feet between them.

Pine felt herself start to shake. The emotions welling up inside were unlike anything she had ever felt before. No, she thought, she was wrong. They were the same set of feelings that she had had when she'd learned that her twin sister was gone.

"M–Mercy?"

As Mercy looked at her, long-ago memories, plastered under years of Desiree Atkins-imposed hate, vitriol, and cruelty, came rushing back to the surface of her brain. It was like the dam had finally burst and all that was important was rushing back to her.

"Lee? Is that really you?"

Pine stared up at a face that was very much like and also unlike hers. Thirty years of life, much of it bad, had impressed itself indelibly on her twin. There was no getting around that. Long gone was the adorably pretty girl with the wonderfully long hair and penchant for frilly dresses and a mischievous smile that could make Pine laugh as if on cue. Yet in every other way, Pine knew that she had just found her sister.

Tears were now streaming down Pine's face and she made no move to wipe them away. "Yes, my God, yes, it really is me."

The women both stepped forward as though connected by the strongest of rope, and finally embraced for the first time in three decades.

57

When Pine stepped away from her sister, she simply stood there staring at Mercy.

"I really can't believe this is happening. After all these years."

Mercy looked her twin over, her happy features slowly fading. "It's been a long time. I doubt I'm like what you remember."

Pine's smile slowly faded, too, as something strange and ill-defined seemed to spring up between the pair, like a border wall built of myriad and substantial components. But she told herself absolutely nothing was going to taint this moment. She was too happy, and she meant to show this to her sister. The smile came back even more forcefully. "The only thing that matters to me is that you're alive and that you're here, right now. Oh my God, this is the day I've been waiting for, for so long."

Mercy put her hands in her pockets. "Yeah, I can see that, sure. So, I heard you were in trouble."

Pine's smile dialed back down. "Yes, I was. Then I got out of it."

Mercy checked out her sister's swollen face. "But not without getting kicked around?"

Pine crossed her arms over her chest, as she saw the euphoric moment of sisterly reunion seemed to be over. "Goes with the territory. I hope to pay them back at some point." She stepped forward and rubbed her sister's arm. "I know a little of what happened to you. And I'm so sorry. And I know how ridiculously inadequate any words are right now."

Mercy shrugged. "I survived it. I got away, too, just like you. They didn't beat me."

"No, they didn't."

"That's what it's about, survival."

"Yes, yes it is," Pine said awkwardly. It was like they were two casual friends shooting the breeze over nothing really important to either of them. In the Hollywood version it would be all smiles, hugs, and tears. In real life, she suddenly realized it was far more nuanced. And complicated.

And why in the hell are you just realizing that now?

She said, "Look, I know the timing stinks, but I need to find my friend. She must be around here somewhere."

"I don't think so."

"What?" Pine said sharply.

"You're talking about Carol Blum? I was with her. We went to see Desiree in jail."

Pine looked stunned. "You saw Desiree?"

"Carol thought she might have something to do

with your disappearance. You know, Desiree's drug friends? We thought they were the ones who grabbed you."

"So what happened?"

"While we were there this big muckety-muck lawyer from New York showed up to meet with Desiree. Carol was smart enough to figure out that Desiree didn't call the dude in, so she wondered who did. So when he left the jail, she had the idea of following him."

"Where did he go?"

"This big-ass house. The dude met a guy there. I got into the house to see what I could learn. The place looked all shut down, you know, like the real owners had left to go someplace else. And maybe these guys were just using it. But then they all left and I was there all by myself. I felt like an idiot because I mostly didn't know what I was doing. I hustled back to the car to tell Carol, but she and the car were gone."

"Gone? Do you think she went after them?"

"I don't know. Have you heard from her recently?"

"No, and I just left multiple messages and got nothing back."

"Then I think something happened to her."

"They might have realized they were followed."

"Yeah, they might."

Pine looked around and found several people standing there staring at them and listening.

She hooked her sister's arm and said, "Let's go up to my room and talk about this in private."

They rode the elevator up to Pine's room. She used her key card to get in.

Mercy said, "My duffel was in the Porsche. All my clothes and stuff were in it."

"I've got some clothes you can wear. You're taller than me, but they should work. We're close to the same build."

Mercy ran her gaze over her sister. "You look pretty strong and fit, able to take care of yourself."

"Yeah."

"Probably helps out with your job."

"It doesn't hurt."

"I do some MMA and local UFC stuff to make money. You do what you have to, you know?"

Pine stared up at her. "I know it's been incredibly hard, Mercy."

"I don't look back. At least I try not to. It's not good for someone like me." She paused. "So, Carol?"

Pine sat down on the bed. "Do you remember where this house was?"

"Not really. Carol was driving and I wasn't paying attention. I used a Lyft to get here but I had to walk quite a bit to a spot where he picked me up. We might be able to piece it together. But it looked to me like they were just using it temporarily. I don't think they lived there. But I did see a guy in the window."

"The lawyer?"

"No, another guy."

"Can you describe him?"

"Tall, lean, forties, well-dressed, classy-looking dude. Did you see whoever grabbed you?"

"The goons, but not the boss. But I'm betting he's the guy you saw."

"What's his beef with you? Not Desiree? Guy didn't look like your typical drug dude, even the higher-ups. He was classier, like I said. He looked like one of those CEO types."

Pine cleared her throat and looked nervously at Mercy. "His beef apparently is with *you*."

Mercy had gone over to the window to stare out. She turned back around. "Me?"

"He was looking for El Cain."

"Why?"

"He said you killed his brother."

Mercy took a few steps toward her. "I killed the guy's brother? He said that?"

"Yes."

"I haven't killed anybody. Just like I didn't kill Joe Atkins. Carol told me you got Desiree to confess."

"We did. The confession is safely uploaded to my personal cloud."

"I was worried when I saw that the FBI was after me."

"They weren't *after* you. They just wanted to *find* you."

Mercy knitted her brow. "Did this dude say *why* I supposedly killed his brother?"

"Not really, only that he deserved it."

Mercy plopped down in a chair. "That makes no sense. The guy's nuts. I've beat some guys up because they deserved it, but I haven't killed anybody. I swear."

"I believe you. But this *guy* is dead set on getting to you. It was really personal to him."

"You think he snatched Carol?"

"I think he might have." Pine rose. "An FBI team is downstairs. They're here to deal with a separate matter involving Tim Pine."

"Yeah, Carol told me about him. And about our biological father with the big bucks."

"Jack Lineberry."

"So what was up with our mother? Was she a slut, or nuts, or both?"

Pine felt her face burn at this blunt question. Mercy seemed to read her mind.

"I'm sorry. I don't really remember her. Carol said she was a mole against the mob or something. But then she upped and left you."

Pine's face burned even hotter at this last statement. "Yes, she did. I'm trying to find her, and Tim."

"If she left you, why bother? You have something you want to say to her, Lee? But would it really matter? After all this time?"

Pine went to the closet and pulled out an envelope

from her jacket. She held it up. "I just got this letter. It's from Mom to Jack Lineberry."

"What's it say?"

"I'll let you read it while I go back down and talk to the agents. I . . . I don't want them to know about you right now."

Mercy glared at her. "You said it was all cool for what happened to Joe! He was stabbed. I didn't do it. I just hit him when he tried to stop me. You said you had Desiree's confession. Carol told me the same thing. Were you two lying or what?"

"No, it's the truth, Mercy. But let me handle this. I know the Bureau. Just trust me. I can work this out. I promise."

"I haven't trusted anybody my whole life. I don't think I can start now. I'm sorry, but that's just the way it is."

"Okay, I can understand that, so just stay here and read the letter and I'll be back."

Mercy took the letter. "We need to find Carol. I like her."

"We will. I like her too. She's . . . she's . . ."

". . . like a mother to you?" said Mercy as she watched her twin closely.

Pine didn't answer. She left, and Mercy sat on the bed and commenced reading the letter.

58

McAllister was still sitting at the same table in the hotel café. He was on the phone when Pine walked in. The man held up a finger for her to wait, then he finished the call and looked up at her.

"What do you got, Pine?"

"Carol Blum *is* missing. We need to put out an APB."

"Neil checked video from the parking lot. Blum was earlier seen getting into her vehicle with a tall woman in a hoodie. Any idea who that could be?"

Pine knew this question might be coming and still didn't have a good answer.

"I'm not sure."

"Okay," said McAllister, not looking convinced. "I'll put out the APB, and then you and I need to talk."

Pine gave him a description of the Porsche and the plate number.

He left her for a few minutes and then was back with Neil Bertrand in tow. They sat down across from her.

"Coffee?" asked McAllister. "We have an open tab running."

"Sure, that would be great."

"You must be hungry, too. I doubt your kidnappers fed you."

"No, I'm good, but thanks."

"Coffee black or the works?"

"Black."

Bertrand went off to fetch it.

McAllister took a sip from his cup and set it down. "You told me to trust you. Okay, I do. But that street runs both ways." He let that sentence hang out there, and from the looks of the man, Pine knew he wasn't going to say anything else until she responded. She would have done that too if their positions had been reversed.

Pine waited for her coffee, and when it came she took a long sip of it and plunged in.

"I've been on leave from the Bureau to look for my twin sister, Mercy Pine. She was abducted when we were six years old. We traced her to Desiree and Joe Atkins' home. She had been given the name Rebecca Atkins."

McAllister's eyes widened and he started to nod. "Rebecca Atkins? Right, I remember seeing the FBI's PSA. Damn, she was your sister?"

"Yes. Anyway, the Atkinses kept her prisoner, but she escaped nearly twenty years ago. We tracked Desiree down in Asheville, and I busted her for imprisoning another young girl. And I also got her to confess to killing her husband, Joe."

"Confess?"

Pine took out her phone and played the recording.

"Is it admissible?" asked McAllister.

"I hope so," said Pine. "Because it clears my sister of any wrongdoing, although in my book she had every reason to harm them—they were trying to keep her imprisoned."

"Well, I think most courts and juries would agree with that. And do you know where your sister is?"

Pine drew a long breath. "The truth is she's upstairs in my room. She was the tall woman you saw in the hoodie getting into the car with Carol. She's the one I've been looking for."

She glanced up to see McAllister's and Bertrand's reactions to this.

Bertrand looked surprised, McAllister did not.

"Two tall women, same build, and both seen with Blum. It doesn't take a Sherlock Holmes. Your sister goes by Eloise Cain now?"

"Yes. She came here to confront Desiree, which she's done. But a lawyer from New York came down to rep Desiree—only someone else employed him. I think that person is the one who snatched me. Carol and my sister followed the lawyer to a house, where my sister saw the man talking to the lawyer. But then they took off. Maybe they suspected they were being followed, I don't know. My sister had gotten into the house for a closer look and to see if I was in there. When the people abruptly left, she ran back to where the car had been, but Carol and the car were gone."

"And you don't think Carol followed them?"

"She would have left a message. She didn't. And all my messages I sent to her a short while ago have gone unanswered. So I think they got to her."

McAllister sat back and glanced at Bertrand, then said to Pine, "And this man—the ringleader, let's call him—he said he was after El Cain, your sister, because she had killed his brother? What does she say to that?"

"She has no idea what he's talking about. She's killed no one."

"And you believe her?"

"Yes."

"And you found her when?"

Pine took another long breath. "About twenty minutes ago."

"After not seeing her for thirty years? And you think you know her well enough to figure out if she's telling the truth or not about killing someone? And would she really confess that crime to an FBI agent, sister or not?"

Pine's professional side knew what answer to give: Of course she didn't know her sister well enough. But her human side provided the answer. "I believe she's telling the truth. And the man said his brother deserved it, so it sounds to me like whether she did something or not, he might have provoked her."

"Did you ask her about anything recent in her past that might have prompted such action against her? I mean, whoever wants a piece of her has kidnapped an FBI agent, gotten a hotshot lawyer from New York, and abducted another FBI employee. There must be a significant motive behind it."

"I haven't gone that deep with her yet."

"While technically this is not my case, I think someone should."

"I'll do it."

Bertrand interjected, "Do you really think you're objective enough to do that, Agent Pine? Under Bureau rules—"

"I know everything about Bureau rules," she snapped, and then immediately calmed. She took another drink of coffee to give herself time to formulate a more effective response. She looked into the liquid as though it might hold a way out of her current dilemma.

"I'll talk to her about it, *objectively*. Then, if it appears that there might be more to it, I can arrange for you to speak with her. Does that sound fair?"

"Fair enough, for now. And about Tim Pine?"

"I haven't seen him or my mother for many years. I thought he was dead. I have no idea where either one of them is."

"How did Ito Vincenzo end up in his grave?" asked Bertrand.

"Have you spoken with Jack Lineberry?"

"He's next on our list. We understand the Georgia police and a Virginia homicide detective have already interviewed him. I don't think they were satisfied with his answers."

"Why is the FBI even interested in this? Homicide is a state matter, unless there's something unusual about it."

"Apparently there is."

"Look, the truth is, my mother acted as a mole for the U.S. government in taking down some New York Mafia bosses back in the eighties. Bruno Vincenzo was one of them. He got killed in prison for turning snitch but not before talking his brother, Ito, into abducting my sister and almost killing me in an act of revenge. Many years later, Ito tracked my father down in Virginia and again he tried to kill him. Only Ito was the one who ended up dying."

"And why didn't your father report this?"

"He should have, but the Mafia has long memories. This would have dredged everything back up again. So he and Lineberry worked out a plan. Lineberry initially identified the body as Tim's and my mother confirmed it. I guess the face was unrecognizable."

"I saw the autopsy pictures. It was," added McAllister, with a repulsed look on his face. "So your mother and this Lineberry fellow *lied* to the police and obstructed an investigation."

"Lineberry worked for the government. He was my mother's handler. I suppose he's bound by some secrecy oath. You may have to duke it out with a sister agency."

"Wouldn't be the first time."

"My only focus right now is finding Carol."

"I can understand that, Agent Pine. Why don't you go and speak with your sister? She may know something useful."

Pine rose. "Thanks for the coffee." She walked off.

McAllister moodily watched her go. "She's a funny one."

"Great record at the Bureau," noted Bertrand.

"Yes, but she's ruffled feathers along the way, too."

"Think she's holding anything back?"

McAllister gave the younger man an incredulous look. "Hell, Neil, of course she is."

59

Mercy set the letter down on the bed, turned and walked over to the window, and looked out at a clear day over Asheville, North Carolina. The beauty of the Blue Ridge Mountains sat like an obedient dog right in front of her, hoping to cheer her up.

It didn't work because Mercy didn't see the trees, or envision a symbolic canine, or feel cheered up. The only things she was seeing resided in her own head.

The little barefoot tomboy in dirty dungarees and a faded T-shirt dropped to the dirt from the tall tree and stood up straight and proud and stubborn. The little girl in the colorful dress sat on a blanket clutching her doll Sally and sipping on an imaginary cup of tea. The dress girl called out in a southern twang to the tall, beautiful woman with the thick hair piled high, "Told you, Momma, Lee figured it out. She got down just fine."

Next, the beautiful woman loomed up in front of her. In the face, Mercy saw parts of her and parts of her sister. She had no idea what this Jack Lineberry looked like, but facets of him were probably in her and Lee's features, too. She bent down and gave Mercy a hug, and her smile was a mile wide and inviting and made everything in Mercy's life the absolute best it could be.

"You were right, Mercy; you seem to know better than your mother about Lee."

"We're twins," little Mercy said. "We share everything. Even our *brain*."

Her mother laughed and called out to her sister. "Lee, come over here, sweetie. I need to look inside your and your sister's heads."

Lee appeared in the picture in Mercy's mind. Tough, little hands almost always balled in fists, itching for a fight with anyone. But when Lee saw Mercy and Mercy smiled, the hands uncurled, and Lee smiled back and laughed in the way she always did that made Mercy happier still.

"In our heads?" said Lee. She bent down so her mother could pretend to open up her head and peer inside.

"Now let me do your sister."

Giggling, Mercy lowered her head, too. Their mother dutifully performed an examination and proclaimed that the girls did indeed share a brain.

"What does it look like, Momma?" said Lee.

"One side has a pretty dress and one side has dirty dungarees," she replied and then commenced to tickle Lee until she screamed, before Mercy joined in and started tickling her mother. Then both girls went after their mom with the tickle bug, and they all ended up on the ground rolling around and shrieking with laughter.

Mercy turned from the window as the tears streamed down her face.

This memory had just come back to her fully after reading the letter. Bits and pieces had been with her for many years, but not all of it, not the most important parts.

All those years, I could have been with her and my sister, having all that fun, all that . . . love. And, instead, I was with the Atkinses.

But as she picked up the letter and read through it again, her mother's words—where she had blamed herself for all that had gone bad—made Mercy feel a sudden burst of anger. Was her mother just trying to get sympathy and money from Jack Lineberry? Mercy thought there was an "oh woe is me" tone to the words.

But perhaps she was being unfair. Being that young and working against the mob had to have taken great courage. And then to have her family attacked, one daughter taken, the other left for dead? Then the man she loved nearly killed, too?

Mercy never liked other people judging her, although they too often did based on her ratty clothes or her old car, or the way she looked, her limited education, the clumsy indelicacy of her manner. To be fair, she had no right to judge others, including her mother.

Yet it was now obvious to Mercy that her mother didn't want to be found. She didn't want to be part of her daughters' lives. That was her choice, Mercy supposed, though she believed it to be a selfish one. Even after reading the letter, Mercy couldn't understand why her sister would want to find the woman. There was clearly nothing there. The woman with the piled-up hair and the tickle-bug playfulness was long gone. She had made her choice, and that did not include being there for her daughters. They all needed to move on.

She looked up when the door opened and Pine appeared there.

Pine sat on the bed next to Mercy and glanced at the letter in her hand.

"Well?"

Mercy shrugged. "It's a letter. Full of regrets, sort of like a sob story. I don't know what you get out of it. She doesn't want to be found, that's clear enough. Okay, fine. Move on. There's nothing there for you, Lee."

Pine's face paled and her features turned troubled. "And what she wrote made you feel . . . nothing?"

"Why would it?"

"Then why are your eyes red and your cheeks wet?"

Mercy dropped the letter on the bed, stood, and

looked away. "I don't need this shit, Lee, okay? I came here to deal with Desiree. I said my piece to the witch. I'm off the hook for a murder I didn't do. Now I just want to go back to my simple little life."

"And what about me?"

Mercy turned to look at her.

Pine's eyes glistened, and in a low, tight voice she said, "*I* didn't choose to lose you. *I* didn't walk away from you. I've been without my sister for thirty years, Mercy. And now that we've found each other you just want to walk away? Just like Mom did to me?"

Mercy didn't wilt under this; she seemed to grow taller and broader. "I didn't have a walk in the park, okay? The last thirty years have not been a piece of cake for me, *sis*. I would've traded with you in a heartbeat." She lifted her sleeve. "Check these beauties out."

Pine looked at the collection of torture marks. "I know what she did to you."

"No, you have no fucking clue what that bitch did to me. Here, here's what she did to me."

Mercy stripped off her hoodie and undershirt. Her arms and torso were covered with blackened marks, scars, and lumps.

"Desiree loved cigarettes. Not to smoke them. But to burn me with them." She pointed to three charred marks close together on her right forearm. "Do you know what she said about these?"

Pine couldn't speak; she just stared.

"She said they were like the three little pigs and I was Goldilocks. This burn was too hot and this one was too cold and the third one was just right, so she held it on me till I thought my fucking brain was going to pop out of my damn head. I was nine."

She pulled down her pants, exposing her legs. "And these?" She pointed down both thighs where there were rows of burn marks. "That bitch wanted to make a column of ants up and down my legs. You know, like 'ants in the pants,' she said. I had ants in my pants. And she laughed her ass off while she's burning ants into my skin. I was eleven."

She tugged her bra down, revealing her breasts. "And she didn't like the way my boobs looked. So she took a knife and carved shit on them. I was twelve. I didn't really even have breasts yet, so all she was really doing was pushing my skin into my bones with a sharp blade."

She touched her underpants. "And . . . and down . . . there." Mercy bent over and started to quietly weep. She angrily swiped at the tears. "Down there she—" She waggled her head, looked like she might be sick to her stomach. "I was only . . . I don't . . . I don't remember how old I was. I just remember it hurt. It hurt like nothing I've ever felt before."

In the face of all this, Pine finally had to close her eyes.

Mercy stared directly at her. "Yeah, Lee, that's right, don't look. I wouldn't. I used to be pretty like you.

I guess I did, anyway, because I don't remember anymore. I've looked like this longer than I haven't looked like this. I'm a freak and I know it. With this body I only get the guy losers of the world, and there are plenty of them. The normal dudes, they take one look at this shit and it's goodbye."

She rubbed her scalp. "I cut this off because Desiree used to pull out handfuls of it, roots and all, or set it on fire while she held me down. And with all the stuff you see on my body, that wasn't the worst that she did to me." Mercy smacked her head. "It was up here that she screwed with me the most. The mind games, the pure shit she poured into my head from when I was little to when I was big. That, *that* was the worst of it. Every nightmare you can imagine, the most evil, disgusting shit you can think of, that woman threatened to do to me and then she *did* do it to me. And then she went to another level to where I think even she was freaked out at what she was capable of.

"Then I got away and spent years getting crapped on by lowlifes who thought they could do anything they wanted to me, and I mostly let them because I didn't know better. And I did stuff I'm not proud of, made the worst choices in the world, and snorted and injected and sucked down every drug you've heard of, and some you probably haven't."

As she kept talking, Mercy's voice was rising and her temper was flaring while Pine kept her eyes shut.

"And I finally get the courage, the nerve, the,

I don't know what the fuck to call it, to say enough is enough. And for a long time I've actually had a damn life. It's not much. I live paycheck to paycheck, I'm homeless sometimes when everything goes to hell, but then I get back on my feet. And I keep going. Alone. Because that's the way it has to be. I'm not good around humans, Lee. Because I'm not human, and haven't been for a long time. So, yeah, you ask me if I want to walk away, you're damn right I do. I want to get back to the little piece of a shitty life that I've carved out for myself *by* myself because it's *my* shitty life. Because people like me, we don't know how much longer the road goes. But we know it doesn't go as long as it does for normal folks. That's just the way it is. I didn't make the rules. I don't agree with the rules. But they are the rules. And I'm not getting screwed over anymore by anybody. And I'm sorry if this little reunion isn't going the way you thought it would, but that's life. You want some fantasy where everyone has a great smile and every house has a white picket fence and the scene ends with tears and hugs and perfection all around, try somewhere else. Because that's *not* me!"

She put the exclamation point on this diatribe by drilling her fist into the drywall and creating a large dent. Then she quickly pulled up her pants and bra, slipped on her shirt and hoodie, and stormed out of the room, slamming the door behind her.

Pine sat there for a bit, her eyes still firmly clamped

shut even as the tears seeped out of them. Finally, she opened them and stared at the dent in the wall, courtesy of her sister's iron fist and brutal temper.

And for the first time in a very long time, Atlee Pine had no idea what to do.

60

Peter Buckley slowly walked around the grounds as powerful recollections flooded over him. This was the land of his birth, literally. His mother, with the aid of a midwife, had delivered him on the second floor of their home here, a building that had been gutted by fire from an incendiary round fired by federal agents during their attack against the compound, but mostly against his father.

Buckley had only partially reconstructed the site. There was a large barn and the jail and the house where he had lived and a couple other buildings. And he had erected the high perimeter fence and the gate and a single guard tower.

When his parents had operated it, and hundreds of people lived there, the compound had multiple barns, cabins for the families, and a three-story bunkhouse for the singles. And there was the ever-important church where his father would preach his version of the Gospel, which was unlike any that one would hear in other houses of worship around the country. There was a small, spring-fed lake on the western edge of the property, a source of swimming and pleasure, and also used for drinking water.

They had crop fields and marijuana fields, and they raised cattle and hogs for slaughter and bred horses and mules for purposes of transportation and farming. And there was the facility where drugs were manufactured and then distributed through a carefully built and cultivated network.

Buckley had learned about that when he was eight and had snuck into the place; he'd been amazed at its illicit efficiency.

Back then the entire compound had been fenced in, with strategically placed guard towers. That was to keep outsiders out, and some of the Faithful, who had lost their way and their faith, from leaving until they could be reindoctrinated by other members who were expert at doing so.

And there was the graveyard, for the Faithful did indeed die, despite its leader proclaiming eternal life for all of them. The deaths were explained as the dead's not being faithful enough, which terrified the rest into recommitting themselves ever more fiercely to Buckley's father.

It was a brilliant setup, Buckley had to concede. And it would have continued unabated except for that fateful day, which he would never forget.

The federal agents had broadcast at them over their PA system for ten hours nonstop, ordering the Faithful to give up and come outside the compound.

Buckley's father had stood at the front gates and fiercely condemned this assault on their religious freedom, along with every other freedom granted by the Constitution—although Buckley Sr. had for years also proclaimed that the Faithful was its own country and the land under his feet no longer belonged to America. But when it suited him, he was more than happy to claim the benefits of U.S. law.

Then the armored vehicles had assembled at the gates, with the federal agents, in full riot gear and carrying assault weapons, arrayed behind them.

Buckley remembered the panic inside the compound that night, the young mothers with children screaming for his father to surrender. In the melee and confusion, Buckley had seen his father drag one young woman, who had been leading this effort, behind a building. He had not seen what had happened next but he had heard the gunshot. Then his father reappeared a few seconds later without the woman, and carried on leading his people against this government assault.

The next moment, the gates had been rammed and came down. And then several hells had broken loose. In the darkness the gunshots roared for hours. Explosions rocked the sky, flames and smoke and the screams of both terrified and dying people punctured the darkness as the chaos continued to play out.

Buckley, all of twelve years old, had grabbed a rifle and taken up his position in the barn's hayloft. He had sighted through his scope and fired on the federal agents, hitting two but killing neither because he had aimed for their armored torsos and not their heads.

When it was all over, more than two dozen of the Faithful lay dead, and his father had suffered multiple gunshot wounds. They arrested the bleeding Buckley Sr., who was still clutching empty pistols in each of his hands. It was a heroic sight, Buckley thought, the leader fighting with everything he had right to the last.

Only three federal agents lay dead, a product of their superior training, weaponry, and body armor, and the Faithful's inability to shoot straight. Buckley had always assumed that his father had killed all three. He was an excellent shot. Buckley had always felt shame that he had failed to kill a single one of them.

The Faithful had either been arrested or, in the case of the mothers and their children, dispersed around the country to begin new lives without the faith. Buckley and his siblings had been placed with family members who had never subscribed to the doctrine of their parents. The time with his parents had been the best of Buckley's life. The time right after, the worst. When he had turned eighteen, Buckley had worked hard to scrape together enough money to bring his siblings to live with him. He had leased a house not too distant from here, and Buckley took it upon himself to raise them in a way that was reflective of their parents' beliefs. But, to no avail. The moment his sisters had turned eighteen, they had fled, never to be seen again. His brothers had grown up to be petty and unsuccessful criminals, slaves to the booze and the drugs and the women who exploited them.

And then only Buckley had been left. Freed of his familial obligations, he had set out building his personal empire. He had done it with a single-minded focus that allowed him to outsmart even those smarter than himself because he simply wanted it more. He outworked everyone because he knew what it was like to lose everything. And that fear burned through him every minute of every day and powered him like a nuclear core did an aircraft carrier.

And now he was here. For something truly monumental. This had gone far beyond merely avenging his sad sack brother's death. This was taking on the federal government and finally holding them to account for destroying his *family*.

An eye for an eye was a remnant of a savage culture, though it was espoused in pretty much every book of religion there was. But it fit his situation perfectly. What he would accomplish here would not change the world, he knew. But it would make the unjust death of his father and his way of life feel suitably avenged.

Buckley was dressed in jeans, a sweater, a tan hunter's jacket, and Wellington boots, for the ground was muddy after recent rains. He walked the perimeter of the new fencing, nodding to the guards in the tower who were armed with AR-15s and watched the land out to the horizon for threats. The place was not thriving with hundreds of people as it had in the past. Other than himself and some select associates, the only other people here were Britt Spector and one other person. Perhaps, for his plan to work, the most critical person of all.

Buckley opened the door to one building that had a sign out front reading, simply, JAIL. Even among the Faithful you had those who needed to be punished, and this was where they had performed their penance. His father had been a stickler on that. Rule violators needed to be made examples of. That was one reason Buckley had rebuilt it, as just a symbol. However, he had never expected to actually use it.

But now, this building housed Carol Blum.

61

She sat on a small, hard bed behind a set of steel bars. Her clothes had been replaced with old-fashioned black-and-white-striped prison scrubs that Buckley had bought and used to stock the jail. Back then his father had favored the striped prisoner uniforms. Wrongdoers needed to stand out and be made to look foolish. Zebra stripes fit the bill nicely.

She looked up at his approach. He could tell she was trying to put on a brave face, but right behind that façade was stark fear. Buckley would be afraid, too. It was just in the nature of human beings facing the end of their lives to be fearful.

He stood on the other side of the bars and looked at her. She didn't have a blindfold on. There was no need of one.

"Are you being well taken care of?" he asked.

"Are you serious?" she asked. "Or did you just come here to play mind games with me? If so, I'm sure you have better things to do with your time."

"I'm sorry if my query offended you. And I believe you're right. It was, under the circumstances, callous."

He sat down in a chair and crossed one leg over another. "So let's get down to it. Tell me about the Pine sisters."

"Why?"

"They're fascinating. I'm curious."

"What do you want to know?"

"Tell me what they're like."

"I just met Mercy," said Blum.

"Still, whatever you can contribute."

"I will tell you nothing that will cause harm to them."

"Not my point. But to show you I'm doing this in good faith, let me tell you about my family. Ken was my youngest brother. I was the oldest. I also have two sisters. My other brothers were also failures in life. They're all dead or in prison."

"And your sisters?"

"They left the family long ago," Buckley replied.

"I've always found that women have far better judgment in certain matters than men."

Buckley smiled, but there wasn't much behind it. He was here to get useful information, but there were limits to what he would accept from anyone. He felt a tremor in his right hand and was somewhat surprised to see it curling in anger. But there had been a lot of anger in this place. Maybe just his being here was allowing it to percolate to the surface, supplanting what was normally his controlled and placid manner. He had truly been an angry child on that horrific night. He had worked for years to subdue those demons. He thought he had; now Buckley was not so certain.

He cleared his throat and said, "Ken had a girl-friend. He was terrible to her. A true monster. Despite my best efforts, he really never became civilized in any appreciable way. Then he ran into Mercy Pine, for let's call the woman by her proper name. They fought. Ken eventually pulled a gun. And she, deservedly, beat him up. Later, in the hospital, he died of the injuries she inflicted on him. She probably has no idea he's even dead."

"So this is simply about avenging your brother? Even though, as you said, he deserved it?"

"There is nothing *simple* about revenge, particularly for a family member. But while it might have started out that way, it has grown into something more . . . symbolic." He looked around. "Do you know where we are?"

"We were on a jet. We landed. I was led here. There wasn't much opportunity for me to *see* anything."

"This compound used to belong to my parents. Peter and Deborah Buckley. Are the names familiar to you?"

Blum's eyes narrowed and understanding spread over her features. "It was over thirty years ago. Your parents headed up a group of religious zealots. But they were also involved in drugs and selling weapons.

And other things. The feds came here. There was a violent confrontation. Your father was almost killed."

"And my 'angelic' mother testified against him, and then abandoned her children. My father was later murdered in prison. By the way, what 'other things' are you referring to?"

She looked him over. "You had to be merely a child back then."

"I was twelve."

"Well, then, perhaps you didn't know."

"Didn't know what?"

Blum hesitated. "It's not important."

"No, it *is* important if it's about my family."

"The FBI had a hand in the arrests and prosecutions, that's why I remember it. I was assigned out west at the time, not too far from where this compound is located. I even assisted in some aspects of the case. It was all hands on deck because of the complexity. That's why I remember it so well. It was a top priority for several federal agencies, including the Bureau."

"And?"

"And your father was also charged with engaging in prostitution and human trafficking. He was selling young men and women into the sex trade. Some of them were members of his sect. I forget the name they used."

"The Faithful. And those allegations were never proved."

"They *were* proved. In court. It was one reason

your father got a life sentence without parole. And maybe your mother testified against him because she felt enormous guilt about it. That's just my speculation."

"I meant it was not proved to *my* satisfaction."

Blum said nothing to this, because she could apparently read in his features that her words would not change his opinion. It would be akin to moving a glacier with a tugboat.

Buckley eased back in his chair. "And now that I have bared my past to you, please answer my questions."

"Agent Pine is a formidable person. An excellent agent. She has never failed on a case, to my knowledge. She is tenacious, smart, and tough."

"And a good friend of yours. She will surely want your safe return."

"Which, I'm sure, is a sentiment you don't share."

"And Mercy Pine?"

"Has been through hell and back."

"Yes, I know something of her background. Tell me about their parents."

"Why?"

"Knowing about the parents can tell much about the children."

"Does that hold for you, too?" she said.

He smiled. "Are you sure you're not an FBI agent?"

"I'll take that as a compliment."

"I will concede that my personal history had a large impact on who I am as an adult. Now, the Pines' parents?"

"When their mother was a teenager she was a mole for the federal government against the Mafia. That put them in danger. That danger came to fruition when Mercy was kidnapped and Agent Pine was almost killed. They were only six years old. It devastated the family."

"The Mafia? Interesting. And where are the parents now?"

"No one knows. Agent Pine has been looking for them, too."

"Their mother must be formidable to have worked against the Mafia at such a tender age."

"I believe she was very scared, but did her duty. But her work came at a high personal cost."

"I assume she or their father was tall?"

"She was six feet tall. Agent Pine told me. She did some work as a model, in fact."

Buckley nodded. "And both daughters are tall, strong—fierce, even, with exemplary fighting skills. I saw Mercy Pine's handiwork. I assume her sister is equally talented. I saw the Wikipedia page. She almost made the women's Olympic weightlifting team. Impressive."

"Both sisters have had to overcome a great deal of adversity."

"Good, good. However, I doubt that your Agent

Pine has ever been physically tortured, as her sister has?"

"No, I don't believe so. But why in the world does that matter to you?"

"Being able to endure pain is a source of great strength, I believe. It gives one an edge over another. Perhaps the critical edge."

"I suppose so, but, again, I don't see the relevancy."

"But you don't have to, Ms. Blum. Because *I* do."

"I'm not getting out of here alive, am I?"

"No, you're not. And neither are the Pine sisters."

Blum now looked alarmed. "They're not here, are they?"

He rose and tapped the bars with his finger, gracing her with an eager look.

"Not yet."

62

Britt Spector had to admit the scheme was brilliant. And risky. That didn't lessen the brilliance; it just made the plan more complicated. And special. Her admiration for Buckley had been displaced by a growing concern for the man. He was taking all of this far too personally. She understood that it was his brother. But it seemed to have evolved into a personal grudge that was now devolving into a terrible, looming confrontation. And she was uncertain of the exact shape it would take.

She had walked the grounds of the compound. Knowing the geography of a place was critical, if you wanted to make it out the other end. She had great faith in Peter Buckley, but when things went sideways with something like this, they often went terribly wrong. And then *faith* was just a word. A useless one. Then you were on your own.

This was her first time here. The place was rugged, imposing. If you didn't know what you were doing, survival out here would not be easy.

He had never spoken of the place. She knew some

of Buckley's background, and she had researched the history of this place once she learned where they were heading. His childhood had been as unusual and potentially as damaging as her own. So how could she judge the man harshly?

She stared out at the distant mountain range, and the less distant foothills. Canyons had been carved in the earth here by once mighty rivers that had vanished over time. She had driven all over this land after they'd arrived, getting a feel for it, trying to understand its secrets. Because one just never knew, did one?

She headed to the new two-story building where, Buckley had told her, the old hay barn had once stood.

A team was already there setting up the structure inside it.

The steel posts had been sunk into the dirt and reinforced with concrete footers. The chain-link perimeter fence was being strung along these posts. It rose ten feet.

She patted one of the posts; it didn't give an inch. Cement shoes on a dead man. Buckley had thought of it all.

Spector went over the plans with the crew chief. He had been well paid, had no idea what this ultimately would be used for, and didn't want to know. As soon as they were finished, he and his men would be on a chartered plane out of here and back to the country from where Buckley had recruited them. This tale, for them, would end with the wheels-up and the beer flowing.

She left the barn and kept walking, turning left and heading down the main street of the place. It really was a wonder that so many people had lived here at one point. And died here. The graveyard held well over a hundred plots simply inscribed with just first names on now-rotted wooden markers. Buckley had told her that these folks had all died of natural causes.

She didn't believe that and wasn't sure he did, either. She wasn't certain how he reconciled that in his own mind. Maybe he never had.

Spector looked up. This was a part of the country where the sky seemed to go on forever. There wasn't another living soul within at least a hundred miles. When they had been coming in on the jet she had looked out the window. She saw flat, rugged land frequently interrupted by buttes, rocky outcrops, a line of foothills, and finally their bigger, blunt-faced mountain cousins in the distance with snowy caps. She saw birds and animals and patches of water and some vegetation among the mostly stripped red earth.

But not a single human being.

She had come to realize that Buckley much preferred that arrangement. He had told her that he would come here for days at a time and just wander. He said that the power of the isolation astonished him.

"We're all hamsters on the wheel, Britt. We never stop long enough to try to understand what we really want, what we're really doing. It's all a mirage based on speed and lack of personal focus and thought."

"If you say so, Peter," she had replied at the time, clearly not pleasing him. Which had been her intent. She was not simply going to agree to agree. That made her trivial and, worst of all, fungible. To matter to the man, you had to be unique. And one way to do that was *not* to blithely follow his lead.

Spector wondered if Buckley had thought of *that* during some of his wanderings here.

It was the simplicity of his plan that appealed to her. Yet, for her, a bullet, a garotte, a blow to the base of the skull, a knife, or even a delicious little poison surreptitiously delivered would have served just as well. In the face of that, Buckley might say that she had no style, no burst of imagination. She would have agreed. Spector wasn't seeking masterpieces. She was no da Vinci. She was more workmanlike. She believed herself more akin to Michelangelo, indisputably a genius, but there was a lunch-pail-and-overalls practicality to his mastery that, in her mind, eclipsed even the dreamy, luminary vision of the *Mona Lisa*'s creator.

She had made additional discreet inquiries with the Bureau that had yielded a substantial treasure of potentially helpful intelligence. Some of those she had disclosed to Buckley and some she had not.

She walked into the little jail, passed the guard, entered the cell area, and stared through the bars at Carol Blum. She had been the one to abduct the woman back in Asheville, pointing a gun at her through the Porsche's window. Blum had been astute enough to know that the look on Spector's face brooked no opposition, and no hesitancy to shoot her in the head. So she had surrendered.

Spector had heard the woman mutter something like "Not again." This struck her as odd, but she had to admire Blum's nerves. She was not one to be intimidated. She had to know her fate was sealed, but she didn't act like it. That in itself was impressive.

Blum looked at her through the bars. "You look familiar somehow. And I don't mean from Asheville."

"I doubt it."

"Can you tell me your name?"

"Not prudent on my part."

"Mr. Buckley had no problem telling me his, or the history of this place and his family's connection."

"That's his choice; I work differently."

"Meaning you're not overconfident. I find men so often are, even the smart ones. Particularly when it comes to women."

"I can't disagree with that. In fact, I *agree* with it."

"I assume he pays you well."

Spector put one hand on the bars. "Sometimes it doesn't seem enough. Like right now."

"Pangs of conscience?"

"What can you tell me about Mercy Pine?"

"Mr. Buckley already asked. I only just met her. I can't say I know her."

"But you spent *some* time with her. I see you as a quick study. If you're admin at the Bureau, you would have to be."

"Do you know the Bureau?" Blum said quickly.

Spector smiled. "Anyone who does what I do has to pay attention to the FBI. Read into that what you will."

"What do you want to know?"

"I understand she had a rough upbringing under Desiree Atkins."

"That's one word for it. And probably not the right one."

"But she got away and . . . built a life?"

"She did. And she allegedly killed Buckley's brother, so in his warped mind, her life has to end as recompense of some kind."

"Did Agent Pine meet her sister?"

"She hasn't as far as I know. I'm not sure what Mercy did when she found out I was gone."

"Yes, we thought you two were together. She was watching the house?"

"I'm not quite sure why you didn't try to take her then."

"You aren't the only one wondering that. But I follow orders, I don't give them."

"Why do you want to know about her?"

Spector rubbed the single scar on her arm, the remaining souvenir of her own personal hell of a childhood.

"It's interesting to me how people facing similar challenges in life turn out very differently, by making very different choices."

"That speaks surely to the individuality of the person in question," replied Blum, looking intently at Spector. "Did you suffer something similar to Mercy Pine? Which led to different choices for *you*?"

Spector looked uncomfortable with the bluntness of the query. "I believe I thought I had made the right choices. I guess you would call it being on the side of right, as silly as that sounds."

"It doesn't sound silly at all to me. What happened?"

"Meaning?"

"Meaning you clearly are not on the side of right any longer."

"To use your own words, surely that speaks to the individuality of the person in question."

Blum cocked her head and looked disappointed. "You know as well as I do that there are limits to how far that argument can be expanded and employed."

"Perhaps I do."

"And just so there's no misassumption on your part: I understand that you're having this somewhat frank discussion with me because I will shortly not be alive to recount it to anyone else."

"But I didn't reveal my name. Does that give you some hope?"

"Not enough," Blum replied bluntly. She was silent for a bit and then said wistfully, "When I joined the Bureau decades ago, I had a family to raise. There was no question of my becoming a special agent. I don't even remember who or when the first female agent was."

Spector said promptly, "Alaska Packard Davidson back in 1922. Her brothers started the Packard car company. She was fifty-four when she became a special investigator for the Bureau of Investigation, the FBI's predecessor."

Blum took up the story. "That's right, I remember that now. But then Hoover became director and got rid of the female agents."

"But in 1972 Hoover died, and the Bureau graduated the first two female special agents since 1929."

"Susan Roley," said Blum. "I don't know the other."

"Joanne Pierce," replied Spector.

Blum gave her an appraising look that simulated the point of a sharp knife, prompting a smiling Spector to say, "That was neatly done, as it now appears clear that you knew *all* of the Bureau history answers."

"But that's beside the point. And with what I now *know* about *you*, I am truly saddened."

Spector's smile faded. "I don't recall saying that your opinion of me was important."

"But it saddens me still. And that's *my* prerogative."

"Everyone makes choices, men and women."

"And you've clearly already made yours. I'm just collateral damage. Some would say I've lived long enough. My children are grown. I'm not married. In the end who would miss me for very long? I'll soon be a faded picture on the wall."

The blunt response hardened Spector's look, but a glimmer of a softer underbelly lingered in her eyes. "You don't strike me as a person who wallows in self-pity."

"If I wallow in anything, it's in *reality*," replied Blum sharply.

"I hope Pine appreciates you as her admin," said Spector.

"She will remember me fondly, I hope. *If* she has the chance to."

Spector put her face an inch from the bars. She was clearly done scratching around the edges of this back-and-forth conversation. "Look, you seem like a nice lady. I have no doubt you're a dedicated public servant. The same with your boss. I have no grudge against Mercy Pine, either. She's obviously had a shitty life. I have no personal beef with any of you."

"But it's the old story, right? You have a job to do?"

"There *is* a lot at stake."

"There always is when you're going to take someone's life. Or at least there should be. It's supposed to be what separates us from all other animals." Blum seemed to stare right through the woman. "But you already know that. And it's not just about *choices*, is it? Even for *former* FBI special agents."

On that Spector pursed her lips, turned, and walked out.

Blum could have felt triumphant with this parting shot.

Yet all she felt was sadness for a life wasted. And more loss yet to come.

63

Mercy sat in her aged Civic gazing out the window but not really seeing much. She had many things she could have been thinking about after walking out on her sister. What her mind was riveted on for some reason was that Sally was in her duffel in the Porsche, and she might never see the doll again. Part of Mercy knew this was trivial, bordering on the ridiculous. But she just could not let it go. She ran her hand over the grimy steering wheel and thought about someone else holding Sally right now. And that thought made her mad.

Only it was not really about the doll, she knew. She had just done a full-blown psycho session on her twin. Those things needed to be said, because Mercy had felt all of them. To keep it all bottled up inside was to invite an explosion of an even more epic nature later. Better to let the pressure valve do its thing. Her sister didn't deserve to be on the receiving end of Mercy's emotional salvo, but she was the only one handy, and thus she had gotten both barrels.

Yet she also knew things could not be left here. But

it was complicated, and that was the reason for the focus on Sally. Dolls were simple. You held them and pretended they were alive and that they loved you unconditionally. It required nothing more than a modicum of imagination to carry it all off.

But then real life intruded and cut you off at the knees. Real life needed to be confronted and dealt with, mistakes and all. She needed three more minutes of Sally time, where in her mind palace she was a little girl again and the only worries she carried were what imaginary tea to use for her imaginary tea party with her imaginary friends, and whether her rambunctious sister would be able to work her way down from a tall tree and set foot back on the earth alive and well.

Mercy took the luxury of the full three minutes, and then Sally and "simple" were gone.

She got out of the car and leaned against the roof, having to bend over slightly because of her height. It was a pretty day, a cloudless sky. She had things to be happy about: Desiree was in prison. She had found her twin. She now knew something of her real father. And that the man who had helped raise her might still be alive and living with her mother—the tall lady with the piled-up hair and infectious smile, an image that had just returned to her after all those years.

She could drive back home and resume her life with those accomplishments in her back pocket, even without Sally by her side. She could do this because for most of her life it had just been her. She'd had no one else that she cared about, because no one she knew cared about her. When you got into that groove, an important set of basic human emotional instincts, like love and devotion, were eroded, like muscles atrophied from disuse. And her Good Samaritan routine now began to make more sense to her.

I give money to people I don't know. I help them because I know what it's like not to have anything. But that's easy. I slip them a few bucks and walk away. There's no other obligation, no lasting responsibility. I don't have to do anything hard. If they live or die, get hurt or sick, it doesn't affect me. It doesn't touch me, because I have no real link to any of them.

But with people who cared about you, who loved you, it was different. That road ran both ways and so did the responsibility. And that suddenly scared her more than anything she'd ever fought in her life.

A direct connection to someone else who really matters, who really counts, so that if I lost it, I would feel the pain. And it would hurt far more than even what Desiree had done to me.

Yes, so much easier, and also painless, to walk away.

Instead, she trudged back into the hotel and took the stairs up. She walked down the hall and rapped on the door.

Pine answered, the fresh tears still sticking to her face like hot wax on a death mask.

She seemed far more surprised to see Mercy standing there than Mercy felt standing there.

Did I always know I was coming back? Probably.

Pine closed the door behind her sister and she sat on the bed while Mercy stood.

"How do we find Carol?" Mercy asked simply.

Pine wiped at her face, cleared her throat, and went into FBI mode. "We have APBs out on her and the car. The Porsche will have been abandoned. She may already be out of the state by now. And as time goes by, maybe out of the country."

"I don't think so."

"What?"

"The dude wants me, like you said. Him just having Carol ain't gonna cut it. She's a means to an end."

Pine pushed her hair out of her face "You're right. She is."

"So he's gonna use Carol to get me."

"At least he's going to try."

Mercy nodded, chewing on this line for a bit. "Since he's using her as leverage, we can use me as bait. *That's* how we get to Carol."

"No, *that's* how you get dead, Mercy."

"Well, Carol can end up dead, too."

"I know that. Which is why we have to handle this really carefully."

"They're gonna contact you somehow. They're gonna want you to give me over for Carol."

"Which I can't and won't do."

"But if I'm cool with it, you don't have a choice."

"That is not how this works," said Pine firmly.

"Why not? It's a free country."

"I can't let you just give yourself up to be killed."

"So you'd sacrifice your friend for me?" asked Mercy.

This blunt statement hit Pine like the punch delivered by Spector had her gut. Her face flamed, her lips set in a straight, unflinching line, and her hands curled to fists.

She looked to Mercy like the little dungaree–clad girl about to assault another tree. And win.

Pine said, "I'm not sacrificing *anybody*. My goal is to get Carol back safe and sound, without losing you in the process."

Mercy sat down in the chair. "And how will you do that?"

"I'm working on it."

"No, you're still recovering from the mental avalanche I dropped on your head just now."

A few moments of profound silence passed between the women.

In a cracking voice Pine said, "You obviously felt the need to say it all. And you also came back. Why?"

The fists had now uncurled to shaky fingers, Mercy noted. The little girl was solidly on earth, but perhaps more afraid than if she'd been up an eighty-foot poplar with no way down and a lightning storm coming.

Mercy shrugged in the face of this question, partly because it was complex and partly because she didn't really have an answer that she believed would satisfy her twin.

"You worked hard to try to find me. Seems shitty to walk out on you when you need some help. And Carol doesn't deserve to get killed over this. It's not her problem. It's mine."

This blunt and honest assessment seemed to wick the tension from Pine's body. She relaxed and looked down. "Carol is really the only good friend I have. I depend on her for everything. She's . . . taught me a lot."

"This dude who took her. Anything else you can remember about what he said?"

"Why?"

"He said I killed his brother. Something you remember him saying might give me a clue as to what the hell he's talking about and who the hell his brother was."

"But you said you didn't kill anybody."

"I haven't. But he sure seems to think I have."

Pine said, "I can't think of anything. And I never saw his face. I got hit twice. But I don't think by him. Whoever did it knew what they were doing."

Mercy said, "Only your face? You look tight in the torso, too."

Pine lifted up her shirt to reveal a mass of yellow and black bruising on the left side of her abdominal wall, bleeding over to her oblique like a stain.

"Fist or some kind of weapon?" asked Mercy, clinically observing the marks.

"Fist. I felt the knuckles." She dropped her shirt.

"Whoever did that had some max power."

"No need to tell me that."

"But two inches over and you could have died."

Pine looked at her curiously.

Mercy said, "Your diaphragm and the aorta behind it. A blow that hard, especially if you weren't really ready for it, could have caused you to stop breathing. And if it had damaged your aorta and it ruptured later? Like being in a car accident and you hit the steering wheel because your seat belt doesn't work or the airbag doesn't come out. You'd bleed out in no time. But where they hit you? That doesn't happen."

"I guess they wanted to keep me alive to answer their questions. And how do you know so much about that anyway?"

"I told you, I do some MMA. Strictly local junior-league stuff because I'm nearly forty pounds over the UFC's heaviest weight class. I studied up on that stuff. A good ab wall makes all the difference. So how do you think they're gonna contact you about Carol?"

"Maybe a note left at the hotel? But they can't expect me to just do whatever they want me to, with no guarantee that Carol is even alive, or that they'll let her go."

"You said there are other agents here. You gonna tell them if you get a note?"

Pine said nothing for a moment. "I'm sure if I do, her abductors will kill Carol."

"Then I guess it's just you and me. Sort of like real, real old times. *Sis.*"

64

An agonizing four days had passed with no word from Blum or her captors. The Porsche had been recovered on a dirt road twenty miles out of town. The forensic team had gone over it without finding the prints or trace of anyone other than Pine, Blum, and Mercy, who'd had her prints taken for elimination purposes.

The APB had produced not one sighting. Because Blum was a Bureau employee, additional resources had been deployed. They had nothing to show for it.

Pine was now sitting across from McAllister and Bertrand in the hotel dining room, which had become their ad hoc operations room.

McAllister's face and eyes showed the lack of sleep. Bertrand looked livelier, but Pine didn't need lively, she needed results.

McAllister cast a look at Pine that made her stiffen.

"Yeah?" she said expectantly.

"I'm going to venture into speculation, speculation that might cause you some concern."

"Fire away."

"Could it be possible that your sister had something to do with Blum's disappearance? By her own admission she was the last person with Blum before she disappeared. And her prints *were* in the car."

"Because she was *in* the car. And what would be her motive?"

"Who knows? You don't really know the woman, Pine, admit that."

"I know her well enough. She was helping Carol try to find me. She couldn't be working with the people who snatched me."

"How do you know that?"

"I *told* you. The man who was questioning me wants my sister because he says she killed his brother. They're not working together. He wants to kill *her*. They followed him to a house. They were probably spotted. They took Carol."

McAllister shot his partner a wary glance. "Okay, so why not snatch them *both* if the guy really wants your sister? Why leave her and take Carol? Your sister said she was in the house where they were. Yet they just take off and leave the golden goose behind? It makes no sense."

"McAllister, they might not have known she was even in the house. They may not have even known that Carol and Mercy had hooked up. It was a spontaneous thing. They probably spotted Carol in the Porsche. And if they'd been following us before, they would have seen me and Carol together."

"So when they took you, they thought *you* were your sister?"

"That's right. With the hair and our height she and I closely resemble each other enough for a mistaken identity to happen, particularly to a couple of strangers like the guys who grabbed me. But then they found my shield and realized their mistake."

McAllister leaned back and rubbed a hand across his chin. "So why no word from the captors about Carol? They must want to make an exchange, don't you think?"

"I would say yes. And I don't know why we haven't heard from them."

McAllister tilted his head to eye Bertrand before turning back to Pine. "And when and if that contact comes we'll be in the loop, right?"

"I know Bureau protocols on abduction cases, Agent McAllister," Pine said more sharply than she probably intended.

"Knowing and *acting* on those protocols are two separate things," was his lobbed response. "And I don't want to be sitting here drinking my hundredth cup of coffee only to find out you're playing the hand all on your own."

"What I'm going to be doing is the best I can to make sure Carol comes back safe and sound."

"No argument there, but you didn't answer my question."

"You know how these things can go down," replied Pine.

"Let's face facts. The odds of Blum coming back in anything other than a body bag are pretty damn low. Do you disagree?"

"Yeah, I do disagree, because *I'm* on the case."

"Bravado is not going to help. But moving on to another subject: Tim Pine?"

"I already told you, I have no idea where he is."

"Have you heard from him or your mother?"

"No."

"Not in any way?" he said, watching her closely.

Pine, sensing a trap, said, "Meaning what, exactly? In a dream? Telepathy? On a Ouija board?"

McAllister cleared his throat, finished his coffee, and said, "Agents have talked to Jack Lineberry. He mentioned a letter that your mother had written to him. And that he had given to you?"

Pine sucked in a breath. "Right. Sorry, I didn't think of that."

"Can I see the letter?"

"There are no clues in it. And . . . and it's pretty personal."

"The whole thing is personal, Pine. And it's the only communication that we know of from your mother after she left you. We believe that she and Tim Pine hooked up after fabricating his death."

"Vincenzo went there to kill Tim. He defended himself and Vincenzo died. They covered it up because they saw this as a chance to finally get away from the mob. I already *told* you all that."

"That may well be the case. But right now all I know for a fact is that the man in the grave was Ito Vincenzo, when your mother and Jack Lineberry lied and said it was Tim Pine. Their motivations notwithstanding, that *is* a crime. And as I'm sure you know, I can't take your word for it that Tim Pine killed Vincenzo in self-defense."

"He kidnapped my sister and almost killed me," barked Pine. "You don't think he would have tried to murder the man he thought was our father?"

"If the killing was justified, he has nothing to worry about. But we're not there yet, as you also well know. If somebody could get off killing another person based on what-ifs and maybes we'd have a lot more murders and far emptier prisons." He reached over and tapped her hand. "If you were working this case on the Bureau's end would you do anything differently than what I'm doing? If so, I'm listening."

Pine shut her eyes, but just for a moment, her mind whirling at warp speed, processing all of this. When she opened them she said, "I'll get the letter for you."

"Thank you," said McAllister, an edge of relief in his voice.

Pine rose and looked down at him. "If you hear anything on Carol's whereabouts, let me know. And I'll do likewise."

"Thank you for *finally* answering my question."

After Pine stalked off McAllister turned to his colleague.

"You stick to her like superglue, Neil."

The younger agent nodded, rose, and headed off.

65

Another twenty-four hours went by with no word about Blum and no demand from her captors.

Mercy and Pine were sharing the latter's room at the hotel.

Over lunch in their room Pine said, "Something is off. It doesn't take this long to communicate."

"Maybe they're trying to put the squeeze on you. Get you uptight, hoping you make a mistake."

Pine put down her coffee cup. Her sister was wearing a pair of her jeans that were two inches too short, and a shirt that was a little tight across her broad shoulders but rode well over the rest of her torso.

"I guess that could be. But they're also allowing us time to come up with a plan of our own."

"And *are* we coming up with a plan of our own?" asked Mercy as she put the last forkful of salad into her mouth. Pine watched with a twinge of heartbreak as her sister sopped up every last bit of salad dressing with her piece of roll before depositing it in her mouth as well. The plate looked clean enough to be used again.

Mercy caught her looking and said, "I don't waste food."

"Yeah, I get that. In answer to your question, it's hard to come up with a plan when you don't know what the other side is going to do. But McAllister has notified the FBI about the situation and they are standing ready, as are the local cops. And the APB is still out there."

"So you think this is going to go down in Asheville?"

Pine looked at her thoughtfully. "Not necessarily."

"What *are* you thinking?"

"I'm thinking that your using your credit card brought the people who took Carol to Asheville."

"Meaning they put a trace on my card?"

"Yes. But they knew other things and I'm wondering where they learned—shit!"

"What?"

Pine held up a hand and made a call. She put the phone on speaker and laid it on the table between them.

Wanda Atkins sounded upset. "Agent Pine, you never called me back."

"I know, I'm sorry, things got a little crazy. But I remember you saying you had something else to tell me? That some 'other' people had visited you?"

"That's right. But first things first, did you find Mercy?"

"Yes, yes I did. And your call was very helpful. Thank you."

"Well, that's good. I'm glad. But that gal scared the bejesus out of me. Are you sure she's right in the head?"

Pine glanced at Mercy with a nervous smile. "Tell me about these other people."

"That was the other reason I called you. Two people came by asking questions about Mercy and you."

"When was this?"

"The same day Mercy came by, only later. They just showed up on my doorstep."

"What did they want?"

"They said Mercy had murdered somebody. They were trying to find her and convince her to turn herself in."

"Who were they?"

"I don't know. They didn't give me their names. But I think they were with the police or something. They seemed very professional. And I told them that you had been by to see me. I gave them your card."

"Who was she supposed to have murdered? Did they give you a name?"

"No, they didn't say."

"Was the man tall and lean, dark hair, dressed nicely, good-looking?"

"Yes, that's right."

"And the other person?"

"A woman. About your height, but leaner. Dark hair. Very pretty. Very intense. She . . . she . . ."

"She what?"

"Well, she seemed to be blaming me for what happened to Mercy. Like laying a guilt trip on me. I didn't care for that."

"Okay." The woman evidently wanted a sympathetic response from Pine, but she wasn't going to get it. "Go on."

"And when I showed them your card the fellow asked the woman if she recognized the name, but she said she didn't. She said something like there are thousands of female FBI agents. I asked her if she was an agent and she said no, but that she knew some."

"So let me get this right. They didn't give you their names. I'm assuming they didn't have badges or credentials showing they actually were police. So why did you talk to them?"

"Well . . . They seemed nice and professional, like I said."

"Wanda, I need to know *everything*. And I mean everything!"

"Okay, okay," the woman said in a flustered tone. "The man paid me two thousand dollars in cash. I really didn't have a choice. I *had* to take it. Me and Len barely get by what with all the medical bills. And let me tell you, Medicare and the VA don't cover it all, not by a long shot."

"Did you see the car they drove up in?"

"No. When I answered the door the lady pointed out that somebody had knocked down our lamppost and I guess that distracted me. I bet it was Mercy. Like I said, she scared the bejesus out of me. Said she wanted to kill me and Len."

"I *did* knock it down," said Mercy. "I did that to the lamppost so I wouldn't do it to *you*."

Wanda snapped, "Is that you, Mercy? I didn't know you were on the call."

"Well, I am."

"What you did was not very nice. It'll cost something to fix that lamppost."

"You came into two grand because of me, so there's that."

Pine interjected impatiently, "Wanda, would you be able to recognize these people?"

"Yes, I think so. They both kind of, you know, stood out, so to speak."

Pine checked her watch. "I'd like to come and see you today."

"Why?"

"You can give us fuller details. And I want to check around the neighborhood. Somebody may have seen the people, too, and the car, and maybe gotten its license plate number. We need to find these people, and this is the only lead we have right now."

"Why do you need to find them?'

"Because I'm pretty sure they're the ones who

kidnapped Carol Blum, the woman who was with me when we visited you."

"Oh my God. I feel like I've been dropped into some damn spy movie or something."

"Only this is real life. So you'll be home this evening?"

"Yes. I really don't go nowhere anymore."

"By the way, we found Desiree. She's in prison."

"What! What for?"

"Keeping another little girl prisoner."

"Christ Almighty. Hope she never gets out."

"I've got some things to finish up and then we'll head out. We can probably be there around seven this evening."

"Are these really bad people? They seemed very nice."

"I'll see you around seven."

66

Pine was driving the Porsche SUV the police had recovered, and her sister was riding shotgun.

In the backseat was Special Agent Neil Bertrand. He was there because Drew McAllister had insisted Pine allow him to accompany them. She had introduced Bertrand to her sister. The tall, lanky agent seemed intrigued by Mercy Pine. He had no doubt learned some of her history, but he asked no questions and rendered no judgments, for which Pine was appreciative.

The day was turning stormy with the clouds moving in and hovering dome-like over them as they passed through Chattanooga, Tennessee, on the wide asphalt strip of I-75. The wind started to buffet the SUV, and Pine gripped the wheel with both hands. The traffic was heavy; tractor-trailer rigs blew past her on both sides carrying the commerce of the country to where it needed to go.

"You really think Wanda Atkins will be able to help you find Blum?" asked Bertrand.

"I'm convinced the people who were there are the

same ones who have Carol. And it's not like we have an abundance of leads." She glanced at him in the mirror. "Do you have a better idea?"

"No," he admitted.

"How long have you been assigned to the WFO?"

"Two years. Before that I was at an RA in Fort Smith, Arkansas."

"Very different from an agent's life in DC," noted Pine.

"Yes it is."

"Which do you prefer?" asked Pine.

"I liked Arkansas. Got to know the people. The work wasn't as challenging as I would have hoped, though they do have drug rings and bank robberies and white supremacist groups in that area."

"Just like pretty much everywhere else," said Pine.

"The WFO has a lot more bureaucracy. But it's an important stepping-stone in an agent's career. I know you were assigned there at some point."

"I was. Then I got out. I like to work on my own. Shattered Rock, Arizona, is my stomping ground and I couldn't be happier. And I can't wait to get back."

The import of her words struck Pine and she glanced at Mercy, who was staring out the window and didn't appear to be listening.

"McAllister said you could have moved up at the Bureau if you wanted to. Gotten a supervisory job at one of the field offices."

"Yeah, move right up to a desk overseeing other

agents' work instead of doing that work. No thanks.
Not why I signed up."

"I get that. It *is* a trade-off."

"And every agent has to make up their mind about
what they want." She looked at him again. "And I can
see you're not there yet."

He smiled. "Nope, not yet."

"Well, you'll get there, don't worry."

It was dark when they got to Huntsville, and the
storm they had been riding into most of the way was
about to unleash its fury on the town. Clouds swirled
into black and gray masses with threads of crackling
lightning embellishing their underbellies, like pulsat-
ing veins in the brain.

"Gonna be a doozy," said Bertrand, staring out the
window. "Glad we didn't fly here."

"I've never been on a plane," said Mercy suddenly.
"What's it like?"

Bertrand glanced uncertainly at Pine before answering. "Um, usually smooth and very fast, of course. Just
don't eat the food, at least in coach class, not that they
give you any food these days. Starvation seems to be
the goal at thirty-five thousand feet. And they pack
you in like sardines. And with your height, the seats
will be a little snug. I'm six three, so I always try to
book the aisle or a bulkhead. That way I can at least
stretch my legs out halfway, or deep vein thrombosis
here I come."

"Sounds great, can't wait to try it," cracked Mercy.

Bertrand smiled as they pulled into the Atkinses' driveway.

As they walked past the toppled lamppost Pine caught Mercy smiling maliciously at her handiwork and couldn't help but smile as well.

A few drops of rain fell and they hurried onto the porch.

Pine knocked and then knocked again when no one answered.

"Place is dark," said Bertrand, glancing at his watch. "It's seven on the dot—they should be expecting us, right?"

"Yes, they should," said Pine, pulling her Glock. Bertrand and Mercy did the same with their weapons.

Pine looked through one of the door's sidelights and saw nothing helpful in return. The rain started to fall harder, and streaks of lightning ranged across the sky with claps of thunder dutifully following.

Pine pounded on the door. "Wanda, open up. Are you okay?" She tried the door but it was locked.

Pine glanced at Bertrand. His gaze was darting in all directions, and he looked ready for whatever came their way. She looked at Mercy, who seemed puzzled but calm.

Pine took a step back, planted her back foot firmly on the wooden decking of the porch, and lashed out with a kick aimed right at the door's hardware. It buckled but didn't break.

Mercy put her shoulder to it, and that did the trick. The portal popped open and swung back hard on its hinges, banging into the wall.

"Mrs. Atkins? Wanda?" called out Pine.

She stepped through the opening, and the other two followed.

Bertrand was the last one through; he groped with his hand for a light switch.

"Wait!" cautioned Pine. In the glare of illumination from the storm she surveyed the front room. There was no wheelchair and no Len. There was nobody. No lights were on. It was like the house had been abandoned. "They could have had an emergency," said Pine. "Maybe with Len. He'd had a stroke."

"Do they have a car?" asked Bertrand.

"I suppose so. Wanda said she didn't really go any-where anymore, but there is a garage. The vehicle might be in there."

"But if there was an emergency, surely they would have called an ambulance," noted Bertrand. "They might be at the hospital."

"Maybe." She pointed Bertrand toward the kitchen. "We'll take the bedrooms and bathrooms," she whis-pered. "You take the kitchen and then the garage."

Bertrand nodded and headed off.

67

The powder room off the foyer was empty. But when Pine and Mercy reached the doorway of the main floor bedroom, Pine hissed, "Shit!"

Wanda Atkins was lying motionless on the bed. Len was in his wheelchair, but hanging off to the side in a way that suggested a total lack of consciousness.

"What's wrong with them?" muttered Mercy.

Pine edged forward and touched Len's wrist with her index finger, holding it there, feeling for a pulse. She next checked his neck pulse, then ran a hand over his face.

Cold. She raised one of his arms. It was supple. He was dead, but clearly not long enough for rigor mortis to set in. That made sense because she had talked to Wanda only about six hours ago. She took out her light and ran it over him. She saw no obvious wounds or other marks and nothing that could tell her how the man had died. She looked over at Wanda to see Mercy standing next to the bed. Pine joined her.

"She looks like she's sleeping," said Mercy.

Pine dispelled that notion when she hit Wanda's eyes with her light and got nothing in return, except the unrelenting stare of the deceased. Still, she checked for a pulse and found none. The woman was cold. She ran her light over her looking for ligature marks, a wound, frothing on the lips to indicate poison.

"She's dead?" asked Mercy.

Pine nodded and then flinched as she sniffed the air. "Do you smell smoke?"

Both sisters turned to the doorway.

"Bertrand!" Pine cried out.

When he didn't answer, Pine gripped her sister's hand as she gazed at the large oxygen tank in the corner, and remembered the others in the front room.

"Bertrand!"

She edged out of the room, with Mercy right behind.

"Bertrand!"

They hustled forward and entered the kitchen.

Pine hit the room with her light. And stopped when it held on Bertrand sitting slumped in a chair.

She raced to him and almost fell. She shone her light on the floor and, with a sickening feeling, saw the fresh pools of blood there. She eased over to the agent, then took a step back when she saw the four-inch incision someone had made across his neck. She looked at his white shirt now turned red; the blood flow had reached all the way to his belt.

She pointed her gun around the space. Pine knew

they had ambushed him as soon as he came into the kitchen, slit his throat so he couldn't cry out, and dumped him to die seconds later in this chair. His eyes stared wide and unseeing at the pebbled ceiling, his jaw was slack, and his skin was already turning pale from no blood running through the veins.

She looked at the back door. It was open. The killer's exit? The storm was raging out there now, and copious amounts of wind were being driven through the opening. If they could catch the bastard who had done this . . .

She looked back at Bertrand. She had lost an agent. The first time ever. Her fault.

"Lee!"

Pine jerked her head at Mercy, who was pointing at the cabinets. After finding Bertrand, Pine had forgotten about the smell of smoke. Now that dilemma was presenting itself front and center.

The cabinets were flaming up, the fire racing across the lacquered wood like someone had dumped gas on paper and struck a match. Pine had never seen a conflagration build that quickly.

She whirled around, forgetting about the fire just for a moment, and with good reason. It had been replaced by something even deadlier to them. For in her mind, Pine once more saw all the large oxygen tanks strewn around the house.

This was no longer a residence in the suburbs.

This was a bomb. Just about to detonate.

She grabbed her sister's arm and pulled her along. "This whole place is going to blow."

They reached the front porch and ran the short distance through the driving rain to the Porsche. Any second Pine expected to be hurled off her feet from the blast wave of a house disappearing and taking her and her sister along with it.

We'll just be ash. Cremated together.

She flung open the driver's-side door and Mercy did the same on the other side.

An instant later everything turned black, for both of them.

68

Pine opened her eyes for a moment and then closed them. She did so again, fighting against the feeling of cement lodged between her eyelids and her face. It was like being in a nightmare and struggling to open your eyes to see the terrible things coming for you.

Finally, they stayed open and she was staring at a low ceiling of whitewashed brick. A brick ceiling was quite unusual. She slowly sat up and stared over at her sister. Mercy was sitting upright on a bunk, her back against the wall.

Pine looked around and took in the barred and chicken-wired window and barred door. "Where are we?"

Mercy shrugged. "We look to be in jail."

Pine stood on wobbly legs, put a hand against the wall to steady herself, then stretched out her back. "Okay, I feel like I was hit by a tank."

"Same here, but I don't remember what happened after I opened the car door."

Pine nodded and glanced out the window at the foreboding terrain outside. She also saw the high fence topped by concertina wire. "What the hell is this place?"

"Saw a guy with an AK walking by out there earlier."

Pine checked her pocket for her phone. It was gone, along with both her pistols.

"Yeah, they took my gun, too," said Mercy.

Pine sat down on her bunk, rubbed her eyes, and said in a bleak voice, "They killed Neil Bertrand. And the Atkinses are dead, too. And we're here."

"Yep," said Mercy. "I think we got played. They were obviously waiting for us there."

"But how could they know we were going to visit Wanda?"

"Don't know. I wonder if the house burned up or blew up first," said Mercy.

"Whoever took us was waiting for us in the Porsche. When I opened the door, I thought I saw something, but then everything went black. They might have hit us with some gas or something."

Mercy nodded but said nothing.

They both perked up when they heard footsteps. It was a man dressed in jeans and a flannel shirt. He was carrying two trays. He put one down, and waited. Then another man appeared, dressed similarly. He was carrying a riot shotgun, Pine noted, like they used in prisons. It was designed to kill over a wide, shallow field of bodies.

The first man unlocked the door and slid the two trays through.

Pine looked at each man; they did not look back at her.

She said, "Can you at least tell us where we are?"

The first man locked the door and they both left without speaking or ever looking at them. It was like they had left food for two invisible people.

Pine picked up one tray and handed it to Mercy while she took the other. They sat on their bunks and ate the food and drank the glasses of water provided.

When they were finished the same two men came back and retrieved the trays. This exact timing made Pine believe they were under surveillance.

Five minutes later another man appeared.

Peter Buckley had on jeans, a white collared shirt, a tan vest, a brown corduroy jacket with olive-green elbow patches, and a pair of all-weather boots.

He pulled up a chair and sat down, facing them from the other side of the bars.

He looked first at Pine and then settled his gaze on Mercy.

"You're the guy I saw at the house, with the lawyer," said Mercy.

Buckley said nothing, he just kept staring at them.

Pine let this scrutiny go on for a bit before saying, "Well, we're here."

Buckley looked at her. He didn't smile, he didn't

chuckle, he didn't look grim or angry or triumphant. He simply appeared curious.

"Yes, you are."

When he spoke Pine's suspicions were confirmed. He was the man who had spoken to her when she'd been kidnapped.

"You killed an FBI agent. And two other people," said Pine.

"No, the Atkinses had a heart attack or a stroke when my men broke into the house. They never touched them."

"And Agent Bertrand?"

"He was supposed to have been anesthetized, as you two were. Unfortunately, things went awry. They're not sure how the fire started, but there's not much left of the house. The important thing is that you are both here."

"How did you know we'd be at the Atkinses?" asked Pine.

"We hid a tracking device in the Porsche after my colleague took Ms. Blum. And we had the Atkinses' line tapped. We heard your conversation."

Pine closed her eyes for a moment, inwardly seething at this oversight on her part.

"And do you also have Carol Blum?" she asked after she reopened her eyes.

Buckley nodded. "She is an important part of this."

"And what exactly is *this*?"

Buckley turned back to Mercy. "You killed my brother."

"No, I didn't."

"What I meant to say was you didn't know you had, but you did."

"That's as clear as mud."

"His name was Ken. You stopped him from hurting Rosa. He pulled a knife and then a gun on you. You beat him up."

Mercy sucked in a breath and looked over at Pine. "He wasn't dead. I checked his pulse. And even though he hit his head, he wasn't a quad. I checked that, too."

Buckley said, "He later died of a brain aneurysm, probably from his head hitting the ground."

Mercy eyed him more closely. "I saw you at that house and thought you looked familiar. It's because you look like Ken around the eyes and jaw."

"You said he deserved it," Pine pointed out. "It was kill or be killed. And she didn't even know he was dead. So what exactly are you trying to do here?"

Buckley crossed one leg over another. "It's payback, but it's complicated payback. Not really connected to the incident with Ken and your *sister*."

Now Pine sucked in a breath.

Buckley smiled at her discomfort. "Yes, we know all about that. What you two represent is symbolic, really."

"Again, clear as mud, as my *sister* said before."

"The government caused my father's death, and turned my mother and my sisters against the rest of the family. I was the only one to really make anything of myself. The payback is against the government. Since I, of course, can't do it directly, I am going to do it indirectly, using you two."

"So you're going to kill us as revenge on the *government*? Doesn't that strike you as a little bit insane?"

"Not at all. It's incredibly logical and has a certain symmetry. And Ken was my brother. Regardless of whether it was justified or not, your sister killed him. In my world, that requires payback. So I'm killing two birds with one stone, at least figuratively."

"So we both die then?"

"Not necessarily."

"What does that mean? And where is Carol?"

"She's safe. In answer to your first question, it will become apparent in short order."

"What will?"

"What I have devised for you. But let me warn you, it will be more difficult than anything you've ever faced."

"We've both faced a lot," said Pine, while Mercy just watched him.

"You've faced nothing like this," said Buckley. "I can assure you."

On that, he rose and left.

69

Two days passed and Pine slept uncomfortably, waking at odd hours. She noted with some envy that her sister slept soundly, seemingly untroubled by the situation they were in. During the day, and knowing that they were probably under surveillance, they discussed things. Mercy filled Pine in on what had happened with Ken.

"I didn't think I hit him that hard," she said. "But he was going to shoot me."

"You did nothing wrong," said Pine.

"Oh, I know that," said Mercy matter-of-factly.

They talked about Mercy's life after she was taken. Her years with the Atkinses were painful for Pine to learn about, and she believed that Mercy glossed over some of it, perhaps to spare her the hardship of learning about it. The years after her sister escaped from the Atkinses were also difficult to hear about, particularly when she had been repeatedly brutalized by people along the way.

"I let it happen," Mercy said simply. "And then I stopped letting it happen."

"You didn't *let* anything happen. The Atkinses kept you in a cage and then you got free. You weren't capable of handling any of what happened to you, Mercy. None of this was fair to you."

"Nothing about life is fair, at least for people like me. But I got things straightened out eventually."

Pine watched her twin closely. "Now I wish you *had* left me. Then you wouldn't be stuck here."

"*I* was the one the dude was after. They would have found me at some point. At least we can face it together, have each other's backs."

Pine reached out and touched her sister's arm. "I just wish I knew where they were keeping Carol. Just because he said she was okay means nothing. I want to *see* that she's okay."

"I wonder what the guy meant about what we would be facing."

"He strikes me as the type to understate, rather than embellish things. So, I guess we're right to be worried."

"Do you think the FBI is looking for us?"

"I'm sure they are. They'll have gone over the Atkinses' house by now. What's left of it, anyway. They'll have found Bertrand's remains. They'll bring everything they have on this one." She said this louder, in the hopes that they *were* being spied on.

Mercy glanced out the window. "Any idea where we are?"

Pine looked out the window, too. "Western U.S.,

I think. If I had to guess, I'd say Utah or Idaho, maybe Colorado. I've been through those states a lot, and I recognize the topography."

"Then we must have been flown here. I don't think we were out long enough to have been driven."

"Which means the man has his own jet with pilots who won't talk."

"He looked like money," said Mercy.

"And this looks like some sort of compound. A jail, perimeter fencing, armed guards."

Mercy said in barely a whisper, "Like the dude from Waco? I read about that."

Pine replied in a low voice. "David Koresh? I don't know. Our guy strikes me as more of a businessman, not some crazed cult leader."

"I guess we'll find out."

Mercy lay back on her bed and put her arm behind her head.

Pine watched her for about a minute, certain things inside of her building, like a jet's engines creating barely suppressed thrust before takeoff. Finally, unable to stay silent any longer, she said, "I'm sorry about everything, Mercy."

Mercy glanced at her. "This wasn't your fault. Dude was after me. I should be apologizing to you."

"No, I didn't mean that. I meant . . ." Pine looked down, gathering the words she wanted to use as precisely as possible. Only her emotion was impeding her effort at logic. Finally, emotion won out.

"I should have looked for you long before now. I just went on with my life and . . . It was like you weren't . . . I didn't deserve to . . . have . . . any . . . fucking thing. I . . . hate . . . myself."

Pine leaned forward, her head nearly touching her knees, wrapped her arms around herself, and started to sob. It was like someone had just dropped an entire world on her soul, crushing it to nothing.

Mercy sat up, looking alarmed, and then her features changed to understanding. She shifted over to the other bunk, drew close to Pine, and finally wrapped her long, strong arms around her. She pressed her mouth to Pine's ear, as Pine was wracked over and over again with sobs, her body shaking uncontrollably. Mercy tightened her grip, trying to quell the guilt-ridden rage inside of her twin.

She said in a low voice, "You're going to get through this. *We* are going to get through this. You always figure it out. Always."

Pine shook her head fiercely. "No, I don't. It took me thirty damn years to find you. I'm useless."

"Look at me, look at me. Lee, look at me!"

A teary Pine finally gazed at her sister.

"Do you remember that old oak tree in our yard? You would climb to the very top and it would make Mom so mad, because she was afraid you were going to fall and kill yourself?"

Pine nodded. "I-I r-remember."

"But you always figured out how to get back

down. Every single time. I watched you do it. You know that, right?"

Pine nodded dumbly.

"Well, this time we're *both* up that tree, but you're going to get us back down."

"H–how can you be so s–sure of that?" said Pine with a pleading look on her face, and sobs still coming jerkily from her.

"I believe in you, Lee. I always did. And that got me through more than you'll ever know."

Slowly, painfully so, Pine's sobs subsided. Her body stopped shaking. Her breathing slowed.

And all the time, Mercy's grip on her held firm.

"I'm here, Lee. I'm here."

Pine let out one additional long gasp of air, straightened, turned to her sister, and wrapped her arms around her. And held her just as tightly as Mercy was embracing her.

"I'll never let you go, Mercy. Whatever happens, I'll never let you go. It's both or none, from now on."

Mercy patted her sister's back and stared up at the ceiling with a troubled look.

Nothing in her life had ever gone as planned. And her features betrayed what she was feeling.

She had found her sister, or her sister had found her.

They were together after all these years.

And now they would probably die together.

★

Mercy

In another room of the jail, Britt Spector sat alone in front of a video screen set up on a desk, with a pair of audio buds in her ears. She had just finished watching and listening to this entire exchange between the two sisters.

She cut the video feed off and yanked the buds out of her ears. And with her own memories wracking her, Spector stared at the screen as the tears rolled down her cheeks.

70

Pine and Mercy were jolted from sleep by the drumming of boots on wood. They sat up on their bunks as the half-dozen large men filed into the room. Four of them were armed with shotguns. The other two held restraints designed to transport prisoners.

Buckley was not with this group.

Pine searched the men's faces. They were all hard, featureless, soulless. They were here to do a job—a well-paid job, no doubt—and they were going to do it. Morals, issues of right and wrong, were never going to be entertained by such people.

"On your feet," said one man. He was the smallest among them, at six one, but he also looked the sharpest.

"Where are we going?" asked Pine. "And where's Carol?"

"We're taking you to her. Now, on your feet!"

The door was opened and both women's ankles and wrists were manacled with the chains, which were then interconnected around their waists, forcing them to do the prison shuffle as they left their cell.

One man nudged Pine in the back with his shot-gun. "Now you know how it feels to perp-walk, FBI."

They were led outside, where it was cold and dark with a raw wind blowing in from the west. Pine shivered and felt sprinkles of rain land on her head.

As they were marched across the dirt she could see other buildings, the guard tower, and a row of vehicles. This clearly was a compound of some kind, stuck in the middle of nowhere. Could the well-dressed and well-spoken man who was doing all this really be some sort of cult leader, like a David Koresh? Or was he the head of some criminal organization? The men surrounding them looked far more like hardened criminals than potential Kool-Aid drinkers. If so, that did not bode well for Pine, Mercy, and Blum.

They were led into a large building that looked like a barn, and there they were separated. Before that happened, Pine had a glimpse of something large in the middle of the space. She couldn't see what it was, because it was draped with a huge tarp.

She was led into a small room by two of the armed men. Hanging on wall pegs were articles of clothing.

One man took off her chains while the other kept a shotgun pointed at Pine.

The man stepped back, coiling the chains around his arm. He said, "Take your clothes off in that little stall over there and put those on." He indicated the things hanging on the pegs.

"Why?"

The other man waggled the shotgun. "Just put them on. We'll be waiting right here. You got two minutes before we come in there, so hustle it up. And no shoes or socks. Leave those behind."

Pine grabbed the items and marched into the stall. She stripped down to her underwear and then looked at the articles of clothing.

What the hell?

She slipped on the Lycra shorts, a chest protector, and the sports top.

She stepped out of the stall and looked at the men. "What is going on?"

They just motioned her to the doorway they had come through.

They returned to the main area, where Pine saw Mercy come out of another area of the building wearing clothes nearly identical to her own. Her twin stared back at her, obviously as confused as she was.

They were led over to the tarp.

And that was when Buckley appeared. He was dressed in khaki pants, a tan sports coat with a yellow crew neck sweater underneath, and sturdy brown boots.

Pine glared at him. "What in the hell is all this about?"

In answer, Buckley motioned to a man standing in a far corner, his hand on a metal lever connected to a machine with a flywheel and a chain. The man pulled on the lever, and the space was filled with the whine of engaged hydraulics.

They all watched as the tarp, attached to a chain at its pinnacle, was slowly lifted. Revealed underneath was something very familiar to Mercy.

A UFC cage. She glanced over at her sister, her mouth agape.

The tarp was swung away from over the cage and deposited on the ground.

Pine looked at Buckley. "That doesn't answer my question."

"This will," said Buckley. He motioned to another man. He disappeared from sight, but came back about ten seconds later, leading a blindfolded and gagged Carol Blum.

"Carol!" exclaimed Pine. She tried to reach her, but a wall of armed men barred her way.

Blum was forced to sit in a chair next to the cage and her blindfold was taken off, but her gag remained. As her eyes adjusted to the light, she saw Pine, and then Mercy, and her eyes widened to the extreme edge of their range.

Pine whirled on Buckley. "Look, just let her go. Your beef is with us, not her. Just let her go."

Buckley stayed silent for a moment and then said, "Are you finished? Because I have a schedule to keep."

Pine just scowled back.

"Good. Now, as you can see, you are about to engage in battle with your sister."

"The hell I am!"

He looked at the man next to Blum and nodded. The man took out a serrated-edged knife and held it against Blum's neck.

"If you don't fight, your friend dies and then you both die, too. It's up to you."

Mercy stepped forward. "*I* killed your brother, not them. Let me fight one of your guys. Hell, I'll fight all of them. But you don't have to hurt my sister or Carol."

Again, Buckley remained silent for a moment. "Are *you* finished?"

Mercy glanced at Pine but said nothing.

"Let me introduce you to your referee."

From out of the shadows stepped Britt Spector. She was dressed in a striped hoodie with a kangaroo pouch, and black pants that hung loosely on her, with a knapsack over one shoulder. Her hair was tied back. She came to stand next to Buckley. Spector didn't look at Pine or Mercy. Her gaze just stared out.

Buckley said, "Now for the rules. There will be four rounds. Five minutes each round. If, at any time, I feel that you are not fighting your hardest . . ." He turned to the man next to Blum. "Jason over there will make an incision on your friend's skin. Each subsequent incision will be deeper and draw more blood. The ending of this is easy to see. The more times I request the cuts, the more blood she loses. A tipping point will be reached and that will be that. But I will be fair in my calls."

"Sure you will," snapped Mercy.

"And how exactly *does* this end?" said Pine.

"If one of you wins by knockout, you live, as does Ms. Blum. And the other one dies. If neither of you clearly wins, you both die. Along with Ms. Blum."

"And you expect us to believe that you'll just let us walk out of here to tell the cops what happened?"

"I didn't say the winner walks out of here. I said you get to *live*. I didn't say where or how."

An enraged Pine bolted toward Buckley, but two of the men tackled her before she could get to him.

She fell at his feet. He looked down at her and then nodded at the man next to Blum.

Pine saw this and screamed, "No, please, don't hurt her."

The man ripped open Blum's sleeve with the knife and cut delicately into her skin. Blum jerked back as the blade sliced into her. She started to shake with pain.

Pine was hauled to her feet and was vibrating with fury, as Buckley looked at her in disappointment.

"I expected better from you," he said. "And your sister is apparently a real killer in the cage. You better bring your A game."

He jerked his head at his men. They force-marched

the two women into the ring. Spector followed and then the door was closed behind them.

Spector finally looked at them. "Are you two ready?"

"What the fuck do you think?" snapped Pine.

"If you don't fight hard, he will do exactly as he said he would to your friend."

"And you really expect us to believe he's not going to kill all three of us regardless of what happens in here?" said Pine.

"I don't know what else to tell you," said Spector, looking at the dirt.

"Great, thanks for the help," said Mercy.

"I'm just doing my job."

"Right, I'm sure he's paying you plenty. Enjoy it along with the memory of a triple homicide," barked Pine.

Spector led them over to the center of the ring. She pulled from the knapsack two pairs of UFC gloves and two mouthpieces. She helped the women get them on and then looked over at a man who was standing next to a large countdown clock set on a table and visible to all in the cage.

"Okay, I'm sure you both know the rules. Knock-outs and armbar stops are in my sole judgment. Your level of fighting is up to him. And Carol is already bleeding some, so keep that in mind."

Both women looked over at Blum to see her

pained face and the swelling patch of blood leaching onto her torn sleeve.

Pine stared at her sister. Mercy looked back at her, with not a shred of hope on her features.

"Well," said Pine. Her voice was garbled because of the mouthpiece. "He was right about this being something I've never faced before."

Spector said, "Okay, step back and then commence fighting on the sound of the horn."

Pine looked once more at Mercy and shook her head.

"Shit" was all she could think to say.

71

When the horn sounded, they marched forward, and each assumed a defensive stance. Mercy looped a kick; Pine blocked it and then threw an awkward punch.

The scream froze them.

Blum's gag had been removed. And the man standing next to her had made a large cut on her upper arm, where blood was streaming down.

"Carol!" screamed Pine.

Buckley called out, "I warned you. Now fight!"

Spector stepped between them and whispered. "Do it, ladies, or she's dead. Just make contact and absorb the punishment. He's not an expert in MMA. Come on. You can do this."

Pine gave her a curious look as she stepped back.

Mercy eyed her sister and said, "Let's give the asshole a show."

Pine launched a right hook at Mercy's left oblique, and she fell back. As Pine charged forward Mercy pivoted and landed a side kick to Pine's jaw. Had her sister unleashed her full power, Pine's jaw would have been broken. It still hurt like hell.

Pine clinched and then pushed her sister off. They landed solid blows with their fists and feet. They kept doing so until the horn sounded and the round ended.

They retreated to separate sides, where a bottle of G2 with a squirt top was hanging from a hook on the fencing next to a white towel. Spector held the bottle to Pine's mouth and let her suck on it. She wiped Pine's face, arms, and legs off with the towel.

While she was doing that Spector said in a low voice, "Just keep doing what you're doing."

Pine eyed Spector curiously.

"Just hang in there," said Spector. "And trust me."

She went over to Mercy's side to provide hydration and toweling off and relayed the exact same thing.

Buckley called through the fence. "Well done. Now keep it up. I want more!"

The horn sounded and the second round began.

They met in the middle of the ring and started kicking and slugging. During a clinch Pine mumbled, "So do we trust her?"

Mercy said, "Hell, do we have a choice?"

They heard another scream and both turned to see the man slice into Blum's arm again. Then they both turned to Buckley, who was now standing at the chain-link fence. "Not a single knockdown yet?"

Pine looked at Mercy, who tapped her chest. A silent communication occurred. It was like they were kids again playing in the backyard in Georgia.

Pine stepped back and then exploded forward with a looping kick that slammed into the left side of Mercy's head. Mercy staggered backward, impacted the fence, and went down to one knee, her taut belly sucking in and out.

Pine sprang forward, but Mercy had already risen and she drove a fist right into Pine's gut. She staggered back and dropped to her butt. Mercy was on her, and the two women struggled, each trying to arm-bar the other. Pine finally kicked free and rose with blood streaming down her face.

It was with both pride and envy that Pine had to admit that though their strength levels were about equal, her sister was bigger, more limber, and a better MMA fighter than she was.

The third round went just like the second did. Mercy and Pine pounded away, but Pine could tell Mercy was holding back on her blows and Pine did her best to both do the same, and physically react as if she was getting the shit kicked out of her, which wasn't all that far from the truth. Both their faces were bloody, their limbs and torsos lumpy with bruises, their breathing ragged, and their bodies, despite the chilly air, dripping copious amounts of sweat.

Standing by the fence, Buckley took all of this in and seemed to be enjoying himself. He even did a bit of shadow boxing, to the amusement of his men, who were hooting and clapping and stamping their feet the whole time.

Before the fourth and final round started, Spector again administered hydration and toweling. As she did so she relayed to each of them the same message.

"Listen for my signal at a minute to go. At the thirty-second mark fight like hell. I'll need the distraction."

Then she had stealthily pressed something rubbery into their ears while drying off their heads with the towel.

Both women readied themselves for the final round. Spector glanced subtly at the knapsack she had hung on the chain-link fence, then stepped back with her hands hanging loosely at her hips. She looked behind her once, first at Buckley, at whom she smiled triumphantly, and then at Blum, who sat there, her arm bloody and a horrified expression on her face at what she was watching.

The air horn sounded and the two women went at it with gusto. They had five minutes, maybe, left to live. They landed blow after blow, arm bar after arm bar. Each of them went down twice, but for both it looked far worse than it felt. To their audience, they looked near death. In reality, they had a lot of gas left.

Pine tried hard not to look, but her attention would flick to Spector every now and then. The woman looked inscrutable every time Pine glanced her way.

"You're both still standing," called out Buckley. "That will not *do*, ladies."

"A minute to go," cried out Spector.

When Pine glanced at Spector, she had positioned herself so that her back was to the crowd. The woman formed a one and a zero with her fingers and then closed her eyes for one second.

Pine instantly got what she was communicating. In a clinch with Mercy she whispered instructions to her.

"Thirty seconds to go," Spector called out a bit later.

On cue, Mercy kicked Pine so hard that she flew across the ring and slammed into the fence opposite Spector. Pine was dazed and slow to get up. Mercy pounced on her sister and started pounding away, as the men cheered and raced over there to get closer to witness the kill.

As all eyes were on the sisters, Spector reached inside the knapsack.

"Ten seconds to go," cried Spector.

Pine and Mercy closed their eyes, so they couldn't see the gun in Spector's right hand and the other objects in her left.

She fired twice between the chain links. Both shots hit their targets, and the man holding the blade next to Blum fell down dead.

With her other hand Spector had already launched twin flash bangs. They sailed over the fence and hit within a foot of where Buckley and his men were clustered together.

Mercy

The devices detonated and the space was engulfed with smoke and a brilliantly lit, decibel-shattering explosion. Buckley and his men instantly collapsed to the ground.

Pine and Mercy, with the earplugs in and their eyes closed and averted, were able to rise quickly, and sprinted after Spector to the door. She kicked it open and shot through the smoke toward where Blum had slumped to the floor.

One of the men on the ground groaned and reached feebly out. Spector flattened him with a kick and Pine made sure he stayed down with another blow to the back of the head.

Spector struggled to lift Blum. Mercy pushed past her, bent down, and lifted Blum over her shoulder.

"Let's go," she barked.

72

Spector sprinted to the door with Mercy right behind. The women had removed their ear plugs. Pine brought up the rear. When a figure loomed up in front of her, she kicked him in the head. As he started to topple, she slammed her fist into his back, causing him to scream and pitch forward.

They met an armed guard as they rounded a corner.

"What the hell is going on?" he shouted.

In answer, Spector shot him in the head.

Pine stopped and grabbed the man's AK and pistol, and she thrust the latter into her shorts.

"The SUV's right over here, come on," urged Spector.

They could hear cries from inside the building from where they had just fled, as well as feet running their way from other parts of the compound.

They reached the black Escalade, and Mercy and Pine loaded Blum in. Spector jumped into the driver's seat and fired up the engine. Mercy climbed in next to Blum. Pine was about to get into the front passenger seat when a man came out and fired at them. The slug shattered the side window and passed right behind Spector's head.

"Get in," she cried out.

Pine did, after placing AK rounds into the man's torso, dropping him where he stood.

Spector slammed down the gas right as Pine managed to shut her door. They accelerated, and quickly reached the gates leading out of the compound. A man in the guard tower called out to them to stop. Before he could aim and fire, Pine, leaning out the shattered passenger window, hit him with two rounds from the pistol. The man toppled over the tower's edge and hit the dirt next to them as the SUV rammed into the gates, popping them open.

Spector aimed the SUV straight ahead, but then started to veer as gunfire came at them from the rear. Pine looked back to see men running after them and firing.

Some bullets slammed into the SUV's body, but fortunately, none of the rounds hit its tires.

Pine turned back around as Spector hung a left and they passed out of their pursuers' sightlines. "Where the hell are we?"

"The middle of nowhere in Idaho."

"Okay, next question: Why'd you help us?"

Spector didn't look at her, choosing to keep her gaze ahead. "You have a wonderful assistant in Carol Blum, Agent Pine. She talks a good, honest game. She made me rethink some things that I thought I was long past rethinking."

Mercy checked out the still not fully conscious Blum and said, "We need to bandage her up. She's still bleeding."

"Shit," barked Pine. She climbed into the back seat.

"In the duffel in the cargo area I've got a first aid kit," said Spector. "And some clothes, food, water, guns, and ammo."

"You thought of everything," said Pine. She searched through the duffel and found the first aid kit. As she worked away on Blum, she said, "Carol, you're going to make it. You're going to be fine."

Blum was obviously still dazed by the flash bangs, and the blood loss had made her weak. But she managed to open her eyes and nod. She looked at the back of Spector's head, and a small, satisfied smile crept across her face.

Pine got Blum to drink some water and then checked the wounds to make sure the bleeding had been stopped. She retaped the bandages down over the gauze, glanced at Mercy with a relieved expression, and climbed back into the front seat. She looked at the speedometer and saw they were doing eighty.

"You ladies did your part well," said Spector.

Pine rubbed her jaw. "Maybe too well." She glanced with pride at her sister. "I know you were holding back. If you hadn't been, you would have knocked me out in the first minute."

"Don't kid yourself, Lee, you pack a wallop," said Mercy, gingerly rubbing her left oblique.

Pine said to Spector, "Where are we going?"

"There's a town, about a hundred and fifty miles from here. It's the closest place. But we're not out of the woods yet. I did my best, took out some of their vehicles, but I couldn't get to them all. But with this head start we should be able to keep in front of them."

"You more than did your part."

Spector glanced at her. "I hope you remember that if we actually survive this."

Pine looked at her for a moment and then glanced at Blum, holding the other woman's weary gaze for a second. She turned back to Spector. "We'd all be dead but for you. I don't care why you were there. I just care that you helped us. It was a big risk. If it hadn't worked, they would have killed you for sure."

"Okay," said Spector, turning her full attention to driving. "Why don't you and your sister change your clothes? It's some of my stuff. You're both taller than me, but it'll do, for now."

Mercy opted for sweatpants and a long-sleeved T-shirt, a lined leather jacket that was tight in the shoulders, and running shoes that were long enough but too narrow. Pine put on jeans, a wool sweater, and a sleeveless parka vest with hiking boots on her feet. She had a pistol and the AK, and Spector had brought along two other pistols, a shotgun, and a long-range sniper rifle.

"I like your choice in guns," said Pine.

"Nothing comes between me and first-class weaponry," quipped Spector.

Pine and Mercy settled into their seats on either side of Blum. As they rode along, Blum began to come around enough to where she sat up straighter and looked at Pine.

"We're going to be okay, Carol."

"I know. I will bet on you every time." She eyed Mercy and put a hand on her broad shoulder. "And you too, Mercy."

"I hope I don't disappoint you then."

"I don't think you could ever do that."

"Are you feeling better? Here, drink some more water, keep your fluids up," said Pine. She helped Blum to drink some water, then recapped it and sat back.

Blum reached out and took each of the sisters' hands in a firm grip as the SUV roared along.

Up front, Spector smiled as she looked behind her in the mirror and saw nothing except the dark. Then she glanced at the gas gauge and her jaw slackened. "We had a full tank when we left. I'm already down to half. Something's off."

"Shit, they must have hit the fuel tank," said Pine. "Pop the cargo window."

She climbed back there and peered out the rear window. Pine could see the trail of gas they were leaving behind.

"We're never going to make that town at this point," warned Spector.

"No repair places or gas stations along the way?" asked Mercy.

"There is *nothing* along the way except what you see right now."

"Don't you have a phone?" said Pine.

"I do, but this is one of the 'no coverage' spots you see on the service provider commercials. We won't have phone service until we're about a mile outside of the town."

Mercy said, "Can we stop and maybe plug the hole with something?"

Pine peered behind them and saw what looked to be headlights.

"I don't think we can stop," she said, indicating the headlights far in back of them. "They regrouped a lot faster than I would have thought."

Spector glanced in the mirror and said, "Well, damn."

"Yeah," said Pine, looking at her. "Damn."

73

Peter Buckley sat in the rear seat of the Jeep looking grim. He eyed the gun in his hand. It had been a long time since he had personally killed anyone. Right now, he was looking forward to it.

And he intended to torture and then gut Britt Spector for betraying him. He chastised himself for not seeing the clear warning signs. She had been acting funny, distracted—no, not distracted; *disillusioned* was a better term. As though she were reevaluating things in her life. Well, she certainly had chosen a different path. Maybe it was because they were all women, and two of them were with the FBI. Maybe that connection ran deeper than even she knew.

They had seen evidence of the gas leak, though, and he knew they would not have enough fuel to reach help. The terrain here was rugged and unforgiving. When they ran out of gas, they would run out of heat. And at night, the temps would plunge into the teens or lower. But he expected to catch up to them long before then.

It would not be a fair fight. He had too many men,

and they were four women, and one was in her sixties. He appreciated the symmetry because the fight
that had nearly killed his father here had not been fair,
either. Buckley had not gotten his revenge back at the
cage fight. He would get it out here. And out here
was where he would bury all the bodies, far, far under
the dirt, and cover them with boulders.

He looked out the window at the bleak sky, and
imagined how it all was going to end. This had
become his single, defining moment, he could see
that clearly now. All of the other things he'd done
with his life—the money, the connections, the bit of
fame, travel and culture—it meant nothing. It was as
if he had wasted his entire life. But now he had a
chance to make it up. He had never felt closer to his
father than he did right now. And the elder son was
finally going to avenge his father, once and for all.

Ten miles ahead, Spector cut into a box canyon that
had been formed by raging water millions of years
ago, and rode the narrow dirt strip as far back as she
could. From the gauge she calculated they had about
five gallons of gas left, and she noted that the fuel
level had stabilized—the bullets must have pierced the
tank above the remaining fuel. However, it was not
enough to get to the town, particularly at the high
speed she needed to maintain. That was why she had
turned off into this canyon. Stopping out in the flat-
lands would mean they would have no chance at all.

She pulled the SUV behind a pile of collapsed rock and cut the engine.

"They might miss this turnoff, which could buy us some time."

"Time to do what?" said Mercy. She looked out the window. "I don't see anyone coming to the rescue."

Spector nodded. "This really is the middle of nowhere except for Buckley's compound."

"Buckley?" asked Pine.

"Yes. I guess you don't know who he is."

"Only that he has a brother named Ken," said Mercy. "I guess Ken Buckley."

Spector started to speak, but, surprisingly, it was Blum who ended up telling them all about Buckley and his family's past.

"This was long before your time at the Bureau, Agent Pine." She glanced at Spector, as if to say, *And yours, too.*

If Pine noticed this look, she said nothing.

Blum continued, "He told me this was not really about avenging his brother, but his father, and everything he stood for. He seemed very excited about it, in a sick sort of way."

Spector nodded and said, "When he explained it to me, he seemed a bit . . . mad actually."

"Have you known him long?" asked Pine.

"I've done other work for him," said Spector vaguely. "But nothing personal like this. And he was never part of those missions. He just paid me to go in and do what needed to be done."

"And your name is . . . ?" asked Pine.

"I would prefer to keep that to myself."

Pine stared at her for a moment, but didn't push the point.

Spector said, "Okay, we need to set up a perimeter. And I'm sure you're hungry after beating each other up. And an army can't fight on an empty stomach."

Later, after they had eaten and had some water, Pine took the first watch. She noted that Spector's choice of locations had been a good one. The road coming in here was narrow and provided her with an excellent sight line. Blum was in the SUV with a blanket around her, and Mercy standing guard.

Pine held the sniper rifle with the attached scope as she lay on top of a flat ledge that jutted out from the wall of the canyon. Spector had taken some things with her and disappeared down the road.

Clipped to her belt was a walkie-talkie that Spector had given her. She'd told Pine that she had taken a set with her from the compound but set them to a different frequency. Pine had used it to check in with her from time to time. Spector had reported back that there was no sign of Buckley and his men. "There are a maze of canyons and switchbacks and foothills around here. They lost sight of us for a bit, and that's when I made my turn into here. We passed some of them on the way here, so they'll have to check those first. Knowing Peter, they'll be very methodical, meaning it will take them time to find us."

But Pine knew at some point they *would* find them.

She looked behind her for a moment, where the two most important people in her life were: Blum and her sister. They really were her family, the only one she was ever likely to have now. And it was at least even money that she was going to lose her family and her life right here. But if it came to that, she told herself, she was fortunate indeed to have found Mercy before her end came.

And if this is our Alamo, at least we'll take as many of them with us as we can.

Later, as she sighted through the scope, Pine stiffened. A figure was running toward her location. Pine's finger slid to the trigger guard and held. Until she could make a definite ID she would not fire. Her walkie-talkie squawked.

"It's me," said the voice over the ether.

She relaxed as Spector reached the ledge.

Spector said two words, the only ones she needed to say:

"They're coming."

74

"I'll take the sniper rifle," said Spector. "They're on foot now, going slow and taking no chances. We've got about thirty minutes."

"I'm good right here," replied Pine.

"I've got something else for you to do. Quick, follow me."

Pine reluctantly handed over the rifle and followed her back to their campsite. They told Mercy what was happening; Mercy gripped her pistol and said, "They'll have to go through me to get to Carol."

Spector popped the cargo door on the SUV and opened a small duffel. She pulled out a small drone and its accompanying remote control.

"Ever use one of these?" she asked Pine.

"Yeah, for surveillance. In the hinterlands of Arizona, it comes in handy. How'd you score that?"

"It belongs to Buckley. He uses it to keep an eye on his property. He doesn't like trespassers. I thought I could put it to better use, so I pinched it."

"Good thinking," commented Mercy.

"Okay, this remote has a screen, so you see what

the drone sees. I want you to take up position behind the boulder next to the ledge where you were."

"And then what?"

"I want you to fly this sucker straight down the road where they're heading in right now. Keep it at about a hundred feet. It's small enough, and it's dark enough that they won't be able to see it very well." She pointed to the drone's underbelly. "Now *this* is the key. When the drone is right over them, hit this button on the remote." She indicated the button on the right. "I'll do the rest."

"You don't have to do it all," said Pine.

"I won't. There are too many of them. They're going to breach our outer defenses. When they do, well, it's going to come down to hand-to-hand and whatever tricks we can come up with. But I'm betting on us."

Pine looked at the sniper rifle. "You sure you don't want me to do that part?"

Spector looked uncomfortable. In a low voice she said, "You know HRT?"

"The FBI's Hostage Rescue Team? Yes, of course."

Spector gripped the rifle. "Well, I was a sniper with them for two years. This is the same model rifle I used back then."

She didn't meet Pine's gaze. At first. When she did look up, Pine's eyes were boring into hers.

Spector licked her lips nervously.

"Then you better get in position. And good luck," Pine said finally.

"Thanks, Agent Pine."

She hustled off. Pine checked on Blum, and then had a brief word with her sister.

Pine handed Mercy her walkie-talkie and told her if anything came up to contact Spector right away. She added, "If this goes sideways . . . I . . . Look, I'm just so happy that we found each other."

Mercy clipped the walkie-talkie to her waistband and looked down at her sister. She put a hand on her shoulder. "It won't go sideways. We've got a job to do and we'll do it. These assholes won't know what hit them."

Pine gripped her hand and squeezed it.

"I just have to get us down the tree, like you said."

"But *this* time, I'll help you do it, Lee."

Pine hurried off with the drone and took up her position. She glimpsed Spector up on the ledge in a prone position; the tripod legs of the sniper rifle were deployed, and she was sighting through the night vision scope. It seemed the woman's focus was complete.

HRT? thought Pine. They were the best of the best. It was good to know about the woman. And also troubling as hell.

Pine set the drone down and fired it up. Manipulating the controls, she watched as it rose into the air, then she directed it toward the road.

She guided it up to a hundred feet and drove it forward some more. Pine studied the illuminated screen closely. Threading across the screen was a cluster of heavily armed men. They were outlined in black and gray on the screen and were making good time, but there was caution in their movements. The lead man knelt down, scanned the ground, picked up a handful of loose dirt, and sniffed it.

The gas, thought Pine. The smell was still in the dirt.

The group moved forward. She thought she could make out Buckley. He was near the front, a shotgun in his hands.

She let the drone hover over the group for a few moments. Then she put her finger on the button Spector had showed her, said a silent prayer, and pushed it.

The darkness over Buckley and his men was ripped away as the drone's searchlight exploded down on them like a sunrise of startling proximity.

A bare millisecond passed before Pine heard Spector's rifle begin firing.

On the screen Pine saw a man shot and he fell. Then another, and a third. The rest scattered, trying to avoid the light from the drone that made them sitting ducks. But Pine moved the drone to keep them in the spotlight.

Spector's rifle roared again and again. And more men fell.

Shit, thought Pine. *That gal can shoot.*

The next moment the drone was blown out of the sky by a shot from one of Buckley's men. The darkness instantly returned.

But the damage had been done.

Spector scrambled down from the ledge as return fire hit all around her position, blowing off shards of rock with each impact. She met up with Pine.

"We need to fall-back."

"The road gets narrower up ahead," said Pine. "We can funnel them into that."

They raced away as shots continued to fly at them, and the sounds of running feet echoed off the canyon walls as their pursuers closed in. The gunfire became so intense that they finally had to stop running and duck down.

"Look out," screamed Spector a few moments later.

A man appeared out of the darkness and charged forward, firing at Pine. She turned and shot him in the chest. He fell dead to the dirt.

Then Pine groaned as a piece of sharpened rock, blown off by all the concentrated gunfire, slashed her in the arm, shredding the skin and flinging blood over her.

Pine grabbed her arm but managed to turn and run.

Spector slung her rifle over her shoulder, pulled a pistol, and sprayed the area behind them with gunfire to buy them some time. They rounded a bend, sprinted ahead, and reached the SUV.

Pine grabbed the first aid kit, and Mercy helped her bandage her arm.

"You gonna be okay?" asked Mercy.

"Oh, yeah," said Pine. "No way I'm missing this shit."

Pine grabbed some spare mags from one of the duffels.

Mercy snatched up the shotgun and held the weapon at the ready.

"I laid Carol down in the back seat," she told Pine. "Figure bullets are going to be flying."

"You're the failsafe, Mercy. If they get past us it's up to you."

She racked the pistol's slide, slid some of the mags into her jacket pocket, handed some to Spector, and said, "Now, let's finish this."

75

Pine was on the left side of the trail and Spector on the right. They crept forward, trying not to make any noise, and pausing and listening in the still air for the sounds of anything coming their way. Pine knew that the fact that they were hearing nothing meant Buckley and his men had hunkered down and were reevaluating things in light of their heavy losses.

Pine looked across the trail and saw Spector pause and kneel down. She glanced at Pine and pointed ahead, held up her pistol, and then made an X with her forearms followed by a sweeping motion in front of her. Pine gave her a thumbs-up.

She took aim with her pistol, pointing it to the far right, about two feet in front of Spector's position.

And waited.

When the two men came into view, Spector's gun fired; a split second later so did Pine's. They were employing a cross-stream tactic, meaning they had overlapping fields of fire covering the entire space in front of them.

They both emptied their fifteen-shot mags, paused to reload, and commenced firing again.

Three men eventually dropped dead in front of them.

The only drawback to this tactic was their muzzle flashes had revealed their positions.

Concentrated gunfire started to rain down on them. It was so intense that both women had to hurl themselves over rocks and fall flat to their bellies. When it stopped, Pine jumped up and ran over to Spector, and helped her up.

"We need to go, now!" barked Pine.

Out of the darkness, two men appeared, guns pointed at them. Pine whirled and kicked the weapon out of one man's hand. The other man fired at her, but missed because Spector had kicked him right in the nuts.

Then they went at it, hand to hand. The men were far bigger and far stronger. And they ended up being no match for the two women because, in a fight like this, physical strength was vastly overrated. Spector ended the life of one by gutting him with a knife. Pine broke the neck of the other man by pinning him with her legs and wrenching his head violently to the right. Both women rose, breathless and hurting. They had won this battle, but the men had managed to inflict considerable damage on both of them. The women were cut, bruised, and exhausted. Pine could barely move her left arm, and her right knee was swollen tight against her pants.

"Let's go," said Spector.

The next moment she grunted as a round pierced her left calf and shot out the back, taking part of her with it. A piece of shrapnel sliced into her cheek, another gouged deeply into her oblique.

As the rounds continued to hurtle down on them, Pine fractured her ankle falling over a rock and cut both her hands and her face when she landed on the hard ground; she also broke one of her fingers. A bullet sliced through her jacket, burning through the surface of her forearm but luckily not entering her body. She jumped up, turned, and emptied her mag across the mouth of the trail. This cover allowed Spector to get up and join her, firing as she retreated.

Pine was breathing hard and gritting her teeth with each step as blood leached from her lips. When she looked at Spector she saw her face was ashen, except where the blood streamed down her face from the wound there.

"Where else are you hit?"

"Calf, oblique, but I'm good," Spector lied. "You?"

"I'm good, too," Pine lied right back.

They both fast-limped toward the truck. Both of them understood this would be their last stand.

They reached the SUV, and Mercy stood up from behind the front of the vehicle. She eyed both women, saw the awkward gaits, the blood, and the gritted teeth.

"How bad?" she said.

"It's not a problem," said Spector, and Pine nodded in agreement. But both slumped against the SUV's side and sucked in air, trying to catch their breath as sweat slipped down their faces and mixed with the blood.

Mercy came around the side of the truck and looked toward the trail. "How many are left?"

Spector said, "Not sure. But probably too damn many."

Pine looked down at the blood all over her, and her damaged hand meant she was having trouble gripping her gun. Spector did the same survey of her body. And by the look on her face, trying to simply stand on her wounded leg was absolutely killing the lady.

"The odds are not in our favor," said Pine. "And we're running out of ammo."

Mercy pulled something from her pocket and said, "Found this under the seat." She also held up the walkie-talkie. "I've got an idea."

Spector eyed Pine, who gasped, "Let's hear it, sis. Because I'm fresh out."

76

Buckley peered around the edge of a rocky outcrop. Thirty feet away was the SUV. He glanced back at two of his men. They looked as nervous as he felt. This had not been nearly as easy as he thought it would be. He had vastly underrated the women.

However, they had seen from the blood trail that both women had been wounded, how badly he didn't know. He figured they would fight to the very last; what choice did they have? He waved one of his men forward.

The fellow joined him and Buckley said, "I doubt they're in the SUV, but they might be on the other side of it and using it as a shield. Shoot the hell out of the damn thing. Maybe we'll get lucky."

The man nodded and went back into the ranks to get the force he needed. A minute later they crept forward, spread out behind a line of rocks, took aim, and, on the man's command, pulled their triggers. The SUV's windows shattered, the tires were riddled, the metal sides punctured. They even aimed fire under the vehicle in case anyone was hidden there.

The screams from the vehicle were clear even over the sounds of the gunfire. As the rounds piled up, the shrieks reached a crescendo and then died out. After hundreds of rounds were expended the man held up his hand. He glanced over at Buckley, who nodded at the SUV. "Sounds like it's over but make damn sure."

Some of the men approached the vehicle, while the remaining group, including Buckley, provided cover. They expected to find at least one body. They shone their lights inside through the shattered glass, but the sight line was jagged.

The lead man gingerly opened the rear passenger door, and another man did the same with the front passenger door. They pointed their guns all around. Then the first man spied the walkie-talkie in the floorboard, with its Talk button taped down and the volume turned all the way up.

His mind processing this, he looked in alarm at his companion.

But then something else grabbed and held their attention.

"Is that something burning?" said the second man.

On the other side of the SUV the long fuse that Mercy had found in the vehicle was burning fast. Its other end had been dropped into the opening for the gas tank, where a few gallons of gas and a ton of explosive vapor dwelt.

The fuse quickly burned down, reached the open fill cap, and disappeared into the tank.

The men turned to run, but it was too late.

A second later an explosion rocked the SUV, lifting it off the dirt and vaporizing parts of the men unfortunate enough to be standing next to it. The concussive force threw the rest of their remains a hundred feet away. An arm hit Buckley in the face; a leg wrapped itself around the man next to him.

"Oh my God!" screamed Buckley as he tried to scramble away. He didn't say any more because he wasn't given the chance.

A size-thirteen foot hit him so hard in the face that his jaw shattered. The man next to him had his windpipe crushed by that same foot. He dropped to the dirt grabbing at his throat, sucking on air that could not pass through the damaged pipe.

Buckley was lifted up by another kick to the side of his head and was slammed against a chunk of rock and slumped to the ground, bleeding from multiple cuts and punctures.

A third man made the mistake of trying to fight with his bare hands against the force that had been unleashed against them. A bony knee drove into his face, crushing his nose. As he slumped down, repeated foot and elbow strikes shattered his skull. He would die a minute later from the hemorrhage.

The remaining men, the fight stricken clean out of them, turned to flee. Or would have, except for the bullets, fired by Pine and Spector, that chased them down and ended their lives.

And then all became quiet except for the moans and groans, and the gurgles of the dying, their exhaled breaths frosting in the chilly air.

Mercy, barefoot and relaxed, came to stand over Buckley. She used her foot to roll him over on his back. He didn't look nearly as handsome now.

As she turned to look at Pine and Spector, who were limping out from cover, their guns still smoking, Buckley abruptly sat up, raised his shotgun, and pointed the muzzle at Mercy's broad back.

A gun fired.

Only it wasn't Buckley's.

The shot hit him directly in the mouth and passed out the back of his head.

He slumped back to the dirt for the final time.

Mercy whirled around to look at him and then turned back, right as her sister lowered her gun.

Pine exhaled a long breath and said, "We're out of the tree, Mercy. And back on firm ground."

She slumped to the dirt, unconscious, where an exhausted and bloody Spector joined her a moment later.

77

Mercy drove them in Buckley's Jeep toward the town. When they finally got in the range of cell service, a revived but badly injured Pine notified the local authorities about all that had happened. When they reached the hospital, Mercy jumped from the Jeep, ran inside, and got a team of nurses and doctors to rush out to attend to the wounded women.

Later, Pine phoned Drew McAllister from a bed in the emergency room and took a few minutes to fill him in.

"I remember the Buckley case," he said. "Worked with some agents who were actually there. They were bad news. Sex trafficking, guns, drugs. The works. And the old man apparently slept with all the young girls to make sure they were 'acceptable.'"

"Well, the son wasn't as obvious, but he was just as dangerous, and every bit the psycho that his father was."

"From what you told me it's a miracle you made it out alive."

"I'm so sorry about Bertrand."

"Yeah. It doesn't sound like there's anyone left for us to arrest."

"The locals are going to go over that compound with a fine-tooth comb, but anybody he didn't bring with him on the hunt is probably long gone by now. Just a lot of clean-up and paperwork."

He told her he would be in contact with the local officials and that he would be flying out within twenty-four hours with a team of agents.

Pine got her wounds cleaned up and treated. They drained the fluid from around her knee; her broken finger was put in a splint and her fractured ankle was placed in a soft cast and walking boot.

Later, Pine, using a pair of crutches, visited Spector in her room, where she was recovering after the surgeries on her calf, face, and oblique.

"Good as new?" Pine said, taking a seat next to the bed.

Spector sat up, wincing a bit. "You bet. No complaints."

"Little dicey back there," noted Pine.

"Your sister really saved us. It was her idea to use the walkie-talkie and the fuse to make the truck into a bomb. Buckley had told me they used dynamite to knock down some of the old, damaged buildings. That's why the fuse was in there."

"Good thing she was there, or we'd be dead."

"I sure as hell wouldn't want to face her in a cage match."

Pine rubbed her jaw. "I feel like I got hit by a tank round. And she was holding back."

Spector slumped down and stared at the ceiling. "I suppose the FBI is on the way?"

"There was no way to avoid it, you know that."

"Yeah, I know."

"They'll be here in about twenty-four hours. The lead agent I know. He's a good guy. Plays fair."

"Right. Okay." Spector smoothed down her sheet and looked away.

Pine studied her for a few moments. "Really, how is the calf? I need the truth. It's important."

Spector looked over at her curiously. "Not bad. Didn't hit the bone. Surgeon said it was a clean in-and-out." She glanced at Pine's crutches and boot. "Unlike you, I can probably actually walk on it now. Be going full bore in a week. But why is that important?"

"Okay, but the big question is: Can you drive?"

Spector sat up and looked at Pine, her features full of confusion. "I'm sure I could. But why do you need to know that?"

"There's a rental car place in town, saw it on the way in."

"Okay, but—" Spector froze as understanding crept over her. "Wait a minute, are you going where I think you are?"

"For some reason I forgot to mention your

involvement to Special Agent McAllister. As far as he knows all the bad guys are dead."

"Just to be clear, what exactly are you saying?"

"There's an airport two hours from here. I looked it up on my phone. You can catch a flight and be pretty much anywhere in no time. Even another country if you're so inclined." She stopped and stared at Spector.

Spector obviously had not been expecting any of this. "Why?" she asked. "This breaks every Bureau protocol, and you know it."

"You saved our lives back there. I have no beef with you. And I've worked on my own at the Bureau for long enough that sometimes I set up my own rules. And most of the time they're better than the FBI's."

"I . . . I don't know what to say."

"Well, on my part, I'd like to thank you personally, only I still don't know your name."

Spector glanced down. "Britt Spector."

"Okay, *Britt*, thank you for saving all of our butts."

Spector said nervously, "Now you can easily find out my history at the FBI. It's not exactly . . . ideal."

"Sure I could, but I won't bother."

"Why?"

"Because I met you in person, under the craziest circumstances ever. So I know all I need to know about you. I don't need to read a bunch of files."

Spector looked concerned. "There'll be questions. The forensics—"

"The crime scene is a mess. I know that, you know that. There's nobody left to prosecute. They'll only be going through the motions. End of story. The locals and the Bureau have no incentive to push it."

"But you're an agent. You're taking a risk. I don't want to leave you hanging out there."

"I think it's a risk worth taking. And I'm really good at landing on my feet when it comes to the Bureau."

The two women stared at each other for a significant moment.

Spector slowly put out her hand, which Pine shook.

"I'm not sure I deserve this, but thank you."

"The only thing I would say is you need to use better judgment in picking the people you work for. You're way too skilled to help the bad guys anymore. We need you a lot more than they do."

Spector slumped back and smiled weakly at the ceiling. "I've already taken that into account. And you're right."

"But really, why?"

Spector looked at her. "Why what?"

"It wasn't just Carol's little speech to you. I spoke to her about that. She's good, but maybe not *that* good. So, really, why did you help us?"

Spector rubbed at her eyes, eliminating a sudden

stray tear or two. "I didn't have the greatest . . . child-hood. And I never had a sister growing up." She looked at Pine, her eyes glistening. In a cracking voice she added, "But I really could have used one. It . . . it would have made things a little more . . . bearable."

"I can definitely understand that. I feel the exact same way."

"I know what happened to you and your sister. In the end, I . . . I just thought you two deserved a lot more time together than Peter Buckley was willing to give you."

Pine rose and put the crutches under her arms. "Well, Britt, I think I just found myself an honorary sister."

Spector held her gaze. "Maybe I did too, Atlee."

78

Just like Spector, Pine hadn't waited around for the FBI to show up in the little town in Idaho. She didn't want to deal with McAllister face-to-face right now. She wanted some distance. So, before McAllister and his team were wheels down, she had caught a flight back to the East Coast with her sister and Blum. She *had* emailed McAllister to let him know of her plans. When he had emailed back to tell her to stay right where she was, she had conveniently already boarded the plane and turned her phone off.

Now, more than two thousand miles away and four days removed from the deadly encounter, Pine had called Drew McAllister to find out what had happened with his investigation in Idaho.

Their phone conversation had been a delicate dance for Pine.

"I told you I wanted to talk to you when we got here. Why the hell did you fly out? And I've been calling you the last four days."

"My assistant, Carol, needed some special medical attention," said Pine. "And I needed to get back to the

East Coast for personal reasons. And I haven't been checking my phone. It's a new one because mine got lost in the shuffle. And I'm having a hard time getting it to work right."

"Right, and they don't have sufficient medical services located in Idaho?"

"I made an executive decision on that. But I'm happy to answer whatever questions you have now. And if you had talked to me before you went to the crime scene, our conversation wouldn't be nearly as helpful to you. By giving you the time to see everything we can be a lot more productive."

"I was warned by several people at the Bureau that you could spin things with the best of them."

"Just trying to be helpful."

"It looks like a war zone out here," McAllister said, his tone turning serious.

"Well, from my point of view, it was. I've been through some crazy stuff in my career, but that one ranks right up there."

"I've discharged my weapon twice in twenty-four years' service with the Bureau. It looks like you beat my number in about four seconds."

"It was out of necessity."

"I could see that. I also saw the cage in the old barn. What was that for?"

"They kept us in there."

"But there was a jail."

"They kept us in there, too," replied Pine.

"You and your sister and Carol Blum?"

"Not Carol, she wasn't in the cage, just in the jail cell."

"We ran tests. We found some of her blood in the barn outside the cage. And we found traces of your blood *in* the cage."

"Well, they didn't treat us nice."

"Why did they bring Carol into the barn?"

Pine decided to simply tell the truth. She explained that Buckley had forced her to fight her sister in the cage and used Blum as the carrot.

"Jesus, what a maniac," said McAllister.

"Spot-on with that one."

"But how exactly did you get away?" asked McAllister.

"We managed to break out and get some weapons. We stole a vehicle, rammed the gates, and the chase was on. They shot out our gas tank. So we had to hole up in that box canyon. That's where the battle really took place."

"We found the remains of a drone and a slew of freaking NATO rifle rounds."

"There was a bunch of weapons in the SUV, along with the drone. We used everything we could to stay alive. And we needed it all."

"And the SUV? It was destroyed."

"Yeah, my sister had the great idea of using the gas vapors in the tank as a bomb to take out a bunch of Buckley's guys."

McAllister said dryly, "Well, it worked. I don't remember seeing quite so many body parts in one place. I'll be seeing those in my head for the next ten years at least."

"Well, the bad guys lost," Pine added brightly.

"Right," said McAllister. "So you're saying that you and your sister took out all of those heavily armed men without help? I mean, I know you're good, but really . . ."

"Well, we had Carol, too—don't forget her. And my sister could kick the crap out of just about every FBI agent you've ever worked with."

"I've heard the same about you."

"And Buckley had an FBI agent murdered. So he got what he deserved. So I'm just a little confused as to why you're giving me the third degree on how I managed to live through all of it."

"No, no, you're absolutely right," said McAllister, his tone quickly changing. He cleared his throat and continued, "Anyway, we're also looking into Buckley's business empire. Seems he had the clean side and the dirty side. And they only became intertwined when he needed to launder the dirty money through the clean storefronts. But it's going to take the best financial forensics guys at the Bureau to untangle all the stuff."

"No surprise. Buckley was a smart guy."

"And now a *dead* guy. Did you do the honors?"

"I did. Good thing I'm on leave, otherwise I'd be

stuck at my desk while the Bureau does a down-and-dirty investigation on me discharging my weapon, which I did quite a few times that day." Pine paused and said, "Now, are we done with that piece? Because I have a question I want to ask."

"Gee, let me guess what that might be."

"How is your investigation going into Tim Pine?"

"Are you cleared to hear all this?" he said. She could almost see his smile through the phone ether.

"I think I am, but you can just give me the non-classified parts if it will make you feel better."

"We had an unusual development on that end."

"What?" said Pine curiously.

"Members of another federal agency came to see us."

"Which one?"

"That's the classified part."

"Okay."

"They filled us in on the whole history of your mother and Tim Pine. Bruno and Ito Vincenzo. The works. Stuff you already told me, but that they confirmed. It was quite a brave thing your mom did, and at age eighteen no less."

"Yes, it was."

"Anyway, they made it clear that Ito went there to kill Tim Pine. And Pine nailed him instead. We were made to understand that the ensuing cover-up was sanctioned at the highest levels of American intelligence."

"So you won't be pursuing Tim Pine anymore?"

"As far as the Bureau is concerned, the matter is closed."

"Did you talk to Jack Lineberry?"

"I did. Quite an impressive man."

"And did he have a hand in getting this sister agency to come forward?"

"I'll let him answer that. I assume one reason you're on the other coast is to see him."

"It is. Did Lineberry tell you anything else?"

"Like what?"

"Just anything."

Like his being my and Mercy's dad, thought Pine.

"Nothing other than what I said."

"Okay, thanks."

"I hope after this all plays out, you're coming back to the Bureau. You're a good agent, Pine. We don't want to lose you."

"Don't lose any sleep over that. I'm an FBI agent down to my bones."

"And stay out of trouble. At least for the next few days anyway."

"I never go looking for trouble."

"I know. It just finds you."

Yes, it does, thought Pine.

79

They pulled up in front of the gates of Lineberry's estate. It was weeks after their return from Idaho. Pine was out of the walking boot and cast, and her assorted other injuries were much better. Blum had healed fully.

Pine was driving the rental, Mercy was in the passenger seat, and Blum sat in the rear.

"Holy shit," said Mercy. "The guy lives here?"

"You should see his place in Atlanta and the pied-à-terre in New York," said Blum.

"A peed what?" said Mercy, looking back at her.

"It's an apartment, a very nice one," explained Pine.

Pine checked in with the security intercom and the gates swung open. When Mercy saw the extent of the massive building and property, she shook her head and looked at her sister.

"Does he live here by himself?" she asked.

"He has a staff."

"Yeah, I guess he would have to. I mean, just to make sure he doesn't get lost going from the bedroom to the kitchen."

"He's also our father," Pine reminded her.

"Not to me. I don't even remember the guy who I *thought* was our father."

They pulled up in front and got out. The door was opened by the maid, and they were led to Lineberry's office.

"He's doing much better than when you were here last," said the maid, an efficient-looking woman in her thirties. She glanced at Mercy. "I understand that you're Agent Pine's twin sister. Mr. Lineberry will be very pleased to meet you."

"Well, it might not cut both ways," said Mercy.

When the woman looked startled, Pine put a hand on her sister's shoulder and said to the maid, "I know the way, thanks."

Pine knocked on the door and Lineberry's voice told them to come in.

When they entered Lineberry rose from behind his desk. He looked like a totally different person, Pine observed. He was dressed in beige linen slacks, a white collared shirt, and a navy sport jacket with a pocket square. His color was healthy, his white hair was neatly trimmed, and though he was still too thin, he looked nearly recovered from his injury.

And his depression, thought Pine.

He smiled, his eyes riveted on Mercy. He came toward them with his arms outstretched.

"My God, Mercy, I can't tell you how pleased I am to see you."

When he moved to embrace her, Mercy stepped back and stuck out her hand for him to shake.

He looked surprised at first, but then glanced at Pine and a look of understanding broke over his features. He shook her hand. "I'm obviously getting way ahead of myself. You don't even know me. I'm so sorry. Please, sit down."

He joined them around a coffee table and looked each of them over before settling his gaze on Pine. "I understand that you have been informed the FBI has closed the matter involving Tim."

"Am I wrong to sense your hand in all that?" asked Pine.

"I had a personal stake in it, too. They were investigating me as well, you know. But I will admit to placing a few phone calls to old comrades, as well as to people on Capitol Hill to whom I have donated liberally over the years. It was beyond clear that Ito Vincenzo came there to kill Tim and Tim merely defended himself. Now, I understand from Agent McAllister that you all had some adventure out in the western U.S., but he didn't elaborate."

"It's classified," said Pine. "But we all survived to make it here."

Lineberry's jaw slackened at this comment, but he snapped it shut and looked at Mercy. "I'm assuming that your sister has filled you in on things?"

Mercy looked him over, glanced around the finely appointed room, the purchased domain of the very rich, and then glanced back at him, unimpressed. "That you slept with our mom and had us? Yeah, got that. So I hear you want to leave us all your stuff. Can I take some of mine now? I got bills to pay and have to get back on my feet. It'll probably be less than what you spend on haircuts."

Blum stiffened, but Pine didn't. She had wondered what her sister's reaction to this meeting would be. And what *had* happened did not surprise her.

To his credit, Lineberry didn't react to this, either. No patronizing smile, no look of anger or disappointment, nothing to show that he felt disrespected in any way by her blunt comments.

But he did glance at Pine and said firmly, "Atlee, would you and Carol mind giving Mercy and me a few minutes alone?"

"You okay with that, Mercy?" said Pine.

She shrugged. "Whatever."

Pine and Blum rose to leave. Pine anxiously glanced back before closing the door and saw father and daughter staring at each other across a span of about six feet. It might as well have been six million. She closed the door after her.

80

"So can I get the money now, or do I have to wait for you to die?" said Mercy.

Lineberry said, "Oh, I'm sure something can be arranged. As you can clearly see, I have a great deal of wealth. You certainly should have your share of it."

"That's not what I meant. I had to quit all my jobs to go back into my past and get stuff figured out. And I got tossed out of my place, so I'm homeless right now. All I need is a little stash to get back on my feet, find some work, and I'm good to go. And you can leave all the rest to Lee. I don't need it."

"So that's it? It's just the money. No other questions for me? About your mother?"

Mercy shrugged. "I know all I need to. When I got taken my mother never looked for me. She left me to rot in a hellhole. Then she abandoned Lee and was never seen again. Oh, and then she wrote some bullshit letter to you to make herself feel better. And in that letter she never once mentioned trying to find me, so screw her. Did I miss anything?"

"You missed a great deal. Like the truth."

Mercy stared at him contemptuously. "Oh, is this where you tell me she was, what, like that Joan of Arc chick?"

"No, she had her faults, many of them, as we all do. She made mistakes—again, like we all do, including me and, I'm sure, including you."

"Don't include me in this, okay?" Mercy said sharply, glowering at him.

"But you *are* part of it." He paused and looked thoughtfully at her. "Your mother blamed herself for what happened to you and your sister. She went berserk with guilt. She pulled out all the stops to try to find you."

"I know that's bullshit. If she had, she would have found me."

As though he hadn't heard her, Lineberry continued, "And then she was forced to *stop* looking for you, at least officially. After that, she was compelled to go underground with her remaining family."

This got Mercy's attention. "*Forced* to stop?"

Lineberry gave her an appraising look. "I've never even told your sister what I'm about to tell you." He paused again, as though to make certain he had her full attention. "Are you prepared to hear it? If not, you can get up and leave. I won't try to stop you." He reached into his pocket and took out a checkbook. "I can write you a check now so you can get back on your feet. Will two hundred thousand dollars do it? If not, just name the amount. A million? Two million? Ten? I don't really care."

Mercy flinched at these absurdly large numbers, but then relaxed. She slowly nodded. "I'm ready to hear it, but that's not the same as believing it. You were in love with my mom and maybe you still are. You'd probably say anything to make her look good."

He set his checkbook aside. "What I'm about to tell you is the literal truth. Whether you believe me or not is up to you."

Mercy folded her arms over her chest, sat back, and waited.

"The Mafia families that your mother helped take down at the tender age of eighteen? They still had many tentacles across the country, in many different forms. Including in law enforcement and the federal government."

"Stop right there. I was told a dude named Ito something or other kidnapped me and tried to kill Lee. Then he dumped me with this psycho family. And he did it for his brother, who was in the mob and got screwed somehow. He blamed my mother for it. That's what Lee told me."

"Bruno Vincenzo *did* get screwed. But *not* by your mother."

"Who then?"

"I'll get to that. Your mother made a deal with Bruno when he discovered her identity. It was the only thing she could have done. If she were exposed it would have blown the entire operation and cost your mother, and many other people, their lives. And apart from that, many dangerous and hardened mobsters would have gone unpunished, free to commit more terrible acts. So she made the deal with Bruno, and that deal was approved at the highest government levels. But when it came time to live up to that deal, Bruno got double-crossed. He was supposed to get immunity and then be placed in witness protection. Neither of those measures ever happened."

"Why not?" said Mercy, now looking interested and engaged.

"Because a very high-ranking official, a man many rungs above me and a name that many Americans would recognize, ordered the deal *not* to be honored. Bruno was tried and convicted, and he was killed in prison by the mob for being a snitch."

"Why would this high-ranking guy do that?"

Lineberry didn't answer. He just looked at her.

She said, "Are you saying because the dude was paid off by the mob?"

"They wanted Bruno," he said simply. "They wanted him to pay for not coming to them about your mother being a spy in their midst. So the deal was deep-sixed, and Bruno died. What we didn't know was that Bruno convinced his brother, Ito, to go after your mother, who he thought was the one to betray him."

Mercy looked at him closely. "Okay, let's say that's

true. But my mom didn't even try to look for me. Nothing you've said addresses that."

In answer, Lineberry held up a single finger. "She left your sister's side at the hospital only once. And that was to fly to Washington, DC, and *demand* that everything that could be done to find you be done. She said that if it wasn't, she would go public with *everything* that she knew."

"Hang on—what exactly did she know?" asked Mercy.

"She knew that the high-ranking official I'm talking about had been bought off by the mob. She knew that he was the one who had, in effect, killed Bruno. And she believed that someone connected to Bruno Vincenzo had taken you. She didn't know it was his brother. I doubt she knew he had a brother. She just assumed it was the mob. And more than anything in life, she wanted you back."

Mercy became noticeably subdued. "How did she find out the government guy was working with the mob?"

"She was undercover. She listened at lots of keyholes and overheard lots of conversations. Folks told her things they shouldn't have because she was very, very good at her job. And she saw people come and people go. He was one of them."

"But if she knew he was involved, why didn't she report him to the authorities right from the start?"

"Because, Mercy, he *was* the authority. And she

wasn't even officially a government agent. She was still a teenager. He, on the other hand, was a legend, grown gray in service to his country. Who would believe her? He could have easily trumped up evidence against her. She used drugs back then. She hung out with criminals. There were myriad ways for him to go after her. So she kept silent. But when you were taken, that was the final straw. She went to see him and confronted this bastard right to his face. Because of *you*. And I can't tell you how brave an act that was. You may not know much about how governments operate, but it was akin to David taking on Goliath. And she did it without a second thought for herself."

"And what happened at this meeting?"

"She made her threats." He paused. "And he made one in return."

"What?" said Mercy a bit breathlessly.

"If she continued to make waves, if she kept demanding this nationwide search for you, if she kept drumming up attention for the matter . . . he would have your sister and Tim . . ." He paused and eyed her knowingly.

"What the hell! How could a government guy do that?"

"It was a different world back then, Mercy. The mob was still a big deal. A lot of muscle. He was in too deep with them. And while your mother helped take down a lot of very bad people, there were a lot of other very bad people still out there. And this traitor was not about to have his entire reputation ruined over this."

"You mean he threatened to tell the mob where my mom and her family were?"

"And that's why they vanished overnight without a trace from Andersonville. She had lost one daughter. She couldn't lose another. But I know that she continued to do all she could, spent time and money, everything she had, in trying to find you. I know this because I tried to help her do so. From the very moment you disappeared, I never saw her smile again. All the life, all the happiness was . . . struck clean from her."

Mercy looked down. Her features had a lost, disbelieving component to them. "Then why didn't *you* out this asshole?" she said sharply.

"By the time your mother confided in me, he was dead. He died quietly in his bed and was given a hero's send-off for many years of faithful public service. He is now buried at Arlington National Cemetery."

"How screwed up is that?"

"Very. And your mother couldn't tell the truth at that point about him. No one would believe her, and it would have alerted the men still after her where she was. It would have put Tim and your sister in terrible danger. Your mother was caught in a box with no way out."

"And you never told Lee any of this? Why not?"

Now Lineberry shifted uncomfortably in his seat. "The easy answer is that I took an oath never to divulge official secrets. But if you want the blunt truth, your sister idolized your mother. She lived with her far longer than you did. Even after Amanda left her, your sister continued to have deep feelings for her. And I knew that if I told her all of this, she would be obsessed with finding her. She would put everything else on hold. She—"

"She wouldn't have had her own life, you mean? She'd just be chasing all of this down and never do her own thing?"

"Yes. And maybe put herself in danger. And your mother believed if Atlee had no idea where she was, that would protect her. That's why she left her."

They sat there in silence for a few moments as Mercy processed all this.

"Look, I . . . I appreciate your honesty. I don't get much of it. People sort of look through me."

"I never will," he said forcefully. "That you can take to the bank as easily as the check I'm going to write you."

She glanced up at him. "You're different than I thought you would be."

"You're *exactly* like I thought you would be."

"Meaning what?"

"Indomitable."

"That's a nice, fancy word. But I wasn't that way for a long time. I let people screw me."

"But no more."

"No. No more." She looked at him. "Will you ever tell Lee what you just told me?"

"I think it might be better coming from *you*. And that decision I will leave entirely to you." He rose. "And if you don't mind, I'd like to have your sister and Carol come back in. We need to take a little trip, a long overdue one."

"A trip? Where?"

"You'll see. All of you will see."

81

The "little" trip was not made by car. It was made in Lineberry's private jet, a Gulfstream G650 with all the trimmings.

Both sisters and Blum looked in awe at the plane's luxurious interior, with its dark wood paneling, colorful carpet, and cream-colored leather seats with gold trim. They were greeted by a uniformed flight attendant and two professional-looking pilots who presented calm expressions and firm handshakes.

As they settled into their seats around a highly polished table Pine said, "Where exactly are we going?"

"It's a very quick trip by jet" was all Lineberry would say.

"This will be my first time on a plane," said Mercy. "The guy who told me what it was like never flew on one of these, I don't think."

"Most people don't, Mercy," said her sister.

They took off like a shot and quickly climbed to forty-one thousand feet. They were served coffee and a light meal, and in less than an hour they were descending through the clouds once more. After the jet cleared them, Pine looked out the window and saw a city down below with a wide body of water to the east.

"Where are we?"

"Savannah, Georgia," said Lineberry. "And that's the Atlantic."

"And why Savannah?"

Lineberry looked at her, a bit sadly, Pine thought. "Just trust me, Atlee. Please. Just once more."

His subdued demeanor only heightened her anxiety.

An SUV and a driver were waiting for them at the jet park. They climbed in and drove off.

They wound their way through the outskirts of the city until they turned into a place that made Pine's heart skip a beat.

"A *cemetery*?" She shot her sister an anxious glance before looking at Lineberry.

"Jack, what the hell is going on?"

Sitting in the front passenger seat, Lineberry simply gazed stoically out the window. Then he directed the driver to stop the SUV on a narrow, patchy macadam road near the back of the cemetery. There were a number of tombstones here, some ten feet tall, several old and massive ornate mausoleums, and some simple bronze grave markers set in the grass.

As Lineberry got out, Pine grabbed his arm.

"You better tell us right now what the hell is going

on, Jack. This . . . this is so shitty of you. I mean, a cemetery? Please God, don't tell me we came here—"

He interjected, "I asked you to trust me. Either you do or you don't. I would never knowingly hurt you, but I am also not going to hide the *truth* from you, not anymore."

He turned and led them over to one section of graves. He stopped at a sunken plot with one of the simple markers. They all gathered close around and looked at the name on it.

"Mark Douglas?" read Pine, before glancing up at Lineberry in confusion.

"He was only forty-eight when he died," noted Blum, reading the birth and death dates.

"Yes, he was," said a voice. "He died far too early."

They all turned as a woman in her midfifties stepped out from behind one of the mausoleums. Her dark hair was shot through with silver and hung to her shoulders. She had on dark jeans, black boots, and a black sailor's peacoat. She was taller than Pine but an inch under Mercy's height. She was lean, and her facial bone structure was flawless, observed Pine; she looked so casually elegant and beautiful that it took Pine's breath away. The eyes were so sparkling a blue they seemed fake. But Pine knew they weren't.

And, Pine knew, she was also their mother.

Both sisters stood rigidly next to each other as the woman they had known as Mom, and Julia Pine, walked up to them. She looked first at Pine and then at Mercy, where her gaze held the longest.

She put out a hand to stroke Mercy's cheek and the woman just stood there and let her.

"I never thought I would see you again, Mercy. Never." The blue eyes filled with tears and the skin around them crinkled, showing off finely etched lines that served to somehow enhance her beauty, giving it the refinement and dignity of an older masterpiece.

Mercy's lips trembled, and she gripped her mother's hand and held it tightly against her skin.

Julia looked over at her other daughter. With her free hand, she intertwined her fingers with Pine's. "Lee, can you ever forgive me for what I did, honey?"

Pine finally found her voice and said, "Back then I couldn't, but I know better. Jack . . . let me read the letter you sent him."

Julia's gaze drifted to Lineberry's.

"I know what you told me," he said. "But under the circumstances, I felt she had the right to know."

She nodded. "Thank you for bringing my girls to me, Jack. You've been a good friend through this entire nightmare."

Pine looked down at the grave and then lifted her gaze to her mother.

Julia nodded and said quietly, "A drunk driver hit Tim while he was crossing the street one night. He was killed instantly."

Pine looked down at the grave and a tear from her face plunked down into the grass.

"In Savannah we were known as Mark and Sandra Douglas. We ran a little floral shop together. Have for years. It was . . . something to do with our . . . *lives*. I still own the shop. Flowers make people happy," she added sadly.

"But I don't understand. How did Jack know to come here?"

In answer Julia looked at Mercy. "I saw the FBI notice on TV. About a girl named Rebecca Atkins from Crawfordville, Georgia? I couldn't recognize the name, of course. But as soon as I saw the face, I knew it was you, Mercy."

"After all those years?" said Mercy incredulously.

"I am your mother. Those were the same beautiful eyes I saw on the day you were born and for six years after, the lovely hair I brushed a million times, the nose I put a tissue to countless times, a million little things that only a mother would notice. I called Jack. Tim had kept his number. He . . . he told me some of what happened to you, Mercy." Her eyes now bulged with fresh tears and the elegant features began to crumble. "I . . . I am so sorry." She moved forward and put her arms around Mercy. Her daughter stiffened for a moment and Pine, who was watching closely, didn't know what to expect. But then Mercy put her arms around her mother and squeezed back.

Mercy said, "Jack told me some stuff today. Why

you had to stop looking for me. You . . . you were caught between a rock and a hard place, it sounds like."

Pine shot Lineberry a startled look, but he was staring at Julia and Mercy.

Julia Pine finally stepped back, turned to her other daughter, and wrapped her long arms around her; both were shaking with emotion as they held the other.

Blum, who was standing back a few feet to give the family their space, looked at the grass as tears slid down her face.

When the women drew apart, Pine said, "In your letter to Jack, you said you figured something out and got someone to give you money. Was that person Jack's old fiancée, Linda Holden-Bryant? She certainly had the money."

"Jack said you were a very good FBI agent, honey," said Julia. "Yes. I finally realized Linda was the only one who could have let people know where we were in hiding." Julia brushed Pine's hair out of her eyes. "I used most of that money to provide for your education and living expenses. It was cowardly how I left you, but I thought the closer I was, the more dangerous it would be for you. Tim almost died, and all I could think was they were still out there. If they believed Tim was dead and I had vanished for good, I thought they would stop looking. I've second-guessed myself a million times since. I debated long and hard about taking you with us, but you were just starting your life and accomplishing so much. The last thing I wanted to do was force you to give all that up and go into hiding again. It would be asking you, basically, to have no life at all."

"I can understand that. And . . . and I think you made the right decision."

"Then you're a better person than I am. Every day I wanted to get in touch. And then the months and then the years went by and whatever courage I had to face you was just gone. You should hate me. I deserve that."

"I finally found my sister," said Pine. "And you found us. I don't really have room left for hate, Mom."

Julia smiled sadly. "I wish your father could be here to see you girls. He loved you so much. Every waking moment of his life, it was all about his girls."

Pine glanced at Jack and then said, "He *was* a wonderful dad."

Then she turned to Blum and introduced her to her mother.

The women exchanged a hug and Julia said, "Jack has told me that you have been a wonderful friend to Lee. I thank you very much for that."

"I'm the lucky one, actually," said Blum.

Mercy said, "So I have to know—why did you name me what you did?"

"Because, honey, you were the first one to come out after two days of excruciating labor and an epidural that never took. It was just the first word that came to my mind."

Julia and Blum exchanged a knowing look.

Mercy smiled. "Yeah, I guess I can understand that."

Julia gripped her daughters' hands. "Would you like to see my little flower shop? It's close enough to walk." She smiled. "It's called 'Twin Pines.' I guess you know where that name came from."

"That sounds wonderful, Mom," said Pine.

Mercy nodded. "Yeah, it does."

"Carol and I will meet you there," said Jack.

"You can walk with us," said Julia.

Blum stepped forward. "No, it just needs to be the three of you right now, Julia." She smiled, her eyes full of emotion. "For a lot of reasons."

She and Jack walked back to the SUV.

The trio of women turned to the west, where the sun was just starting to set, throwing the sky into luxurious eddies of red and gold.

And they slowly walked arm in arm toward that luminous glow.

Acknowledgments

To Michelle, finally, the truth about Mercy. Thanks for all the help with this series! Atlee could be you!

To Michael Pietsch, Ben Sevier, Elizabeth Kulhanek, Jonathan Valuckas, Matthew Ballast, Beth de Guzman, Anthony Goff, Rena Kornbluh, Karen Kosztolnyik, Brian McLendon, Albert Tang, Andy Dodds, Ivy Cheng, Joseph Benincase, Alexis Gilbert, Andrew Duncan, Bob Castillo, Kristen Lemire, Briana Loewen, Mark Steven Long, Thomas Louie, Rachael Kelly, Kirsiah McNamara, Nita Basu, Lisa Cahn, Megan Fitzpatrick, John Colucci, Alison Lazarus, Barry Broadhead, Martha Bucci, Rick Cobban, Ali Cutrone, Raylan Davis, Tracy Dowd, Melanie Freedman, Elizabeth Blue Guess, Linda Jamison, John Leary, John Lefler, Rachel Hairston, Tishana Knight, Jennifer Kosek, Suzanne Marx, Derek Meehan, Christopher Murphy, Donna Nopper, Rob Philpott, Barbara Slavin, Karen Torres, Rich Tullis, Mary Urban, Tracy Williams, Julie Hernandez, Laura Shepherd, Jeff Shay, Carla Stockalper, Ky'ron Fitzgerald, and everyone at

David Baldacci

Grand Central Publishing, for running on all cylinders for me.

To Aaron and Arleen Priest, Lucy Childs, Lisa Erbach Vance, Frances Jalet-Miller, and Kristen Pini, for making my life so much easier.

To Mitch Hoffman, for continuing to make me dig deep.

To Anthony Forbes Watson, Jeremy Trevathan, Lucy Hale, Trisha Jackson, Alex Saunders, Sara Lloyd, Claire Evans, Sarah Arratoon, Laura Sherlock, Stuart Dwyer, Jonathan Atkins, Christine Jones, Leanne Williams, Andy Joannou, Charlotte Williams, Rebecca Kellaway, and Neil Lang at Pan Macmillan, for upping your game with every book.

To Praveen Naidoo and the stellar team at Pan Macmillan in Australia. When I see what you've done for me there it is truly amazing. I am so grateful.

To Caspian Dennis and Sandy Violette, for being absolutely pefect at what you do.

And to Kristen White and Michelle Butler, without you, things would not be nearly as much fun. And I'm not just talking about the margarita machine!

Coming Soon

Read the opening chapters of
David Baldacci's upcoming thriller . . .

The 6:20 Man

Meet Travis Devine, a thirty-two-year-old
decorated survivor of Afghanistan and Iraq, who
left the Army mysteriously under a
cloud of suspicion.

Now his journey takes him to a new hell, in the
cutthroat world of New York's high finance. A new
danger lurks and old friends can't be trusted.

CHAPTER

I

Travis Devine took a shallow breath, ignored the heat and humidity that was rising fast along with the sun, and rushed to board the 6:20 train, like it was the last flight out of Saigon. He was wearing an off-the-rack pearl-gray suit, a wrinkled white shirt that needed laundering, and a muted dark tie. He would rather be in jeans and a T-shirt, or cammies and Army jump boots. But that couldn't happen, not on this ride.

He was freshly showered although already starting to perspire; his thick hodgepodge of hair was as neatly combed as he could manage it. His face was shaved and mildly scented with a nondescript cologne. He wore cheap tasseled loafers shined fore and aft. The imitation leather briefcase held his company-issued laptop with special encryption and no personal use permitted thereon, along with breath mints and a packet of Pepcid AC. He no longer took the neat little power pills he'd popped when suited up to fight for his country. The Army used to give them out like gummy bears so the grunts would battle longer and harder on less sleep and less to eat.

Now they cost money.

His primary weapons, instead of the Army-issued M4 carbine and M9 sidearm of yesteryear, were twin Apple Mac twenty-seven-inch screens, connected by digital tethers to mighty, encrypted clouds seeded with all the data he would ever need. It was all bullshit, really, and, strangely enough, more important to him than anything else on earth right now.

What they taught you in the world of high finance was simple really: win or lose. Eat or starve. It was a binary choice. No Taliban, Al-Qaeda, ISIS fanatic, or Afghan soldier pretending to be your ally before banging a round into the back of your head. Here, his chief concerns were quarterly earnings projections, liquidity, free and closed markets, monopolies and oligarchies, in-house lawyers who wanted you to stick to the rules, and bosses who insisted that you didn't. And most significant of all, the persons sitting right next to Devine at the office. They were mortal foes. It was him or them in Wall Street's version of mixed martial arts.

Devine was commuting south to the big city on Metro North's Harlem Line. At age thirty-two, his entire life had changed. And he wasn't sure how he felt about it. No, he was sure. He hated it. That meant things were working according to plan.

He sat where he always did when commuting into the city—third row, window seat on the starboard side. He switched to the port side on the way back. The train puttered along with no real ambition, unlike the humans it carried. Sleek trains ran like cheetahs in Europe and Asia, but here they were snails. Yet they were faster than the cars stuck in the murderous traffic that piled in and out of the city morning, noon, and night.

Generations before him had ridden this very same route to make their living in the sweatshop spires of Manhattan. Many had died along the way from the usual suspects: widowmaker heart attacks, strokes, aneurysms, the slow death of neurological disorders and cancers, a liver painfully scuttled by too much alcohol, or self-inflicted deaths among those who could take the strain no longer.

Devine lived in Mount Kisco in a saggy town house shared with three twentysomethings trying to forge their futures in various ways. He had left them all asleep as he tried to shape his future day by day. The train would continue to fill as it wended its way along to Manhattan. It was summer, the sun was well on its way up, and the heat was building. He could have lived in the city, and paid a lot more money for the easier commute. But he liked trees and open spaces, and being surrounded by skyscrapers and concrete at all times was not his preference. He had actually been mulling over where to live when a Realtor who knew a friend of his had called out of the blue and told him she had found him a room at the town house. It was cheap enough that he was able to save a bit. And lots of people commuted into the city, even though it made for long days and nights. But that philosophy had been beaten into his psyche for most of his life.

"You work till you drop, Travis," his father had told him over and over. "Nobody in this world gives you a damn thing. You have to take it, and you take it by working harder than anybody else. Look at your sister and brother. You think they had it easy?"

Yes, his older brother and sister, Danny and Claire. Board-certified neurosurgeon at the Mayo Clinic, and CFO of a Fortune 100, respectively. They were eight and nine years older than he was, and already minted superstars. They had reached heights he never would. He had been told this so often, nothing could persuade him not to believe it.

Devine's birth had clearly been a mistake. Whether his father forgot the condom or his mother didn't realize she was ovulating and failed to keep her lustful man at bay, out he had popped and pissed off everybody in his family. His mother went back to work immediately at his father's thriving dental practice in Connecticut, where she was a hygienist. He'd learned this later, of course, but maybe he'd also sensed his parents' indifference to him as an infant. That indifference had turned to fury when Devine was a senior in high school.

That was when he'd been accepted into West Point.

His father had roared, "Playing soldier instead of going out into the world and earning a living? Well, boy, you are off the family payroll starting now. Your mother and I don't deserve this crap."

However, he'd found his place in the world of the military. After graduating from West Point he'd gone through the arduous Ranger School, passing the crawl, walk, and run tests, which was how the three phases were described. By far the hardest part had been sleep deprivation. He and his comrades had literally fallen unconscious while standing up. He'd later qualified to become a member of the elite Seventy-Fifth Ranger Regiment. That had even been tougher than Ranger School, but he had loved the special forces and the dangerous and demanding quick-strike missions that came with being a member.

These were serious accomplishments and he had written to his parents about them, hoping for some praise. He had never heard back from his mother. His father had sent an email asking him what national park he would be assigned to now that he was a *ranger*. He had signed the email, "Proud father of Smokey the Bear." He might have assumed his dad was utilizing his sense of humor, only he knew his father didn't have one.

Devine had earned twin Purples, a Silver Star, and a slew of other bits of metal and ribbons. In the world of the Army, he was known as a combat stud. He would only term himself a *survivor*.

He had gone into uniform as a boy and come out as a killing machine. Six foot one and one-quarter inches, as the Army had precisely measured him. He had entered West Point a lanky 180 pounds of average physique. Then the Army, and his own determination, had transformed him into 225 pounds of bone, muscle, and gristle. His grip was like the jaws of a croc; his stamina was off the charts; his skills at killing and not being killed placed him at the top of the food chain with orcas and great whites.

He'd risen to Captain right on schedule and had worn the twin silver bars proudly, but then Devine had called it quits because he had to. It had torn him up back then. It still tore him up. He was an Army man through and through, until he could be one no longer. Yet it was a decision he had to make.

After that he had sat in an apartment for a month wondering what to do, while old comrades phoned, emailed, and texted, asking him what the hell was he doing leaving the uniform. He had not gotten back to any of them. He had nothing he could say to them. A leader who had never had an issue giving orders and being in command, he couldn't find the words to explain what he had done.

He did have the Post-9/11 GI Bill to help him. It paid for a full ride to an in-state public university. It seemed a fair trade-off for nearly dying for his country. He'd gotten his MBA that way.

He was the oldest person in his class at Cowl and Comely, the minted powerhouse investment firm where he worked at an entry-level analyst position. When he'd applied at Cowl, he knew they had looked upon him with suspicion because of his age and unusual background. They had outwardly thanked him for his military service, because that was always automatic. But they probably had to fill a veterans quota, and he was it. He didn't care why they had picked him so long as he got a shot to make himself as miserable as possible.

Yes, he thought, *as he stared out the window. As miserable as possible.*

He had tried later trains into the city, but there were too many suits on board just like him, heading to work, heading to war. He needed to get there first, because whoever got there first, with the most, often was victorious. The military had also taught him that.

And so he stepped onto the 6:20 train every morning, and traveled to the city as punishment. And as much as he hated the work and the life that came with it, that simple punishment would never manage to fit his crime.

CHAPTER

2

THE 6:20 TRAIN PASSED THROUGH bucolic countryside lurking outside a metropolis of unequaled breadth and complexity. Along the way, it picked up people at stations set in affluent small towns that existed solely to serve the hungry beast due south. It finally chugged past an enclave of homes that were some of the most expensive in this or any other country. It seemed unfair to call them mere homes. A place nearly as large as a shopping center should have a grander name, even *mansion* or *estate* didn't cut it, Devine thought. *Palace*, maybe, yeah, *palace* seemed to work.

He lifted his gaze from his laptop, as he did every morning when passing by this area. Every time he looked out, another structure was going up, or an existing one was being made even more lavish. The cement trucks drove in with wet loads for larger and more elaborate pools, the houses went higher or wider, or a guesthouse was being built or a putting green added. It kept the working class employed, so there was some good in the greed and pretentiousness, he supposed.

The train slowed as it approached a bend and snaked upward over a lazy, heat-struck knoll. It slowed some more, coming nearly to a stop. There was a signal-switching hitch here that the train people either couldn't or wouldn't do anything about. To say they had a monopoly was to say the earth revolved around the sun, so why would they give a damn?

And as they came to a complete halt, Devine *saw* her. He had seen her only a few times before, and only when the weather turned warm. He had no idea why she was up so early, but he was glad she was.

The privacy wall was high, but not high enough to block the sight line of those on the train at this point on the knoll. He knew who the owner of this particular palace was, and he also knew that there were height limits on perimeter walls and fences here. The owner had planted trees along the rear wall to compensate for this, but because of the space between the bottom of the tree canopy and the top of the wall, there was a fairly large gap that one could see through.

It was an oversight, he knew, that the owner would no doubt rectify one day, though Devine hoped not, at least while he was riding the 6:20. He felt a bit like Jimmy Stewart in *Rear Window*, the champion voyeur movie of all time. But he wasn't looking out the window because his leg was broken and he was bored, as was the case with Stewart's character. He was looking out the window because of *her*.

The woman had sauntered out from the rear door of the largest palace in this enclave. *Sauntered* was the only word that worked for how she moved. It was a smooth, leisurely pace, like a panther just getting warmed up before breaking into a sprint. The hips and glutes and thighs and shoulders all moved in the most gloriously primal choreography.

The place looming behind her was all modernistic, with glass and metal and concrete whipped into odd geometric shapes. Only the mind of an architectural savant snorting nostrils of coke could have conceived it.

She had on a short, white terry cloth robe that clung to her tanned thighs. When she took it off, revealed was an emerald-green string bikini and a body that seemed too flawless to be genuine. Her hair was all blond highlights with intricate cuts and waves that had probably cost more than his suit.

Devine looked around to see who else was watching. All the guys were, of course. One of the women had glanced up from her computer, seen the lady in question, looked at the gents with their faces burned to the glass, and turned back to her screen in disgust. Two other women, one in her forties and dressed like a hippie, and one in her seventies, didn't look up. The former was on her phone. The latter was diligently reading her Bible, which had plenty of warnings about sins of the flesh.

The bikini lady placed her painted toenails in the water, shivered slightly, and then in she dove. She did a graceful arc under the water, pushed off the other side, and came back up to where she had started. She hoisted herself out and sat on the pool surround facing his way. She didn't seem to notice the train or anyone staring from inside it. Devine could imagine at this distance all she might see was the train's glass reflecting the sunlight.

With her body wet, the tiny bikini seemed to have shrunk, and her breasts hung heavy and firm in the twin pockets of the swimsuit top. She looked to the left and right and then behind her at the house. Next, she slipped off her top and then her bottom. She sat there for a long moment totally naked; Devine could glimpse comingled white and tanned skin. Then she jumped once more into the water and vanished.

It was about this time that the train started up again, and the next palace in the enclave appeared, only it didn't have a beautiful woman skinny-dipping in its pool. In fact, this homeowner had planted not trees but tall, thick holly or Leland cypress that left no gaps through which one could peer.

Pretty much every other man on the train car groaned under his breath and slumped back with a mix of ecstasy and disappointment. Devine eyed some of them. They looked back at him, smiled, shook their heads, and mouthed things that sounded basically like, *Dude, WTF was* that?

Devine had never seen her strip down before. He wondered what had caused her to do it beyond some sort of playful impulse. He wondered about many things in that particular palace. It was fascinating to him what people did with all that money. Some were philanthropic; others just kept buying bigger toys. Devine told himself that if he ever got to be that rich, he would not buy the toys. He would give it all away.

Yeah, sure you would.

At the next station more people got on. And then at the next station still more.

As he looked around at the mostly twentysomethings on the train, who were already on their fired-up computers and yanking down data clouds, and scanning documents and fine-tuning presentations and excelling at Excel, Devine knew that the enemy was everywhere. He was completely surrounded. And that should have panicked the former soldier.

And yet this morning, all Devine could think about was the naked woman in the water. And it wasn't for the obvious reasons.

To the former Ranger and Army scout, something about the lovely woman just seemed off.

You took my sister.
I've hunted you for 30 years.
Now . . . your time's up.

Discover David Baldacci's bestselling series featuring Special Agent Atlee Pine

  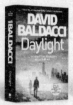 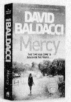

LONG ROAD TO MERCY

Thirty years since Atlee Pine's twin sister, Mercy, was abducted from the room they shared as children, Pine starts the pursuit of a lifetime to finally uncover what happened on that fateful night.

A MINUTE TO MIDNIGHT

Seeking answers in her home town, Pine's visit turns into a rollercoaster ride of murder, long-buried secrets and lies . . . and a revelation so personal that everything she once believed is fast turning to dust.

DAYLIGHT

When Pine's investigation coincides with military investigator John Puller's high-stakes case, it leads them both into a global conspiracy from which neither of them will escape unscathed.

MERCY

FBI agent Atlee Pine is at the end of her long journey to discover what happened to her twin sister, Mercy, and must face one final challenge. A challenge more deadly and dangerous than she could ever have imagined.

In a town full of secrets, who can you trust?

Discover David Baldacci's new historical crime series featuring straight-talking WWII veteran Aloysius Archer.

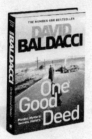 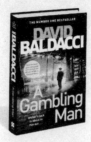 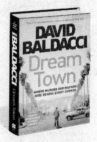

ONE GOOD DEED

Poca City, 1949. Aloysius Archer arrives in a dusty southern town looking for a fresh start. After accepting a job as a local debt collector, Archer soon finds himself as the number one suspect in a local murder. Should Archer run or fight for the truth?

A GAMBLING MAN

California, 1949. Archer is on his way to start a new job with a renowned private investigator. Arriving in a tight-lipped community rife with corruption, Archer must tackle murder, conspiracy and blackmail in a town with plenty to hide . . .

DREAM TOWN

Los Angeles, 1952. Private investigator and WWII veteran Aloysius Archer returns to solve the case of a missing screenwriter during the Golden Age of Hollywood.

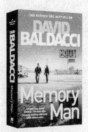
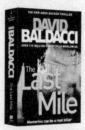

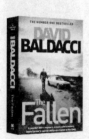
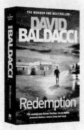
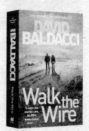